The Third Heaven

The Rise of Fallen Stars

By

Donovan M. Neal

God bless you Brян
I hope you enjoy the

© 2012 Donovan M. Neal

For permission requests, write to the publisher, addressed "Attention: Permissions Coordinator," at the email below.

TornVeil
email: tornveil@donovanmneal.com

Ordering Information:
Quantity sales. Special discounts are available on quantity purchases by corporations, associations, and others. For details, contact the publisher at the email above.
Orders by U.S. trade bookstores and wholesalers. Please contact Lightning Source: Tel: (615) 213-5815; Fax: (615) 213-4725 or visit https://www1.lightningsource.com/

Printed in the United States of America

ISBN 978-0-9894805-0-5
Library of Congress Control Number 2016917350

Cover Design by Roger Despi
www.pintado.weebly.com

Dedication

I want to dedicate this book to all the dreamers, to those who have an idea and work to see it to completion. For better is the end of a thing, than its beginning. May your imagination, ever lead you to new realms.

2 Cor. 12:2

I knew a man in Christ above fourteen years ago, (whether in the body, I cannot tell; or whether out of the body, I cannot tell: God knoweth ;) such an one caught up to the third heaven.

Ecclesiastes 1:9, 10

The thing that hath been, it is that which shall be; and that which is done is that which shall be done: and there is no new thing under the sun. Is there anything whereof it may be said, See, this is new? It hath been already of old time, which was before us.

Table of Contents

Acknowledgements

To the Lord Jesus Christ, who for some reason loves me.

To Pastor, Charles Hawthorne, who nurtured my preexisting love of the Bible.

To my children - Candace, Christopher, and Alexander - you can do great things!

To the authors, comic book artists and writers, game developers and filmmakers who have come before and unknowingly have breathed on the embers of my imagination.

To all my beta readers and friends who gave me critique, and encouragement.

To Nettie who cheered me on when I had nothing and said, "Wow!" after reading the prologue of my book.

To my cover designer Roger Despi for doing such an awesome job on giving me a standout cover.

To Adele Brinkley for her editing and for finding out where I live, sneaking into my house, and stealing all of the commas, semicolons, hyphens, and "as" off my keyboard to make my work even better.

Preface

When the desire to write this book was birthed. It was to provide a form of wholesome Christian entertainment and to answer several questions. How could Lucifer who dwelt in the very presence of God elect to rebel against his creator? What could have gone so wrong that a third of Heaven would turn their backs on God?

The answer to this query is the *fictional* piece before you now. To my beloved Christian reader— this work is *not* scripture. I do not profess divine inspiration, nor would I ever attempt to place this work alongside the word of God. The story is a fictional exploration of the fall of Lucifer, and by taking part in this fictional account, you as a reader and I as the author are in no way implying that we must have theological agreement. The work does presume certain doctrinal beliefs (the existence of the Trinity for example) but this novel is not meant to be a point-by-point exposition of biblical truth. Nor an exact attempt to create a chronologically correct depiction of creation and the events depicted in the Bible. It's an exploratory look into a biblical event and imagines, "what if?"

Mythology is purposely utilized in some portion of in the book. The rationale here is that ancient or modern mythological creatures and gods have their basis in some level of "fact" or are the result of the actions of fallen angels.

When possible, I have tried to be consistent with the teaching of scripture and with what church fathers have said concerning Angelology. Overall, I have taken the liberty to use my *sanctified imagination* to tell a story that might not only spur further interest in the Word of God but also, create an entertaining tale.

In the end, I desired to tell a story full of wonder, and to tell it in such a manner; as I might want such a story told to me.

Toni Morrison has stated, "If there's a book you really want to read, but it hasn't been written yet, then you must write it." I am attempting here to do just that.

I hope this work is enjoyable to you and spawns your further desire to possibly learn more about God, the Bible and maybe even to follow Jesus Christ. God Bless.

Donovan M. Neal

Prologue

I will always remember the screams, the untold billions of screams.

The cries of the damned reverberated off the canyon walls. The sound of their wails stretched over miles with each moaning breath mingled into a cacophony of pitiful, tortuous laments. I beheld in fascinated horror as billions upon emaciated billions of humans and Elohim languished in agony. Their rotted and burning flesh stank as the winds made the hellish perfume waft across the skies, causing the air to reek with putrefaction. Blistering heat sizzled from the white-hot lake of molten rock and fire. Fire that licked and bit at each captive's smoldering flesh, flesh forever burned but never consumed. Therefore, they screamed the residents of this canyon did — it was a sickening sound.

Is this how Moses felt? I wondered. *To behold a thing that burns but is not consumed?*

They see me.

"Please make it stop," said one.

"I am sorry, oh God! Please, God, listen! Jesus do you hear me," said another.

"Aaarrrgghhhh!"

"I hate your guts! Do you hear me angel of God? I hate you!"

The voices melded and flowed, morphing into a singular pitiful cry for relief and of anguish.

I watched as some fought to climb atop others in a futile struggle to escape the horrifying affliction. It was a fruitless skirmish from which none could expect release.

I suppose that it could be possible to flee. I saw neither bars nor chains to hold these souls captive. Straining and squinting, my angelic eyes viewed no doors that would prevent escape. Selfish preservation run amok, pain, and hope-

3

lessness prevented them. As one soul approached optimism and the border of freedom, another wretch dragged it back within the bowels of smoke and flames. The grotesque scene of twisted, writhing bodies, moved as the tide in this sea of fire and brimstone.

I observed them dance, the denizens of this canyon. Dance a relentless waltz of hope deferred. For there was no respite to soothe one's pain, no aid to come to one's side. None could leave, and salvation had forgotten this place.

The Lake of Fire consumed each incarcerated soul held captive by the insatiable passions of lust and self: a twofold punishment forever administered on these prisoners for all time. A memorial by El, forever to be remembered by us all.

The lake was an eternal smoldering monument of our war: a token of El's wrath upon all those who had held back the truth in unrighteousness. My eyes were older than much of creation, and as they darted over the vastness of this everlasting torture, I remembered when I first saw the flames of the Kiln run amuck.

Yet even now, I found that I looked for him: my beloved, my brother, my friend, and my enemy — he whom my soul delighted.

I stood at the precipice of this jagged maw in the Earth's crust of heat, smoke, and fire. I strained that I might see the Adversary. It has always been an easy thing for a creature such as I to find my own kind, and with Lucifer even more so — quite easy actually. Knowing my brother, I needed only to look towards the heart of this mass grave of the spiritually dead.

Our eyes met.

He was still a creature of pride, and even here, even after all this time, Lucifer sought to be the center of all things. He smirked as he looked at me, but I am not deceived. I know that joy does not dwell in this place. The human

Dante was prescient when he penned, 'Hope had abandoned all those that entered here,' here in the Lake of Fire, even Hell herself could not flee.

Lucifer's face I knew with intimate familiarity. The smirk on his lips masked an unspoken yet seething hatred from the inner knowing that he was "superior" to all in creation, elevated to stand in the very presence of God, yet cast down as rubble to be stared and looked upon, a creature to be pitied.

Oh how art thou fallen O Lucifer son of the morning. How art thou cut down to the ground, which didst weaken the nations.

It was this knowing, which I knew forever would gnaw at him...the reason for his smirk. Our gaze was short as smoke enveloped him, yet through the veneer, yes, I saw it— a tear.

Then he was gone; veiled in smolder and fire; and pummeled by the legions he once sought to rule. Forever crushed underfoot by those he deemed chattel — forever humiliated.

Never in all my days did I believe my eyes would behold such a sight.

I turned away as I could behold such suffering for only so long. Even one such as I had limits.

I am relieved that the war is over.

The kingdoms of this world are become the kingdoms of our Lord, and of his Christ; and he shall reign forever and ever.

But at what price?

This victory was not without loss, not without pain.

"Have you come to mock me, Michael?"

Lucifer's voice could not be mimicked or masked. There was one being in creation that sounded thus. Only *he* could speak so that even from the Lake of Fire my attention could be garnered.

I am hesitant to reply. I do not wish to look upon this—murderer.

5

We will not speak again after today. I know this, therefore, I turned to face him for the last time.

"What manner of conversation would I engage with the King of Lies?"

As I looked upon his face and body now disfigured, I steeled myself. There was a time when I shed tears for my brother, but that was millennia ago. Too much blood had been spilled between us, too many wounds. Mercy no longer beat within my breast for him, yet even now, I could not help but ruminate on more pleasant times. I drifted into reflection and daydreamed back to the beginning of it all—still questioning—still wondering.

How did it come to this?

Chapter One

In the beginning...

Day Five

The sun's heat broiled and beat upon Michael's pale skin. The mountain cliffs radiated the thick humidity as he wiped the perspiration from his face. The haze moved to escape the swelter in a vain attempt to flee. Long turquoise streaks of sweat beaded upon his forehead and streaked his muscular jaw line to cover his face in lines of blue sweat. He shook his head to keep the perspiration from getting into his eyes, and his golden hair sprayed a mist of as he tried to cool himself. His white robes were soaked, and his golden bands steamed and burned his forearms as the heat baked him and his men. The group had labored all day to fit the new Cadmime beams to the sides of the cliff in order to expand Heaven's foundation.

Michael looked down at the whirlpool of hurricane winds, dangling high above their howling wails. Each gust ascended the canyon walls as the tempest below rotated in cyclonic fury swirling around the black eye of the Abyss. The Abyss — the bottomless pit where all reality ended. A heavenly body so dense that not even light escaped its grasp. It was a natural phenomenon of such destructive might even angels dared not venture near. Yet here Michael and his kind did the work to build Heaven. His race of Kortai alone answered El's call to work so close to the Abyss. Within the bottomless pit, there was no space, no heaven, no time. It was a gaping mouth of a null void. There was no escape if one fell in. El had deemed it so that any who ventured to fall would fall forever.

Gusts buffeted him, slamming him against the rock face. The downdrafts stood ever ready to drag him into the waiting mouth of the bottomless pit. Despite its howls, Michael enjoyed the coolness of the breeze the winds generated against his skin.

Michael cocked his head in an attempt to stretch his neck, and scrunched his lateral muscles, each tendon aching from the harness strapped tightly to his back. He tugged at his belt straps to loosen his gear. The straps pinched his skin forcing him to adjust them constantly from nipping his 10 wings. Work this close to the Maelstrom was dangerous, but he had carefully clamped and tied his harness. He tugged on it again just to be sure.

It was secure. The wind battered and shoved him against the craggy rock of the canyon's wall.

I am going to be so sore today, he thought.

Lucifer also was hoisted and attached to the cliff wall and hammered a brace into place. "I believe this to be the last one, brother. Is your beam secure?" His voice resonated with melody and the alto of his inquiry chimed in Michael's ears.

Even in the exhaustive heat, the tabrets and pipes in Lucifer's body gave off a pleasant tune; each dimpled pore of his skin opened and closed with every syllable from his operatic voice.

Michael pushed off against the cliff and rappelled sideways, hurtling through the air while the whirlwind raged below him. His feet landed on the crag, and he leaned over to inspect his brother's work.

"The strut will hold. Well done, and I think it is time for a break."

"Agreed," said Lucifer. "Michael, when you said you could use my help you neglected to mention that it would take all day."

Michael laughed. "You are so busy I rarely get to spend time with you. Besides — work using your own hands and not relying on your servants could do you some good."

Lucifer rolled his eyes and then smiled.

"Next time you desire to spend time with me try to think of something less dangerous."

Michael laughed. "Oh come now would you have me believe that you would prefer being in the palace composing sonnets, and miss all this?"

Michael opened his hand to present the spectacle of nature that surrounded them.

Lucifer eyed the stretched landscape of the canyon. The splendor of the chasms walls awed even him. He noted that they all stood as mites on the underside of the mountain that was Heaven. Lucifer turned his eyes to look below and surveyed the Abyss beneath them. The winds of the Maelstrom churned in its claw-like attempts to sweep them away. Stars, uncountable as grains of sand, splayed themselves like crystal across the canopy of Heaven's golden and black sky, each a visible reminder of the barrier that separated the realms. Lucifer had to admit it was indeed an impressive view.

Michael yelled over the whine that came from the Maelstrom so that his brother could hear. "Alas, I do confess that I enjoy the sound of your voice. Your melody is soothing, and who else could I trust to extend the cliff face — these lazy friends of mine?"

Michael thumbed in the direction of his smiling three comrades while they hammered spikes into place.

They laughed in retort, "Hey! We are right here!"

Lucifer chuckled.

"It would seem that our work here is complete," said Michael, "Everyone take a rest. I shall attend shortly."

Michael watched in satisfaction as tendrils of new ground sprang from the sides of Heaven as living rock grew to embrace the Cadmime extension.

Good, Heaven will have more room for the changes El hast command-ed.

The ground began to groan. The earth swelled, buckled, and stretched to overtake the beam planted in the canyon's side. Michael and his men smiled from the familiar sound of the land expanding.

Michael loved building, to see the results of the fruit of his labor. The Lord had given him the plans to the city, and he had overseen every aspect of its growth.

El would be pleased, he thought.

Michael prepared himself to release the buckle that latched him to the side of the mountain. The winds of the Abyss were but yards below him, and he could hear the howl of the hurricane that separated the heavens. A dimensional barrier crossed only by Ladder or special dispensation from El. The winds rotated in cyclonic fashion as a whirlwind: a Maelstrom that encircled the Abyss, a realm of bottomlessness and the flux from which the second and third heavens met. El had said that dissolution was the natural Ladder to enter into the realm. A peeling away of one's mortal coil would send one careening from the reality of the First to the Third Heaven, the Kingdom of God, a realm superimposed over all other layers of reality.

Michael knew that expanding the ground was dangerous work, for the Abyss pulled at two realms and sought to consume within itself anything that lay on its outskirts. Michael was careful not to stray too close to the event horizon.

Lucifer and the rest of the workers unlatched their harnesses and pushed against the cliff wall. Outstretched wings allowed the updraft of the wind from the Maelstrom to jet them upwards to the edge where they landed safely, still tethered to the stakes on the cliffs.

"Secure these lines," commanded Lucifer. "The ground will shift soon."

Lucifer looked down to his brother who still inspected the strut supports. He yelled below. "Michael quickly, get out of there!"

Michael had already unleashed his tether when the ground shook, and the mountain heaved outward encasing the implanted beam. A cropping of rock jutted out, striking Michael in the face and knocking him backward. Untethered, Michael waved his arms in a vain attempt to balance himself, but the rock slid and collapsed from under his feet, and he plummeted into the winds of the Maelstrom.

All watched in horror as the winds of the hurricane swept Michael away and rushed to drain him into the Abyss.

"Michael!" Lucifer yelled.

Lucifer's face grew anxious, and he turned to a worker behind him. "Quickly give me your harness," he said.

The angel unlatched the golden rope and lanyards that overlaid his garments and handed them over to the Chief Prince.

"Lucifer ... Michael is lost —"

Lucifer looked at the angel and raised his voice. "He is lost when I no longer draw breath."

Lucifer buckled the clamp to his waist, pummeled a spike into the ground, turned, and then rappelled back down the side of the cliff.

He untied the grappling ropes. Each rope held a twelve-inch metal spike to latch onto the rock face. He placed the harness over his body, secured each fastener, and latched the hooks into the rings of his belt to support his weight.

El — please give me strength; let me not be too late.

Lucifer looked out towards the center of the Abyss; the blackness was enveloping, for not even light escaped its edge. He knew that there was no survival if he fell in. He would be lost in the bottomless pit that separated the realms. Lucifer shed his garments and the light from his skin burst in all directions. His flesh transformed into living diamond, and the colors of the rainbow skipped about him. His twelve tendril-like wings unfurled and waved, as each vine of energy caught the gusts that blew from the Maelstrom. Stripped of his raiment, his skin reflected the light, and he gleamed so that onlookers fell to their knees and raised their hands to shield their eyes.

Lucifer lifted the grapples over his head and swung them, each spin gaining increased momentum. Each wave of his arms vibrated the air, and a screeching sound rang in the ears of all about. He released the grapples, and they flew across the expanse of the whirlpool and stuck into a crag on the other side.

He tugged on the rope. It held fast, but the winds from the Maelstrom buffeted the line, making it move and shift. He tied the end to a boulder near him until the rope became taut and held firm. He oscillated his breathing in his ears so that his body would pulsate as a beacon for Michael. He turned down the brightness of his flesh, and all ceased from covering their eyes. He threw another line towards his workers. They caught it, latched their bodies around it, and braced themselves against a boulder.

"Watch the line," he yelled to the workers. "Do not let it give way!"

The angels nodded. Lucifer looked into the Abyss, attached himself to the rope, and climbed up on the line, dangling upside down. His ankles and hands were wrapped tightly over the line as he shimmied himself towards the center of the pounding gales. The squall beat at him; its force and his weight made the rope buckle. It gave way some. He looked in the distance to see his fellow angels struggling to hold it tightly against the stone. He turned his face rearward towards the opposite end, and he could see the line starting to slip.

He opened the pores of his back, howled from the vocal cords that lined the muscles of his trapezoids, and yelled. "Michael! Raise your hand that I might see you! Michael, can you hear me?"

He strained his eyes to see any hope of his brother, but could not see him. He focused himself to look for movement in the whirlwind and beheld Michael tossed about by the gale force winds and struggling to release the straps from the harness that held his wings against his back. Lucifer watched as Michael's body swirled around the edge of the whirlwind knowing that he would have but one pass to rescue him, for with two passes, he would drain into the Abyss. Lucifer lowered his hand to prepare to hoist his brother from the storm.

Michael headed towards him, tumbling and tossed about, his body thrown aloft like a piece of driftwood on crashing rapids. Closer, Lucifer lowered himself down the more. Michael raced towards him; yards removed and then with increasing swiftness mere feet away. Timing his reach, Lucifer lunged to grasp his brother from the grip of wind and gale, strained to extend himself without also falling into the whirlpool. Michael reached up and grasped his brother's hand and they interlocked wrists.

Lucifer struggled to hold onto him, but the Maelstrom would not let Michael go, and they stood in stalemate with Lucifer hanging on suspended over the canyon of typhonic winds.

"We cannot both be saved—leave me," yelled Michael.

Lucifer struggled to fly with his brother, but Michael was too heavy and the winds too strong. The squall howled their disapproval, and with a gust that smashed into them both, the line snapped, and Lucifer plummeted with Michael into the circling storm.

Lucifer held fast to Michael and spoke as they hurtled towards the event horizon of the crushing black that was the Abyss.

Lucifer spoke into Michael's ear. "Never ask me to leave you, nor from following you, for where you go, I will go, and if you die, I will die."

Michael hugged his brother as they spun uncontrollably and jetted towards the event horizon of the Abyss. Michael closed his eyes as the darkness edged closer to overtake them. "Surely El will save us," he said.

Lucifer looked up and beheld that the Waypoint of Argoth was within view, and his mind raced with a plan to escape.

"No...El hast given us means to save ourselves." Lucifer struggled to lift his finger and pointed to the Waypoint of Argoth. "Look, do you see?"

Michael nodded. "Hurry, there is not much time!"

"El tore, shay crom mere ley," Lucifer roared.

Speaking in the draconic tongue, Lucifer commanded the doors between the realms to open and summoned a Ladder.

In obedience, a thunderhead gathered, swirled, then encircled above the duo, and ejected bolts of lightning. A storm birthed from the billows and stoked the winds of the Maelstrom even more. Winds howled to one another in competitive shrieks as the new tempest fed the gale already running through the canyon. The force was such that the cliff face started to shred for the might of the winds.

The ground around the cliff's edge buckled and heaved in response. Workers watched with mouths agape as a rainbow colored funnel cloud crackled with thunder, lightning, and reached down as a great hand into the cyclonic drain that was the Maelstrom.

Michael and Lucifer spun closer to the event horizon of the Abyss, carried adrift by the current of the gale. The vortex of descending light twisted, screamed, and whined as the winds of the maelstrom fought against the winds of a Ladder summoned by the word of El.

Hurricane wrestled against cyclone, and when Lucifer saw that they approached the event horizon, he heaved Michael into the air with all of his might. Michael quickly ascended and lifted away from him as the funnel of light gripped him and held him fast. The Ladder sucked him high into the sky and tore him free from the clutches of the Abyss.

Michael screamed in agony and reached out as he watched his brother flail helplessly into the enveloping shroud of darkness. The black dragged Lucifer into the whirlpool that was the bottomless pit.

Michael lunged across the sky, falling through a tunnel exploding in color and hot white bursts of plasma. The Ladder then folded on itself, hurtled towards the ground, and slammed Michael into the dirt on his back.

Workers round about ran to their leader.

Coughing, wheezing, his muscles throbbing, Michael struggled to rise to his feet. "Get this harness off me!" He yelled.

The workers raced to unlatch the straps that bound their master's wings. Michael moved in agitation, for despite their swiftness, they moved still too slow for his taste. The harness then fell to the ground, and with wings unfurled, Michael ran to fly to his brother's aid, but several angels tackled him so that he would not plunge headlong back into the Abyss.

Michael struggled against them, and tears welled in his eyes as he listened, for the sound of music that echoed from Lucifer's body, music that sprang from the soft motion of winds against his skin, faded into silence. Nothing remained but the incessant howls of the Abyssal whirlwinds. Slowly, the sparkle that emanated from Lucifer's crystalline flesh, dissipated in the blackness, and he was seen no more.

Michael let loose a wail despairing in self-crimination. Gripping loose dirt in his palms, he smeared his face moaning and coiled over weeping.

15

Suddenly, the ground shook, and howling and lightning burst from the Abyss, making Michael to cease his self-flagellation and take note.

For the Ladder had still not dissipated, and though its base was lost within the darkness of the bottomless pit, lightning arched from the funnel cloud and bolts of plasma struck out blasting the landscape in all directions. Michael and the workers watched as the Maelstrom turned bright white, and the earth underneath them buckled, heaved, and collapsed beneath them.

Each ran as the earth opened and chunks of the cliff fell into the Maelstrom. They lifted themselves into the sky to escape, when suddenly an explosion rocked across the canyon, and a blast of heated wind flung them all backward into trees and rock. Michael fell crashing to the ground and turned to his rear to see the land behind them was gone, and the Maelstrom was all that the eye could see.

The Ladder then lifted into the sky, twisting, screaming in howling fury. A figure gleamed at its base, and Michael watched as the Ladder turned, hurtling towards them.

Each angel ran and flew to escape the ensuing beam of light and plasma and leaped out of the way to prevent from being struck. The familiar sound of Lucifer's body echoed across the canyon.

The funnel touched the ground, and then Lucifer followed and slammed into the earth. The impact from his fall cratered the land, throwing rock and trees aside while fire and white smoke hissed from his frame. Lucifer was on bended knee as the colors of the rainbow skipped around him as fallen snow. Flecks of prismatic light followed him and settled on his person, and Lucifer glowed as light from a star.

Onlookers mouths dropped at what they had witnessed and bowed in awe that the Chief Prince had survived the Abyss. "Lightbringer," an angel said.

Others whispered the words about them and bowed themselves in respect for their prince.

Lucifer rose from bended knee. His body shivered uncontrollably; sore that two of heaven's forces had vied over him. His face twinkling in light, Lucifer turned to speak to Michael in the melodic tenor that was his voice. "Are you all right," he asked.

Michael coughed and turned towards his brother. "I am — thanks to you. Are you ok?

Lucifer replied, "Aye, sore, very sore, but El be praised we survived."

"I thought I had lost you," said Michael.

Lucifer laughed. "I thought I had lost me too."

"There is something that you should know," said Michael.

Lucifer scrunched his face while massaging the back of his neck. He shook his head and looked at his brother curiously. "And what might that be?"

Michael hesitated to answer but looked at his brother, paused, and then spoke quietly under his breath. "That brace — well it fell when I unlatched from the cliff. Sorry."

Lucifer's eyes widened as he looked at Michael in disbelief. He lifted himself from the ground, as he wiped grime and dust from himself. "Michael Kortai! I am *not* going to do that work all over again!"

Michael bowed his head slightly; his eyes darted from Lucifer to the ground and then back again. He hunched his shoulders and pulled from his robes the spike that had dislodged from the wall. He held it up and tossed it to his brother.

Lucifer caught it, looked at it, looked at Michael, and then chuckled. Michael too found himself snickering, and like a viral infection that spread; each broke out in stomach bursting hilarity as workers who beheld their rescue and escape ran to assist them and gathered round to see the two laid out, flat on their backs laughing.

Suddenly a flash of white light appeared. The group covered their eyes as Gabriel stood before them in shining white robes and a staff in hand. "The Lumazi are summoned to court," he said.

Lucifer and Michael rose to stand in their brother's presence.

Lucifer stopped laughing, and his tone grew somber. "Of course," he said. "We shall leave at once."

Gabriel looked at them and pinched his nose against the odor that floated about them; grime and dirt covered their face, and dust fell from their clothing.

"You both stink," Gabriel said.

They laughed, and Michael pointed at his brother, "It's him."

Lucifer cocked his head and gave Michael a scowl.

"Well, you *do* stink," said Michael.

The sound of falling rock came from their rear, and Gabriel peered to his left to see behind and past them. Quickly, they moved to his left to block his view: and when he moved to his right to see, Michael and Lucifer also moved.

Gabriel frowned and placed his hands on his hips. "This is not funny."

Lucifer took the spike he held in his hand and tossed it to Gabriel, who caught it.

"Indeed, you know not the half of it," Lucifer sniggered.

Michael and the rest of the work crew burst out in laughter. Gabriel looked upon them all as if they were all mad. Each walked past him laughing.

"You really missed it," said one.

"If you had just come a bit earlier," said another.

Once again, Gabriel heard the sound of crashing rock to his rear. He turned his head, and Gabriel's eyes widened at the spectacle before him. The cliffs face and large chunks of land fell into the mouth of the Maelstrom, and the gale ripped and shredded boulders apart until nothing but sand remained. Gabriel looked at his brothers as they walked away and then turned to look once more at the chaos they had left behind. He shook his head in disbelief and made his way to run after them.

"You two are something else. Ok, this one I've got to hear."

****

The Lord God's command was clear. "Assemble before me and report of thy stewardship."

Propelled by instinct, the high princes traveled from the farthest reaches of creation as salmon to their stream of birth.

Michael walked through the outer court of the palace. Light permeated every nook and cranny of its colossal, white granite halls: each ray of luminance sprang from the person of El whose mere presence glowed and projected brilliance above the brightest sun.

"Hail Michael!" said a familiar voice from his rear.

Michael turned to see Raphael floating from the Hall of Annals towards him. He smiled wide upon seeing his brother.

Raphael ran to embrace him. "Ah, it is so good to see you!"

"The feeling is mutual," replied Michael.

"You have been so busy with the business of the Grigori that I feel neglected. It has been too long since we have spent time together. I miss hearing the tales of what El is doing throughout creation."

Raphael nodded and spoke. "Indeed, we have been apart too long. Perhaps after the report, we might converse in the Hall. I can show you the creation of a new nebula. Michael, I tell you, never have my eyes seen such sights. El honors my people by allowing us to record all. We are, after all, the most traveled of Elohim."

"The Lord is wondrous, and I look forward to exploring the new realms," said Michael. "I must admit I am excited to travel. To see the wonders of creation in person is indeed a thrilling prospect. As Archon over the city, my management of Heaven leaves little time for anything else. Perhaps I may request from El a temporary leave from my assignment."

They laughed as they walked towards the veil of the throne room.

As they walked from the outer court of the palace into the inner court, the Seraphim cried out to greet them. Michael and Raphael adjusted their inner ears to prevent deafness.

The Seraphim roared to the approaching angels and to each other. "Holy, Holy, Holy, Lord God Almighty, which was, and is, and is to come!"

Michael was used to the Seraphim repeating this ear-splitting chant day and night. The sound was so loud that it would deafen all but the most powerful of Elohim. Flame covered the entirety of the Seraphim's bodies. Each had six wings. With two they flew, with two they covered their eyes, and with two they covered their feet.

There were four of the creatures in existence, and they were always in El's vestibule or outside the temple doors. Eyes filled their bodies, and each was half man and half beast. Fire emanated from their frames, and dark smoke ushered from them. They stood 20 feet tall and were muscular in build.

Michael and Raphael continued to converse and heard the sound of music in the distance before them. Lucifer had come to greet them.

"Michael, it's good of you to join us. Late again I see?"

Michael eyed with admiration his elder brother. Lucifer's porous and scale-like skin glowed, and the multicolored moving patterns of his body mesmerized so that one did not want to look away. His twelve glowing wings were aburst in color, and each follicle of his hair captured the slightest movement, and like wind chimes created melodious sound with each of his approaching steps.

"Ah my brother never has sarcasm sounded so sweet," Michael, teased.

Raphael let out a laugh.

Lucifer's pitch changed, and the beautiful scowling of a hundred-voice choir replied, "I would not see you rebuked. Come, we do not wish to be late."

Lucifer scratched at his chest as if irritated. He motioned the two princes to follow him. "Come, El awaits the council."

Michael and Raphael turned to follow. Michael eyed his elder brother, for his organs were musical instruments, and as Lucifer walked, every movement made one want to dance or sing. The sound was pleasant to the ear, and Lucifer could create any sound within creation in any key, with any pitch and volume. Lucifer did not speak; he sang.

Michael studied Lucifer, mimicked his gait, and waved his hands with flowing motions through the air.

"Michael, what are you doing?" Raphael whispered.

Michael fluttered his wings like his elder brother but still nothing.

Raphael looked at him wondering if Michael had lost his mind.

"Michael," said Raphael.

Lucifer turned around to see that his brother mimicked him. With eyebrows raised, he spoke. "Would you for a second stop fooling around, and come on!"

"There it is," said Michael.

Lucifer looked at Michael with irritation and put his hands on his hips. "There is what?" he said.

"That thing you do with your voice — that twang. How do you do that?"

"Ugh, you are as incorrigible as Jerahmeel." Annoyed, Lucifer shook his head and walked away.

The brotherhood knew Lucifer was the most serious-minded of them all and possessed little humor. However, no one could irritate Lucifer more than Jerahmeel, whose brashness and disregard for protocol irked him to no end.

El never rebuked Jerahmeel, as if El knew the high princes needed his sage, yet frank advice. Jerahmeel always told Lucifer to "lighten up." Yet, despite all of his seriousness, no one among them was more devoted to the service of El than Lucifer.

"See! He did it again," said Michael.

Raphael walked past him laughing. "Lucifer is right; you are incorrigible."

"What? I think it's the pipes in his throat and forearms. That's what's making that sound! I want some too!"

Passing through the veil of the inner chamber, they entered the throne room: the seat of all power in the multiverse. Four members were already assembled and on bended knee waiting for El to summon them.

Michael lifted his hands to his eyes to block the glare from the blinding white light as waves of intense heat overtook them as they neared El's presence. Lucifer's company never helped, for his mirror-like skin just heightened the effect.

Michael looked over and whispered to Raphael, "I will never get used to this."

"Hush, Michael," he replied.

The three princes traversed the throne steps and arrived at their apex.

The steps of the throne were made of the same material as the street of the city: a translucent gold. All streets in Heaven found their paths ending at the mountain of God and the throne room. Before the throne, the floor was as a sea of glass similar unto crystal. In the midst of the throne and round about the throne, a mist filled the air, and a rainbow arched above the throne.

Seven basins of fire were set before it, a place for each high prince to sit before the fire. Within each lamp lived a Virtue: living smoke, whose foggy presence filled the chamber, yet did not emit the smell of burning or make one choke. The fragrance of the Virtues was akin to frankincense, and they wafted about the throne room with transparent eyes and moved as fish swim in formation.

The white marble pillars of the throne room shook from the voices of the Seraphim outside. Behind and beneath the throne were the Ophanim; living creatures that looked like wheels within wheels. Two of these creatures were underneath the throne as if its entire weight rested on them, and two were horizontally behind it.

Each had four faces. As for the likeness of their faces, each of the four had the face of a man and the face of a lion on the right side and the face of an ox and an eagle on the left side. They sparkled like chrysolite.

Two rotating wheels with wings crisscrossed by two other wheels with wings surrounded them. Moreover, they moved in any one of four directions the creatures faced; and all four wheels were full of eyes all around.

Each Ophanim generated powerful gusts that propelled the throne at El's whim. When the Ophanim moved, the wheels beside them moved, and when Ophanim rose from the ground, the wheels rose. Wherever the Lord God went, they went too, and the wheels rose along with them because the spirits of the living creatures were in the wheels.

Affixed to the top of the throne were two Cherubim; each faced one another with backs arched and heads bowed. With outstretched wings, they covered the throne as if it were possible to provide shade for the God who is light, yet they stood ever ready and awaited any command from El. El's train filled the temple, a living blood red cloak that draped round about the throne and flowed down unto the crystal floor below.

The angels of his presence, the Lumazi, had assembled and stood before the Lord. In unison, the seven princes bowed, as was protocol before the Lord of all things.

Others could not look upon El without blindness, yet their eyelids as High Princes allowed them to filter the luminance and made it possible to see an outline or, at least, a partial visage of his form. The Shekinah Glory surrounded El, and those who looked upon him directly would invoke blindness, for the Shekinah was the residue of God's breath. A living shawl of breathing light that enveloped and irradiated the person of God. The Shekinah illumined all that came near the Lord and left an afterglow on anyone who attended Him, even after one had left his immediate presence.

To describe El was difficult. All angels were in a manner of speaking a reflection of Him, yet He surpassed all intelligible attempts to describe Him.

Michael looked upon El, and He appeared as a bearded Elohim of 10 cubits height: whose hair was as wool, youthful in looks yet ancient beyond understanding.

Michael observed that El possessed two legs, two arms and that there was no form, comeliness, nor beauty that He should be desired, just an all-encompassing gentleness and power. When El walked, he did so with a slow deliberate and steady gait. Only on the most momentous of occasions did he even leave the throne room.

24

When Michael asked what his brethren saw, each saw a different thing. Raphael said that he saw a two-legged figure with a blindfold over his face, having four arms; each arm held four objects: a book a stylus, an inkhorn, and a balance.

Gabriel swore he saw a feline-like creature with wings on each foot.

Lucifer— Lucifer never discussed how he viewed El. He was always reluctant to speak of what he saw. Michael always thought his reluctance strange, but if he were not confident of Lucifer's devotion, one would say contempt would be the look Lucifer displayed whenever Michael broached the subject.

Then El spoke and awakened Michael from his daydreaming.

"I am the Alpha and the Omega, the Beginning and the End. Stand before me and give account of thy stewardship. Approach, Michael."

Mindful to bow, Michael walked towards the Lord, sat before him, and gave his report.

"Lord, the additional housing that you have directed has been completed. There are one billion new units now available for occupancy. The granaries have been expanded for increased food storage, and the city expanded by an additional 25% by your orders.

"Lord, it would appear that we have more than enough room in the capital and clear that we have more living space and food production capabilities than is necessary. May I ask the purpose of these additions to the kingdom?"

Michael waited for a response. El smiled at him. Michael remembered El once told him that his trusting and inquisitive nature was one of the attributes that He most enjoyed about him.

"Soon all will be made clear, my friend. I will announce my intentions at the next assembly. By then all preparations will be complete, and on the seventh day, I will rest from all my labor."

I knew it! So an announcement is forthcoming! Michael thought to himself.

Michael shook his head, knowing that by the time he understood what El wanted done, El had been planning the outcome from the very beginning.

Michael continued until he concluded his report.

"I am pleased with the progress to the city my son. Well done."

Michael stood to his feet, bowed, and walked backwards until he was again with his waiting brothers at the steps below.

"Lucifer, Son of the Morning Star, approach."

Lucifer was titled "Son of the Morning Star," and other than God Himself, there was no object brighter in illumination, thus the title of honor. God had named each member of the Elohim and had written their names on their flesh.

Then the Lord said unto Lucifer, "Whence comest thou?"

Then Lucifer answered the Lord, and said, "From going to and fro in the Earth, and from walking up and down in it."

"And how fares the happenings on Earth?" the Lord asked.

"Lord, per your orders, the seas have brought forth great beasts after their kind, and the skies filled with fowl. A particular species glides for several furlongs with a grace that rivals even the Elohim my Lord.

"I am most impressed by your designs and creativity. To pattern this planet after some of the same flora and fauna as in Heaven, I would not have thought to do that, especially in light of the variety of worlds that you have allowed us to administer, but this world is particularly beautiful, Lord. I thank you for allowing me over-site as its Archon."

Michael shook his head and smiled at his brother. *Look at him as giddy*

26

As soon as he knew the importance of this assignment, Lucifer fawned all over it. Michael had never seen Lucifer so pleased with himself than when El titled him Archon of Earth.

Michael was happy for Lucifer: proud even, for he had assisted him since the very beginning. Lucifer was always there always helping each new Elohim that God created to acclimate to their new assignment. Initially, it was a daunting task when the Elohim were fewer. However, nothing was too much for El. He was their Father, and they happily obliged Him in all things. Never would Michael have thought to see the wonders that they now behold.

In each of the last assemblies, the council had come to learn more about the thing El had called *Time* and that He would create a sphere of creation that would be subject to it.

Each member of the Lumazi was to explain to their race the meaning of all that they learned and commit to their knowledge the conduct required to operate within each realm. They adjusted over time to the knowledge and reality of these new heavens and the limits that El had directed as they roamed within each one.

Lucifer continued his report and in a twinkling of an eye displayed to his maker all the wonders of Earth's beauty. He noted how the planet had angels making sure that each river ran its course per the explicit directions of El.

Michael listened awestruck as to the level of involvement that El had in every aspect of creation. He never realized how his duties in the capital dulled him from appreciating how much design went into the massive undertaking of creation.

Four days they had all labored, and Lucifer gave his report on the latest day's efforts, detailing to the Creator information on new flying creatures, wingspans, and even the number of feathers each one needed to remain airborne.

Michael leaned forward absorbed as Lucifer elaborated on the difficulty in achieving the color combinations that El commanded in certain species of flowers. On and on, the First of Angels relayed the intricate details of life that was quickly enveloping the planet El had named "Earth." God nodded his head in approval and saw that it was good.

"Well done, Lucifer. You have done all according to my will. Well done indeed."

Then it happened.

El stood!

With a wave of his outstretched hand, the throne room suddenly disappeared. The walls vanished before their eyes, and all that remained were seven angelic princes still on bended knee floating within the second heaven El had named "space."

El's eyes turned towards one of the many galaxies He had created, and for a moment, any equilibrium the princes possessed failed them as the motion of stars, planets, and other phenomena too wondrous to describe flashed before their eyes.

Then within full view of them all, El reached for a small blue orb of a planet, which encircled the now familiar star named Sol, and lovingly held it within the palm of his hand.

Once again, they moved and found themselves partially submerged in water.

Michael became off balance as a sea of water surrounded him, and waves crashed over his face. The whole group struggled to swim, fly, and adjust to the instantaneous nature of how they traveled from the throne room of Heaven to this planet with its teeming oceans.

Panic-stricken, Sariel cried, "Look!" and pointed to several large creatures moving with great speed towards them.

Then they appeared: great whales—giants gliding in the great deeps of the watery world, and littering the sky above them were countless fowl whose numbers were too abundant to tally.

With arms outstretched and a voice of gentleness and satisfaction, God saw that it was good. The Lord God blessed them, saying, "Be fruitful, and multiply, and fill the waters in the seas, and let fowl multiply in the Earth."

Then with a flash after having reached this planet of teeming life and having adjusted to the state of water and motion, the group found themselves instantly atop the Mountain of God in El's throne room.

"Wow," said Jerahmeel, soaking wet with the biggest smile on his face. "Now that was fun! Can we do it again?"

Gabriel lost all sense of balance and immediately toppled over. El's unique method of instantaneous transport was finally too much to overcome. Michael laughed aloud and Gabriel shot him a hot frown.

"I am not amused," said Gabriel, who then put his hand over his mouth: his cheeks turning green.

Michael smiled, looked up, and noted that the Lord had settled into his throne. Lucifer also was sitting before the Lord and had continued his report while the rest of his brethren; pale and queasy attempted to compose themselves.

"Show off," Michael whispered to Lucifer.

Lucifer grinned and continued his report.

Michael glanced up and noted to his astonishment that El was chuckling at them.

And the evening and the morning were the fifth day.

Chapter Two

Finishing Touches

Day Six

"What is wrong with you?" asked an angel.

I had never thought that I was different, never until someone pointed it out to me.

"What do you mean?" I asked.

"Why is your stone broken?" the angel replied.

I reached my hand into my robes and pulled my sigil stone from my chest for inspection. It felt fractured, even coarse in some parts, yet there was a clear delineation of smoothness to half of it. A quarter of the stone was missing, but it was clear that two halves of the stone were stitched together. I looked down to see the gouged hollow absent from the whole. My Heartstone warmed my hand as it pulsated in my palm. The ginger-colored stone shimmered with a crystal glint; it had firmness and heft to it. The outer skin of my heart rose and fell. Something moved within that strained to get out of the stone. Smoke and ash floated from it, and it crackled with a sizzling sound. It gave off an aroma akin to burnt charcoal.

My self-inspection showed that nothing seemed amiss.

"I do not know," I said. "It has been this way since my creation. What's wrong with it?"

"Your stone is broken," the angel said. "Something is wrong with you."

Your stone is broken. Something is wrong with you: that is all he ever said. It's funny as I think back, but I never did get that angels name.

"Apollyon are you ready?"

Perhaps now after all this time I will gain the respect I have always

30

wanted.

"Apollyon, stop day dreaming. Are you ready?" Saesheal said.

"Yes, my friend. You fuss over me like I am going to forget!"

Saesheal laughed, "No — I fuss over you because you *do* forget!"

I laughed because I knew Saesheal was right. He was the first to take any interest in me: my truest friend. He has always been so protective, and I had to admit I enjoyed how he doted over me.

"Leave him alone. You can mock about someone else's stone when you acquire the power to create one yourself. If El does not worry, then neither should you." The angel scowled and walked away. I turned to my benefactor and looked upon the smaller Arelim who had come to advocate for me.

"My name is Saesheal," he said. "We will be serving together in the Sol system. What is your name?"

"Apollyon," I replied. "El has titled me Son of the Dawn."

"Truly?" Saesheal said. "Impressive—that name is similar to Lucifer's. It is my pleasure to meet you. My quarters are not far from here. Care to get a bite before training?"

"That would be nice. Thank you," I said.

"By the way, I happen to think your stone makes you unique. It has an orange color to it."

I tried my best not to roll my eyes. I hated orange.

"Thanks," I replied.

How ironic, that after all this time, I find myself now bathed in the orange glow of this star. Saesheal interrupted my daydreaming.

"I always knew that you looked good in orange Apollyon." Saesheal teased. "You are now Archon of Sol, I am proud of you."

I positioned myself in the center of the sun and reveled in the blanket of its warm embrace: its flames soothed tendons and muscle. I was now officially the Archon of Sol. I could feel my jaw widen with the grin that I knew stretched across my face.

Archon: I liked the sound of that. My assignment as archangel over El's prized star would give me great prominence among my people. Perhaps now, I might command respect and no more be called, "broken stone."

I looked at Saesheal, who smiled at me, and remembered the angels of times past who sneered at my difference. "Shhhh, here he comes," laughed an angel.

I winced as I thought back on the memory. I suppose they never did truly care if I heard them or not. Ashtaroth was always quick to remind me of my difference with his constant and grinding ridicule of me. I had resigned myself that I would best him in seeking title as Archon of this star.

"Eh, pay him no mind Apollyon," said Saesheal. "There is something to be said about being different from everyone else. It sets you apart. You would do well to consult with Lucifer. He might aid thee to understand how one so different might abide. No one understands this more than the First of Angels."

"Perhaps I will," I said.

Lucifer always supported me. He made sure I had the best training and took a personal interest in me. I knew he saw how others treated me. He was quick to rebuke when anything occurred and swift to offer me words of encouragement I was grateful for his mentoring. I appreciated the kindness he and Saesheal showed me.

"Bear Ashtaroth no mind, my friend, as he too covets to be Archon of Sol," said Lucifer. "He has petitioned Master Breagun for the role. I suspect he desires to impress me by overseeing the sun, which warms my own charge. I believe his behavior towards you is but his way to show his own desire for thy

32

status," said Lucifer. "I will talk to him. He is rife with possessiveness whenever I speak of another angel in fondness or admiration."

"Am I to understand that you admire me then Chief Prince?" I asked.

Lucifer smiled. "I have come to see how similar we are, my friend. I would see such potential cultivated and steered. You are the 'Son of the Dawn'. I would see you shine."

I paused from my past reflections and waved to Saesheal as I bathed within the fires of this orb of gas and flame, but nothing warmed me more than the smile that beamed back approvingly from my friend. I no longer could afford such lapses in thought as I slowly assumed control of the star.

"Saesheal, we both know that orange is *not* my color. And you, dear sir, well, let's just say I can't wait to see you in grey."

Saesheal chuckled at me. "Let me enjoy this moment I can't help it if you look silly in orange."

"Oh so after so many days together, the truth comes out! I knew I looked funny in orange!" Saesheal snickered and covered his mouth to hold back the laugh he was attempting to squelch. He did well at first, but as I gave him the eye, the reflex was finally too much to control, and he burst out in laughter and revealed what we both knew to be true.

"Ok, ok—you do look funny!"

"Humph, laugh as you will. I am sure your assignment to administer the moon will give me much amusement. That is just rock. Nothing to control or watch over there."

"I beg to differ," said Saesheal. "If Luna wavers in orbit, the tides of Earth, the continents themselves will shred. It is a vital role. Besides, I had requested to be near my friend."

"Well, you are welcome company indeed. I still remember what Master

Breagun drummed into my head. 'Celestial oversight of planets stars and other phenomena could be for some Elohim extremely lonely. Mind your thoughts for your concentration must forever be attentive to maintain El's laws. El has flung into motion all things, and we must *not* allow even one word to fall!'" I said in my best mimic of his barking voice.

Saesheal laughed. "You do a remarkably good imitation of Master Breagun. However, he is right, and that is the exact reason why I am here. To keep that straying mind of yours focused on the task."

I knew he was right.

Every aspect of creation had an overseer, and nothing was made without an Elohim to administer it. El had dispatched untold Elohim to the four corners of the universe to watch over his creation, to keep it, and to govern every orbit and every shift of climate on all worlds.

I was glad to be here with my friend, both of us chief administrators of the sun and moon. I enjoyed my service to El and felt privileged to bring warmth to His prized possession.

I had studied and prepared myself, isolated for time to accustom myself to the solitude and quietness as Archon of this star. Learning to hone and focus my thoughts on the Elomic commands needed to fuel this star's flame. Now positioned within Sol's core, my mind expanded as it trained to control every nuance of Sol's temperature, contraction, and the processing of its fuel. I was ready to begin my work.

I surveyed the length and breadth of this new solar system. There was beauty in the quietness. My eyes darted across each celestial body, each administered by an angel with specific instructions.

There was a third body to which I was ever to be mindful, a fragile speck from my vantage point, but lush and teeming with life. El had a great interest in His mote.

I looked also upon the fourth planet and gazed upon it. It seemed similar to Earth in its ability to hold life.

I wondered—

I exercised my will, now trained to manipulate stars. I flexed my twelve wings, and my Heartstone glowed and pulsated.

Hmm—a slight adjustment here...

The ball of stellar fire and gas bowed in submission as hydrogen and helium harnessed Sol's power of fusion and complied with my whim. I reveled and basked giddily in my newfound supremacy. I watched from afar, as Saesheal settled in Luna's core, and I was happy.

While my attention focused on this mere indulgence of joy, in my momentary drift of concentration, Sol's energies flashed before my eyes, and the giant's fury reached out towards the fourth planet. Then the fiery outstretched hand of Sol raced away from me into the black.

A long tendril of the newly formed star stretched forth into the vastness of space, and its spark and heat dashed off to fulfill my will. My heart beat faster, and panic quickly engulfed me. Sol reacted violently to such emotion and glowed to the notice of Saesheal.

Saesheal's eyes opened wide with astonishment, and his jaw dropped. He looked at me frowning and with apprehension in his face.

"Apollyon, calm yourself...what have you done?"

"I think I misjudged the degree to which the temperature must be the controlled!"

"Well, get it under control!" he screamed back. "We cannot fail!"

The heated cord sprinted its way into the blackness, and both of our eyes turned to trace its projected destination. Realization and panic gripped us as we saw the blue speck, Earth laid directly in its destructive path. Saesheal voiced the dread that now lay in both our thoughts.

"In El's name, no," he cried.

Suddenly Saesheal launched himself in pursuit of the flaming tendril.

"Saesheal, what are you doing? You are spirit; you cannot stop it!"

He looked back towards me, and I could see his forehead tense as he pondered the gravity of the situation.

"I can if I become flesh," he cried back.

Flesh? I thought.

The flare was part of the physical realm, and although it presented no mortal danger to Saesheal as spirit, I knew that the fragile blue world created by El was in imminent danger of ruin.

Faster and faster, he flew as I watched him close in on the blaze. I sensed that my friend might actually be in danger.

Apprehension began to flood my soul, and I could feel movement within my Heartstone. I felt Sol leap in response ready to unleash further destruction. I fought to smother my anxiety. I could afford no further loss of control. I could sense my training reasserting itself, and the sun settled in its churning.

Oh maker of all—El hear my cry. We need you to intervene.

Closer the strand of solar energy reached to grasp the planet for annihilation. Quickly Saesheal's wings carried him, now propelled by the power of the living God. Soon he overtook and distanced himself from the flare and hurriedly flew around the planet. He paused and posted himself as a defense: a living barrier between the Earth and the power of the new sun's fury.

He frowned and with a look of determination, spread wide his angelic wings, inhaled, and I watched his lips mouth the Elomic command necessary to draw upon the power of his spirit. Intuition informed me that I was watching my friend's last moments, and my countenance fell.

"Kodor en-chi El-khan El-khan"

Repeatedly he pronounced each word, and with every breath, the flare coursed nearer to embrace him in its destructive hold.

El's power emanated and crackled around Saesheal, and a visible bluish white light enveloped him. Wave after wave rippled from his body, and soon he rivaled the brightness of the flare itself.

I stared in horror unable to move, helpless to render aid unless I was relieved of the responsibility to watch Sol. I could not risk leaving to assist my friend, or the sun would flare even further.

An indescribable ache washed over me like a wave. A woe. My belly hurt as if I had been pummeled in the gut. Sol responded in kind, and its core slowed and darkened. I struggled to hold back a tear that I might keep the sun in check. I then pleaded aloud my lament to my creator.

"Oh, God of all, where art thou?"

****

Saesheal looked into the sun to see Apollyon overwhelmed with emotion: anxiety, mixed with frustration and birthed out of a womb of helplessness to act. Saesheal longed to be with his friend.

He was afraid for Apollyon, afraid that the shackled passions he knew beat within his troubled heart would one day erupt. Lucifer had asked him many days ago to watch him when he himself could not. Saesheal grinned as he remembered that befriending Apollyon was an assignment he initially did not care for. For Apollyon's stone was broken, and like the rest of Heaven, Saesheal wanted no part of him. However, he grew to care for the Arelim, and they had become the best of friends.

Saesheal could say he had honestly come to love him. He always wondered why Lucifer assigned him to watch him. Was not Apollyon's own Grigori enough?

"Who am I to be a *Watcher?*" he asked his Lord.

Lucifer's reply was ominous, "His Heartstone is an abscess of pain waiting to rupture. I fear what lies within. We must not let Apollyon succumb to emotions of despair and anguish, or it shall be to the ruin of us all. Guard his heart with all diligence, for out of it proceeds the issues of life," he had said.

Saesheal looked into the distance and saw that Apollyon's eyes fixated on him. As a slave fastened and bound, he stood chained, helpless to do nothing but watch the actions of his friend, and Saesheal knew him well enough to know that fear coiled itself around his friend.

Who would watch after him now? He wondered.

Saesheal smiled at Apollyon and whispered to himself, "Be strong, my friend. I have faith in you. Do not give in to despair."

Saesheal turned from Apollyon's eyes and launched himself into the flare's course, his body outstretched, head down, and wings tucked dense against his frame. His trajectory designed to place himself squarely in the lane of the flare's fury.

Closer they marched toward one other, an irresistible force against an immovable object. Saesheal closed his eyes and mouthed the oath of all his kind.

"Thy will be done."

The decision to transform had arrived: to fulfill the will of El or to allow His grandest creation to sink into ruin. But for Saesheal, there was no second-guessing, or need for reassessment. With a thought, Saesheal became a powerful, physical being of flesh and blood.

With gritted teeth and clenched fists, Saesheal collided with the deadly mass of heat and flame, absorbing the kinetic power of gas projected at the speed of light. Saesheal's wings unfurled to soak up as much energy as possible. Flesh burned and clothing cindered Saesheal's body now a shield to deflect the fury of the newborn sun. Then he turned limp and plummeted to the Earth below.

Apollyon searched for movement in Saesheal's fall, looking for any sign that he might recover from the descent that hurtled his flaming body into Earth's atmosphere.

Apollyon's hope failed him as he watched to see that when spiritual flesh is altered and meets the might of the celestial realm that only mortality is birthed.

Light exploded and encroached on the blackness of space that blanketed the Earth. The collision created a shock wave that smote the planet's atmosphere and irradiated the sphere. Wave after wave of light burst across the night sky: a cacophony of greens, yellows, and purples entertained the now alerted and curious Elohim who attended to their various tasks below. Polar ice caps melted, and seas rose in response. Angels hurried to control the ensuing chaos that raged beneath them, and for a moment, all beheld two great suns in the sky.

Apollyon observed the charred and scorched shell that was once his friend. He wanted to cry out, to scream, yet he could not. Concentration on the sun had to be absolute, but his eyes shed a tear as he watched Saesheal grimace. Apollyon could only imagine the pain that flooded the body of his friend, falling into the blue sky of the planet below.

As quickly as the scene began, it came to an end: and from the midst of the crackling flames which surrounded him Apollyon heard Saesheal's scream break through the silence of space and he watched as his friend plummeted into Earth's atmosphere.

****

"GGGAAAHHH!" screamed Saesheal.

Lord and Master preserve me!

The consciousness of El suddenly filled Saesheal, and peace flooded his soul. Time slowed to a crawl while the Almighty spoke to Saesheal's quickly disintegrating mind.

"Go thou thy way till the end be, for thou shalt rest, and stand in thy lot at the end of days. Be not afraid, for thine journey is not yet complete."

When the Lord had finished speaking, Saesheal loosed himself from the tether of his life. His spirit emptied from his body, which became as a flailing husk plummeting to the ground.

Drained of the power of El, Saesheal's lifeless body penetrated the atmosphere. Earth's troposphere welcomed the fiery ember that breached its clouded walls of oxygen and carbon dioxide. Saesheal's body then woke the stratosphere from its rest. Sonic booms disturbed the once previously tranquil blue sky. The friction of powerful but frayed angelic wings created commotion upon the planet's new aerial inhabitants. Thunderclaps from his fall sprinted as a jaguar across the lower levels of the sky, and dark smoke and lightning trailed his descent.

Saesheal's body fell on the newly formed land below, and rock and earth heaved to make way. Trees flung themselves aside like discarded kindle and snapped trunks screamed in creaking disapproval. The ground itself cried out with the explosive sound of fire and shrieked its objection to the violent intrusion. A "mighty one" had fallen, and Saesheal's body autographed itself with fire in the earth.

Dust and debris jettisoned into the air, and after the passage of time gently settled back to earth covering both leaf and blade of grass. The breadth of the crater burned of charred wood and grass whispering to onlookers with the sizzle of steam and nestled silently and motionless within its core, the empty, crusted husk of Saesheal lay still; smoke lifted from his frame like a hovering phantom.

Angels in the area of impact moved to investigate the site. By the hundreds, they came open-mouthed and eyes wide.

"Saesheal, can you hear me? Saesheal," one said.

"Wake up, Saesheal! Wake up," another cried.

Another looked upon the charred remains of his comrade. "How is such a thing possible? Why does he not answer?"

"I saw a flare of light come from the sun. He looked as if he was trying to stop it," said another.

"But he does not breathe! The Arelim does not breathe," shouted one.

Apollyon still cradled in a bath of stellar fury looked on in anguished dismay. Passion and sadness overwhelmed him: yet he dared not express himself, for he knew the sun would broadcast his pain to the solar system's ruin.

So silently, he ruminated, embroiled in a mental cauldron of grief and angst. Looking into the distance of the black star-filled canopy of space, he strained to see past the second heaven into the third and wondered to himself, *El why didst you not save us?*

****

"My Lord," said Michael.

"Yes, my son?"

"You seem preoccupied. Is all well?"

El sat on his throne, his eyes looking past them all, looking elsewhere.

"Saesheal has thwarted a threat to Earth, and Apollyon now wonders within himself my actions."

Each archangel collectively looked upon one another questioningly and in amazement then turned to their Creator. Unanimously they responded as one. "And your will in this matter Lord?"

El closed his eyes for a moment. He sat in silence, then opened his eyes, and spoke. "Raphael come forward and report of thy stewardship."

Like his fellow brothers before him, Raphael stepped towards the throne and sat. He waved his hands, and volumes of books appeared above their heads and filled the room. Raphael stood across from El and pointed to a small window-like opening, and images began to flash before their eyes.

Raphael displayed the record of each Elohim. Each volume was open before him and floated transparently yet occupied no space. Pens and stylus moved of their own accord, never ceasing in their writing. Each pen updated the book upon which they wrote, and in the window before them, Grigori stood everywhere, taking note of all things: watching. Each carried a book, an inkhorn, and a stylus. Each screen showed the cowled and blank face of the Grigori, a race of Elohim that possessed neither eyes nor ears. They could see, but they did not. They heard, but they did not. Gifted with divine sight and hearing, they were absent the instruments normally associated with a species that experiences sight or sound.

El spoke, "Raphael, please display the Grigori assigned to Apollyon's attachment."

Raphael once more raised his hand, and one image came to the fore-front of all others.

The image showed Apollyon looking up, and his Watcher barely perceptible in the background, faithfully recording every word and the thoughts of Apollyon's heart. The Lumazi collectively viewed this crystal display; the show of thought and action hovered above their heads as Apollyon's innermost thoughts were made known for all of them to see.

"*El why didst you not save us?*"

Each was amazed; startled even that El would even be questioned.

El spoke, "Lucifer."

Lucifer stood to attend to his master, "My Lord?"

"Please assist Apollyon to understand."

El's eyes fixated upon the person of Lucifer and El began to com-municate to Lucifer the words and the voice tone upon which he was to speak the word of God. Nothing was left to chance, and in the seconds that passed between them, Lucifer's reply was straightforward and familiar.

"Yes Lord."

"Thou art dismissed to see to the matter. Make haste," said the Lord.

Lucifer scratched at his chest. "Thy will be done," said Lucifer.

Instantly Lucifer rose to his feet and began his descent from the throne room, deep bass sounds   echoed with his every step. Melodious sounds emanated from the motions of his wings, and as he left, the sound of his presence faded.

"Jerahmeel, Talus, and Sariel, I will commence later with your reports. You may each retire for a time, and I will call for you when I am ready. Raphael, I have an assignment for you. Michael stay as you also have a new assignment. Gabriel, Saesheal, has —fallen. Recover what remains of thy brother's body and bring him here. He has honored me, and I will honor him. Tell your brethren that I am with them and let not their hearts be troubled."

Each cherub bowed to the Lord and exited the throne room.

El turned to Raphael. "Raphael, thou art commissioned to find all instances of thought, conduct, and or speech similar to Apollyon's. You and your attendants shall bring to me a volume which lists all Elohim and research on your findings."

"Aye, Lord. And your desire as to when you would have this complete?"

"Report thou to me on the conclusion of the 6th Earth day at which time I will take my rest."

"As you command Lord," replied Raphael. Bowing, the mighty cherub turned to leave the presence of the living God.

Michael stood and looked at his Lord. El noticed his glance.

"Speak Michael."

"Lord I have served you without ceasing day and night. You have allowed me to oversee as Archon the expansion of the city. I have seen wonders as you spoke the stars into existence, yet I perceive that something is amiss."

The Lord looked upon his beloved of angels, smiled, and studied him. El's gaze penetrated Michael, and for a brief moment, Michael thought that the

Lord would speak. El stood instead.

Immediately Michael bowed with his face towards the ground.

"Rise, Michael, O beloved of angels. Rise and walk with me."

El left the throne, and both walked to the upper floors of the palace.

"Understand my son, that I declare the end from the beginning, and in the day ahead, that will be called 'ancient times,' *the things* that are not *yet* done. My counsel shall stand, and I will do all my pleasure. The words that I speak unto you, though they are unclear, they shall be revealed later."

"Yes Lord," was Michael's reply.

"So, Michael, speak your mind."

"Lord, I do not fully understand what I have just seen. Raphael showed us what Apollyon's Grigori witnessed. I was not aware that such thoughts would be contemplated among the Elohim."

El looked upon his son and smiled. "My friend, thou art ever with me and have my heart. Thou art continuously in Heaven laboring in the work to which thou hast been faithfully assigned. Apollyon hast experienced for the first time a force capable of injury to his person. This new awareness of *self*-preservation hast brought with it questions. Questions about, why I would create such a thing? Why might I risk his person to accomplish my own ends? Apollyon has been thrust into a new set of circumstances, and as you all were created with a free will, such lines of reasoning must inevitably encroach upon his thoughts."

Michael nodded. "I see."

"All that can be done will be done. And all that will be will be," said El.

"All that will be will be, aye, Lord."

Lucifer arrived at the Cliffs of Argoth, a cropping of rock that overlooked all of Jerusalem: one of several waypoints that El had allowed for travel between the realms. The waypoints were essential. Failure to use a Ladder directed at a waypoint could result in the mistaken destruction of a structure in Heaven or worse, the possible dissolution of an Elohim. Several waypoints existed throughout the realm, and each was wide enough to accommodate the displacement of the heavens when Ladders formed. Lucifer closed his eyes and focused his thoughts. His mouth moved, and he recited the Elomic command that would transport him from the capital city to the second heaven called "space."

Lucifer felt honored. As the first created sentient being, he was one of a select few given an Elomic command. Each command allowed a creation event, a method to affect reality. Every syllable and each word added to reality or even allowed travel between the realms.

By this word, El created reality. El, however, was the living Word itself. All creation sprang from his mouth. El spoke, and what he spoke came to pass. He was *the* Elomic command.

Carefully, Lucifer pronounced each syllable, and with every utterance, eternity began to fold back upon itself. The pitch in Lucifer's voice was flawless, his volume perfect, and with the authority of El, he evoked the realms to hearken and to permit passage to the celestial realm.

As if on cue, creation itself came to attention and bowed to fulfill the word. Light danced around Lucifer's person, and slowly Heaven dissipated and revealed the barrier that separated eternity from time. Energy crackled around the mighty cherub, and wave after wave pulsated until a *schuuuup* sound blasted the air; similar to the sound expected when air vacates a room. Then it opened—the Ladder.

Lucifer's scales retracted into his body to reveal a powerful armor that surrounded him. The luminescent and translucent flesh of his wings glowed bright and, his legs and arms grew muscular, and with the revealing of his talons, he completed the transformation into the warrior angel necessary to survive the environment of the thing El had called space.

Looking down into the pulsating chute of light, Lucifer began his descent down the Ladder, and galaxies and stars soon littered all that he saw. Lucifer moved his body to adjust his path and made his way towards the planet that he had come to call home: the lush place El had called Earth. Lucifer had been responsible for its administration, and as chief Archon, he was the arm of the Lord overseeing all things concerning El's will.

Lucifer soared past worlds seeded with new life; each waited expectantly with an attentive ear for any command from El to bud. Some planetary bodies were pleasant to the eye, and all assisted in the guidance of what was now dubbed times and seasons.

He turned to a star in the distance and, able to recognize its unique signature among the billions littered in space, motioned his body towards the third planet. He entered the solar system and flew past the outer planets.

Then it appeared; the lush planet filled with aquatic life lovingly handcrafted by El. The young atmosphere quickly enveloped Lucifer, and its searing heat embraced his angelic skin as if to welcome him home. Red and green flashes of light skipped before his eyes, and then blue skies filled with wispy and majestic clouds. The familiar clap of thunder announced his entry. His twelve broad wings, used to cover El himself, slowed his approach, and he lightly touched down a stone's throw from the location of Saesheal's plummet. The

Ladder then dissipated and retracted to lift back into the Third Heaven.

Lucifer approached the scene and eyed with curiosity the thousands of angels encircled above and around the crater of Saesheal's impact.

One angel of God was a remarkable sight; a legion was a thing of wonder. Each Elohim was as different in function, power, and beauty as the snowflakes that filled the Earth. There were the Arelim; massive, four-armed muscular creatures, bi-pedal with cloven feet. With the faces of rams, their leathery wings made them perfect for the building and movement of planets, a species to which both Apollyon and Saesheal belonged.

There was the Harrada, Issi, Satyrs, Kortai, Draco, and Grigori–so many present to behold this sight.

All noticed Lucifer's presence as they surrounded the crater and bowed to the Chief Lord Prince and planetary Archon.

Lucifer surveyed the enormity of it all. There was a central black impact crater bordered by scorched and flattened trees of one-furlong roundabout. Apollyon lay within the center of the deep crater; holding the charred remains of his friend weeping uncontrollably. Apollyon refused to be comforted, and his wails filled the air.

"Eleah, Eleah, kknada sabathkunar?" Which in the Elomic tongue meant, "My God, My God why hast thou forsaken me?"

Lucifer turned to one of the gawkers. "How long has he been this way?"

"My Lord Prince, you honor us with your presence on this dark day."

"Forgo me the chatter—how long!"

"He has been discomforted since Master Breagun commissioned Ra to relieve him not moments ago. He then ran into the center of the crater, held Saesheal, and would not release him. Master Breagun has suspended Apollyon's post as Archon of Sol until he receives instructions from Prince Talus."

"Indeed?" Lucifer replied.

Suddenly, with a flash of immense light and clap of thunder, Gabriel stood over Apollyon, his white linen still bright from the glory of God. Gabriel stood nine feet tall, with twelve white flowing wings. His hair was solid white, and his skin spotted with flakes of black on dark grey skin. He looked upon Apollyon and spoke.

"Oh, Son of the Dawn, fear not, nor be thou troubled. Saesheal though fallen is not without a future, for El has declared that his journey is not yet complete. I have come for his temple to return him to the Lord."

Apollyon looked upon Gabriel, and the Shekinah glory still irradiated Gabriel's face, for he was still fresh from the presence of the Lord. Peace slowly began to fill Apollyon. Apollyon held the body of his friend in his arms, wiped what remaining dirt and debris encrusted his face, and lightly brushed Saesheal's cheeks.

"And what does El intend to do with the body?"

"El has stated that as Saesheal has honored him thus shall he be honored. More I do not know. My task is clear; make way not to deter me from it," said Gabriel.

"Aye, Lord Prince," said Apollyon.

Apollyon gently gave the body of his friend into Gabriel's waiting arms, and with equal care, Gabriel wrapped Saesheal's body within the linen of his robes and prepared himself to depart.

"Hear all ye Elohim, for the Lord is not without pity. Believe in your God, let not your hearts be troubled nor let them be afraid, the Lord thy God is with thee."

Gabriel and Lucifer looked upon one another. Gabriel nodded with respect, and Lucifer returned the acknowledgment. Gabriel looked up and lifted himself from the gravity of the mass of spinning ore, and all looked upon him as his figure slowly diminished into the distance. Then the light of a Ladder was seen bridging the realms, and Gabriel was gone.

"My prince, what does this mean?" asked a bystander.

Apollyon spoke before Lucifer could reply. "It means that *I* have injured my friend. It means that *I* have failed. It means, Orion, that I must live with the knowledge that my brother has perished because of my hand."

Orion and the others looked on Apollyon with curious stares, but Orion spoke for them all. "Explain, Apollyon. How are *you* responsible for this?"

"I attempted to manage the sun's power to make life habitable on the Marxzian surface…"

"You fool! Did it not occur to you that you would boil the oceans just made? I cannot imagine that Master Breagun would have authorized such a careless act…"

"He did not, Orion, for I had thought"…

Livid, Orion cut Apollyon off. "Think no more, '*Broken Stone',* as it is ruinous to us all. If you …"

"Enough!" Lucifer said.

Lucifer's deep and powerful voice overwhelmed them all and shook the ground. All present immediately stopped all talk and took notice as the Chief Prince roared at them. Silence surrounded the area, heads bowed in obeisance.

"I find that I have had enough and that this conversation edifies not. Accusations against a Son of God will not be leveled in my presence! Cease from this prattle and return to your posts, all of you!" Lucifer barked.

The ground quaked as Lucifer's command was issued. Startled and shocked back into the normalcy of reason, angels dismissed themselves from the area until none remained save Lucifer and Apollyon.

His countenance now softened, Lucifer turned to Apollyon and spoke, "Be encouraged, my brother; you did what you thought was right."

"My Lord Prince, I..."

"You Son of the Dawn are tired, and it is apparent that you are overwhelmed with the events of today. Come, seek solace at my palace, and be refreshed. My attendants will see to your needs, and we will talk after you, have had a chance to meditate. El knows of our friendship and of all the princes that he might send during such a time; He knew I would be the one most apt to comfort you."

"Your pardon, Lord Prince, your hospitality is appreciated, however..."

"Speak," said Lucifer.

"But I seek no meditation on the person of El."

Lucifer looked curiously upon this angel never having heard such speech in all his days. "I see. Then seek consolation within my halls. Come."

"Aye, Lord Prince."

Lucifer took flight, and Apollyon followed, heading towards the central city Lucifer had built on the Earth.

Lucifer's mind churned with questions about the day's events. *Why would El allow this to happen? With a thought, he could have easily dispatched the flare. He needed never to have even left the throne. Why even show us Apollyon's thoughts? Are my thoughts on display to those of the court as well?*

Lucifer noticed that their Grigori silently followed them. Their gaseous form made them easy to forget that they were there. Knowing that Lucifer's own thoughts were logged and recorded, he chose to meditate on thoughts of intrigue that he might provide sport for his own Grigori, Lilith, to write.

Why would the Lord even create such a creature? Lucifer was sure

51

Lilith's pen would record his thoughts and, in so doing generate, some intriguing logs.

Ahh to know the innermost mind of a Grigori.

Lucifer chuckled at this prospect, for Lilith, his watcher was ever with him, yet Grigori never spoke or interacted with anyone but their own kind. Lilith, however, was of no immediate concern to the Chief Prince, but they would have words later Lucifer thought. Of that, he was sure.

Clouds bypassed them, and Lucifer was relieved to see in the distance the majestic spires of Athor. *Ah, it is good to be home.*

Athor stood over a thousand cubits high. Designed as a series of five pyramids interconnected with the tallest in the center and surrounded by the other four, the city was constructed out of diamond and pearl. Lucifer demanded nothing less for his home, an abode worthy of God's Chief Prince, a glorious center where the Lord's beauty made the planet shine with his radiance should He ever choose to sit upon Earth's throne.

Athor dazzled in the distance, and no matter from which way one approached the city, it captured and refracted all light, displaying the entire spectrum. Its walls were as a stone rainbow comprised of quartz, diamond, and pearl.

Lucifer saw his citizens as he came near. They saw his approach, and the tower bells announced his return. Lightly, Apollyon and the First of Angels landed in the central courtyard. Lucifer's three attendants rushed to his side. Mephisto, Ashtaroth, and Dagon knelt before him. Mephisto was the first to greet them. His black hair contrasted against his tinted red skin, and with a cloak of silver and gold, he lowered his gaze and bowed as he spoke to his master.

"My Lord Prince, Son of the Morning Star, we bid you welcome home.

What word is there from Jerusalem, and is there a new command from El?"

Lucifer replied, "Apollyon has been through great distress. Please have quarters prepared for him. Also, prepare a banquet in his honor, and I will dine with him later. As far as command from El…it is yet to be known, but when it is, we shall obey."

"Aye, Lord Prince, a banquet my Lord—for him?"

"Are my instructions not clear Mephistopheles?"

"They are clear, my Lord"

"Then proceed with their execution," Lucifer said.

Mephisto motioned to Apollyon to follow him. "Son of the Dawn, please come this way."

Apollyon was visibly uncomfortable over the fuss made over him and spoke to object.

"Oh, my prince, I am not worthy…"

Lucifer held his hand up to silence him and interjected.

"Speak not to me of worth my friend. El has deemed you worthy as we all. Hence, silence yourself of this speech and accept the graciousness of El on my behalf. Rest and we shall speak more soon."

Apollyon sighed and resigned himself to his chief's command as he and Mephistopheles left Lucifer's presence.

Ashtaroth and Dagon looked at their master and awaited instructions.

"Dagon, how fares the ground? Will it yield manna for the denizens here?" asked Lucifer.

Dagon's hulkish frame looked up at his master, his bronzed skin shown in the sun, and he was draped in all manner of gold and silver jewels. His bull-like face snorted in irritation.

"Nay, Lord Prince. I have continuously nurtured the ground here per your instructions, and though it yields herb-bearing fruit of every kind, manna will not spring from this soil. It is as if El has not designed this world with the Elohim in mind, for it does not produce the food we consume. We have coordinated with Prince Michael for shipments of manna as needed. Upon review of the granaries, he said he could provide us all that we require, for it is limitless in the heavenly city and grows without measure in the Elysian Fields."

Lucifer lowered his head and pondered. "Curious. It will *not* yield manna you say? I will speak with Michael upon my return to Heaven. How much more do you require to sustain the populace?"

"We have enough for two more creation events at the current rate of consumption. However, we increase each day in the need for Elohim as El expands this planet's attributes. There are countless Elohim monitoring from the east wind to every tree."

Dagon continued his assessment. "Those within the planet itself report that this world has oceans of magma upon which the land floats. It is assuredly unique from Heaven, for we have nothing like it at home. The land breathes fire in some sections. We have dispatched per El's command and your word Elohim throughout the planet."

Lucifer could not help but meditate on what Dagon had told him; "...*as if El has not designed this world with the Elohim in mind...*"

It occurred to him that Ashtaroth stared at him and sought to anticipate his master's will.

Ashtaroth was slim in build. His skin was solid white, and his wings were feathery and shimmered with a yellow tint when the light from the sun touched them. Necklaces from the translucent gold mines of Heaven draped his neck, which was as long as his arm and each collar glowed and moved around his neck of their own accord, never touching his skin. He looked with concern at his lord.

"My Lord Prince," he said.

Lucifer replied, "I am fine, Ashtaroth, thank you. Tell me how fares your coordination with Breagun's attachment?"

"My Lord, we have received word why the flare from Sol was unleashed upon our world. Thus, we are swift to ask why you have brought this simpleton to our door. Should he not be brought before Prince Talus for inquiry?"

"Save your interrogation for one who tolerates it Astarte, for I will not. I possess a word from El to Apollyon; the will of El be done."

"My apologies, Chief Prince, but by now all of Heaven knows of his failure. How can it be that an error of such magnitude is not dealt with?"

"Astarte, you have my leave. Coordinate with Breagun's new overseer of the moon. I do not want its proximity to disrupt our work here. You are both dismissed to see to your matters"

"Aye, Lord Prince. El's will be done," said Astarte.

"El's will be done," Lucifer replied.

El's will be done–curious.

****

Gabriel, Prince Lord of all Malakim, carried within his arms the body of Saesheal. He walked reverently past the gate of Heaven, through the city streets, and solemnly toward the Mount of God. All of Jerusalem emptied as angel after angel vacated Gabriel's path that he might pass. Angels bowed to the prince in accordance with royal protocol. On this day, the lifeless body of an Elohim existed in Heaven. With a look of steel, Gabriel made his way through the center of the city; the Towers of Praise stood quietly in their annunciations of

God's glory as all Elohim looked on in stunned silence. The only sounds heard were the footsteps of Gabriel and the flap of wings that held each angel aloft.

Gabriel made his way towards Michael and his brethren. Talus stood next to Michael while Raphael was away occupied on official business, but with the exception of both Raphael and Lucifer, all were present and accounted for: Talus, Jerahmeel, Sariel, Gabriel, and Michael. Talus, who was Prince Lord of all Arelim: and no one — save the Lord himself — grieved this loss more. Saesheal was of his race, and all of Heaven grieved for the Arelim, an experience to which none were accustomed.

Michael looked upon the multitudes and was moved with compassion. He, like so many who now looked upon the empty shell of their friend, contemplated the enormity of such loss in Heaven. Michael saw the confused looks on his brethrens' faces. Each struggled with the thought that an immortal could die, that an error of judgment could lead their hurt. The reality of the concept was affirmed by the testimony of the voiceless body carried by Gabriel through the street. Michael noted that he would remember this day for all time: the day when everyone acquired this new awareness, the day when grief and fear entered their collective consciousness.

Gabriel drew closer, and Sariel and Jerahmeel fell in behind him as he made his way up the flight of glass steps. Gabriel stopped where the brass altar lay. Talus stood prone, and Gabriel handed the body of Saesheal to his fellow prince. Talus gently took Saesheal's body and placed it on the Altar of Sacrifice.

The Altar of Sacrifice, all had wondered why El had named it thus, but the reason of its identification was now evident for all to see. Never had the altar been set aflame before, never until now. The great doors of the palace opened, and the Spirit of God flew out from within. All of Heaven bowed in reverence as the Holy Spirit lighted on the altar. The Holy Spirit was impressive to behold. His flaming wings outstretched and dwarfed the altar itself, the length of which was 100 cubits long. His eyes blazed with fire, and his pupils were as balls of lightning, and like a bird of prey, he flew and a trail of fire and the colors of the rainbow followed him.

To look upon the Holy Spirit of God was as if to look upon a dove and an eagle simultaneously. Yet the similitude of a man appeared within the image of the raptor-like image. The Spirit lighted upon the altar, and fire immediately raged both under and on either side. A *woof* sound sparked as it ignited, and Saesheal's body illuminated within the blaze. Then the air filled with the aroma—a scent, a smell not of ash or charred remains—but sweet and cinnamon like. Then the aroma changed, and almond filled the air, and again the nostrils of all became enthralled as frankincense wafted across the emporium. Michael could tell that he was not alone in his curiosity and surprise as he looked to see that all Elohim present seemed enraptured as the aromatic mist filled the mountain and spread outward in every direction.

A vial was set towards the altar's front side again, but for what purpose none were privy. El ever directed them to build, to maintain, and to create; later they learned for what purpose.

Higher the flames climbed, but the body of Saesheal was not consumed. Smoke filled the area, which neither stifled nor hindered breathing, yet all around, the smell was sweet and saturated the air. All of Heaven was bowed down in reverence to the Holy Spirit of God and basked in the midst of the potpourri. The third person of the Trinity spoke and waves of visible sound ushered from his outstretched wings.

"Sons of God arise and let your eyes look upon the sacrifice. Behold the great Saesheal, Keeper of the Word of God. He was to be chief overseer: Archon of the lesser light of the moon. His bravery that my will not be thwarted placed him in harm's way. Thus, shall all of Heaven now honor him."

The mountain itself quaked as the Spirit of God spoke and seven thunders thundered. Lightning and smoke filled the mountain of God, and all stood captivated as the Spirit arose from the altar. Sparks of flame leapt from his wings and torched the body, which did not burn; instead, it smoldered while lying in state atop the altar at the foot of the Spirit.

Every eye looked to the person of the Holy Spirit, and all of Heaven either stood or was in flight, huddled like anxious participants to a great coliseum match; each struggled to see the spectacle before them. An innumerable company of angels filled the emporium and surrounded the mountain, ten thousand times ten thousand, and thousands of thousands. Michael watched astonished as mouth after mouth opened in response to the scene before their eyes. He, too, found himself overcome with wonder, his eyes fixated on the Altar of Sacrifice, and all of Heaven looked on with fascination, transfixed as Saesheal's body began to move.

****

"Is the manna to your liking, Apollyon?"

"Indeed, Lord Prince, this particular flavor is of exceptional taste and refreshes me. Your hospitality is much welcomed."

Lucifer took a cup of ale to drink and held a sapphire chalice to his lips. Decorated with some of the planet's flora, the banquet table impressed Apollyon. Tapestries imported from Heaven draped the walls and ornate ceiling, ready for the day that El himself might seek to fill this temple. The floors were made from the finest ores of gold, silver, topaz, jasper, beryl, and onyx. Diamonds and emeralds adorned the walls like grout all ready to reflect the temple's steward Lucifer.

Lucifer sat, covered himself, and pulled his robes tighter over his person so that his beauty did not distract. He was careful to stay covered when outside of the presence of God; therefore, he wore coverings that he might never draw attention to himself. Lucifer knew that were he to uncloak or otherwise reveal his appearance, the reflection from his mirror and diamond-like skin would overwhelm the whole palace in light, for the place was crafted that he might reflect God's glory.

"Think naught, my friend. El has commanded me to share with you his word. It is my intent to carry out my master's will. However, before I speak his word, I'd like to ask you a question if I may?"

"Of course, Lord Prince, please."

"El heard your cry and dispatched me to respond to thee. I will, of course, share with you El's words, yet I find myself with a desire to hear *yours*. I hold particular interest of your account of this event."

"It is very simple Lord Prince. Master Breagun received and gave me orders from Prince Talus to serve as Archon for this system's star and Saesheal for the moon. Each one of us was to appoint seven attendants to our cause. After receipt of said orders, Saesheal and I determined to go and scout our posts and personally see to them. I relieved Ra who was temporarily assigned at the time."

"I see, and once fitted within Sol's core what then?" asked Lucifer.

Apollyon looked down, his eyes closed and his head in his hands, his voice cracked with sadness as he replied.

"I saw the beauty of Earth, Lord Prince. I saw the lushness that inhabited the planet. I saw the whole of the system seated in the center of Sol, and when I looked upon each world, I was moved with compassion. So I reached out to bring warmth to the fourth planet. I failed to remember that my thoughts themselves bound me to the star and that it would obey my will. The flare was an oversight, an impulse of my mind reaching out for what I saw. When I realized the magnitude of my actions, the flare had already approached your watch. I could neither pursue nor recall it once unleashed. Saesheal also knew this and sacrificed himself to save Earth."

"Am I to understand Apollyon that *you* let *your* will slip? Did I hear you correctly, or did you just inform me that you exerted *your* desires and will over El's?"

"Nay, Lord Prince, I am truly submitted to my master and king. I would never defy Him," said Apollyon.

"Your words leave me little comfort, Archon. You were assigned to *my* sector of space, and your actions have endangered the success of *my* watch. This temple an edifice in which I have invested much toil. All that I have created here over the course of these past five days would have come to ruin, all because *you* determined that one planet out of the countless specks in this cosmos should support life.

Let me ask you, Archon, would your desires have extended warmth to the gas giant in this system, and what of the nether planets on its outskirts? Did it not occur to you that each one is set in its course by El himself? Or did you think yourself omniscient to know how and which planets should support life?"

Silence engulfed the room.

Apollyon visibly shook and covered his ears as the volume of Lucifer's words made his ears pound. Although Lucifer could conceal his visage so as not to blind, his voice boomed so that others could hear. His interrogation drew the notice of the attendants outside his chambers. Belial, a servant of Lucifer, poked his head inside the chamber door.

"Lord Prince, is all well?"

"Nay, Belial—nay, it is not. You may take your leave nonetheless."

"As you command, Lord Prince," said Belial.

Belial departed and shut the door behind him, leaving the two Elohim alone to continue.

Lucifer stood to his feet and removed his royal robes; each wing slowly unfurled, six to his right and six to his left. He opened the pores of his flesh to reveal his true form, and light raced to his body as iron fillings to magnetic ore, and colors projected from his skin like spotlights on the room walls.

The walls themselves absorbed and amplified the light. Each beam bounced off the glass of the temple. Brighter and brighter, the temple glowed, sparkling as a lamp within the darkness. The building radiated a hum, and every-one within the city knew that Lucifer had become uncovered, and each bowed to shield his eyes.

Apollyon kneeled in front of such a display, and although his strength in a physical altercation would equal or even surpass Lucifer, his mind was quickly overwhelmed by the brightness of his glory.

Lucifer spoke. "I am Chief Prince Lucifer Draco, Lightbringer, and Son of the Morning Star. I walk within the midst of the Stones of Fire. Hear the word of the Lord!

Oh, Son of the Dawn, thou who is the blossom of the Morning Star, be still and let your soul be at ease, for this thing was done that others might be made manifest. For you shall twice be tested and have once been vexed, the flame, which thou, hast controlled, shall indeed mirror your own as it doth consume; let not your own flame thus burn. But be thou warned that if sorrow persists, then on your shoulders shall indeed a new dawn come, the breaking of a new day. And he to whom you would seek solace shall be your King, and your infamy shall indeed be known even unto the end of days.

Lucifer shuttered the pores of his flesh and covered himself with his robes; the light from his person vanished, and the room grew dim.

Apollyon rose to his feet, the drumming from Lucifer's voice still echoing in his ears. "This is the word from El: a riddle? But what does it mean?"

Lucifer motioned towards Apollyon and placed his hands on his shoulder as a gesture of comfort.

"I know not the meaning of his words. I only carry them per his will."

"Ugh, I do not wish to meditate on riddles," snapped Apollyon.

"I think, Son of the Dawn, that your heart *was* in the right place: you simply wanted to see life where none existed. It is evident that you have been misunderstood. Where others might see failure or a simpleton, I see before me an Arelim who merely wanted to be as his Creator. A sentiment all who behold El: would understandably aspire. You made a mistake. I do not profess to know El's mind in this matter, but He is right that judgest, and surely He can see that your heart is sound."

"Thank you, Lord Prince. I shall return to Heaven and solicit from Him myself the meaning of these words. I wish to see my friend's body once more and determine my status as Archon with Talus."

"Then return, my friend, and may El grant you audience to understand His word, but, Apollyon, tell me —"

"Yes, Lord Prince?"

"How fares your consolation," said Lucifer.

"My consolation Lord Prince? My *consolation* would improve if my brethren, such as your attendant Ashtaroth, did not whisper injury behind my back. For I am neither deaf nor without feeling. I am sure he would not like me to reciprocate. It is not with honor I bear this failure."

"I will speak with him," said Lucifer.

"May I take my leave, Lord Prince?"

"Of course. May El's presence give you comfort Apollyon."

"Not today, Lord Prince, not today."

Lucifer looked upon this angel and noted that his manner was so different from all he had seen, his spirit so similar to his own. Lucifer perceived movement to his rear as light waves changed, and he turned to face his now visible Grigori.

Lilith stood as all of his kind, cloaked in black, non-descript in appearance save he possessed no eyes or ears. A golden sash lined his waist, and a silver pen ever writing in a tome hovered slightly above him to his rear whilst an inkhorn hovered opposite him. His folded hands were covered in his dark cloak.

"I have yet to record what I have witnessed."

"And?" said Lucifer.

"*And*, you have *not* dispersed the entirety of El's word," said Lilith.

"Indeed," was Lucifer's reply as he warily observed his 'Watcher'.

"El's command regarding His word is clear Lucifer. "Ye shall not add unto the word which I command you, neither shall ye diminish ought from it, that ye may keep the commandments of the Lord your God which I command you."

"That Grigori is *your* command. I walk within the Stones of Fire. El grants me great autonomy to function in his name. I have exercised said privilege now."

"Take care, Lightbringer, as to diminish El's word is to trifle with reality itself."

Lucifer walked towards his Grigori, and his eyes narrowed as he inspected him. "And you, Lilith, why warn me at all? Are you not in violation of your own oath to speak with me? You are my watcher; since when would you be my counselor?" said Lucifer.

"Ah, but my liege…" Lilith bowed mockingly, "I acquire enormous benefit from watching you. Your thoughts are most shall we say – intriguing: to be sure. Therefore, I record your journals that I might *continue* to watch your thoughts and deeds. I am sure if I *fully* recorded what I see, then those within the royal court would be as equally distressed as when Apollyon's own thoughts were revealed."

"Indeed," said Lucifer. "However, I am curious, Lilith."

"Yes, Lord Prince?"

"Who watches the watchers?"

Lilith grinned, and his form began to fade and slowly disappear to its non-corporeal state until all that remained visible to the eye was an angelic yet impish grin.

****

Apollyon walked through the halls of Athor: its corridors gleamed in light, and tapestries adorned its walls. His large frame made each Elohim that he encountered make way for him to pass. Each one-eyed him. He noticed the sneers as he stepped toward the outer court; however, none of them understood. He could tell that their eyes followed him when they thought that he was not looking. Who among their kind had ever lost a brother? How could they know his pain he wondered? Apollyon thought to himself, *what could have been El's plan but to watch Saesheal's ruin? I know that El heard my cry. If he had but been there, my brother would still be alive. I must return home. El must answer me.*

It is not fair! We both should be basking in the glory of service and helping to prepare this world for its next stage of creation. Instead, I find my mind consumed with anxiety and thoughts of what could have been. Lord El, hear thy servant's plea. Why did you not prevent this tragedy?

Lucifer at least cares. He recognizes that it as an error. He knows. Why God? Why is my mind filled with doubts and criminations of my actions? I saw the planet: reached for it, and Sol reached with me. How could I have known that this would happen? I just want to go home, to speak to You. You will give me words for this situation. Not the babble of nonsense Lucifer delivered to me earlier. El will, but, El, why did you not save me?

Tears fell from Apollyon's eyes, and he reached down toward a bench to steady himself. Grief soon overwhelmed him, and he placed his large hands on his face. He was Arelim, and Apollyon looked to notice if anyone had seen him. He composed himself and wiped the tears from his eyes.

It was then in the midst of his moment of sadness, in the instant where the weight of his actions filled him with heartache that he heard the spiteful words uttered to him for the first time.

"What? A mighty one cries? Does the *Destroyer* shed tears?"

Apollyon winced at the remark. Slowly he rose and turned to face Ashtaroth who stood behind him; his disdain evident in his stance and face. His hands were on his hips, and his eyes conveyed to Apollyon that he was being given a visual dressing down.

"You would dare speak to me in such manner?" said Apollyon.

"I do, Son of the Dawn. You are a testimony to all that Elohim aspire *not* to be: a failure to your race, a shame to your prince, a *Destroyer*. How El would even consider manna on one such as you baffles me. How a noble, such as Saesheal, ever would call you friend is beyond fathomable. Leave this place, Destroyer, for destruction indeed follows you, and I would have none of it in Athor."

65

As Ashtaroth turned to leave, Apollyon quickly looked upon this out-spoken and contemptuous angel and reached to seize his arm.

"You will never utter Saesheal's name again in my presence, Astarte—never! Yes, I called you Astarte. That is what Lucifer called you, is it not? I see he values you so little that he does not bestow you enough honor to speak your full name. And you, servant of the High Prince, have not enough value for yourself even to object. You are indeed a vassal designed to serve."

Ashtaroth flung his arm away to break free, but Apollyon's grip was sure.

"Unhand me immediately, you buffoon!" Apollyon removed his hold from Ashtaroth's arm only to grasp his throat and lift him from the ground.

Ashtaroth struggled to breathe and speak, his speech gagged from the hold of Apollyon. He grabbed Apollyon's forearms and struggled to wrest free from his captor's grasp.

Apollyon raised his figure to his lips. "Shhh, hush, little angel."

His eyes narrowed, and Apollyon looked upon him as a cobra might view a coiled mongoose as prey.

Ashtaroth squirmed in discomfort, his vocal cords constricted by Apollyon's grasp.

"I wish to thank you, Astarte. You have made me aware that not all would praise my elevation as Archon of Sol, a position of honor that I know you sought as well. Indeed, little angel, I may be a simpleton as I overheard you say earlier, and yes, I did hear you, but intelligence aside: between the two of us, I am Archon of Sol."

Apollyon smiled and glared at Ashtaroth. "How it must gnaw at you, to be relegated to serve the tables of Lucifer while this simpleton, who grasps your throat, commands the very stars. You, Astarte, are not worthy to be Archon of flatware: you, little angel, are chief administrator and archangel of nothing—nothing but Lucifer's tactful derision. For too long, I have been the butt of your ridicule and spite."

Ashtaroth squirmed and tried to raise his voice, but he released only a squeal of a sound.

Apollyon smiled. "What was that? I cannot hear you. Perhaps, you would care to speak louder?"

Apollyon looked with disdain upon Ashtaroth: his control of Ashtaroth's throat absolute. He released his grip, and Ashtaroth fell to the ground, wheezing and gasping for air. Apollyon spit on the ground where Ashtaroth lay and leapt into the air: he summoned a Ladder and turned to face him a final time. "You would be wise not to approach me again, Astarte, and do not think that your position with Lucifer will cause me pause if you do."

The giant Elohim then stepped onto the Ladder and was gone.

Ashtaroth's need to fill his lungs overpowered his ability and desire to make immediate reply; he looked up in humiliation and resentment as the Ladder carried Apollyon away. Thoughts quickly turned over in Ashtaroth's mind and plans within plans formulated, as he slowly regained his composure.

"This is *not* over Arelim—far from it."

****

Gabriel and his fellow princes looked in awe as the body of Saesheal rose into the air. Lightning crackled, and thunder clapped. A cylinder of light surrounded Saesheal, and the Holy Spirit hovered, his wings outspread, his eyes focused on Saesheal's body.

Jerahmeel leaned toward Michael and quietly spoke, "What is He doing, Michael?"

"I know not," Michael replied. "I stand as puzzled as you."

The charred flesh of Saesheal slowly began to heal, and even the smell from his remains began to fade.

The ground quaked, as the colossal wooden doors of the palace flung open. All eyes shifted to the illuminated figure that stood in the archway's midst.

Michael lifted up his eyes and behold a certain man was clothed in linen. His loins were girded with fine gold, and his body was like beryl; his face was as the appearance of lightning, his eyes as lamps of fire, his arms, and his feet likened to polished brass in color, and the voice of his words like the voice of a multitude.

"Verily, I say unto you…"

Immediately the citizens of Heaven knelt, the host of Heaven went prostrate as the Logos second person of the triune God, had determined to speak, and all of Heaven was hushed, eager with an ear to hear.

"Saesheal has honored me. Thus, he speaks even before the beginning: the things that shall be. For with faith, he hath quenched the dart of Sol and so prophesied of darts yet to come. For as Saesheal gave himself that others might live, so too shall the Son of Man lay down his life that the world might be saved."

Perplexed, the Elohim looked upon each other at a loss for comprehension; their shoulders shrugged in confusion as the depth of Jehovah's word plumbed their minds. He continued, and none spoke.

"Saesheal is not lost but away in the wilderness that I might have voice in all things. To be first among many that would do my will, and thus, it must be suffered him that all righteousness might be fulfilled. He shall stand with his lot at the last day. For indeed, He that loveth his life shall lose it, and he that hateth

68

his life shall keep it unto life eternal.

I am the resurrection and the life: he that believeth in me, though he were dead yet shall he live. Saesheal believed in his God and shall be given a throne, and these things are done that those to come might believe that Jesus is the Christ, the Son of God and that believing they might know that life is through his name."

Like the crash of waves upon a rock, Jehovah's voice echoed throughout the realm, and as suddenly as He had appeared, He was gone, the palace doors shutting fast behind him.

All rose, and Saesheal's body was now fully healed of all injury and slowly lowered to the ground. From each vial, water began to pour, and the waters weaved a maze-like course into spouts that put out the smaller flames.

"The sacrifice is accepted," spoke the Holy Ghost. Lightning crackled, and thunder boomed overhead. Suddenly, a wall of flame erupted in front of Saesheal's body and obscured all from view, a dark barrier of smoke engulfed the altar, and a searing curtain of fire erupted and created an impenetrable wall of flame.

Talus, who was closest to his charge, stepped back, overwhelmed by the intensity of the seething heat. Gabriel and his brethren also backed away, and the immediate area of the emporium emptied until the smolder of the altar cleared away.

All stood in silence at the image before them. None of them knew whether to weep or to break forth in cheers. Those close enough moved towards the altar hands outstretched and raised their hands to grasp the image of light.

The image of light stood—100 cubits high, surrounded by six other smaller pillars: one of violent, blue, green, yellow, orange, and red. Each pillar-shaped to form an Elohim and each pointed to the innermost figure. A translucent image of Saesheal appeared, but Saesheal seemed engaged with another Elohim. Michael and his brethren made out its features; its ram's head and hoofed feet were unmistakable. It was an Arelim.

Beneath them, were two small creatures huddled and cowered under the protective stand of Saesheal. Each had two arms and two legs, and one was shapelier in the hip and torso than the other. Neither had scales or flesh as the Elohim, and a mane of hair flowed from the crown of one creature's head to its shoulders; both grasped one another for comfort and was on bended knee as if in fear. Each image represented the seven species of Elohim, and inhaled and exhaled as if alive. They all moved and *breathed* except the two small bipedal creatures at the base. They were motionless, inanimate in their state of cower and worship.

Talus looked at Michael and then back at the sculpture of light, which lived yet, did not.

"What are those words on the base?"

Michael glanced and knelt down to read a golden plaque hung from its base and words written in angelic script were emblazoned in the fire.

'S-e-p-h-i-r-o-p-t-h'

Michael finished reading and his hand stroked his chin, puzzled as to the term's meaning, and in the instant of his wonderment, he rose and turned his head at the voice in the distance that thundered across the emporium; the irate roar of a tormented and anguished soul.

Apollyon had come home.

Chapter Three

I Am the Potter, You Are the Clay

Day Six

"Saesheal!" Apollyon screamed out. Saesheal's features were easy to distinguish even from this distance. The monolithic breathing sculpture sat near the brass laver and altar at the foot of the mountain of God. Apollyon flew towards the object frantically and moved those who barred his path. The other Elohim made way for the giant as he approached.

Gabriel and the rest of the princes eyed Apollyon as he landed before their presence. Too overcome with grief, Apollyon abandoned protocol and failed to bow. There was no regal welcome, no sign of submission in his posture: only confusion rested in his voice as he spoke in interrogation.

"What has been done to him? Prince Michael? Why is he thus?"

Michael walked towards him. Michael's frame was similar to Apollyon's and in a show of compassion, Michael rested his hands on Apollyon's shoulders to comfort him. Apollyon looked closely at the breathing monument. Apollyon's eyes squinted in response to his mind's curiosity as he attempted to comprehend how a structure of light was alive but was not. He passed his hands through the illuminated form of his friend, and his hand grasped ether, but there was substance to the eyes. The monument gave off an aromatic sweet smelling savor: fragrant and intoxicating to all present, causing Apollyon's confusion to rise even more.

"Please, Lord Prince. How is he thus?

Prince Talus came forward. Michael looked at him to answer on his behalf, and Talus spoke.

"Saesheal is yet alive Apollyon. We know not where nor do we understand how. This is his body recreated by the Holy Spirit of God Himself. We all stood to see our brother restored in the flesh. El has spoken by his Spirit concerning his person."

Talus paused and looked upon the great emporium of assembled Elohim, each still fixated at the sculpture. The mighty Cherub lifted his voice and spoke as if to the wind. "Grigori of Heaven, you who have witnessed what has been seen and done here today. Speak the record that our brother may hear. A Throne Prince of Heaven commands you!"

There was no immediate sound or action for a moment. A sense of indecisiveness and expectation hung in the air. Soon visible mists of air moved and stirred, and by the thousands the Grigori uncloaked. Their hooded and veiled forms became visible for all of Heaven to see. A group of shimmering ghostlike personas rarely noticed, but whose presence was always there. Each flew without wings and stood next to its assigned Elohim of record. Their dark cowled figures flooded both the emporium and the sky round about. With a voice never before heard in Heaven, the Grigori spoke as one man.

"Saesheal is not lost but away in the wilderness that I might have voice in all things. To be first among many that would do my will, and thus, it must be suffered him that all righteousness be fulfilled. He shall stand with his lot at the last day. For indeed, He that loveth his life shall lose it, and he that hateth his life shall keep it unto life eternal.

I am the resurrection, and the life: he that believeth in me, though he was dead yet shall he live. Saesheal believed in his God, and shall be given a throne, and these things are done, that those to come might believe that Jesus is the Christ, the Son of God; and that believing they might know that life is through his name."

Then when the record of El's word was spent for all to hear: the Grigori faded from view and returned to their state of hidden observation. Their tomes and styluses faded with them. Then they were gone; an entire race of angels invisible to the naked eye.

Apollyon looked upon his prince and spoke. "Lord Prince if Saesheal is alive have you word on this 'wilderness' El spoke of? How might I see my brother again?"

"I know not my friend. This word is beyond me, but I trust in El. There is nothing covered that shall not be made known and nothing hidden that shall not be revealed. However, Son of the Dawn you are here while Sol is left attended by another. Speak your reason for coming to Jerusalem."

"My desire Lord Prince is to speak with El to determine the meaning of the word I have received from his Lord, Prince Lucifer. I am also come to see to my charge of Sol."

Talus looked upon his friend, smiled, and took him by the shoulder. "Walk with me."

The emporium slowly emptied as angels returned to their respective duties. Talus and Apollyon walked to a more private area of the steps away from all earshot.

"Archon of Sol, and yes I called you Archon and Archon you shall be unless you determine that you are no longer qualified for the post. I see within you enormous potential, my friend. God did not name you Son of the Dawn for naught. Thus, with his wisdom, I have named you Archon of Sol. Twas, not a foolish thing to appoint one such as you, for you, have the stout heart necessary to execute the will of the fires of Sol."

"Thank you, my liege yet—"

"Do not interrupt your Prince. I do not pretend to know the fullness of your grief. I know not what would cause you to question the very goodness of

El. Yes, your Grigori does indeed record all, and El is aware of your thoughts concerning Him, as are the Lumazi. Yet he has not repented of his command to position you Archon of Sol, and it is not my place to question his decision. If *you* must question it, then do so. However, know this: that you question alone, and take comfort that the gifts and calling of the Lord are without repentance. You are Archon. You shall remain thus until either you or El determine otherwise."

Apollyon bowed in submission, grateful for his prince's words. "My Lord Prince, I request that my station be held by another until and if I may speak with the Master."

"Permission granted my friend. Remain within the capital until word is given of thy petition."

Apollyon once again bowed to his Prince and turned to take his leave. Talus left his charge and returned to the rostrum near the laver to see Gabriel, Michael, and the others still staring at the new monument El had erected in Heaven.

"All right how long will you all gawk? Enraptured by the smell I take it?" Talus laughed

Michael looked at him, but there was no humor in his face: just a sadness that seemed to portend grim news. "I think you must come and see this," said Michael.

Talus walked towards his friends and stopped to observe what they were looking at.

"What is it?" he said.

Gabriel pointed to the figure of Saesheal.

"Aye, it's Saesheal. This I already know. There is nothing of interest here, so why the to-do?

74

"Look here," said Michael.

Talus then followed Michael's pointed finger and realized that no eyes were on the figure of Saesheal at all, but of the unidentified Elohim of whom he wrestled. The cloven feet and ram's horns suggested that it was an Arelim. The monument's features were not quite complete; still developing even as they spoke. Talus looked upon the breastplate of the Arelim in mortal combat with Saesheal.

"You see it now?"

"Aye, but I do not believe it," said Talus.

Talus looked upon the breastplate of the warrior who was attacking Saesheal, and at whom the small figures underneath him cowered. God had given all Elohim a stone or sigil with their names embedded in it, a symbol that could not be duplicated. This sigil held one name only.

Abaddon the Destroyer

"Who bears this sigil?" asked Gabriel.

"I know not," said Michael, "yet I find it incomprehensible that that one of our kind might raise himself against another."

"Agreed, but the combatants are unmistakably Arelim," said Jerahmeel.

Talus breathed deeply, visibly disturbed by the sigil.

"I have seen this symbol before, yet I know of no Arelim or Elohim with the name of Abaddon. I must meditate on this."

Michael spoke. "In all of Grigoric history, there has never been a record of an Elohim engaged thus with another. It is unthinkable to me. We stand in the shadow of a grave portent."

"Aye, and no Elohim hast ever been brought to not. We walk in new times," Sariel spoke.

Michael nodded.

The palace doors opened, and the sounds of the Seraphim's chants of "Holy, Holy, Holy." came from the throne room and escaped into the open air.

Raphael emerged from the palace doors and spoke. "Brethren, El has reconvened the council — come."

Each began to ascend, into the great hall to attend to their Master's call. Michael looked back to see Talus unmoved, still transfixed in intense study of the fixture.

"Talus?" said Michael.

"Michael, I am positive that I have seen this sigil."

Michael studied the face of his friend, "I am sure you will remember. Come — El summons us."

Talus followed still deep in thought. His eyes glanced back at the monument and his mind flooded with questions. However, there was only one word that clamored for his attention; one word that plagued his mind as he walked into the great hall — *Destroyer.*

****

Heaven bustled and stirred as angels went about their business. Apollyon waited in line at the Grigoric Hall of Records: a building where the walls themselves projected the current happenings of the universe. Each attendant was a Grigori clearly visible and who diligently wrote the schedules of the times and seasons of creation.

The room held hourglasses and other devices that displayed time. El had a Grigori assigned to determine when to schedule his appointments. Raphael's work was extensive as he managed the mammoth task to record the goings on of all of Creation. The Grigori was the most numerous species of Elohim yet the ones who had the least interaction with the creation itself because they primarily recorded and were schedulers. Apollyon approached a desk and spoke to an attendant behind the counter.

"Hail brother, I am Apollyon. I come from Earth with inquiry for El"

The cowled creature looked at him. "One moment please."

He turned to his rear and reached for one book settled on a shelf among many. He opened the Elomic Record, which contained the name of every Elohim ever created. Scores of names and entries dotted the pages. His finger deftly went through each name until he located Apollyon.

"Ah yes. Name: Apollyon. Title: Son of the Dawn. Office: Archon: Administer of the greater light. Assignment: Sol system." He thumbed through the pages and frowned. "Hmmm it would seem that you have had shall we say, a unique start as Archon. I see that you are on temporary leave from Sol. Good. I doubt the system could endure another failure."

Apollyon felt the anger within him begin to rise. "I do not need your rebuke. I simply seek inquiry from El. When am I scheduled to enter his presence?"

The attendant searched for his name, cross-referenced it with appointments that El had and then spoke. "I see no invite to grace His presence."

"That's not possible. All Elohim have access to the personal presence of God. Once access is requested, it is simply…"

"Apollyon, I seek not to deter you from your duties, but there is no future record of your entrance to see His eminence after your entitlement as Son of the Dawn. In fact, I see no further entries for you beyond day six of the Earth creation date."

"How is that possible? I do not simply cease to exist. All Elohim must return to see El at some point in time for renewal!"

"There is only one entry recorded after today, yet it seems to be incom-

77

plete. There is one word and it cannot be made out as of yet."

"And what is it?" Apollyon asked.

The attendant turned the book for Apollyon to inspect for himself.

Slowly burning into the book were the angelic script and marks of three letters not yet complete in spelling. Each letter emblazoned in reddish hues of orange.

"D-E-S..."

"I am sorry Apollyon, but you are currently denied access from El's presence. You might try to intercede through Prince Talus or one of the other Princes for a direct audience."

Apollyon walked away, with his head held heavy. His thoughts churned with questions. Leaving the door of the Library, he saw the crackle of a Ladder atop the mountain of God; evidence that Lucifer had returned to join the council.

Apollyon thought to himself. *Surely, El will hear Lucifer. I will petition him.* Encouraged with this option and hopeful that Lucifer would give heed to his word. Apollyon headed towards his home for respite, and to wait for an audience with the Chief Prince. Yet there was a foreboding that haunted him. The words of the record attendant still echoed in his mind...

"*I am sorry, Apollyon, you are currently denied access to El's presence.*"

Apollyon turned the words repeatedly in his mind and ruminated on one question.

Why do I have no scheduled future records?

****

The council sat before their Lord and waited for El to speak. They were not long in their wait.

"Rise and bear witness, for the end of all things draws near," the Lord said.

El then turned his back away from his cherubs, and the walls of the throne room became transparent. The room and floor disappeared, and they rested upon the earth not far from Athor. The gleaming city sparkled in the distance, and El opened his mouth to speak.

Earth quieted, and all of creation waited with anticipation for God to verbalize.

And God said, "Let the Earth bring forth the living creature after his kind, cattle, and creeping thing, and beast of the Earth after his kind," and it was so.

Out of nothing they came: four legged beasts of every description. The dismayed angels watched as sea, air, and land filled with living creatures. Lucifer moved as a tiny spider scurried over his foot.

The beasts' locomotion was as varied as their color and skin. Some ran, others hopped; still more galloped, slithered, and crawled. They were two legged, four legged, eight-legged, and multi-legged. Some had the ability of flight. Some were as tiny as a speck; others lumbered along with large bony protrusions from what were apparent nostrils.

Immediately the air filled with sound. They roared, chirped, squeaked, and growled. Some barked, and others purred. The Earth filled with new denizens, but they were but automatons in comparison to the Elohim.

Their colors matched the spectrum, and the eyes could not capture the fullness of their beauty.

Each cherub marveled and praised God that life had sprung from El's word. Each prince then lifted up his voice: sang a song of praise and blessed His name. Heavenly voices rose up, and fowl stopped to listen. The animals quieted as the Lord's chief council broke forth into song, and God was pleased.

The Lord smiled upon his council and looked upon all that his hands had made. For God had made the beasts of the Earth after his kind, the cattle after their kind, and everything that creepeth upon the Earth after his kind, and God saw that *it was* good.

All of the cherubs except Lucifer began to play with the new creatures, and from the rear of them came the bleating of a small; four-legged animal in a white coat of puffiness that found itself in front of the First of Angels. Michael watched as Lucifer, the creature stared at one another: and as the creature moved towards Lucifer; Michael looked at the face of his brother and noted that disgust appeared on his face.

"Lucifer," God said, "I have a special task for you."

"Yes my Lord?" Lucifer replied.

"I am determined to honor the greatest of all mine creations with a home on this planet. What shall be done unto he whom the Lord delighteth to honor?"

Lucifer gleamed with excited anticipation, thinking to himself, *whom would the Lord desire to honor above myself?*

Lucifer's mind pondered what he should ask the king of the universe. What would he desire? How could El honor him, his first of all creation? Then it came to him.

"My Lord, I believe that a garden should be created: a lush green place on Earth that would yield every fruit bearing tree. Let it be surrounded in a weather pattern that is most comfortable and cooled by a mist. Within the confines of the garden should also stretch flora that is not just pleasant for food but also to the eye.

"There is a river near Athor, my Lord, that runs east of Eden, and my mind is that whole region would serve as an excellent palatial abode, a realm of spectacular comfort and ease. I also believe that your greatest creation be bequeathed with the deed to Earth. Although you have allowed me oversight as steward, to have title to Earth: to this gem of creation would be of ultimate honor." Lucifer continued.

"And finally, as your image and likeness is so august; I would propose that this creature be unique in all creation and that it would carry *your* image and likeness and that none other may yield it."

El looked upon Lucifer. His eyes penetrated his first creation, and Chief Prince assigned to his most important of deeds. Slowly, he looked upon Lucifer, and Lucifer bowed his eyes to the ground; his brethren also bowed in obeisance. El studied his son, and for a while, the group wondered if He would speak.

"Please you may all rise," He said.

The group rose to see that they were once again within the throne room. El was seated high and lifted up as his train filled the temple and looked down upon them.

"Does the thing that Lucifer hast proposed seem acceptable in thy sight?" asked the Lord.

All replied even as one man, "Oh Lord, thou knowest. Doeth what seemeth right to thou."

El bowed his head, and Michael ever so attentive to his master looked upon El curiously. *Why does El look sad?* He wondered.

El turned to Lucifer, "You have indeed spoken well. Do all that thou hast said, and when the fullness of time is complete return to me, and I will announce my intent to honor my greatest creation."

Michael and Lucifer caught each other's eyes, and Lucifer's glance quickly turned to the throne room doors. The Chief Price left immediately, headed out the palace to assign his detachment their orders, and was quickly out of sight.

"The rest of you are released to your duties. After completion of Lucifer's work on my behalf: return. Then I will announce the future plans I have for Earth, and we will break bread together before I take my rest."

The group bowed in concert; each one dismissed himself and leisurely exited the throne room. The cherubs made their way out the palace, and down the steps, towards the newly formed statue of light.

As Michael and Jerahmeel conversed with one another, Talus motioned for his friends to come near. Talus stood at the statue and gawked his gazed transfixed.

"Michael—that sigil!" Talus said.

"What of it?"

"I think I know to whom it belongs!"

"Who?" Michael replied.

"Apollyon! In El's name — the sigil belongs to Apollyon!"

****

Lucifer walked towards the entrance to the mouth of the mountain of God and noticed the gaseous disturbance that trailed him.

"Your bold desire to manifest and speak is ill-timed Grigori, for we are not in private. What troubles you, Lilith?"

"Remember 'Lightbringer', you do not have things hidden from me. Your disgust of His form grows more apparent even as you pounce at the opportunity to have him honor you."

"I look upon Him Lilith, and I can't help but wonder of the vanity that

82

would cause Him to create *me* first. My presence magnifies His own. My mere existence gives credence to his *need* to be glorified. I am sure El desires to honor the one for helping Him to look so magnificent."

"Do not presume upon El, Lucifer. He is the Word. He is The Father, and you are the son."

"Aye, El indeed is the Word, yet how my creator would make a creation that surpasses Himself seems to reek of weakness and folly."

"It affected you didn't it?"

"That woolish creature? Of course not," Lucifer said.

"Remember 'Lightbringer' I know you as no one would. Do not patronize me."

"Dismiss yourself watcher; an attendant arrives."

Lucifer knew that his thoughts had grabbed the attention of Lilith. Apparently, this image was the one that El chose to reveal to Lucifer, for El had manifested himself differently to each of the Chief Princes.

Running quickly up the steps Basus, an attendant of Lucifer's detachment in Heaven approached the Chief Prince and bowed.

"My Lord, your presence has been requested by the Archon Apollyon. He awaits you within his residence and seeks an audience. If you consent, he will come upon your command to your abode."

"Bid him come, but tell him do not tarry, for I leave for Athor upon the conclusion of our business."

"Aye, Chief Prince," Basus replied.

****

Apollyon walked the streets of his home. Each building of Heaven was carved out of precious stones. One dwelling was fashioned of onyx, another topaz, still others of beryl or sapphire: each home reflective of the qualities of its host. Apollyon walked the streets of glass and gold. Heaven was a wondrous place filled with various flora and fauna. There were birds and exceedingly beautiful beasts that flew. Pegasi filled the air as Elohim transported various building materials to parts unknown. Jerusalem the capital city was a thing of majesty itself. It stood at the base of the Mt. Zion. There was no stellar source of light as with the skies of the second heaven, for the Lord God lit the realm. His brilliance radiated all about. Thus, there was no night in Heaven. God was light, and in Him was no darkness. The city was twelve thousand furlongs in width and height.

Moreover, the city lay foursquare, and the length was as large as the breadth. The length, breadth, and the height of it were equal. If one were to measure the wall thereof, it would be a hundred and forty and four cubits. The building of the wall was of jasper, and the entirety of the city was made of pure gold, like unto a clear glass. Decorative stones adorned the foundation of the walls of the city. The first foundation *was* jasper; the second, sapphire; the third, a chalcedony; the fourth, an emerald; the fifth, sardonyx; the sixth, sardius; the seventh, chrysolite; the eighth, beryl; the ninth, a topaz; the tenth, a chrysoprasus; the eleventh, a jacinth; and the twelfth, an amethyst. Moreover, the twelve gates were twelve pearls; every gate was made of solid pearl.

Michael constructed each road so that if one were to travel on any street, he would arrive at the base of the mountain of God. To the left of the city were the Elysian Fields, vast acres of manna leaf. It was from here the manna leaves grew a never-ending supply to feed the multitudes of Heaven. Elohim came at their leisure. However, as of late Michael had commissioned groups to harvest at intervals and to store the manna in granaries. For what purpose was not clear to Apollyon, for the Elohim had not had a need to store in the past.

Apollyon looked past the fields to the mountain of God. The massive home of El stood and towered over the whole of Jerusalem. God's palace rested upon the top; the mountain itself served as the foundation and chief cornerstone of the immense structure. None could set foot on the mountain of God, for it was the home of El. None approached it, and each Elohim held an instinct to avoid the mountain. Those among Apollyon's kind who ventured too close had found themselves ill and suddenly surrounded by the Ophanim who escorted them quickly away from the vicinity. It was said that the Ophanim at El's command would destroy anyone who dared breached the temple without permission to enter, assuming that one would have first escaped the Seraphim who guarded the entrance to El's throne.

Looking across the Elysian Fields, Apollyon could see the Cliffs of Argoth, a cropping of rock that protruded and overlooked the capital.

Argoth, an Elohim of illustrious renown and mystery was an angel of prophetic praise. Legend says that when the Lord created him, Argoth looked upon his maker for the first time and was so stunned, so overwhelmed and so awed by his beauty, that he became as a man in a deep trance or a waking slumber.

Argoth then walked to the edge of the mountain of the Lord, looked out over the expanse of the Kingdom of Heaven, and proclaimed,

"The LORD, The LORD God, merciful and gracious, longsuffering, and abundant in goodness and truth Keeping mercy for thousands, forgiving iniquity and transgression and sin, and that will by no means clear the guilty, visiting the iniquity of the fathers upon the children and upon the children's children, unto the third and to the fourth generation."

After this proclamation, the Lord said to him, "For nothing is secret that shall not be made manifest; neither anything hid that shall not be known." El immediately silenced him, and the cliffs muzzled from echoing what Argoth had uttered. The cliffs are the only place of permanent silence in Heaven. The cliffs have come to represent a place where secrets are uttered. Afterward, Argoth became a Grigori with an unusual assignment: he now stands mute within the Great Library, his stylus and inkhorn yet to record

Next to the cliffs was a massive cave-like furnace called the Kiln: the place where the 'Stones of Fire' lay and where new Elohim came into existence. It has fired without ceasing since before Apollyon's own creation, a never-ending womb that breeds the host of Elohim who administer the affairs of Heaven and Earth. Only El and the Chief Prince may enter the Kiln.

Apollyon turned down one of the gold laden streets to walk past the living quarters of his deceased friend Saesheal. He turned the door to enter and quietly closed the door behind him. Apollyon walked carefully as if he were stepping over a sleeping patron. Apollyon viewed the flowers picked from the grounds of Heaven: colorful plants that responded to one's touch. Each petal hummed in a quiet melody and emitted a tiny iridescent light. A table with flatware adorned the dining room. Tapestries, linens, chairs, tomes, Apollyon slowly realized how much Saesheal's quarters were highly decorated: so unlike his own.

Apollyon had never found the need for such trivial things. His function was to serve. There was little need for beds, flowers, or living creatures to accompany his solace in his moments of rest. Saesheal, however, was not so. There were volumes of books on his shelves, the record of the commands given to the Elohim upon their exit from the Kiln. The Grigori have created a library within the capital that provides public access to the records of the ever-expanding creation. Each record displayed was either projected as an image or stored in written form. Apollyon noticed that Saesheal had spent time studying his assignment of Luna. Records of Luna's creation and instructions to its oversight littered the table of Saesheal's dwelling.

Apollyon's heart saddened as he walked the room, reminded of the many days of laughter Saesheal and he shared within. The mirth that Saesheal and he enjoyed usually came at Apollyon's expense. Apollyon smiled in remembrance. He would miss those days.

However, a frown found him as he remembered his loss. The absence gnawed at him like a sore. It was a consuming thing this emptiness. Saesheal was closest to him, for they quartered across from each other. Apollyon ached from his loneliness, for none sought to see to his well-being, and none cared for his companionship. Those who would call him brother centered only on his failure. Apollyon missed his friend. He left Saesheal's quarters and turned towards his own home to see one of Lucifer's attendants knocking on his door.

"Apollyon?" The attendant said.

"Yes. I take it you come with word from Lucifer on my audience?"

"Indeed. He has agreed to speak with you. Be swift, as matters of state require his immediate attention. He only waits for you."

"Then let us make haste; lead on," Apollyon said.

Both made for the sky and arched themselves towards the northern part of the city. Lucifer had made his home as close to the mount of God as possible without causing the Ophanim to be irritated. He was also removed far enough from the hustle and bustle of the city to warrant privacy. It did not take long for the two angels to enter into Lucifer's court. Apollyon followed the lead of his guide, and as they walked up the steps, which lead to the mansion, Apollyon could see from the corner of his eye that Ashtaroth attended.

Warily they eyed each other. Ashtaroth glared at Apollyon from the distance. Their eyes locked in a waltz of mutual disdain. Neither spoke. Apollyon finally turned his gaze when Basus beckoned him to enter a great room.

"Chief Prince Lucifer Draco, I present to your eminence, Apollyon Arelim, Archon of Sol, Son of the Dawn."

"Thank you Basus. Apollyon please come in."

Basus left the two alone and slowly closed the door behind him.

"I have urgent business to attend to Apollyon. Basus tells me you have desired an audience with me?"

Apollyon rose from his kneeling position. "Aye, Chief Prince. By your own hand were you sent by El to relay His majesty's word to his servant."

"Indeed. I also recall that you wanted to query El as to its meaning," Lucifer said.

"Yes my Lord. I have also received permission from Lord Talus temporarily to forego my duties until I have entreated the Lord."

Puzzled, Lucifer looked upon Apollyon. "Continue."

"After coming from Lord Talus, I sought counsel to request an audience with El. Upon doing so, the Grigori present stated I was not scheduled to see El, nor is there record after the conclusion of the six-day for me to enter his presence."

"I see — so why trouble me Archon? Submit your entreaties on another occasion. We all must come before his throne at some point."

"That is my quandary, my Prince. There is *no* future occasion where I seem to have access to El. It is as if I no longer exist. How can such a thing be possible?"

Lucifer turned away from his guest. His brow scrunched as he pondered Apollyon's words. He turned back to face him and spoke. "I do not know, yet I muse then that you seek me to intercede on your behalf?"

"Yes, my liege. Thou art the Chief Prince. To company with El and petition him is nothing for one such as you."

Apollyon bowed in submission.

"Rise and fear not. Your fealty is rewarded Son of the Dawn. All that thou sayest I will do," said Lucifer.

"I am in your debt, my Prince. Twice now, you have honored me. I have nothing to return your kindness."

"Nothing is necessary. I consider you a kindred spirit. If El had not assigned you to Sol, I would have you associated with my work on Earth. Perhaps I will still petition for your release into my charge. In the meantime, I must depart for Athor and prepare my work. Reside here within my hall if you wish, and upon my return, I will attend to your request."

"Thank you, Chief Prince. El's will be done," Apollyon said.

"El's will be done," replied Lucifer.

Apollyon bowed and slowly backed away from the Chief Prince and closed the door behind him.

Lucifer stared silently for a moment and thought to himself, *El's will be done.*

****

The statue continued to morph slowly into shape. Mesmerized, each of the high princes watched the light and movement of the figure.

"We must find him!" Talus implored.

Sariel looked at Talus and had never before seen his brother speak so anxiously.

"Talus, what is it that plagues you?"

"I looked and looked at the figure; perhaps my own desires caused me to hold back the truth. I know not. What I do know is that this sigil belongs to Apollyon! Of this I am sure."

Sariel looked at Michael and his brothers.

"Talus did you not say, and can we not see, that this figure who wrestles with Saesheal is *not* Apollyon? Is it possible that this is an Arelim not yet formed? And if it is Apollyon, what of it? What would you have us do? He has not committed offense short of his own failure to questions El's goodness."

"Sariel surely you don't think that questioning the goodness of God is a trite thing?"

"Nay — yet El himself has the power and means to deal with Apollyon if He sees fit. Was it not He that informed *us* of his thoughts? If he knew this would he not know if more would be wrong? Was it not the Lord of Heaven and Earth whose hands crafted the figure we gaze upon? And Talus tell me — has El mentioned any assignment, action, or concern about Apollyon that we or anyone else are to pursue: other than the Chief Prince himself? Nay my brother. Do not seek to stir the flame of doubt where none exists."

Sariel stepped away from the figure and headed down the steps towards the entrance to the city. He paused and turned to speak. "However, I suggest that you find Apollyon. If his Prince concerns himself with his welfare, then Apollyon should be allowed to hear his concerns."

Jerahmeel turned to speak to his brother. "Sariel is correct. You are his prince. You should find him and talk with him."

Raphael placed his hand on Talus' shoulder. "Do not avail yourself to fret. I will scour his tome to see if his watcher has entered anything new that should be brought to the court's attention."

"I appreciate that Raphael. He is on leave from his duties when last we met. He wanted an audience with El. Therefore, he should still be here. I will begin to look for him. Within the Great Library is a good place to start. Michael, would you assist me?" Talus asked.

"Aye, I also wish to see his sigil for myself. Come, let us go." Michael said.

****

Apollyon relaxed in the great hall of the Chief Prince. It was apparent that Lucifer was a connoisseur of beauty. His personal lodging almost rivaled that of Athor. The finest of Elysium tapestries decorated his walls and silks from the Adonis trees draped his windows. The silk was the finest quality and laced with gold, and shimmered. The floors were purple and radiated an orange hue as they glowed. Lapis lazuli was used to grout the diamond tiles on the walls.

Lucifer's furniture was of Chittim wood. The wood's pores dripped a sap that perfumed the room, and the wooden couch's frame conformed to whoever sat or laid on it. Floral pelts adorned Lucifer's tables and couches. Books upon books littered his shelves, and various instruments of measurement were strewn about his desk. A plumb line and other devices used to build were nestled in a case. Apollyon traveled upstairs to his bedchamber, and it became

91

apparent to him by the number of hand carved instruments that Lucifer was an adept minstrel and psalmist. In addition, to more books, Cora leaf pages of song after song of handwritten praise and worship lay near his bed. Lucifer seemed to possess a Grigoric record on every aspect of creation.

"Am I disturbing you Archon?"

Apollyon recognized the voice: a voice which last time he had heard it, he held its bearer by the throat. He turned to see Ashtaroth standing in the bedroom doorway.

"I was not aware that the Chief Prince had granted you right to grope through his affairs. Or am I to take it that your being in the masters chamber is due to some infatuation that I know not of?"

Apollyon embarrassed, smiled sheepishly.

"I meant no disrespect to his lordship. I will leave immediately."

"So once more your actions show a lack of forethought. Yet again, does the Archon display his propensity to waywardness? Be not deceived. I will of a surety bring this to my Lord's attention." Ashtaroth turned to leave, and Apollyon's mind was rife with the words of this angel who presumed to be so smug and superior.

"Ever the servant, are you not Astarte?" Apollyon said.

Ashtaroth stopped and turned to face Apollyon. He slowly walked towards him. Fear was not in the nature of an Elohim. Apollyon towered over him, but Ashtaroth did not fear for his safety and spoke.

"Aye, a servant am I. I serve the Chief Prince, the Lightbringer him-self. He, who stands in the midst of the Stones of Fire. It was he that held both you and I in the Kiln. Yes, simpleton; I serve him. You, on the other hand, serve only foolishness and carelessness, and you have your reward. You are neither worthy of the title of Archon, and I personally hope…"

Ashtaroth paused to point at the cracked stones that beat within Apollyon's chest. "El never again seeks to utilize the stone with which caused your creation."

Apollyon leaped at Ashtaroth to grab him.

Ashtaroth stepped to his side, and Apollyon went flying past him into a desk smashing the desk of soft Chittim wood to pieces.

"You mocked me upon our last encounter Archon. Do not presume that your physical stature impresses me. You caught me unawares before. I will not be so caught in the future."

Apollyon rose from the floor, kicking the soft legs of the broken desk away from him. "Do not concern yourself with being unaware Astarte. I want you to know that it is I who will pummel you into submission!" Apollyon replied.

Apollyon rose from the floor and heaved the large pieces of the desk from before him. Stray portions flew out the second story window and crashed to the golden streets below.

Startled denizens looked up as two Elohim could be seen grappling with one another. Apollyon and Ashtaroth then broke through the walls to fall from the upper balcony and joined the mangled pieces of wood and brick on the street below. Dozens of onlookers scattered as the entangled bodies of the duo crashed onto the street.

Onlookers watched their mouths agape, as Apollyon grasped Ashtaroth by the throat, and lifted him as he squirmed into the air. Coughing and gagging, Ashtaroth contorted his body and used his tail to wrap itself around a piece of wood lying on the ground, and like a whip smashed it across Apollyon's face.

Apollyon screamed in pain as the wood broke the soft tissue of his face and bluish liquid oozed from the corner of his lip and cheek.

Ashtaroth did not wait for a response and moved quickly to kick the large angel in the torso knocking him back through the door of a merchant's store.

Once again wood, stone, and metal gave way, and Apollyon found himself covered in rubble. Slowly, he rose dazed from the debris while vendors scurried to flee.

Ashtaroth laughed, "You called me little angel Archon, yet it is you who sits on his rear in disgrace. Come to me fool, and let us see how buffoonish you truly are!"

Apollyon clenched his fists and his eyes narrowed and enraged, and the power to control a sun welled within him: and one thought alone filled his mind towards Ashtaroth, the angel who had taunted him for so long.

Dissolution.

****

"What if we do not find him here?" asked Michael.

"Michael my being tells me that we will find Apollyon. I just hope that it is not too late," said Talus.

"Too late for what?" Michael asked.

"That, my friend is what concerns me. I do not quite know. All that I know is that right now I need to see his sigil."

"Well, El's audience chamber is up ahead, so we can inquire shortly as to Apollyon's scheduled time for meeting."

The two high princes lightly touched down in front of the door to the great chamber. All Elohim nearby bowed in submission, and the two quickly stepped inside the building.

The chief keeper of the hall ran towards the pair and bowed before the two princes.

"Lord Talus — Lord Michael! You honor us by your presence within our halls. Please, please how can we help you?"

"Rise my friend; we are in need of some answers. Have you seen an Arelim by the name of Apolly…"

"Apollyon? Yes, High Prince. He was in here not too long ago and asked about his scheduled meeting with El."

Talus asked, "Can you tell us when he is scheduled to meet with the Lord?"

"Of course, Prince Talus. There is nothing within our power that we would withhold from you. We cannot remember ever having two from the royal court within our place of business. It would honor us if…"

Michael interrupted, "We are in swift need of this information, Chief Scheduler. Please make haste."

"Of course, of course, High Prince: Apollyon yes. Let me find his—oh, yes. I distinctly remember our conversation; Apollyon has no scheduled meeting with El—ever."

Michael and Talus looked curiously at each other and then at the record keeper.

"No meeting? What do you mean *ever*? You mean he came here and didn't make an appointment?" Talus asked.

"No, High Prince he came here, but we couldn't make an appointment. You may see his tome if it pleases you."

"Show us quickly!" Talus demanded.

The Chief Scheduler turned to the shelving behind his desk, reached, and pulled down a book. He found the entry for Apollyon and turned the tome around for his two patrons to view.

"See Apollyon's record has no entry after the 6th day. And there is… oh my this was not like this before."

"Speak. What troubles you?" Talus commanded.

The attendant turned the book around and pointed to the letters that emblazoned slowly within its pages.

Talus looked, and his countenance paled.

"Michael, do you see?" Talus asked.

"Aye," Michael answered. "There can be no doubt now. Sariel and the others must be informed immediately."

The text of the page was unmistakable. There was no listing for any future meetings with El past the sixth creation event. Only one word stood out in blood red cursive angelic script.

D-E-S-T-R-O-Y-E-R

****

"Apollyon Son of the Dawn, stand down immediately!"

Morael an angel who stood by the bridge between the third and second heaven, and who granted entry into Heaven had come. He stood now in front of the gaping hole made by Apollyon's impact.

"You and Ashtaroth have caused enough damage this day. Do not compound your failure. Stand down now and be judged!"

Apollyon looked upon him, scowled, and wiped the spittle from his mouth to speak.

"Judged? Which of you would dare judge me? False you are! Depart from me! None here I call kindred. For my brother is shame, my sister failure. No Guard of Heaven; you all have disdained me. You all are simply too cowardly to admit it. I am alone. Ashtaroth was correct when he named me 'Destroyer' and rightly so."

Apollyon's voice grew shrill and harsh, and his sarcasm filled the ears of any present to listen.

"Come let us reason together Morael. You will be the first to witness the 'New Dawn'." Apollyon reached into his chest and revealed his sigil the carved stone that bore the name given by El to every Elohim.

"I renounce Apollyon, the name of my creation, and my creator; a new name shall I now pronounce."

He used his talon and deliberately began to deface and scored out his given name, and Heaven beheld an act of sacrilege never before seen.

"That creature no longer exists...," Apollyon declared.

Morales screamed, "Apollyon, No!"

Apollyon saw Morael standing before him, but his words were ignored. In the sight of all, Apollyon scarred his sigil. His Heartstone darkened from the alteration, the burning light of the sun contained in its fire went out, and his stone became disfigured. His body rapidly changed color to a dark and fiery hue. Bony protrusions emerged from his spine, and mouths of flame erupted from his shoulders. His Heartstone pulsated violently, and there swirled a blackness within as if something alive, wanted to escape.

"...Abaddon shall I be."

Abaddon then charged the angel, this creature who dared position himself between predator and prey. Abaddon flew headlong into Morael and slammed into the would-be protector of Ashtaroth. Disbelief filled with fear overwhelmed Morale's mind on his witness of Abaddon's purposeful self-injury. Morael placed his hands in front of him to try to protect his face and screamed out in pain upon Abaddon's bearish assault.

The two angels flew into a wall of another building, and stone and mortar blew apart around them. The explosive impact shook the ground and shattered nearby windows. The affected structure began to teeter, moan; and ache as its shifted weight buckled under pressure and duress. The roof collapsed and buried Morael and Abaddon in a blanket of rubble.

A momentary pause of silence allowed injured onlookers to move quickly in order to escape the destruction. The rubble began to heave, and the sound of movement emanated from the center of the debris field.

Abaddon soon rose from the wreckage, as a person come ashore from the raging sea; dirt and fragments of wood and stone slid off his large frame, and as a man might hold a cat by its scruff: Abaddon held the unconscious Morael by the collar of his heavenly robes. Blood and water streamed from his limp body. Abaddon dragged the broken and bruised body of the angel from the rubble and stood defiantly as his leathery wings projected a dark shadow over him so that only the luminance from his eyes were seen, eyes which smoldered with a yellowish glow. Abaddon threw with disdain the bruised and broken body of Morael, Guard of Heaven, into the street for all to see and then contemptuously spoke to the gathered crowd.

"Interfere, and you shall all likewise perish."

****

"Attendant, did Apollyon see this script? Michael asked.

"He did High Prince, yet it was not this complete when he was here. There were only three letters when last I opened the tome. There are now nine, and the word is complete.

Michael rubbed his chin and turned to his brother. "Perhaps it is a progressive revelation. The title might be dependent on his actions; therefore, perhaps it is not too late. We must find him quickly."

"If I might be so bold my Prince, too late for what?"

Talus looked at the attendant and spoke. "What is your name record keeper?"

"Hariph, sire."

"Hariph, do you know where Apollyon was headed when he left here?"

"Nay Lord Prince; however, I did inform him that he should entreat one from the royal court. I had specifically mentioned that he might entreat you."

Talus looked at Michael. "Michael, we were in session when he came here, and he has already spoken with me. I think we should scout Lucifer's quarters. Perhaps he might have gone there."

Talus closed the book and returned it to Hariph.

"Thank you Hariph. You have been of immense help to the court this day. Your service shall not be forgotten."

"Anytime, High Pr...."

Suddenly an explosion rattled and shook the building. Books and vases not otherwise secured fell and crashed to the floor.

Michael and Talus ran to the front door, and those within the building ran to several windows to look outside. Flames and smoke rose off in the distance of Lucifer's home, and for the first time in recorded history, there was fire on the streets of Heaven.

****

Elohim after Elohim gawked and stood in disbelief, stunned in dismay that two of their kindred grappled in mortal combat. A crowd had gathered to witness the spectacle, and others attempted to hold Abaddon down as the mighty angel tossed several angels aside like rag dolls. Ashtaroth, Lucifer's attendant, stood aloft as a wall of Elohim surrounded him. A contingent of others attempted to hold off Abaddon's charge towards him.

"Move from my path or be moved!" Abaddon roared. His eyes focused on his quarry.

Talus and Michael arrived, touched down to the street, and took a position to stand as a buffer between the two combatants. As more and more Elohim came to both hear and see the spectacle before them, many stood frozen in disbelief. Elohim that held him were tossed aside as a dog shakes water from its body. With open hands and claws unfurled, Abaddon reached once again for the throat of Ashtaroth who saw the charge of the deranged angel, ducked, and then backed away.

Michael screamed, "Apollyon! No!"

In seconds, it was over and the broken body of Corlus fell to the ground. He was Illuminati, an angel devoted to art, wisdom, and beauty. He had waved his hands as a conductor might lead an orchestra, and expected that the mighty Arelim would follow his lead, and stop his maddening rampage. He believed against hope that despite his fury, Abaddon would take notice and hear him. But when words were not enough, Corlus placed himself in the direct path of Abaddon's blow.

Corlus, his pleas but a tiny voice of wisdom crying in the wilderness, attempted to reason with the howls of Abaddon's rage. Yet reason had abandoned Abaddon, and the hard concussive sound of a fist hammered deep into Corlus' soft flesh.

There was a hush over the attending crowd as Corlus' eyes were open, his breathing turned shallow, and the bluish fluid of his life force drenched the transparent gold street now stained with Elomic blood.

Two had become one as Corlus stood impaled, the arm of Abaddon running through his exposed chest. A small whirlpool of cyclonic air whipped around him, light escaped the dying body as if sucked into a vacuum, and in moments, the spirit of Corlus was gone. Abaddon tossed the lifeless husk of his corpse aside and the body sprawled in the street. While Abaddon held in his bloody hand the beating Heartstone of Corlus now still.

****

"Lord Lucifer, as always it is agreeable to see you again."

"Thank you, Mephisto. There is much to do. El has commanded that Eden be primed for creation. A garden of renown is to be planted and shall serve as the personal abode of El's greatest creation."

"Your instructions my Prince?" Mephisto said.

"Gather a legion of Creyun for this task. They are adept at building and gardening. Spare no one Mephisto. Pull everyone off the expansion of Athor. I want the garden completed before the end of the day."

"Yes, Chief Prince. El's will be done."

Lucifer flew towards Athor and settled into his study to ponder the series of maps made of this new world. He spread one across a desk to view the region around Athor and saw that the area of Eden was near and well watered. His eyes glistened with childish anticipation.

"This shall be the greatest of my feats yet. I will make a garden so lush that it will rival the palatial comforts of El himself."

****

"Argh!"

Abaddon lashed out at several Elohim and overcame them. Those captured in his grip found themselves thrown against stone and glass. Dozens of nearby Elohim attempted to restrain the angel now run amok.

"Talus!" Michael said.

"I see him, Michael. Attack from the rear and I shall engage him directly. He must be brought down!"

Flames leaped from Abaddon's body and engulfed all he touched. Elohim screamed in pain as angelic flesh burned. Some wallowed in pain, for their hands, feet, and limbs were violently hacked. Apollyon ignored all pleas to stop and cut down all who stood between him and Ashtaroth.

"Apollyon, yield or be bound!" Talus demanded.

Abaddon looked upon his prince, and his eyes glowed with flame. Where faculty of reason once rested, rage did now abide. Where a command from a high prince might once have made the Arelim bow in reverence, reason was now lost to rage. Abaddon raised his hands and moved to attack his prince.

Talus braced himself and summoned the sharp bony protrusions from his forearms, and he raised his arm to block Abaddon's attack.

Abaddon's blow found its mark, and angelic flame engulfed Talus's arm. The force of the blow forced Talus back, and his feet slid over the gravel. Talus attempted to use Abaddon's momentum against him and reached to grab his arm to pull him forward.

Abaddon lurched forward as his center of gravity shifted and he tumbled to fall on top of his Lord. Talus fell to his back and used his strong legs to throw Abaddon forward and sent the rogue Archon reeling into a nearby house.

The home burst into flames and engulfed the inhabitants within. Screams and panic emanated from the dwelling as several occupants ran out to escape to safety.

Abaddon then shot from the roof like a cannon; his body glowed, and fire spurted from him as he hovered in the air. He clapped his mighty hands together sending a shock wave that knocked all but Talus to the ground and leveled the flaming structure below him.

Burning wooden shards sprayed Talus and those nearby, shredding flesh and scorching wood, cloth, and stone.

Talus yelled to his brother, "Michael now!"

Apollyon's rage blinded him to the presence of Michael behind him. Michael jumped on Apollyon's back, and wrapped his powerful arms around the Arelim in a chokehold and held him fast.

Apollyon struggled to break free, but Michael used his own weight to drag Apollyon down to the ground. With a thrust of his wings, he turned Apollyon's body downward. The two plummeted to the ground, and Apollyon slammed face first into the earth.

The glass street below them buckled and cracked from the impact of their fall.

Apollyon wrestled with Michael to grab hold of him and to break free, but Michael's grip was sure, and with one arm wrapped under and around Apollyon's neck and chin: another interlocked for surety. Michael refused to release him.

Apollyon moved backward and smashed Michael into wall after wall in an attempt to break away from his hold. He bucked, like an untamed stallion to shake Michael from off his back.

Michael tightened his grip the more and frantically struggled to hang on using his wings to stabilize him and keep him balanced.

As Apollyon struggled to escape Michael's hold, lightheadedness flooded him, and his thoughts became disoriented. With each step, his movement slowed: he staggered and swayed until the behemoth of an angel passed out and crashed to his knees. Michael, relentless in his determination and with his grip still taut, cautiously released him.

The rogue angel was now unconscious and collapsed at Michael's feet.

****

"This area will do nicely," Lucifer said. "Spugliguel, create a perimeter 100 furlongs long by wide. This area shall be your charge, and never shall the cold breach this realm. I command a perpetual season of spring be in this place."

Spugliguel bowed in obedience. "Aye, Chief Prince."

Lucifer walked the ground, and his eyes darted back and forth while hundreds of attendants in tow surveyed the land. He gestured with his hand in a sweeping motion.

"I want this area seeded with grass. When my feet walk its surface, I desire to feel nothing but lushness beneath. Caracasa and Commissoros see to the flora. I command that every tree and vine which bringeth forth fruit and is sweet to the taste, every tree which delights the soul be planted within."

"El's will be done," they said and swiftly flew off to parts unknown.

Lucifer looked to his Archon of agriculture and fecundity Habuiah. "Let us begin my friend. El's will be done."

"As you command, Chief Prince," Habuiah replied.

Habuiah flew into the air. His transparent wings created wind gusts around him. He rose to a level so that he could see all of the region commanded by Lucifer and spoke the Elomic commands unique to his charge as Archon of all agriculture.

"Let there be growth."

The ground of the region, all 100 furlongs square, beckoned to his command. A pulse of light emanated from Habuiah. He dove into the ground and drove his giant fists into the earth, and as a stone is thrown into the water, wave after circular wave emanated from him and dissipated only at the edge, of the soon to be garden.

Each wave pulsated across the landscape leaving behind acres of green and lush grass throughout the region. A blanket of emerald green: a 100-furlong meadow of jade and blossoms, soft to the touch and ripe with the smell of freshness, covered the dark earth of Eden. The Elohim present with Habuiah flew into the air to prevent crushing the new growth that rose from beneath their feet.

Commissoros and Caracasa returned from gathering the selected seeds from the earth. As honey bees returned to the hive, the duo released the various seedlings from the pouches within their flesh. Each grasped a handful and tossed the assortment of seed into the air.

Yoniel, one of the keepers of the Northwind, then blew, and the seeds flew gently throughout the air, ever so delicately. Yoniel blew in such a way that each seed moved to its appointed place and rested on the grass below. The coverage of the seedlings was uniform throughout Eden.

Habuiah spoke to the ground and all that lay therein. "Come forth!"

The kernels within each shell split and roots shot into the earth. Tendrils of plants delved to find a home in the black soil beneath the carpeted grass. Like a legion of undead rising from the grave, trees clawed through the surface and reached skyward. Limbs yawned, as one would awake from a morning sleep. The yawns of banana, pear, apple, and various other trees cracked and groaned as bark snapped and splintered in their desire to accelerate and grow, racing to fulfill the will of El.

Smiling, Lucifer looked upon the new forest made before him. His created work sang with the sounds of new life and moved to the tempo of his directives, as an orchestra would follow a conductor. He was pleased. The vision of his mind became a reality before his eyes; Lucifer smiled and saw that it was good.

Michael had never seen Heaven so somber as in these last few hours.

First, there was Saesheal who was and then was not.

Apollyon, who exercised his own will above El's, and now had caused the horrific dissolution of a fellow Elohim.

Angels of all castes, races, and station had come to witness this new sight. A crowd formed as silent and confused onlookers watched several members of the royal court force march Apollyon towards the mount of God.

Sariel and Jerahmeel walked behind him, and each held a chain from a hook attached to an iron collar clamped tightly around his neck. Apollyon staggered as he walked with his head held high and pulled reluctantly in defiance while Michael and Talus yanked forcibly on chains attached to his wrists to drag him forward. He walked slowly, for manacles bound his ankles and wrists.

Apollyon writhed like a rabid dog and cursed obscenities at his captors and those spectators who looked ruefully upon him.

Apollyon could hear their sneers.

"How could he?" one said.

"Look at him!" said another.

"Let him reap what he has sowed!"

Then out of the crowd, Apollyon heard the words that now defined him. "Away with you, Destroyer!" an onlooker cried out.

Apollyon smiled and reveled in the acrimony.

"Dogs of El," he said, "thank the creator that I am restrained, or I would bring dissolution to you all! False brethren you are. I call Heaven and Earth against you that I shall see Heaven razed, and I shall bask in its flames. Look upon me and see. You will all beg to allow me to release you to join Corlus."

Apollyon laughed, and some angels picked up pieces of earth and rock to throw at him. Apollyon covered his face but allowed the tokens of his tormentor's angst to fuel his rage.

"Yes, remember this day. I have committed slaughter in Heaven. Let my name be chronicled throughout Grigoric history. My hands have brought dissolution this day, and my vengeance shall find you out. Remember Corlus, for he shall not be the last!"

Michael and his brethren finally arrived at the foot of the mount of God. They approached the stairwell to escort Apollyon to the altar. The doors of the temple flew open, and the Ophanim descended like lightning to the gold steps below.

They flung great arcs of voltage about them and formed an impenetrable wall to prevent Michael and the others from bringing Apollyon any closer. They screeched, as their wheels turned as a grating sound as irritating as the scraping of fingernails over slate. Their eyes moved as they scanned and probed over every person within sight. They were living balls of rotating lightning, and they crackled, flashed, and barred entry to the temple of God.

The glorious figure of El then stepped through the temple doors.

His presence made all shades of darkness flee as the new day's sun banishes night. The multitudes of Heaven prostrated themselves to the ground.

The Ophanim moved like hummingbirds, and the sound of swarming bees emanated from their bodies. They darted like Dobermans over the congregation, and with a bloodhound's tenacity, they scrutinized any gesture or body movement from anyone who would dare raise their head to look at El.

No one moved.

All sat still, knowing that the creator of the ends of the earth had stepped from the temple, and He was not pleased.

Some Elohim shuddered in fear of attack.

All peripherally watched as the Ophanim explored the corners of the city and whizzed like giant mosquitoes over the heads of the populace.

Then as if recalled to heel, they dashed like a school of fish disturbed and rested in front of the princes who held Apollyon to form what could best be described, as an impenetrable electrified screen.

Apollyon stepped back and covered his face to shield himself.

The Ophanim seemed anxious to shred him in their wheels of grinding flesh.

Like guard dogs leashed yet itching and ready to attack, they aggressively moved towards the party; their mouths salivated and with scarlet eyes. They stood by on El's command, ready to devour them all.

Then El spoke. "Lumazi release your charge."

Michael and his brethren quickly released their chains and without prompt slowly backed away from Apollyon, grateful to place distance between themselves and the Ophanim.

Apollyon, who had boasted earlier, now kowtowed like the rest; and where his swagger had arrogantly flaunted itself throughout the public square: now cowered with his hands over his head and his face bowed down. Where brazen and predictive declarations once ran away from his lips, only pleas of mercy now filled his mouth.

The princes backed ten paces away from Apollyon; then the Ophanim swarmed him.

They whirled around his person, cut into his flesh, and lifted his body from the ground. As their gyroscopic bodies attacked him, his chains severed and disintegrated before they could touch the ground.

Like a cloud of locusts, they ripped into his flesh, biting, gnawing, and stabbing him with teeth that retracted in and out. Apollyon's body twisted in agony, and his screams mingled in a horrific harmony of song to the buzz of the Ophanim's grinding wheels.

His tortured screams echoed across the palace courtyard, and the host of Heaven could do nothing but look on in intimidated wonderment, awed by the wrath of the living God.

"Apollyon Son of the Dawn, thou hast been warned of rage's specter. Only he that is of a pure heart shall find me; yet now thy search hast found me as Righteous Judge and what is this– that Corlus' blood crieth to me from Limbo? Because thou hast scarred thyself and defiled the name of your birth, and thy rage against me and thy tumult hast come up into mine ears, therefore, I will put my hook in thy nose and my bridle in thy lips, and I will turn thee back by the way which thou camest. 'Destroyer' thou hast embraced, and Abaddon shalt thou be. From the furnace of the Kiln wast thou taken and to the furnace of Hell shalt thou return."

All of Heaven then shook. The mountain of God rocked violently, and the waters from the mountain that fed into Poseidon's Fountain, the aqueducts to the city, and the Elysium fields ran dry as if shut off at a spigot.

The ground then cracked and from the rearward of the city a chasm opened up and a geyser of fire spewed high into the sky; the elevation shifted, a craggy peak exploded from the ground and jetted into the air as rock and dirt fell to the ground as it rose.

Conically the mountain grew, and the earthen mount lurched upwards until it belched rock and fire. Pyroclastic flows ejected from the side of the peak, and molten blood vomited from its surface. Smoke rose from a cavernous mouth and belched dark smolder into the sky.

Where previously there had been flowers and shrubs that changed colors, now the flora withered in the wake of an advancing march of sulfur and ash. The small mountain continued to grow, and its acidic noxious stench withered all life that could not escape its path: grass and plants caught unfortunate enough to be in its shadow withered to ash.

Animals that had played around the area previously ran to escape the onslaught of fire that rained down from the mountain's craggy face.

A tall plume of smoke rose and blanketed the area. Shattered only by glimpses of lightning: thunder pounded, and the peak roared as if awakened from some great slumber.

The fires of the Kiln leapt forth in eruption to embrace this lost distant cousin: A mutual kiss of heat and flame that would sear all who dared to draw near.

Black, gritty ash and flakes of powdered sulfur-lined the sides and mouth of the new summit. The body of the volcano inhaled and exhaled like a thing alive. And all of Heaven beheld God create a new thing, a living mountain!

Panting for the choking stench of sulfur, the mount oxygenated itself: its forge of a heart pumped heated magma into granite, and craggy veins umbilically tied it to the Kiln.

Hell was a breathing crucible of arid combustion and steam, and like a newborn babe waited to suckle at its mother's breast. The furnace hungered and salivated magma and brimstone, yearning to consume and wailing in titanic rumblings of starvation.

Knowingly, the Ophanim turned to the mouth of the great breathing cavern now linked to the Kiln itself.

The Ophanim held Abaddon aloft, lifting him towards the mountains

110

mouth, and he pleaded; nay screamed for mercy and pardon. Yet El was silent: stoic in his flowing robes of light and power.

El had spoken, and there was nothing to add to His word.

The Ophanim carried Abaddon, lacerating him as they went. His clothing became tattered from their relentless onslaught of incisions into his flesh. Then when they reached the summits great mouth, they dangled him helplessly over the mouth of Hell where a tongue of lava waited to greet him.

Lapping like a dog at its first morsel: stalagmite teeth bared, ready to swallow whole the now pitiful creature who once had commanded a sun.

Mercilessly, the Ophanim released him and Abaddon fell screaming into the cavernous mountain. The echoes of his ear-splitting cries stretched across Heaven cut short by his drowning in the gastric acids of the abomination of punishment.

Hell's lava bubbled and spittle flowed over its heated mouth, and the stygian hue from its entrance collapsed in on itself.

The magma of the mountain's surface cooled, and steam hissed from the rock. A flash of lightning raced across the sky, a clap of thunder followed, and the peak went mute. The mountain was now quiet in hellish digestion as black smoke billowed from its rocky pores. The smell of burnt flesh wafted through the air. The sky darkened slightly from the smoke that escaped from the mount; suddenly, Heaven was silent once more.

It was here in that moment that a collective epiphany overtook them all. El was power on a level they had never grasped. His anger was terrible, and His ways beyond measure. He was indeed worthy of all honor and glory. They had witnessed the birth of a living realm, its hunger satiated only by their own kind.

El is Alpha. El is Omega.

All watched in fear and trembling. For when Heaven was formed none was present, yet now each bore witness to the creation of Hell. An added feature to the landscape of the realm, and they all looked at the mountain knowing what now *lived* inside.

El turned to return to the temple and as he stepped the "Holy, Holy, Holy is the Lord God Almighty," of the Seraphim could be heard from inside, and the ground quaked with the reverberating of the sound.

The Ophanim flew quickly overhead, zooming low over the knelt populace in the emporium, and each angel instinctively ducked to avoid injury.

Twain settled underneath the feet of El and he rose on their backs as twain covered his rear. Their eyes stared in all directions, never blinking, ever watching.

Watching until the temple doors shuttered fast behind him, and El was out of sight.

****

Lucifer looked upon the Garden of Eden and smiled upon his creation of pristine beauty.

Surely El will be pleased.

He walked the length and breadth of it and took in every smell and sight. The songs of birds fluttered in the wind, the light breeze grazed his flesh, and each scent of cumin and lily filled him with vigor. He tasted one of the grapes from the many vines within the expanse and savored its sugary flavor.

Ahh, this tastes so much better than manna.

He walked and admired the various trees unique to this world. The willow tree and aspen, the birch and the pine; each grew in an environment that would allow it to thrive, each environment compatible with the other.

This will be my new home.

112

From the distance just past a clearing of trees, Lucifer looked and saw them.

A flock of ruminating even-toed creatures draped in yellowish-white fleece for hair. Each sported short tails, and their eyes possessed slit-shaped pupils and set in faces of black. They seemed to be aware of his presence, yet they bleated while they ate the grass under foot.

What an intriguing animal.

"I take it, Chief Prince, that you are not impressed with the creature?"

Lilith had noticed Lucifer's thoughts, saw that they had a measure of privacy, and decided to make his appearance.

"Impressed? No Lilith, impressed is not the word that I would use to describe this creature. Look at it. It grazes in peace unaware of the dignity of my presence. I could but speak a word and the creature would be razed, yet it chews the cud with oblivion. If I but move my finger, the flute within would sing alto and soprano within the breeze. This—this thing neither roars with the power of the great Leviathan nor thunders as Behemoth. It—it bleats. It does not glisten against the sun, nor does it stand erect. Its function baffles even one such as I. I despise its existence; it reeks of weakness, dependence, and docility. It ravishes the lush emerald I have gone to great lengths to create. There is nothing that would engender me to such a thing."

"I have recorded your thoughts Lightbringer, but never until now can I say that I have understood them. This then is how *you* see El?"

Lucifer paused for a moment and then spoke. "I will say that there are *others* more suited to govern this realm."

Lilith laughed. "Of course my Prince. No doubt you would have insight as to *who* might be worthy?"

Lucifer raised his eyebrow and turned around to look at his watcher.

"Do you mock me, Grigori?"

"Nay, Chief Prince, I would not presume to tell you that which you know so well. Your thoughts are open to me, and I know that thou are not satisfied in your status."

"I am the first creation, and I yet I walk amongst the docile, those who chew manna as these creatures here chew the cud. I would see El's plan for me accomplished, and it is to be more than this…this grandiose orchestration of husbandry."

"And what *is* thy desire, Chief Prince? What would satisfy you?" asked Lilith.

Lucifer thought for a moment. His eyes scoured the land and surveyed the sky. His gaze looked past the second heaven and deep into the third.

"That I might ascend into Heaven," he said. "That my throne be exalted above the stars of God. That I would sit also upon the mount of the congregation, in the sides of the north: To ascend above the heights of the clouds…"

Lilith smirked, amused and somewhat startled by Lucifer's reply.

"You already walk within the Stones of Fire, and you are first among your brethren, nay above all creation save God himself. Would *you* be God?"

Lucifer turned to continue his stroll through the Garden of Eden, walked to inspect the small helpless sheep before him, and softly replied to himself, "Indeed."

****

"Speak," said El.

Sariel was the first to enter the fray.

"Lord, in thine wisdom I see why you showed us the vision of Abaddon. He was a portent that you saw; a warning of what could befall us all if we were to deviate from thy will. Yet the Destroyer has taken the life of my charge Corlus. Why then hast he been allowed to live? Will not the judge of all the realms do right? How does captivity in Hell requite the deeds done this day?"

Talus and his other brethren gazed upon Sariel with displeased looks; never had El been queried thus. The events of the last several days were new in a way none had ever imagined or experienced.

"Sariel, mind your tone. Your words offend. El is Alpha and Omega. How shall Kilnborn ask its creator, why hast thou made me thus?" said Michael.

El looked at Michael and smiled. "Michael, Sariel hast obeyed me in all things. I know his heart as I know yours. Speak."

Talus was quick to comment. "My God I take issue that an Arelim, even one as Abaddon would be destroy…"

Sariel was even quicker to interrupt, "Nay and why should you? Your people were not made sport of as Abaddon was quick to make with Ashtaroth; Lucifer's own aid the Chief Prince of us all. Perhaps if the heart of Breagun, your own attendant, had been clutched in Abaddon's hand, then might thy heart desire vengeance! Perhaps the death of an Arelim such as Saesheal does not move *you* with compassion?"

Talus rose and moved towards Sariel as if he might strike him. Michael jumped to stand between the two. Gabriel sensed the passion of the moment and stood at the side of Talus ready to restrain him if necessary.

115

Jerahmeel looked at El and spoke. "I say let 'em go at it. Maybe they might knock some sense into one another."

Never had Michael witnessed such a careless abandonment of protocol. He glanced at El and hoped that they would not all join Abaddon for their foolishness. Michael wished that Lucifer or Raphael were here; surely, their words would bring reason; for zeal now seemed to fill these two.

El stood in the front of his throne, and a cool mist ignited from the heat that El's presence emanated. The rainbow from the refracted light filled the throne room. His immediate movement made all the brethren to kneel before their Lord.

He stepped down from the mercy seat and walked before them; his crimson train followed as he turned to the side of the throne room towards the door that housed the Kiln.

The Kiln was a simple chamber. There was only one entrance, which was from El's throne room, and one exit out a hollowed fiery channel that led only to Hell. Strewn on the Kiln's floor were white-hot coals called the Stones of Fire.

"Michael," said the Lord, "come walk with me."

Never had Michael actually entered the Kiln. It was a privilege of the first Kilnborn, the Chief Prince. Michael looked curiously at El, but he rose and followed his master into the Kiln. Michael could feel the eyes of his brethren on his back and was sure their jaws dropped in wonderment of El's actions.

The presence of El within the Kiln simply fanned the flames hotter. Like a match sparking gas, the furnace of heat blistered. El was the fuel that kindled it. Even his absence was such that the Kiln blazed from the presence of his embers. It never extinguished, and it never went out.

Michael watched as El walked among the stones as he had done in times past. Each stone was a separate element. Littered on the floor were stones of alkali metals - actinides such as uranium, and neptunium, halogens - and nonmetals, each was alive and containing the stuff from which the universe was composed. Stones upon stones, colors vibrant and hot to the touch, all called to El like schoolchildren who clamored for their teacher's attention, all competing for the chance to *be*.

El pointed to one stone and motioned to Michael to pick it up. Michael walked over to take it and placed it into his Lord's hands. It was a stone of iron and he handed it face down to the Lord. El took the stone into his hand and covered it with another as if to mold it. A figure soon developed and El returned the small sculpture to his angelic son.

"Place it within the wall's flesh," said the Lord.

Michael placed the figurine within the wall of the Kiln as commanded and watched in amazement as the sculpture slowly transformed and germinated from a smooth stone of rock to a figure that grew with arms and legs.

Boney wings sprouted from its back, and powerful cloven hoofs attached themselves to muscular legs. Sinew and veins of cast iron chains soon appeared. Links of rusted iron composed what looked like a rib cage.

Its face was like the bleached skull of a mare. Its body was clothed in a tattered dark cowl; putrefaction and rust slowly dripped from under its robes, and its arms were like hammers and it held a bladed curved steel scythe in one hand. It had three tails composed of what looked like rusted manacles, and from its chest dangled six steel chains that were like the tendrils of a squid.

Like a stillborn child, it fell from the walls of the Kiln to the floor, covered in a white, red, and black filmy and fiery membrane.

El said, "Stand before me and be thou charged."

Obediently, the pitiful creature rose to its hind legs; its height cast a shadow and darkened the Kiln. The clanking sound of its dangling chains joined the sounds of the fires of the Kiln. Each step it took was as a hammer would hit an anvil; its chains scraped the ground, and Michael looked in horror at this hollowed out shell of an Elohim, an automaton of celestial life. Throughout his entire existence, there was only one thing in creation that he truly feared.

Today there were now two, and both stood next to him.

This new horror of an Elohim stood erect before him, 20 feet tall. El then spoke to the creature.

"Thou art ferrous in nature. Thou art the wall and none may pass. Stand between the darkness and the light. Thou art Archon of Hell, the ferryman of doom. Charon shalt thou be.

"Now go to and stand thou at Hell's mouth and watch. Journey thou through the umbilical to Hell's womb and exact mine fury on all that lay therein."

From the fires of the Kiln and flesh of Charon, the Lord then fashioned two glowing keys. One to control Death, and the other Hell, and gave them to Charon that he might bind and loose the forces of Hell.

The Godstones shook as the heavy weighted creature turned to march away; its manacled legs, somehow able to bear its weight. Charon trudged and dragged his dangling chains behind him. Unmoved by the heat and seething flame: Charon plodded slowly towards the Kiln's fiery exit.

Blistering heat engulfed the creature as black acrid smoke swirled from around it. Where others of Michael's kind, might flee such a blaze; Michael realized that here within the furnace of both the Kiln and Hell. Charon was home.

He watched as this myrmidon of El slowly marched across the umbilical of Hell, this newly formed tunnel of fire, a passageway that connected the Kiln with the new prison of fire and brimstone El had named 'Hell'.

Fated to crawl through volcanic intestines only to exit from its sulfu-ric throat, Charon dragged his charcoal staff with its anvil like arms to journey through the bowels of the mountain. Forever a guardian to Hell's infernal maw, Charon became a sentinel that none within could ever hope to pass.

Michael discerned that Charon, this warden of Hell sent to execute the vengeance of God and Abaddon would meet somewhere inside.

Michael thought about that encounter and shuddered.

The Lord stood in the midst of the Stones of Fire and flame draped around his form as one might wear a shawl. He looked back on the members of the court that were present and who peered through the doorway of the Kiln and spoke in authoritative finality.

"Vengeance is mine," said the Lord. "I will repay."

No one dared to speak a word.

Chapter Four

New Additions

Day Six

Receiving word that his master was Heaven bound, Ashtaroth stood at the waypoint near the cliffs of Argoth anxiously awaiting his Lord's arrival. His wait was not long as the familiar *boom* of a Ladder and the concussive wave of spectral light penetrated the realms.

"Welcome back Chief Prince," said Ashtaroth. "I trust that your time on Earth was fruitful?"

"Indeed," said Lucifer. "I have completed my task as assigned by El and am returned to acquire the Lord's next assignment. Report of thy stewardship."

Ashtaroth lowered his gaze and ceased to look his master in the eye.

"My stewardship Lord Prince?"

Ashtaroth gulped and staggered backward, his eyes darted feverishly as the wheel's of his mind turned to develop an explanation of all that had transpired in his master's absence.

The second floor of your residence is in ruins, and I am responsible.

Lucifer looked upon his attendant with irritation. "Ashtaroth, I await a report."

Michael and a few members of the royal court left from meeting with El and upon their exit crossed paths with their brother.

Michael spoke first. "Lucifer, I am glad to have you home. I missed you brother. I surely could have used your wisdom."

Michael turned his head and looked at Talus and Sariel, who both looked away and pretended to neither hear nor see him.

Michael extended his arms wide and walked to Lucifer; they embraced and kissed each other on the cheek.

"It *is* good to breathe Heaven's air once more, but I must admit that I am becoming ever fonder of Earth," said Lucifer.

"Well, much has transpired here in your absence."

Michael pointed behind to the section of the city near Lucifer's palatial estate. Lucifer turned and followed the direction of Michael's finger. The neighborhood and market were riddled with debris. What was more intriguing was the dark and fiery peak that now towered behind the city. A mountain of fire that spewed out black smoke and flared heated plumes of scorching magma.

Taking in the totality of what he saw, Lucifer stood dumbstruck. His mouth partially open, he turned to Michael to speak, but Michael raised his hand to prevent him.

"El has charged that Jerahmeel informs you of the events of today."

"Indeed?" Lucifer sighed. "A conversation I am most eager to have."

Jerahmeel took a couple of steps forwarded and gave Lucifer a large firm smack on the back with his hand. "I can't wait to see your house." Jerahmeel snickered. "I heard it got banged up pretty good!"

Lucifer looked pleadingly at Michael. Michael leaned forward to whisper in his ear. "This too shall pass. Just listen and it will go quicker." Michael chuckled and continued to walk down the stairs towards the emporium.

"I must see to the ward's damage and its repair, but after my assessment I will see you shortly," said Michael.

Lucifer nodded, and Jerahmeel hugged Lucifer one more time on the shoulder and scrunched him up like a doll.

"Just means I gotcha all to myself is all!" said Jerahmeel.

"Oh, the joy," Lucifer replied sarcastically.

Lucifer glared at Ashtaroth. "I will expect a full account of my estate Astarte."

Ashtaroth bowed. "Yes, my Prince."

"Oh leave him alone Lucy," said Jerahmeel. "Let's go."

Jerahmeel and Lucifer walked down the steps from the Cliffs of Argoth to the emporium. Jerahmeel explained to Lucifer all that had transpired in his absence as they went. Ashtaroth trailed several paces behind them.

"So am I to understand that Apollyon wrought this destruction without cause? Surely there must have been something to have sparked such grave action on his part?"

Jerahmeel looked at Lucifer as if to study him.

Lucifer noticed Jerahmeel's gaze and became uncomfortable from his stare, "What is it?" he asked.

"He is Abaddon now, and quite frankly I am trying to figure out what you think could *justify* this destruction?"

"Nothing justifies it Jerahmeel, yet there is a cause for it. What has your investigation determined?"

Jerahmeel stopped to look at Lucifer in disbelief.

"*Investigation*? Lucy, Michael, and Talus saw Abaddon rip the Heart-stone from Corlus' own chest. I figure there was not much to investigate myself. Of course, if you think you need a trial, I suggest you take it up with El. Abaddon was brought before El in chains for judgment. You see that mountain over there? I suspect Lucifer, that the mountain expelling ash over there will be El's answer to your question of a trial. On the other hand, do you not see that Abaddon destroyed an Elohim? Abaddon set himself on a path to destroy and injure. My apologies Chief Prince: if I'm not inclined to know his motives in this act."

"Do you think me a fool brother?" Lucifer said. "I indeed understand what has transpired; however, without understanding *why* we risk similar behavior in the future. How have the other Elohim reacted to this—this Hell construct?" Lucifer said.

Jerahmeel stopped and turned to face his brother. "You know something, Lucy? You've become a little different since you started your assignment as Archon of Earth. You seem — I don't know — more aloof to me. Well, more aloof than usual let's just say that. But since when do we seek an *opinion* about El's actions?"

The two angels had reached the entrance to Lucifer's home and Ashtaroth stood a respectable distance as to be within earshot to attend to his master if needed.

"If you wish to know the origin of Abaddon's act, then look no further than your own servant," Jerahmeel said. "For Ashtaroth held his own when Abaddon raised himself against him."

Lucifer looked confused. "Why, do you cite Ashtaroth?" Lucifer asked.

Jerahmeel grinned and pointed to the damaged upper level of Lucifer's abode.

"Behold the hole in the upper level of your palace and be it known that Ashtaroth had a hand in its making." Jerahmeel patted Lucifer on the back again, started to whistle, and walked away. He chuckled as he looked at Ashtaroth as he passed by.

"Boy, are *you* in trouble."

****

Raphael managed to locate Michael before he left the palace grounds and saw that he was ready to leave.

"Michael, are you headed out?" asked Raphael.

"Yes, I am. I need to see about the damage to the city," said Michael.

"Before you go I'd like to show you something."

"Of course." Michael turned to walk with Raphael back up into the temple.

Raphael darted back and forth as if he was in thought.

"Is something the matter?" Michael said.

"I am not sure. I only know that in all my days I have not seen anything like this. I would like you to bear witness to my conclusions just to make sure."

Michael looked at Raphael curiously, "Conclusions?"

"I know. I know. I'll explain when we reach the Hall of Annals."

Michael followed his brother; curiosity now fully gripped him.

"You are scaring me, brother," said Michael.

Raphael paused before he replied, "I am scared myself, Michael."

They entered back into the great hall and walked down a corridor into one of the many rooms of the temple mountain. They approached two wooden arched doors; each overlaid in transparent gold. Etched in their frames was the angelic symbol for the word *Light*. The door's hinges were of silver and adorned with ruby handles.

They entered the room, and barrenness was all Michael saw. The room was completely empty.

Raphael spoke an Elomic command upon their entry, "Sh-un-to" which means to "Seal."

Michael looked at him curiously, "Raphael, why have you sealed the door?"

"Follow me and move exactly as I move," He replied.

Michael watched Raphael, "Uh, Raphael the room is empty are we in the…"

"Quickly, take four steps forward." Raphael had already started to move.

Raphael immediately made a move to his left towards the north wall. "Michael, move or the Zoa will fall upon you!" Raphael then pointed slowly to the ceiling.

Michael looked above his head and realized that barely perceptible to the eye was a ceiling full of creatures with eyes. Their jaws were in their belly and they walked with tentacles on the roof ready to drop on the unsuspecting. They quietly hissed and slithered. Michael hastened his gait and mimicked Raphael's steps exactly.

"Hurry, Michael: touch the wall quickly."

Several of the Zoa dropped to the floor. Their jaws opened wide to reveal a series of razors. Each tentacle held stingers with barbs.

One slowly inched towards him, and its eyes sized up its prey. As a coil, it wound up and stood poised ready to pounce and devour the Prince of Heaven.

Michael quickly moved to touch the wall at the spot that Raphael indicated and stumbled forward, tumbling through the wall.

The tentacled creature with a mouth of razors for teeth swooped down to follow; its jaw open, ready to devour.

As Michael slid back and raised his forearm to shield himself, a twinge of fear crept through him. Inches from his body, the creature was repelled backwards as if deflected by some invisible force. Its body hit the floor, but it still eyed its prey and launched itself to attack again.

Michael did not wait for the creature to land and immediately scooted farther back, but the result was the same. Once more, the creature was repelled.

It growled in frustration and leaped back unto the ceiling, its presence disguised to pounce upon any who might enter the room unawares.

"You are safe Michael. Come I must show you something," said Raphael.

"Like I haven't seen enough already, and exactly *why* is there a creature like that in the temple?"

"Michael, within this room contains all the recorded knowledge of the universe. Therefore, only those who are invited may traverse the room without incident."

Michael guffawed. "*Incident*? You call what happened back there 'without incident'?"

Raphael laughed, "Well let's just say that it would not be wise for you to enter without my presence. Come."

Raphael motioned for Michael to follow him as they walked down a corridor. It winded for about 20 cubits and ended in a hallway, which was black and filled with stars.

Michael observed that the room had no perceptible ceiling, floors, or walls. Only the opening from which they came offered any bearing that there was a room at all. He entered the chamber and with each step; his feet caused tiny ripples to move across the floor as if he walked on pools of water in the night sky.

Stars filled the ceiling, the floors, and the walls. There was a central sun, and all things revolved around it. All the stars had tendrils that ran from them to the star. The central stars heat and light radiated to the others, and each received its life from the one.

"Welcome to the Hall of Annals, Michael. This is where I do my work."

Michael stood speechless.

"This is a representation of the second heaven, the area devoted to the wondrous cosmos that El hast created. This room contains all records that I may see all. If there is a Grigori assigned to a portion of creation, I am able to see what they see. The room itself is a partial expression of the mind of God. In it, one may observe all that is current or has happened within the realms. By it, the creature within may understand what the creator sees, but there is a level of sight beyond what even I may behold within these halls. Of course, El has no need of such contrivances, for He sees all things. But it is only one level to this room."

"What can't you see?" said Michael.

Raphael looked at his friend and said, "Those things which shall come to be are denied me. Only El has knowledge of the future. Feel privileged for you are one of a select few who has seen this room. Only Gabriel and Jerahmeel have seen the wonders inside. Even Lucifer has not stepped foot into this hall."

"Why is that?" Michael asked.

"El has denied the Chief Prince access. His words to Lucifer when petitioned were '*Abide in thy calling, wherewith thou hast been called.*'

"Lucifer expressed his preference, but El would no longer speak on the matter. Lucifer dropped the issue after that. However, when he found out that Jerahmeel could enter, and *he* could not. He looked incensed to me. I know he will not admit however how he feels."

Michael laughed. "Jerahmeel could do something that Lucifer could not? Oh yes, I am sure our brother was *most* displeased, but you did not bring me here to discuss Lucifer. What did you want me to see?"

"Actually Michael, Lucifer is *exactly* the subject that I wanted to discuss with you." Raphael waved his hand and spoke.

"Rescind to Third Heaven. Seek Lucifer Draco."

The room immediately moved in the same fashion that El had transported the royal court when He had blessed the fowl of the Earth. Michael beheld the expanse of the Third Heaven and slowly was able to determine his location. They were inside the mountain of God. Of that, he was sure, yet the orientation of the room was such as if they looked from the very top of Mt Zion. The view was breathtaking.

Michael surveyed the topography of Heaven and saw The Three Mountains: Mt Zion, the Kiln, and Hell, the great city Jerusalem, the Elysian Fields, the Cliffs of Argoth, the River of Life the Valley of El, and the gates of Heaven. All were within his field of view.

Immediately the room zoomed in and Lucifer was kneeling before the Lord. The room's picture of El was so different from Michael's own eyes, for El was so bright; the light washed his visage from view. Both looked as lights. However, Lucifer's light was so much dimmer as to be almost imperceptible. Michael covered his eyes slightly in order to partially block out the light.

Raphael spoke. "Regress"

Immediately Lucifer left the throne but walked backward from his meeting with Michael and Jerahmeel. His speech became unintelligible, and various scenes rewound in their order from his landing near the cliff waypoint to his ascent from Earth. His walk through the Garden of Eden, meetings with attendants — on and on it went until Raphael stopped at one point.

"Proceed from here." said Raphael.

Lucifer's image stood in front of the duo and his glory was fully revealed. Apollyon was on bended knee, as Lucifer communicated the word of God to Apollyon.

"I am Chief Lord Prince Lucifer Draco, Lightbringer, and Son of the Morning Star. I walk within the midst of the Stones of Fire. Hear ye the word of the Lord!

'Oh Son of the Dawn, thou who is the blossom of the Morning Star, be still and let your soul be at ease. For this thing was done, that others might be made manifest. For twice, you shall be tested and once have been vexed. The flame, which thou hast controlled shall indeed mirror your own as it doth consume, let not your own flame thus burn. For be thou warned that if sorrow persists, then on your shoulders shall indeed a new dawn come, the breaking of a new day. And he to whom you would seek solace shall be your King. And your infamy shall indeed be known even unto the end of days."

Michael stood for a moment speechless. Thoughts swirled within him and he spoke. "Ok? I am not quite sure what I'm supposed to understand from this."

Raphael nodded in acknowledgment. "Watch more. Regress." Raphael commanded.

Immediately, the images marched backward in time. Slipping further and further until they stopped at the day when the council knew of Apollyon's thoughts. Michael watched as El looked at Lucifer and imparted to him the message he was to deliver to Apollyon.

Raphael spoke, "Proceed from this point; reveal Grigori."

Michael watched as each Grigori floated quietly behind their prince writing meticulously in his tomes. Lilith was behind Lucifer and diligently recorded every event.

"Reveal and interlock Grigoric record: Lilith."

Lucifer's tome appeared before them, and as El spoke to him, El's every word faithfully notated. Emblazoned in angelic script Lilith had written,

"Oh Son of the Dawn, thou who is the blossom of the Morning Star, be still and let your soul be at ease, for this thing was done, that others might be

made manifest: for you shall twice be tested and have once been vexed, the flame which thou hast controlled shall indeed mirror your own, as it doth consume, let not your own flame thus burn, for be thou warned that if sorrow persists; then on your shoulders shall indeed a new dawn come, the breaking of a new day. And he to whom you would seek solace shall be your King. And your infamy shall indeed be known even unto the end of days.

Resist the taunts of thy brethren. For I have sent Lucifer as a comforter to thee. Abide with him for as I liveth. If thou leaveth him, know that ruin liveth not far behind, and my comforter shall be thy king"

Michael looked carefully at the text of Lucifer's Grigori and then looked at Raphael. "They are not the same. Lucifer has diminished El's word."

Raphael nodded in the affirmative.

"And El knows?" said Michael.

Raphael nodded again.

"I'm not sure what to make of all this. I want to talk to Lucifer."

"No, Michael. Something is indeed amiss, but I shall be giving my report to El soon, and I'm sure he will address Lucifer in time."

"When did you know this?" Michael asked.

"I have learned of it just recently. I am almost prepared to give El my report on the search He wanted to be done."

"But Raphael, it makes no sense: none whatsoever. Why would El request such a tome when He already knows the answer? And why would Lucifer do such a thing?"

"I cannot fathom El's mind. His ways are past finding out, but I suspect that the tome is not for Him as it is for us. Lucifer's actions, however, warrant further scrutiny. I have also determined that Lilith is also involved."

"Lilith—his Grigori—why do you say that?" said Michael.

Raphael turned to the wall and pointed. The wall displayed Lucifer and Lilith's conversation. "When have you ever known a Grigori to engage in talk with their study?"

Michael looked and realized that Lucifer and his Grigori *were* in in-depth conversation.

"In fact, when have you ever discussed anything with your Grigori Michael? Do you know if he's even here?" said Raphael.

Michael thought for a moment. He *had* never interacted with his own Watcher. It simply never occurred to him. As each Elohim had a specific call-ing, Michael was too involved in his own affairs to concern himself with affairs, not under his charge. A Grigori's duty was to record history; Michael's was to see to the city's needs.

"No never. A Grigori does not interfere with his charge's activities: they pledge only to observe and document that which they see. They are neither to add nor subtract from an account."

"Correct," said Raphael. Then Raphael spoke into the air. "Athamas, reveal yourself please."

Immediately, Michael's Grigori showed himself hovering; draped in a dark cowl with an inkhorn and stylus in one hand and a floating book in front of him.

"Michael, I present to you Athamas. He is the ward I have assigned to you and has been faithful in all his doings."

Michael nodded in respect and Athamas bowed in return.

"You may return to your duties," said Raphael.

Upon command, Athamas disappeared from sight and continued tran-scribing.

Michael cocked his head and turned to look at Raphael. "So let me understand this; when that thing in the other room was about to attack me…"

"Athamas was documenting yes."

"Ok, at some point you and I really have to sit down and talk more about this job you and your people are assigned to do."

Raphael laughed. "I just wanted you to notice what I saw when Lucifer was with El and why I am even more concerned than you could possibly know.

"Show present status of Lucifer Draco. Reveal assigned Grigori," commanded Raphael.

The ceiling fluctuated and showed an image of Lucifer in discussion with El in the throne room. Lucifer appeared pleading before El for Apollyon.

Michael strained to see if anyone else was in the throne room apart from the norm.

"Lucifer's Grigori is not with him," Michael remarked.

"Indeed. This record is from the Virtues within the throne room," replied Raphael.

"Is it normal for a Grigori to leave his charge?

"A Grigori never leaves the side of his charge, Michael — never."

Michael looked at Lucifer and listened to his entreaty for Apollyon's freedom. He studied him carefully.

Raphael looked Michael squarely in the eye and took him gently by his shoulders. "Be careful around him Michael — just be careful."

Michael laughed. "Lucifer would never harm me. I trust him as much as I trust you. I'm sure this is nothing." Michael turned to leave.

Raphael watched his brother depart.

I hope you are right Michael — I just hope you are right.

****

132

Lucifer bowed to his Lord and gave his report on the construction of the Garden of Eden.

"Lord, I have completed my charge and am greatly disturbed to hear of Apollyon's actions."

"Abaddon was warned," said the Lord. "He had ears but did not hear. His eyes beheld yet they did not perceive. His ears waxed gross, and he became dull of hearing. His eyes he did close, lest at any time he should see, and understand that he might be converted. Do *you* understand this, my son?"

"Lord, I do not understand why you have made this prison. Was Apollyon so far removed that there was no hope for him?"

"My son, your natures are such that once thou hast made the decision, to depart from thy design; then you may never be restored. Thou and thy kind are taken from the Kiln. You are a living *stone* of fire and ministers of flame. Thou art not clay."

"You are as the paintings in the Gallery of Issi; if defaced, the canvas is irrevocably spoiled. It cannot be recreated or restored. Thou art as the salt in the earth, but if the salt has lost its savor, wherewith shall *it* be salted?

When Apollyon thus changed his name and sigil, he determined that he would not live in a realm where I was his Lord. He would run amok, destroy without purpose, without remorse, and in time destroy himself. Thus, I created a realm in my mercy to allow for even his existence, a habitation made unique to him."

"But Lord, surely you could have erased him from creation! He is too dangerous to keep even imprisoned in Hell!"

"That Lucifer is not my spirit. To obliterate him is not my way, for with purpose was he created and thus shall still, an illustration to all: that mine will shall not be thwarted. Hell is the most merciful answer I may give to all that would choose to live apart from me. Do *you* understand this, my son?"

Lucifer pondered the Lord's words for a moment and spoke. "May I see him, Lord?"

The creator of Heaven and Earth looked lovingly upon his first created, the, first of all, Kilnborn.

"Your love for Abaddon is laudable. His choices were his own; the Apollyon you knew is forever lost. Only Abaddon remains. His actions were wrought of pain and anguish. He is now self-injurious and destructive to those around him. Grieve him if you must. Yet before thy brethren, thou shalt not mourn nor weep, neither shall thy tears run down. For I will be sanctified in them that come nigh me, and before all the people I will be glorified."

Lucifer held his peace on the subject and continued to bow face down to the Lord.

Michael suddenly walked into the throne room and knelt before his King.

"My Lord, Charon has traversed Hell and was seen stationed at the opening of Hell's gate."

Lucifer looked at Michael confused. "Charon?" Lucifer said.

"Did not Jerahmeel inform you?" asked Michael.

"Nay, our brother seemed more interested in my scolding of Ashtaroth and the damage done to my home than informing me of anything on this wise. Again, what — who is this 'Charon' that you speak of?"

The Lord interrupted. "Charon is my voice in Hell. He executes my will. He guards Hell that none my leave and none may pass."

Lucifer continued to look perplexed. "*He*? Then he is an Elohim? If he is Elohim, then he was made in the Kiln?"

"That is correct my son," said the Lord.

"I was under the impression my Lord, that aside from thyself no Elohim was formed without my presence in the Kiln; that I over all Elohim walk within the Stones of Fire. Have I been stripped of my title of Chief Prince?"

"Nay my son. Thou art first among thy brethren, and I repent not in that decision. Yet you were absent seeing to the charge of the Garden of Eden. A garden that *thou* wast most determined to see done. Therefore, another was chosen to stand by my side."

"Forgive me Lord, and I pray that thou not be angry with thine servant. Who was selected to walk in my stead?"

"Your brother Michael stood as proxy for thee."

"Michael? But Lord, none other than myself hast ever walked in the Kiln ..."

El looked upon Lucifer and spoke gently but firmly. "Lucifer, I do thee no wrong. Didst, not thou agree with me to walk when I walked in the Kiln? Take what is thine and go thy way: I will give unto this last, even as unto thee. Is it not lawful for me to do what I will with my own? Is thine eye evil because I am good?"

Lucifer held his tongue, and rose to leave, but El stopped him.

"Gather all thy brethren to the emporium. For the day draws to a close, and I must announce my plans. You will herald my presence."

"And the garden Lord?" said Lucifer.

"Yes, what of it my son?"

"You said that it was reserved for your greatest creation. I would like to have the attendants of mine house prepare to move my palace to Earth."

The Lord paused and studied Lucifer. "I see."

"My Lord?" said Lucifer.

"Lucifer, the garden is not for you, my son, but for he who shall follow

135

thy kind and who shall hold the deed to Earth and be given my image and likeness. He shall be called; 'Man'. He shall be made a little lower than the angels yet crowned with glory. Thou and thy brother art first to hear. As it is my will that the first be last and that the last shall be first."

Lucifer replied. "But sire…"

Michael raised himself from the ground and took Lucifer by the arm to go with him and spoke to the Lord. "Thy will be done," said Michael.

Michael tugged on Lucifer to follow. He reluctantly turned to leave and then spoke. "Thy will be done," said Lucifer.

Lucifer followed with little enthusiasm and walked out with Michael to the hallway of the temple as the throne room doors closed behind them.

Lucifer and Michael walked further to the edge of the temple doors where nothing but the booming chant of the Seraphim echoed. Lucifer noted that no one was looking, grabbed Michael by his arm, and spoke. "Never again cut me off when I address El. *I* am Chief Prince. *You* are not. How dare you presume to interrupt me! Do you think because you hast set foot upon the Stones of Fire that you have now surpassed me?"

Michael bowed his head in submission. "My apologies brother; El had spoken. He would neither add nor take away from that which had been said — to say more…"

His teeth clenched, Lucifer walked closer to Michael and glared at him. His grip on Michael's arm tightened, and for several moments he looked deeply into Michael's eyes, and Michael's face contorted from the discomfort.

"Lucifer, you are hurting me!"

Lucifer thought to speak, but slowly the features of his face softened. He released Michael's arm and spoke. "I—I am sorry brother. Please charge this not to my account."

Michael massaged his arm, now sore from Lucifer's grip. "Of course, I would not see you rebuked by El."

"Indeed — come," said Lucifer. "Preparations must be made for El's announcement."

"What would you have me do?" asked Michael.

"I need you to gather the other princes, and I will usher a call to assemble everyone shortly."

"But Lucifer did not El say that you were to…."

"Michael, do you plan to supplant me as Chief Prince?"

Michael looked at Lucifer with a look of confusion on his face. "What do you mean?" He asked.

"Do you challenge me as Chief Prince? Only the first of the Kilnborn has ever walked on the Stones of Fire. You must know that I will not abdicate Michael. I will not yield as Chief Prince."

Michael bowed in obeisance. "Nay brother, I have no desire for thy throne."

"Would my own brother raise arms against me? Would thou besiege *me* as Apollyon?"

Michael knelt and took his brother's hand to kiss it. "As the Lord liveth, El called me into the Kiln. Thy throne I do not desire brother."

Lucifer looked upon his younger brother. His eyes studied him. Lucifer's thoughts reflected on his work with Michael when they labored together to lay the chief cornerstone of Heaven. How Michael had assisted him in the construction of his own palatial estate, and his face softened.

"Rise brother, for I sense no taint of Apollyon's treachery in you. I apologize."

"Lucifer, you are my beloved. We have been with each other from the

137

beginning. Never could we be at odds."

Lucifer rubbed the shoulder of his brother and embraced him. "We have not spent enough time together lately. We must rectify that. I miss you."

"As do I," said Michael. "As do I."

"Michael, I must first do something before I herald the Lord. Please gather our brethren while I attend to this matter."

"Of course, I'll see you in say—an hour?"

"That should be fine. I will see you at the temple doors upon my return."

Michael opened the doors in front of them and stepped through; Lucifer followed and suspiciously eyed Michael as he flew off from the steps to assemble his brethren.

Lucifer turned, looked straight ahead, and saw the newly formed mountain of seething heat and flame. He adjusted his flesh to the light waves that emanated from El that allowed daylight to exist in Heaven. His pores soaked in the light and saturated themselves; they swallowed the light around him. Lucifer with a thought; changed his skin and light wrapped around him to conceal and camouflage him from all eyes. Only a small distortion would give his presence away as he effectively became a mirror that reflected all that surrounded him. Lucifer took his cloak off and placed it out of sight near a ledge of steps.

Unencumbered, he flew into the sky of Heaven. His twelve wings propelled him both with swiftness and with ease. He moved towards Hell determined to see this 'Charon'.

His thoughts raced within him. *Man! Who is this 'man' that El wouldst be mindful of him? Have I spent my time and labor only to grow a garden for a new species? A thing that would be crowned with glory he said! His 'greatest creation' that is what he called it!*

I was the one that suggested that, this, this thing be given, El's image and likeness! Yet El knew! He knew, and Michael... he let Michael assist in the creation of Elohim! Who but the Chief Prince walks within the Kiln?

Lucifer saw the croppy outgrowth and the dark figure standing tall with an onyx scythe. Hell's maw was clearly a tunnel that went deep into the mountain. The whole area bristled with heat. Living stalagmite-like teeth barred all that would dare seek entry.

Lucifer would speak with Apollyon. He lowered himself to the ground and stood in front of the giant creature. It stood 10 cubits tall, and its face was as the skull of a stallion.

Lucifer looked on in curiosity at the abomination El and Michael had created. Its arms were powerful and looked like hammers. Black, ashy, tattered vestments covered its body, and chains dangled from underneath its robes. It was then Lucifer realized it possessed none of the regality that all Elohim possessed. Lucifer was disgusted.

Such a creature should not even exist.

Lucifer was invisible and thought it easy to slip around it and the earthen teeth of the maw to the fires within. Lucifer moved to the left of the guard towards the cave's opening.

The creature moved to block his path.

Lucifer undeterred moved to his right to go around.

The creature moved with a swiftness that defied its size; again to deny him access. Its gaze fixed straight forward as it stood.

Perhaps this ruse is not necessary. Lucifer thought to himself.

Lucifer retracted his porous flesh within himself and stood revealed to Charon.

"I am Chief Prince Lucifer Draco, Son of the Morning Star. I walk on the very stones from which thou wast created. Move aside that I might have words with thy prisoner."

Charon neither acknowledged Lucifer's presence nor moved, and silence filled the heated air.

"I shall repeat myself this one last time. Move aside for the High Prince. Or thou shalt be moved." Lucifer said.

Charon gave no response and continued to stare straight ahead.

Lucifer irritated at the snub and slight in protocol attempted to shove him aside that he might pass.

Charon's face looked down at the archangel, and from underneath his cloak metal chains moved to swiftly coil themselves around Lucifer's hands and legs.

Lucifer surprised, but more offended that he might be touched, struggled to escape the manacles of iron.

Yet Charon's grip was sure, and the sentinel of Hell tightened his hold around Lucifer's wrists and ankles.

"How dare…"

Charon lifted the cherub into the air as if to study him from all sides and then slammed him on his back hard into the ground.

Lucifer felt a rush of pain wash over him from the sharp craggy rock that cut and scraped at him.

Charon towered over him as a mantis might devour its prey.

Lucifer now pinned to the ground; attempted to lift himself with his great wings, but the weight of Charon was too much to overcome.

Charon lowered his face to look upon his quarry. His skeletal face bowed within inches of touching the Chief Prince. Charon sniffed Lucifer as if to catch his scent.

Lucifer turned his face to the side; for Charon's pungent breath suffocated him.

"Release me! I command you!" Lucifer screamed, and the ground shook from the vibrations of the bass in his voice.

With a snort, Charon raised his powerful cloven legs and lifted Lucifer from the ground.

Charon looked upon him as a corpse might look upon the living.

"Dost thou know whom thou hast handled? I am first born of the Kiln. I will see you remanded for this outrage! I command you to release me!"

Charon used one if his tentacles to grab his onyx staff and slammed it firmly into the ground. Lava bubbled up from the black soil beneath, as blood might ooze from a wound. Slowly Charon turned Lucifer's body that he could see, and with his staff began to carve words into the ground.

If thou enter — you may not return.

Slowly and gently, Charon released Lucifer, stepped away from the Chief Prince and bowed.

The realization struck Lucifer that Charon sought to do him no harm but only to protect him.

"So I am to understand that if I were to enter I would not be allowed to exit?'

The cowled figure nodded.

"Very well then, creature. If thou did not unhand me, my wrath would thou hast incurred. I am he who has walked on the very stones that created thee. If I were to grace your presence again and my commands are not obeyed, know that your ruin will not be far behind."

Charon stood mute before the Chief Prince, unmoved.

"This is not over," said Lucifer.

Lucifer turned to walk away and enveloped himself as a chameleon might camouflage into its background. Lucifer lifted into the sky to return to the mountain of God and ruminated on what had happened.

This shall not stand.

****

"Lucifer is all prepared," said El.

"Yes Most High. All of Heaven hath assembled themselves. Those stationed throughout creation hath received sight into the realm to see the emporium as thou hast commanded."

"Well done my good and faithful servant, well done. Go, for the day draws quickly to a close."

"Yes, my Lord."

El commanded the Ophanim and they lifted the throne. Slowly the doors of the throne room opened and the power of the Seraphim's voices boomed into the emporium. The procession of the royal court began. The Seraphim moved first and like giant golems, they made the ground quake before them. The colossi marched towards the front of the temple and the attendants of the palace opened the doors, and cheers and celebratory music could be heard from outside. The air filled with shouts of praise and melody and Elohim began to sing in harmony with the Seraphim.

The royal court followed in rank: each in his assigned order within the procession. From the youngest to the eldest they came. Talus entered first bearing the angelic standard of the Arelim. He raised the flag of his sigil, and the sapphire light bathed the emporium in a soothing tranquil blue. There were great cheers as he showed himself. Talus waved to the crowd, and they roared their approval.

"He is Alpha and Omega; let all the heavens praise him!" said Talus.

Heaven erupted in applause. Cloven feet pounded the streets of gold and the tremors rumbled to the top of the temple steps. The power and gentleness of El represented in the making of each Arelim.

Sariel immediately followed his brother and wore his standard of purple. His race of Centaurs and Pegasi leaped, galloped, and raised their fists high into the air. Then Sariel hoisted his sigil into the air and addressed the people. "We praise the Lord according to his righteousness: sing praises to the Lord most high! All hail El Elyon, the Most High God!"

In response, all Heaven shouted the same. "All hail El Elyon, the Most High God!"

The Princes representing El's Power had started the procession and the princes who symbolized El's knowledge followed. Jerahmeel, Lord Prince of all Harada, stepped onto the platform and spoke.

"Blessed be the Lord God almighty. How great are his signs! How mighty are his wonders! His kingdom is an everlasting kingdom, and his dominion is from generation to generation. Blessed be the name of the Lord!"

"Blessed be the name of the Lord!" All shouted once.

"Blessed be the name of the Lord!" They shouted again.

Jerahmeel took the purple flag that bore the symbol of God's knowledge and his people and waved it in a circle for all to see. His linen robes of indigo and mauve glistened in the light. Amethysts and sapphires adorned his staff, which he held high aloft in the air.

The congregation of the sons of God roared. Heaven became as a stadium cheering in jubilation and convulsed in praise.

Jerahmeel took his place beside his brother Sariel. Raphael was next to come into view. His dark purple robes etched in gold with the Elomic words for wisdom, dignity, nobility, and creativity. He hovered and waved his hands. Immediately his inkhorn, stylus, and tome of record can into view, and Raphael spoke. "Every word of God is pure: he is a shield unto them that put their trust in him, for the word of God is quick and powerful, it divides asunder soul and spirit. It is a discerner of thoughts and intents of the heart. He is Alpha and Omega, Beginning and the End. For He spoke and it was done; he commanded, and it stood fast. All hail the living word!"

"All hail the living word!" the crowd roared.

Raphael stretched forth his hand and said, "Let the invisible thing be clearly seen!
For nothing is hidden from his sight!"

Suddenly the sky of Heaven teemed with Grigori. Like specters they emerged; thousands upon thousands of books filled Heaven's air. Pens and inkhorns moved on their own recording all that transpired. Like ghostly stenographers, nothing escaped the Grigori's notice and with the voice of one man, they that rarely speak spoke. "El watches over his word to perform it. All hail the living word!"

Heaven celebrated, applause filled the air, and the Arelim broke out in a spontaneous militaristic cadence.

"Power and Glory and Honor to God!" They stomped in the emporium, and their precision made the ground shake with thunder. One by one Harrada, Arelim, and the rest of the host of Heaven chanted in pandemonium at the cacophony of praise of all creation's Elohim. Their mantras muted the chants of even the mighty Seraphim.

Raphael took his place on the dais, and Gabriel entered.

The cherub had a boyish look; his blonde hair sparkled, and his robes scarlet representing the color of conquest and royalty. He stood for all the species of Malakim and represented the omnipresence of God. His were the messengers of Heaven, and like the Grigori, they spanned the universe and ran the vision and word of El to the four corners of existence.

The Malakim were the only species allowed to create Ladders from Heaven to specific points in creation. They could move instantly between the realms, and there was nowhere they could not reach.

Gabriel held the standard of the Malakim: a pruning hook in his hand, the blade and handle encrusted wholly in ruby. He raised it high for all to see. The light of the crimson sprayed out like blood, and he spoke. "Bless the Lord, ye his angels that excel in strength, that do his commandments, hearken unto the voice of his word. Bless the Lord!"

Roars of adulation rang throughout the emporium. Angels began to throw strips of parchment. Various Malakim took their staffs and struck the ground fiercely, and crimson sparks rocketed into the air and dispersed into flowers of orange and yellow hues.

Gabriel, like those before him, settled into position and Michael strode into the podium and Heaven exploded as they chanted his name.

"Builder of Heaven!"

"Hail Archon of Zion!"

"Michael! Michael!"

Michael waved and held his peace, his cheeks flushed, embarrassed to receive such praise. *I am but a servant to El, who am I that I should receive such adulation?* He thought to himself.

Michael bowed his head in acknowledgment to the citizenry and lifted the standard of scarlet as his brother Gabriel had before him, and once more Heaven thundered approval.

The archangel of Heaven lifted his hands and motioned to quiet the excited crowd. He looked over the populous and was moved with compassion; these were all his people and friends. Harrada, Kortai, Grigori— they all— like him were servants of El.

Overcome by the privilege of serving so great a people and selected by El to do him honor in Heaven was simply too much, and the spirit of worship befell him. All of Heaven grew quiet, watched, and listened intently as Michael bowed his head and sang aloud.

Praise Jehovah — Lord God Almighty.
Praise Jehovah — Everlasting King
We praise your name.
We praise your name
Lord Jehovah we praise you.
Praise Jehovah — in his entire splendor
Praise Jehovah in all his majesty
We praise your name
We praise you.

Without prompt or sign, Elohim throughout the realm joined him in worship. Trancelike the host of Heaven lifted their voices, the harmonies of a thousand angels — no ten times, ten thousand, thousand: melodiously echoed throughout creation.

Their notes of beatific reverence sailed, and their praise vaulted to every star, every mote of dust, and to every lily and robin, and all of Heaven and Earth swayed to worship at the choral inspiration of one cherub.

As extemporaneously as it had begun, the song slowed until nothing but the soft melody of a single voice sang.

Michael's head was bowed, his palms outstretched and his arms rose high crying while tears of appreciation glistened from his face. Softly he closed the worship with one verse that was sympathetic of all. "…we praise you."

He finished singing and with those words, Michael quietly moved aside to take his place with his brethren.

Heaven was lost deep in communion, euphoric and awash in the afterglow of worship; and no one—not even El himself: wanted to progress further.

****

Who but the Chief Prince may lead Heaven in song? The impudence! Lucifer looked upon the residents of Heaven and rage swelled up within him like a tumor.

Now I must wait to come before the people.

His own procession, now an afterthought to all, diminished because of the worship that Michael had unleashed.

If I advance now, I will break the spirit moving upon the congregation. My presence would seem as an intrusion, yet the longer this persists, the less my own entrance will command glory.

Lucifer folded his hands and his eyes narrowed with malice. His breath raced as the ruminations of his mind caused increased malignance towards Michael and the scene which he was helpless to stop that unfolded before him.

This was supposed to be MY moment of glory! Thoughts raced through Lucifer's mind.

Circumvented. Dishonored.

Emotions of anger and offense churned within him and Lucifer — consumed in his thoughts of self-martyrdom did not see his master motion for him to advance.

"Lucifer." said El.

My glory I will not give to another!

147

"Lucifer," El spoke again,

Lucifer awoke from his daydreamed flagellation of Michael.

"Yes, my Lord?"

"Lucifer, you may proceed my son."

"Yes Lord. I apologize."

Michael and the other princes looked back at their brother curious as to the delay. Raphael whispered to his brother, "Lucifer, is everything well?"

Lucifer smiled. "Aye, brother, I just desired to stay in the thralls of worship."

Raphael smiled and replied. "Ah of course. It can be difficult to return to one's senses once lost in communion."

Indeed. Lucifer thought.

Lucifer walked towards the podium and uncloaked before all of Heaven. Free of his robes, light raced to embrace him and enshroud his perfectly formed body. His skin when not a living mirror was bronze-like with tints of red: and to look upon him was to desire him.

Lucifer arched his back and flexed his muscles, and his twelve flowing wings extracted to cover the entire rostrum.

He rose into the air and with each flap and movement; the veins of his white tentacled wings chimed in the wind.

He positioned his scales to open up his porous flesh that he might both absorb and reflect all light simultaneously; and as a newborn sun, the mighty cherub illuminated the entire emporium.

El had not even entered the lectern to address the people, but Lucifer's visage was so bright that it was difficult to look at him. Elohim across the city covered their eyes as the colors of Lucifer's bioluminescent flesh radiated in patterns of gold, blue, and scarlet.

He breathed in the warm air of Heaven, his vocal cords and tabrets in his body animated, and music poured from his body. The sound of cornet and flute rang into the air, and Lucifer's voice thundered and made vibrate the golden street below. Each member within earshot felt the bass of his pronouncement as a physical force upon their own chest.

Lucifer was perfect in representing all the power, beauty, and wisdom of all Elohim at once, but his strength was not resident in the meager demonstration of his physical qualities.

Lucifer's physical prowess could easily rival the majority of Heaven; however, his true power was in his ability to mesmerize and blind any who might even look upon him.

His power to reflect light could penetrate and cause blindness even with one's eyes closed. He could bend light to project a visage so real that one would question reality itself.

His voice so potent it could split the ground if he chose. His sway of suggestion was virtually without resistance, for he could modulate his voice to compel one to praise, and enraptured by his voice one would immediately desire him to speak more.

Between the assault of one's senses in sight and sound, he could bring any to their knees. He did not need to touch an adversary, for most could not even *approach* him. He represented the cumulative of all Elomic power, wisdom, and beauty.

He was perfect in all his ways.

Lucifer then annunciated the entrance of the King.

"Glory and honor and majesty belong to God Most High! Power and praise blessed be the name of the Lord! From everlasting to everlasting. All hail the King!"

The Lord God of Heaven then entered; concealed by the clouds of living smoke and the Shekinah that surrounded him. His visage was yet somehow clear. Bathed in light and heat, He walked to address his people and all of Heaven, and those who saw from waypoints while they remained on duty in their respective areas of the universe bowed, and prostrated themselves before the Most High God.

Lucifer became even brighter as El entered his presence and waves of light and heat pulsated in all directions: sparks of lightning arched and jumped across the emporium, and seven thunders echoed from the clouds in the sky.

"Holy, Holy, Holy!"

Lucifer flew to the Lord and with his expansive wings he perched himself above the throne. He hovered above the mercy seat and took his role as the anointed cherub that covered and affixed himself to the throne. Ophanim flew to the left and right of El, and the most High God spoke.

"Host of Heaven, on this the sixth of days; we will declare a thing never before heard. Much has gone into preparing Earth to be abode to him whom the Lord would delight to honor. Lucifer, our faithful servant hath overseen its preparation and has completed the task according to our will.

Thine court was entreated as to what honor we should bestow. In their wisdom, they spoke, and we have hearkened according to all their word. We have thus made a garden of such beauty to house as a palace for him whom our soul would love.

Therefore, let us make man in our image, after our likeness: and let them have dominion over the fish of the sea and over the fowl of the air and over the cattle and over all the Earth and over every creeping thing that creepeth upon the Earth."

The Lord God then moved suddenly and instantly to the Earth, and all of Heaven saw him, but somehow, he still stood at the lectern. The angels watched as El placed his hands in the garden that Lucifer had prepared and formed a man from the dust of the ground.

Like the many times of formation in the Kiln, he shaped and cut away and molded until bone was formed. Carefully El made hands, arms, and two legs, and he fashioned sinew and placed flesh upon the man.

The man lay motionless and still, and El neither gave it wings that it might fly nor did he fashion the man's flesh after the flesh of Elohim, but a light brown thin layer of porous soft tissue did he weave as skin.

El knelt over to his new creation and breathed into its nostrils the breath of Life: and the man became a living soul. Heaven looked on in astonishment, and everyone erupted in a horde of cheers.

Lucifer looked upon the man silently from atop the throne of the Most High. He glared scornfully upon this new rival in bitter silence.

Chapter Five

Murmur Not Among Yourselves

Day Six

Lucifer watched from atop the throne and looked on in spite as the mud creature El had named 'man' stood and reached up to embrace the King of the Universe. El hugged the man and then softly kissed him on his forehead.

Lucifer looked down upon the legions of Elohim before him perched from a vantage point that none other but he possessed. Gazing from the Third Heaven into the totality of all realms Lucifer eyed his people; watching as they celebrated in adulation over El's creation of the man.

Lucifer beamed approvingly at them who were as countless as the stars. Then he eyed the man and saw his frailty and the fawning that El spent upon his new creation. Contempt grew as pus within him, and his thoughts teemed with bile towards his maker. Lucifer noted that the people applauded a creature that neither flew nor possessed the power of Arelim, the voice of the Draco, but was made from the dust of the Earth. When he saw the man and his own people cheering in senseless applause, Lucifer noted that none thought for themselves.

A multitude of bleating sheep you are: huddled and flocked together. Like the wheat fields on Earth, as chaff carried aloft with the breeze. Ah, my people, alas thou art blind to the truth, nor do you perceive, but lost in the mesmerizing bask of worship to El. If only thou might see what I see. Then would you be loosed from His chain.

Lucifer marveled at their docility: the Elohim simply obeyed, never questioned, and now they stood baying in applause at a creature beneath them in beauty.

Is this how El sees us?

Lucifer basked in his perch above the throne. All of creation seemed as a quilt spread out before him and all realities appeared at once. He reveled in the sense of knowledge. It was intoxicating.

Swallowed in his pride, Lucifer looked upon the people: proud that he alone could see the truth that they truly were all slaves to the whims of the Almighty. Sadness began to flood over him. Sadness that El had created a source of labor to carry out his dictates, sad that his people were relegated to serve this 'greatest creation'. Angry that El would in his selfishness hold back such knowledge. Lucifer then looked upon El and despised him. His countenance changed towards his maker while he questioned the goodness of God and ruminated with thought after thought in his mind until one seeded itself above all others. *I will be God.*

Lucifer continued to look upon El, and El's continued fawning over the man gnawed at him.

Lucifer then looked upon the man. He was indeed beautiful: soft not hard like the diamond and scales of himself. The man, however, was limited, mortal even.

Lucifer's mind reeled with unbelief and disgust. *Surely, El would not turn over such a realm as Earth over to a creature, which was of mud and clay. No true King should behave in such a way! This — this is the creature that should bear El's image and likeness?*

Lucifer looked upon El, and the form that he had despised for so long revealed itself to him. He attempted to rid himself of the image, yet the vision would not cease. Like a persistent apparition, he saw El through the veil of fog.

The servant looked upon his master and disgust began to fill him. *This represents El's true form?*

All of Heaven watched as God personally created two trees from the

153

rich soil: one that released the knowledge of good and evil and a companion tree of eternal life. Each was set within the midst of the garden. The Lord then gave the man instructions concerning the trees and of what he could eat.

Then the Lord God brought every beast of the field and every fowl of the air unto Adam to see what he would call them, and whatsoever Adam called every living creature that was the name thereof.

Adam then gave names to all cattle, to the fowl of the air, and to every beast of the field.

Lucifer became incensed.

Adam bestowed on every creature a name, and with each act of naming: God further sealed man's dominion over them. For Heaven's code states that he who names a thing defines and administers the thing. Lucifer observed as man steadily and with little effort gave each creature a name, which defined it.

The Lord saw that there was no mate for the Adam and said, "It is not good that the man should be alone; I will make him a help meet for him."

The Lord God then caused a deep sleep to fall upon Adam, and he slept. Then He took one of his ribs and closed up the flesh thereof.

And the rib, which the Lord God had taken from man, made He a woman and brought her unto the man. And Adam said, "This is now bone of my bones, and flesh of my flesh: she shall be called Woman because she was taken out of Man."

The Lord was pleased with the form of them, and the Shekinah moved from El and hovered over the man and the woman. The brightness of his glory covered them that they shown as the stars, and the shawl of living light covered their face and skin, and they glowed even as the Lord.

They were both naked, the man and his wife, and were not ashamed. And the Lord walked in the cool of the day with the man and the woman and fellowshipped with them, and they with him.

Moreover, Lucifer made note of the name that Adam had named the white, docile creature that nauseated him, the creature that in Lucifer's mind was the identical image of El.

He pronounced the word aloud to hear it for himself, speaking it into the air. He now had a name to assign to his image of El, a designation that symbolized all the weakness he now came to despise in his creator. There was only one word, which perfectly described his repugnance: *Lamb.*

****

El ceased from talking with the man and his companion, and as the hours marched onward on Earth mere seconds passed in Heaven, and El immediately continued to address the congregation.

"Behold the pinnacle of our creation. For with great thought have plans been laid to secure man's future. Know that we shall accomplish all our will. Therefore, we will watch over his coming and his going.

Thou great Elohim, birthed from the fires of our Kiln, shall also serve to aid man to understand all things. As we have taught thee, go to and teach thou Adam and his seed that he might have dominion."

El turned to enter the temple again; smoke, lightning, and thunder echoed in his steps. Lucifer immediately lifted off the throne and covered El's backside and the Ophanim propelled the throne back into the great hall of Mt. Zion.

As El departed, Lucifer's own glory diminished, yet he continued to pronounce the majesty of God, and Heaven rang with cheers of, "Praise the Lord! Praise the Lord!"

Slowly, each member of the royal court left the dais; from the eldest to the youngest until only the seraphim were all that were left to march into the great hall. Their, "HOLY, HOLY, HOLY" echoing across the emporium. When all parties left, Lucifer alone stood on the rostrum and watched the crowd as they dispersed.

Lucifer scratched at the burning that ached in his chest and his mind raced with just one thought: *Thou must decrease that I might increase.*

****

Lucifer settled into the center hall of Athor prepared to address the elders of the city. He stood behind the raised platform so that he could adequately see all the participants. The elders of Athor slowly made their way into the chamber hall.

The room was circular with seats made of white marble. The floor was lapis lazuli, and the ceiling was gold etched in silver with cursive angelic script, which pronounced the glory of El. The walls were quartz and reflected the light, not just of the noonday sun but also of Lucifer himself, who stood high in the center of the chamber surrounded by the marble stadium seats.

In the course of time, all sat and Lucifer began to speak.

"Fellow Sons of God — I as Chief Prince and Archon of Earth have asked you here that I might assign to you the tasks necessary to complete our mission to instruct the humans. We have...."

Lucifer was interrupted by Srosh, one of his fellow Draco. He was tall and muscular; his species shimmered in scales of bluish silver. His blonde hair draped his shoulders as he raised his serpentine-like body for attention.

"My pardon, Chief Prince, but perhaps you would enlighten the elders on the rumors which circulate Athor, for much has been made of Apollyon and his deeds."

156

"And what would you know Srosh that has not already been reported?"

"Chief Prince, is it true that El has closed the mouth of the Kiln? Reports from Heaven say that a living mountain of ash and fire now draws power from that which is our womb. Is this so?"

Lucifer eyed the crowd. They too fastened their eyes on him, fixated and waiting on his every word.

"That which thou hast heard is true. There is a mount of breathing rock tied to the Kiln itself and which lives off the flesh of Elohim."

Gasps echoed across the room. Mouths dropped. Whispers circulated within the center hall.

"My Lord, then are we to be no more? Is this the end of the Kilnborn? Will there be no more stones to fire our ranks?"

Lucifer pondered the words and turned them over in his mind. *Will there be no more stones—is this the end of the Kilnborn?*

Another angel arose to speak. "My Lord, is it true that Apollyon now lives in punishment within the belly of this mountain?"

Then another, "And what of this dark creature reported at the mouth of the new mount? What is he? He does not present as other Elohim"

"Master…"

"My Lord Prince…"

"I have a question…"

Lucifer found himself suddenly barraged with demands from all fronts. Shouts of angels quickly filled the chamber, each vying and clamoring for attention, all in query. Lucifer looked upon his people and pity welled up within him, for they were as sheep with no shepherd.

Does El even understand what he has done? He thought.

Lucifer's Heartstone pained him, and he clutched and scratched at his

157

chest for relief. He staggered as the pain became more intense. He looked up at the crowd that now argued amongst themselves and spoke to regain order. "Silence!" he roared.

Immediately, the room fell mute as the power of Lucifer's deep voice shook the ground, and the south quartz wall cracked. However, Srosh a fellow Draco did not move. He did not cow upon Lucifer's rebuke. Like all Draco, he was regal in stature and able to project his own voice. Despite the command of his Chief Prince, Srosh spoke the mind of many within the room.

"Are we to be servants Lucifer, forced to serve a creature of mud and clay?" Srosh's statement emboldened another to speak.

"I do not wish to serve."

"Free Apollyon," cried an Arelim.

An Issi elder immediately retorted, "Let him burn within the mountain!"

Lucifer frowned; his brow tightened in anger. Anger, that El has placed him in such a position; anger that he would have to answer for his creator. Anger that despite all his desire to give an answer, he had none with which he could defend his Lord's actions.

Anger — that was unleashed.

Once more Lucifer spoke, but spoke with such force that the floor opened its mouth, and Srosh and several of the assembled elders cried for help and struggled to find release from the fissure, which now raced across the floor. Panic quickly ensued, and the Chief Prince stretched his wings and lifted himself from the ground to address his audience.

"It is true that the Kiln now fuels Hell's belly and also true that Apollyon now lies trapped therein. It is true that El hast made Earth, home to the humans: a home that *you* have carefully maintained and assisted in its very

158

fashion."

"Was it not *you* who ferried flora across the world to populate the garden that the humans now occupy? Was it not *you* who mined the floor of Earth to encase Athor in gold and glass: its beauty and illumination a floodlight in the night sky? Its luminance seen even from the second heaven of Sol?"

"Aye," said Lucifer. "It is true that El hast made a creature of such hunger that it feeds off the very life of Elohim, and lo, within the span of one day we see two abominations. One — a guardian to keep our brother imprisoned. And two, a creature so beneath us as to be made from El's spittle and the mud that *we* walk upon. Yet were *we* given the title to anything? No. We serve."

"We praise a master who rewards us not according to our works nor celebrates our accomplishments. Nay my brethren, *our* reward is clear. *We* will no longer be fashioned to seed the heavens."

Lucifer looked each in the eye probingly. "No longer will the Kiln burn to fire *our* creation." Lucifer pointed hard at his chest repeatedly. "Nay, the Kiln now burns to fire *our* prison! It exists to remind us that those who refuse to serve will burn therein!"

"*I*," said Lucifer pointing again at his chest, "Am Chief Prince, Lord Lucifer Draco, and First Kilnborn of all Elohim. I alone walk upon the Stones of Fire. I will not serve, and I will not burn. I pledge to free our brother Apollyon!

For I will ascend into Heaven.

I will exalt my throne above the stars of God.

I will sit upon the mount of the congregation, in the sides of the north.

I will ascend above the heights of the clouds.

I will be like the most High!"

Raphael walked into the throne room, sat before his king, and looked at the enormous book within his hands, which contained all the information the Lord El had requested.

"My Lord, the task wherewith I have been charged is complete. I have tallied all as thou hast commanded."

El looked upon Raphael and smiled, "And what did your examination find, my son?"

Raphael's face became angst-ridden. His heart and mind burdened by what he knew, knowledge he must now dispense to the Lord. Never had he given the Lord a negative report. Now he must be the first Elohim to broach the subject of treason with his king.

"My Lord, your instruction was to find all instances of thought, conduct, and or speech similar to Abaddon's. To bring to you a concise volume that lists all Elohim and the result of my findings."

El saw that Raphael's lip tightened and that the cherubim struggled to choke back tears.

"Raphael, speak my son, for there is nothing covered that shall not be revealed and hid that shall not be made known. Fear not."

Raphael straightened himself, wiped his eyes, cleared his throat and spoke as directed.

"Lord, of the host of Heaven there is a number whose mind is pure and whose fealty my King can command without question. These whose names are written therein are not so. They number almost a third of Heaven. Those who dissent to thy rule speak of displeasure with Abaddon's sentence, the existence of Hell, or take issue with relations with the humans. They say that the humans are not Kilnborn, not of the Stones of Fire. There are some who are displeased to serve a creature of mud and clay."

"And what of the Grigori?" asked El.

"My God, again the Grigori as a whole are with thee my king, yet it pains me to report that all are not so. I regret that I have yet to determine the extent to which my own kind has departed from the way."

"I do know that entries of several tomes have made me concerned. There are records, which seem to do more than simply state the observations that the Grigori have heard or seen. I have found several Grigori whose records have added commentary to their accounts. Some no longer seem content to only document the observations of their charge but to annotate as well."

Raphael looked away from the Lord and paused.

"Continue, do not hold back that which thou hast found." said El.

"I have traced the genesis of this corruption my king. Moreover, I am afraid that one of the Lumazi is the seed to the fruit from which all springs. In a review of which tomes no longer hold true, they point back to one Grigori. Lilith and his tomes are no longer valid, thus out of the mouth of two or three must they now be established. In a review of the tome of Lilith on the Chief Prince, I have seen an entry that hast given me pause.

Lilith's entry was not journaled in accordance to Grigoric law, but because the Grigori are abundant in number; another was in proximity at the time and reveals an inconsistency.

"I believe this entry is the accurate one my Lord, and that which I present now to thy light: the copy of which I hold in my hand. Its record compels me to further investigate any new additions in Lilith's accord of Lucifer."

"And the entry; what did it contain my son?"

Raphael tossed the book into the air, and the voluminous work stood

161

vertically as if coming to attention. The manuscript separated into cover and pages; its sheets flew across the throne, and the pages assembled themselves so that the recorded journal entry was chronologically on top.

Light glowed on the first page. It floated higher to touch the ceiling and the image of Lucifer and Lilith walking in the Garden of Eden appeared. A Grigori assigned to watch a flock of sheep observed the occurrence and documented a portion of the unauthorized conversation.

"And what is thy desire, Chief Prince? What would satisfy you?"
Lucifer looked skyward. His eyes aimed upward as if he gazed directly at God and Raphael.

"That I might ascend into Heaven; that mine throne would be exalted above the stars of God.

That I would sit also upon the mount of the congregation, in the sides of the north: To ascend above the heights of the clouds..."

The image then dissipated, and the mammoth book flared with a flash of white light, reassembled itself, and then fell with a loud thump to the floor.

El stood, Raphael kneeled, silently waiting on any command from his Lord. Then El spoke. "Go, Raphael. Summon thy brothers as there is much to do, the seventh-day approaches, and I must take rest from all my labor."

"Yes, my Lord." Raphael bowed, picked up the book, and turned to walk away. Leaving the sanctuary through one of the many side chambers, Raphael returned to his home within the mountain itself. He walked through the corridor of Mt. Zion and entered the Great Hall of Annals.

He passed by multiple stacks and shelves of records and books until he came to a desk, sat, and placed the completed tome he had just recently finished down; it hit the stone slab of the desk with a thud.

He looked over and noticed that Lucifer's tome was still recording.

New information was penned in angelic script. The letters were in flames, and Raphael's eyes fixated to one passage that leapt off the page.

Raphael's eyes grew wide and his mouth opened, but his tongue could not form words.

His mind raced with thoughts and then froze in disbelief and panic, as he lifted the book and reread each new passage. Hope dashed away as he read, and the horrible truth dawned on him with each sentence, words that he knew somehow would forever change creation. *'I will be like the most High.'*

****

"But my Lord, you cannot possibly hope to defeat El! El is Alpha! He is Omega. We are but Kilnborne. He is Author of all!"

The Chamber hall was raucous, for the elders could not believe their ears.

"Treason!" said one.

"Blasphemy!" said another

"What you say is not possible!"

"Defeat El — can such a thing be done?"

Lucifer looked upon his brethren and spoke. "Thou hast been chosen above all Elohim to serve me. I have selected you all. You alone have raised Athor from the dust. Consider now my words. *El,* not *I,* has shown himself to be traitor."

"Traitor to all Elohim; for he has created us that we might be slaves to another. If we were but servants to El, I would serve happily. However, we are Kilnborn. Are we to teach one who knows not the majesty of those from whom they even learn? Are we to serve those whose sight reaches not into the Third

Heaven? Who tread the ground, but possess not the power to fly amongst the stars?"

"I say nay. El is no longer worthy of rule. He fawns over the man as he walks with him during the day. He has withheld from us and knowingly done so. Why are the granaries expanded? Why hast Jerusalem itself been enlarged? Would he elevate the humans to displace us? Soon will we not have even home in Heaven? Why doth this Earth *not* bring forth manna? Why? Because *we* were not in His mind when it was made. Indeed, we have been an afterthought."

Many in the room nodded in agreement.

Lucifer continued, "Of a surety El is mighty. He cannot be destroyed through strength of arms."

Tiriel, an Issi, and an elder, of the rivers, rose to speak. "You speak the truth. El cannot be defeated, yet I have no pleasure to serve the humans. How then would *you,* Chief Prince, bring down God?"

The room grew quiet, and all eyes turned to Lucifer and listened expectantly for his reply. "El cannot be defeated by sheer power. However, power is not necessary to defeat El. The throne cannot be taken by force. It must be freely surrendered. El will abdicate it willingly."

Kaspiel rose, waved his hand angrily and in disbelief.

"You are mad Lucifer!" he said.

"Am I?" replied Lucifer. "What is the *greater* madness Kaspiel? To serve a God who seeks to enslave us for eternity and sing happily for the privilege? Is it mad to desire and fight for one's freedom? Am I mad that I refuse to bow to a creature of mud and clay?"

Another elder arose and spoke, "Lucifer, you have not yet stated how you would accomplish what you purport. Words alone will not the overthrow of El achieve."

"I indeed have a plan," said Lucifer, "but it cannot be accomplished alone. If thou be with El then go, and I will not think the less of you. However, if thou would hear my plan, I will offer a pledge of mine ability to accomplish my will. Stay and I shall say on."

Each elder in the room looked at the other. Lucifer also looked about the hall. His eyes scanned to see which of his elders might leave. Everyone contemplated if he should be the first to depart. Each knew that something special was taking place, and all wondered if they were destined to herald freedom for their race.

Excitement began to fill the air with a palpable sense that the destiny of their species was at hand. Then Tiamat, an angel from Lucifer's own species Draco stood to speak. He was silver and grey hair ran down the whole of his snake-like back.

"Say on, Chief Prince. We would hear thee on this matter. What proof would you offer this assembly that we might show thee fealty as God?"

Lucifer smiled, looked upon his brethren, and spoke.

"I will brave Hell's maw, release Apollyon, and convey him safe before you. If I return with him, you will alter your sigil in thy flesh, bear my seal, and shall serve me. You will then be my people, and I will be your God."

Tiamat looked around the room, and the other elders nodded.

"We will do as thou hast said. Yet Chief Prince...what if you fail?"

Lucifer looked upon them all and spoke with fire in his eyes.

"Then if I perish—I perish."

****

Ashtaroth waited for his master near the waypoint of Argoth. Lucifer's Ladder materialized, and he strutted off the platform. Ashtaroth took note that his master's countenance was serious even for him.

"My Lord Prince, welcome home."

"Thank you, Astarte. You are my most trusted servant, and in the days of ahead, I will lean on your faithfulness to accomplish a task of great importance."

I am at your service my Prince," he said.

Lucifer and Ashtaroth made their way to his home.

"Astarte how go the repairs to my estate?"

"I expect them to be complete upon our return my Prince."

"Well done my friend, well done. When all this is over, I will see that you are greatly rewarded."

"I am ever grateful, Chief Prince. You honor me."

Lucifer entered his home through the great doors and made his way upstairs while Ashtaroth saw to matters elsewhere in the mansion.

Lucifer stood outside his bedroom door and looked at the two angels sent by Michael to repair his palatial bedroom.

"How are you coming with the repairs?" Lucifer inquired.

One of the two Arelim builders turned to the Chief Prince to respond.

"Well, we are almost done, Lord Prince. We should be off the premises shortly. If I may be so bold sire, it grieves me that an Issi would be the cause of such destruction. It never fails that an Arelim must clean up their mess."

Lucifer looked curiously at the worker. "Elaborate."

"Well sire, it's not that we don't appreciate and respect the Issi. We just know that one such as yourself should have builders around you, not swift-tongued angels who don't know their place."

Lucifer stroked his small beard. "So you disapprove of Ashtaroth an Issi, as my attendant?"

"I pray that my Lord would not be angry with me. It is not our place to judge. However, all one need do is look at thine wall, my Prince. In the very repairs that we make, your answer lies therein."

Lucifer chuckled. "*My* understanding of events is that Apollyon was bested by Ashtaroth."

Both workers stopped, looked at each other and one walked slowly towards Lucifer. "Chief Prince, an Issi: even one who serves within thine house — can never best an Arelim. If Apollyon was bested, it was through guile, not strength of arms."

Lucifer stood unmoved. The Arelim was strong and imposing in demeanor and like all his kind possessed muscular arms, cloven feet, and a bull's head.

Just like all his ilk, Lucifer thought.

Lucifer was not intimidated. He was the Chief Prince, and he walked on the Stones of Fire. He moved forward, but the Arelim stood his ground.

"Elohim do not harm other Elohim, and on the day such were to occur, my wrath would most assuredly ensue on the angel who would lift up his hand against another. Am I understood?"

The Arelim stepped back, "My apologies Chief Prince. I meant no disrespect…"

Ashtaroth entered the chamber and spoke, "My Lord your presence is requested by the court. El plans a repast for the council and…"

Both Arelim workers spread their wings, and the hair on their backs raised as their bodies prepared themselves for battle.

Ashtaroth's stance became poised for defense, and the two angelic species warily eyed one another. The Arelim looked with loathing at Ashtaroth; each dropped their tools and clenched their fists, their wings unfurled and grew tense ready to leap.

Lucifer spoke, "Ashtaroth, you will accompany me to the mount. As for the two of you, your work here is complete. Know that your Chief Prince is pleased. You may leave my presence now."

Lucifer sat down at his desk and began to write within his journal and without looking at the two workers or Ashtaroth, spoke.

"And my *wrath* would assuredly ensue on the angel who lifted up his hand against another."

The two workers relaxed, bowed to the Chief Prince and stepped out the room, scowling at Ashtaroth as they left. Lucifer and Ashtaroth heard them make their way downstairs and out the front door.

Ashtaroth relaxed and his color returned to him.

"My apologies Chief Prince, the Arelim are a most brutish lot. They know not the subtleties of protocol. I fear that tensions have risen since the altercation between Apollyon and myself. There is a growing division amongst the Issi and Arelim. Our exchange, I am afraid, has only inflamed contention over his person and his sentence. Some believe that I too should have been thrown into Hell for my participation with Apollyon. I fear that our altercation is a sore point between our two races. My mere presence incites tension in Heaven's midst."

Lucifer stroked his chin then spoke. "Indeed, but this may be used to my profit," Lucifer said.

"My Lord?" said Ashtaroth confused.

"Ashtaroth, I have changed my mind. I will go alone to the mount. You will assemble the most trusted and loyal of my household, and thou and thy company shall leave for Earth. Await me in the palace, and I shall give you understanding of my will."

"As you command my prince." Ashtaroth turned to leave but then paused and turned to speak. "Thank you my Lord."

Lucifer turned around to face his servant: curious for the expression of gratitude.

"Thank you Chief Prince for calling me by my name," explained Ashtaroth.

Lucifer smiled. "I have always loved you, my friend. You have faithfully served me."

Ashtaroth bowed, turned then left the room. Lucifer closed the bedroom door behind him and looked out the window on the city of angels beneath him. His brow wrinkled, for the path that he was about to take weighed heavily upon him.

Lilith uncloaked behind him and spoke. "He really is quite slow isn't he?"

Lucifer grinned then replied. "He is, yet he is faithful. His obedience is all that is necessary for my purpose." Lucifer continued to look upon the throng of Heaven's populace as they scurried to duties unknown.

"He will serve as will all the rest. But Grigori this would I know…" Lucifer turned to face his watcher. "Are you with me or for mine adversaries?"

Lilith bowed to the Chief Prince.

"You have been a charge most intriguing, Lucifer Draco. Thou sealest up the sum, full of wisdom, and perfect in beauty. If thou can indeed walk through hell-fire and steal Apollyon away to defy El's prison, to walk within the maw and come out again —I would sit watch over thee to see what the end shall be.

"By now Raphael hast learned of my entries, for your actions have become more *difficult* to document without a level of bias on my part." "Aye," said Lilith, "I shall be he which chronicles thy work."

"Thou art wise Lilith," Lucifer said.

"Nay, Chief Prince. My wisdom hast yet to be found in this decision. What I am is an angel who hast violated Grigoric law. Your complicity hast become my own. I simply rise and fall on thy doings, but I must admit, to cease to be under the heel of Raphael's dictums — that I will most enjoy."

"Then I bequeath to you Lilith his position upon my ascension to the throne. All Grigori then shall call *thee* Lord Prince."

Lilith bowed. "I am thine to command."

"Then let us go; El and my brethren await me. Let us not tarry for there is much to do. A kingdom overthrown I must begin."

Chapter Six

Choose ye this day whom ye shall serve

End of day Six.

The Lumazi had gathered for fellowship over a meal. El desired to celebrate the working of the past six days and to share the company of his sons. It was not often that all seven princes gathered with El. The work of creation had taxed them all, and El was now prepared to take his rest, a day when the Holy One of the universe would cease from all his labors.

Raphael had asked the Lord God about his *resting*. El replied, "There is a pattern that must be set, my son." El would not elaborate more.

The banquet hall was immense, with a long circular table set in the midst of the room. Servers attended to every need as an Elohim of a different race waited on each prince. Michael often grew extremely conscientious when others doted upon him. He was Archon of Heaven and constantly looking to see how he might best benefit El and all Heaven. He was a servant and not accustomed to pampering. Gabriel loved to engage in conversation. It took constant reproofs from El to keep him seated and not to assist the attendants in the preparation rooms. Both Talus and Sariel salivated over the incoming meal, yet when Talus eyed Sariel served by an Arelim, he frowned, but both Talus and Sariel managed to do nothing to provoke El to speak disapprovingly to them.

Jerahmeel was, of course, at home. He loved fellowship, and he loved the brethren. His unprovoked laughs were contagious, and he could infect others with his joviality. For no apparent reason, one would find himself spontaneously laughing uncontrollably. Jerahmeel was a praiser. He loved to sing, whether Heaven wanted to hear him or not, and sing Jerahmeel did, especially a song to honor El's designing of creation.

Soon the banquet hall was festive with laughter and song.

Finally, Jerahmeel settled down enough to realize that his plate was empty.

"Are you going to eat that?" he asked Lucifer.

Lucifer shook his head and slid his plate to his brother.

Jerahmeel happily took the plate and gleefully filled his mouth, an orifice that never seemed to close.

Talus was quick to remind him that his own plate of manna seemed mysteriously diminished by one loaf.

El sat quietly at the table.

Michael noticed that both Lucifer and El had not eaten and that each was eerily hushed. El had his hands folded and his eyes closed; he seemed to be listening to each of his sons with a smile was on his face.

El exhaled, opened his eyes, and spoke.

"I will miss these meals."

Everyone around the table looked at him perplexed.

Gabriel asked him, "Lord, what do you mean?"

El somberly looked at each of his seven sons, these beings of power and light. Longingly, he gazed upon them and smiled, but his demeanor changed as a look of seriousness appeared as he glanced down and spoke.

"One of you will betray us all."

Silence engulfed the room

Lucifer shifted nervously in his seat.

Once again, El had introduced a new word to everyone. With blank stares and shrugged shoulders, each looked at one another for answers. When they all looked at Michael, he realized that the group had quietly drafted him to speak the question that they all were too timid to ask.

"What is '*betrayal*' Lord?" asked Michael.

El looked at them and said. "I have many things to say to you, but you are not able to bear them right now. In time, all will be revealed. Although you do not know what I do now, you will know later. The one with whom I share the sop of my cup, he will betray us."

El slowly dipped his bread into his cup and passed it to Lucifer.

Lucifer stared quietly at it and then stared at El.

Each prince in the room watched as El and the Chief Prince looked upon each other. Silence stood between them. El looked at Lucifer, smiled lovingly and seemed to communicate instructions to the Chief Prince as he had done so many times before.

Lucifer looked away from El and rose from the table. He quickly headed towards the door. Michael ran to catch up to his brother.

"Lucifer, where are you going?"

Lucifer took Michael by the hand, hugged him, and whispered into his ear. "Where I go you cannot follow." And a tear ran down Lucifer's eye.

"Lucifer...," said El.

Lucifer turned to gaze upon his Lord before leaving.

"What thou doest," El paused. "Do quickly."

Lucifer nodded in acknowledgment and glanced at his brothers. He stared at each one's face, released Michael and turned to walk away.

"Lucifer?" Michael cried.

Lucifer paused momentarily; clenched his fists, closed his eyes and contorted his tear stricken face, but he did not turn. He gritted his teeth and continued with a quickened pace down the marble corridor.

"Lucifer please...," begged Michael. But his brother continued to ignore him. He lifted himself into the air and quickly flew away.

Michael stared at his brother and watched him disappear; confusion gripped him. He spun around to look at El, his eyes pleading for an explanation.

El stood with none.

All immediately stood as well, and El spoke.

"Come ye have much to do."

"Lord, the meal is not yet finished," said Jerahmeel.

"Aye, but unless we depart, he who is revealed will not reveal himself, and so that all might be made known. I must leave you for a season. Fear not; I will not leave you comfortless. Michael has charge during our Sabbath for war will be unleashed upon you soon."

"Lord?"

"Yes, Michael?"

"What is '*war*'?"

"You shall find out soon my son."

Lucifer walked with a hurried pace and quickly left the banquet room. Attendants of the temple bowed in respect as he passed a corridor and went into the throne room. He gazed at the ceiling of onyx, which showed stars, galaxies, and all the planets of the celestial universe.

When next I enter this chamber, this shall all be mine.

He walked towards the right side of the throne and to the latticed gold doors of the Kiln. He could feel the heat emanating from inside. Lucifer turned the diamond handle to the large vault and entered the Kiln.

Dry air rushed towards his face and the temperature changed immediately from room temperature to boiling as Lucifer made his way into the chamber. He walked down a small corridor that erupted in flames. He had been this way before. Only those empowered by El to walk this hall could survive it. As he entered the chamber the stones stood before him and laid spread out at his feet.

Once more Lucifer walked amidst the Stones of Fire. They called to him, each beckoning to *be*. He had been here countless times before. The sentient stones knew him. They welcomed him, calling out to him. They made a hum against the backdrop of the roar of the great furnace. White-hot flames jetted in front of him. The heat of the whole universe trapped in one room: the source of Hell's fire.

Lucifer, however, was not here this day to assist El in the creation of another Elohim. No, he was here for one purpose only: to cross the long umbilical cord of fire and brimstone that stretched from the Kiln to the living mountain of Hell.

Lucifer stood to hear the songs and opened the pores of his flesh. The flame soothed him, and he sang with the stones as he basked in the heat of the fire. Smiling, he looked at the stone in the center of the room, a gemstone of much larger substance; he listened. For its song was different from all others. Temptation gripped him to touch it, but he had not come here to partake in the stone's song—not yet.

Soon, he said to himself.

He saw the wall still fresh with the imprint of Charon's frame. Lucifer looked down at the steaming floor and saw the manacled tendrils of Charon's footsteps.

A trail, Lucifer thought.

To find Apollyon would require him to walk a path of heat and flame, to follow the path of Charon and to traverse a path through Hell.

Determined, Lucifer looked on. The entry to Hell opened and closed, pulsating like the beating of a human heart. The sulfuric air scorched lung and eye. Lucifer hardened into his Draconian form and closed the pores in his flesh.

Hell was a living prison designed to feed off the flesh of Elohim. A thought that caused Lucifer to take pause. He stared at the orifice and realized how his task would reverberate throughout Heaven.

The opening widened and Lucifer steeled himself and stepped through.

Lucifer ducked his head and followed the footsteps left by Charon through the moist heated bile of Hell's umbilical. The hotness of the channel grew more intense as he walked. The umbilical itself served as an exhaust or as a flume with roasting wave after wave of intense heat.

Lucifer began to grow increasingly uncomfortable: he had walked in the Kiln with God and had survived. Now he stood within the twisted veins and arteries of Hell's furnace. Gooey liquid slowly oozed from the ceiling as Lucifer trekked ever deeper towards the creature's belly.

Finally, he thought. Lucifer saw, at last, the entrance to the mountain. He was horrified. "What abomination is this?" he said to himself.

At the end of the channel, he could see rows of razor sharp teeth. Flames licked ever higher, for the room beyond the teeth was vast. Geysers of sulfuric acid ejected from the walls and floors. Eyes were sprawled on the mountain's floor. Moreover, many mouths lined the walls, each filled with rows of razor-sharp teeth. The openings salivated and waited for any morsel, any opportunity to engorge on Elomic flesh. Lucifer quickly realized that the umbilical was simply one mouth, a mouth that he attempted to exit.

Where does each opening lead? He wondered.

Heated streams of lava coiled a membranous skin of ash and smoke. It became increasingly evident that within the craggy outer crust of the mount, Hell was a creature of flesh.

Lucifer cautiously walked towards the opening, and the fluid of the chamber became more thick and sticky as he approached. He walked towards the razor sharp teeth and slid his serpentine body through the various rows. Pain immediately befell him; the teeth sliced into his diamond flesh as a razor would slice through paper.

The Prince of Angels screamed in pain. The teeth of the maw clawed at him ripping clothing and dug deeper into his skin.

Teeth of diamonds how is this possible? He thought.

More agony.

Few among the Elohim had experienced such a sensation: the termination of life. Saesheal was the first. Lucifer began to understand the allure and intoxication to take life. Abaddon had stumbled upon this level of forbidden knowledge that El sought to deny them. Lucifer would have this secret as well; he would know the knowledge of life and death.

Here within the veins of Hell, Hell tutored Lucifer that death was power. The ability to *both* create and destroy was strength. Here in the hungry clutches of teeth and volcanic gums, where brimstone spittle drenched his face: Lucifer understood the pleasure of Apollyon's fascination with destruction.

Yet he was not Apollyon, and he refused to bow to destruction this day. His was the feet that walked on the very stones that powered the Kiln. Moreover, his would be the feet that would walk through the colon of Hell.

Lucifer called upon the power of his vocal cords and the tabrets and percussion instruments buried in the soles of his feet. Lucifer roared and slammed his feet into the umbilical floor. The sonic waves dispersed in all directions and rippled towards the row of teeth that barred his path. The tone of Lucifer's pitch assaulted the creature's mouth, and the teeth shattered as glass against the frequency of a tuning fork.

Injured but undaunted, Lucifer continued to track the path of Charon, deeper into the bowels of a creature that fueled itself on the digestion of angels.

Lucifer walked on the floor of Hell. His feet burned, and smoke rose as he took each step forward. The floor moved underneath him as lava licked at his soles.

Hell had become aware of his presence, alerted to this strange menace.

As a body struggles to fight a virus, Hell unleashed its brimstone antibodies to fight off this intruder. The immune system of a living mountain unleashed to do battle with the First of Angels.

They came without warning, and they came without concern for title or respect for protocol: centipedes of lava and brimstone hissed as they moved and slowly inched their way to consume the First of Angels.

Lucifer stepped back, for the eyes in the floor followed his every step. Each mouth within the walls of Hell snapped and gnashed teeth and waited to snatch a bite from his flesh, an Elohim whose taste was rife with lusciousness.

Lucifer was quick and moved speedily around the creatures. Soon more appeared, Hell increasingly aware of this contagion. With each step, he took; another creature of volcanic bile appeared, ready to devour him.

One-step, a new creature formed from the floor. Two steps forward and two creatures appeared. Each squished eye of the floor formed into a creature ready to consume. Lucifer stopped moving. Each creature moved and hissed as they converged on his position, but when he stood still, no new creatures formed.

Aha, so they are activated by my steps!

Lucifer lifted himself from the floor out of reach of the mindless creatures. Their movement stopped and the eyes melted back into the fiery floor.

Lucifer flew through ash and smoke careful to avoid the ceiling or walls: and as he made his way through the fiery digestive tract, he heard screams. Lucifer followed the anguished cries until he exited the antechamber and entered a room filled with tendrils that crisscrossed the entire room.

He hovered just outside the lattice of flame and acidic goo and stared to behold Apollyon centered within a netting of pain, caught like a fly within a web.

Tendrils of white-hot magma and sulfuric acid shackled his ankles and wrists while vines of molten lava filled his mouth: he struggled to breathe. Bile secreted from his ears and dribbled down the side of his face to his shoulders. Chain link impressions covered his chest and the back of His chest was lacerated, leaving his flesh exposed. His wings were stretched and ripped, spread wide like an etymological specimen and pierced with needle-like stingers as a butterfly mounted for display.

And the mountain fed.

Lucifer watched as the eternal life force of the Kiln sucked Apollyon dry, yet the mountain also gave life and infused him with life from the Kiln in a perpetual cycle of draining and giving.

Lucifer watched as Apollyon burned and writhed in agony. His body weakened, and his framed diminished from Hell's insatiable appetite. Hell suckled on Apollyon's stone of fire.

Lucifer gawked at the cruelty of El. His mind angered that a creator who portrayed himself as the ultimate expression of benevolence would be evil enough to fashion a prison so torturous.

Enraged, Lucifer extended his claws and assumed his diamond form ready for battle. He launched himself headlong into the web.

"Release him now!" Lucifer shouted in defiance against the engorgement before him.

Acidic tendrils recoiled and snapped to attention. Cut asunder by the claws of the Chief Prince.

Lucifer entered the lattice and immediately his skin burned. Pain wracked his body as heavy fluid rushed in from a side chamber to fill the room and drown the duo in magma and acidic brimstone.

Lucifer's fight to rescue Apollyon came to a swift halt, as more tendrils shot from the walls. Hell would have the First of Angels; she would taste new flesh.

Lucifer hacked coil after coil, keeping each from ensnaring him as he marched ever closer to within inches of Apollyon.

Hell raised a wall of fire before Lucifer, and the concussive force knocked the angel from the air; his body slammed into the moist ground. Eyes liquefied underneath him and again the march of pyroclastic antibodies rose up from the floor ready to consume him. They wrapped their bodies over his feet and his arms as the Chief Prince lay prone, his back against the floor.

Lucifer looked up to see the same tendrils that held Apollyon slowly lower to entangle him. He struggled and the experience of fear for his own person gripped him for the first time, but only for a moment as panic slowly dissipated, and pride and anger filled his mind once more.

"I will not be denied! I *will* be like the most High!" Lucifer opened his mouth, exposed the trumpets and other horned instruments in his belly, and let out a shrieking cry. The sound blasted away the brimstone antibodies and smashed the lattice that held both him and Apollyon.

Hell heaved and lurched as its internal organs contorted from pain. Apollyon crashed to the magma floor. Lucifer grabbed Apollyon by the arm and lifted the barely conscious Arelim to his feet.

Lucifer looked to his rear as the hissing sound of the pyroclastic antibodies made their approach to engulf him. He quickly opened his mouth and recited the Elomic command to open a Ladder to Earth. White light bright as a star, formed around the battered duo and lightning crackled around them.

Hell again convulsed in pain as the eyes of the cavern floor turned red and the antigens multiplied and raced to swallow angel flesh.

Lucifer continued the chant and completed the command, and with the last phonetic utterance, the boom of a Ladder surged through the heated cavern. A flash of light sprayed across the chamber, and a ball of lightning engulfed the two. Lucifer staggered as he carried Apollyon, and as a man might jump from a cliff Lucifer leaped into the swirling drain of light, power, and magma. A chute that connected momentarily the realm of Hell with Earth.

Lucifer and Apollyon fell down the winding tunnel as galaxies and stars shot passed them. Lucifer gritted his teeth as he descended. Hell's connected entrails intermingled with the Ladder made them streak like a comet through

Earth's atmosphere.

His strategy to escape Hell was sure and with a great explosion, the foot of the Ladder touched the green earth with the sound of a thousand tree limbs snapping at once. The flames of Hellfire followed and scorched the ground.

Lucifer and Apollyon immediately materialized and slammed into the ground as the shock wave of their impact tossed redwoods and boulders to every side and blackened the soft ground beneath them.

Smoke, ash, and brimstone lined the crater. The sound of steam wafted into the air, and the crackle of burnt grass and wood filled the area while the acrid smell of ash and sulfur crammed the nostrils of all things that could smell.

Lucifer surveyed his surroundings, and as the ashy fog lifted, he saw Apollyon semi-conscious and sprawled out at his feet. The former Archon of Sol looked groggily upon Lucifer with dazed eyes and strained to speak.

"Thank you Chief Prince," said Abaddon. "I am in your debt."

Lucifer smiled as smoke slowly lifted from his diamond frame. His skin shown brilliantly against the sun's reflected rays, and he replied.

"Then let us go my friend, and wreak havoc on they which imprisoned thee."

****

"In this day I shall take my rest," said El.

"In this day you will have great tribulation, but be of good cheer. I have placed my faith in you. Rest your faith in me, and you shall come forth as pure gold," said El.

Michael and the rest of the council kneeled before El and listened to their Lord. El smiled and looked at them.

"My children, I leave you but for one day that all should be accomplished in accordance with my will." El then closed his eyes.

Immediately, the Shekinah Glory grew dim, lifted from off El, and rocketed out the palace flying over the city and towards the edge of Heaven, then dissipated to parts unknown. The light of Heaven retreated as the setting of the sun. The mountain of God grew dim and darkness crept over all the land. As the host of Heaven looked upon the dimming sky a fog rose from the ground. The temperature dropped and all of Heaven felt El's immediate presence no more.

The princes continued to kneel before their Lord and waited for dismissal, but word never came. Eventually, Michael looked at his master, walked towards the throne, laid prostrate before him and kissed his feet, but El did not stir.

Michael walked down the steps back towards his brothers who looked upon him with confusion.

Gabriel spoke first. "Michael, what shall we do?"

Sariel added. "How shall we function without El?"

Jerahmeel stood, walked towards Michael, hugged him and said, "Well, since Lucy's not here, looks like you're in charge. So what are your orders?"

Michael looked at them all. "We continue in our assignm…"

The sound of a hammer hitting metal came from the side chamber of the Kiln. Michael and the others quickly made their way to the Kiln door with its bronze exterior latticed with gold. They stared at the door and wondered.

It bulged outward as if impacted from the inside. Michael touched the protruding warped shape, his mind curious as to what force could damage the gate of heavy bronze.

"Perhaps Charon?" Michael said.

Raphael stared at the door, studied the bulge and observed how the door strained to stay attached to its hinges, and his countenance grew grim. The air moved from the escaping heat that blistered inside.

"Or something else," said Raphael.

"What else could it be, and what then of Charon?" asked Gabriel.

Suddenly the mountain of God shook from a tremor and they all shifted to keep from falling over.

The princes turned and quickly raced from the throne room. They exited the temple and stopped at the entrance to the temple doors outside. Each clamored to view Mt. Hell, which erupted and shook the ground of Heaven. Its roar was heard for miles, and they looked with telescopic eyes to see if Charon's dark statue of a figure was still present.

"Do you see him?" Talus said.

"No," Sariel replied.

Michael turned to his brother Gabriel and spoke.

"Gabriel go to Hell's maw and report what you find, but go quickly."

Gabriel nodded and vanished before them. In the distance, they saw that he now stood at the Maw. Gabriel stood atop the black rock of the entrance. The stench of sulfur bristled and pricked at his nose and made his skin itch. The mountain exhaled and wheezed as heated vent pockets rife with acidic steam shrouded the area in a warm dense blanket of fog.

Gabriel cautiously stepped over the ashen covered rock that jutted out from the jagged mountain floor. He groped to find the cliff walls and scrapped his hand as he looked to see Charon through the heavy mist. He strained and looked closer down the narrow channel and saw a bright reddish glow.

The Maw, he thought.

He walked closer and with every step, he could feel the heat of the Maw swipe at him. Closer he moved and the opening to Hell's mouth loomed ever larger. The heat blistered his skin and sweat began to bead from his brow.

Where is Charon? He wondered.

The air began to move as distortions from the heat; waved, danced, and shooed away the fog. The entrance was open and unguarded, bidding welcome to all that might brave entry.

The black and yellow lined stalagmites stood and threatened oblivion to all who might travel through her teeth. Lava oozed from between the caves stalactite gums like plaque.

The heat was unbearable, and steam began to hiss from Gabriel's boiling skin; his very flesh would be simmered alive if he dared remained much longer.

What was that?

Gabriel moved closer to the entrance, and Hell instinctually aware of angel flesh; opened her mouth to invite Gabriel in that she might savor him.

Gabriel inched closer.

Yes, there he is.

Deep within the throat of the mountain: plodding and dragging his intestine of chains and anchors of bondage behind him. The great dark cloaked figure of Charon burrowed deeper into the magma and acidic bile, his destination unknown. Gabriel watched as Charon disappeared into the fiery dark and he turned to return to his brethren.

Then Hell screamed.

****

Abaddon looked haggard. His face was pale and his eyes and extremities had turned a greenish pink. His body was a living welt, for marks from Hell's intrusions and Charon's lash had lacerated and decorated his frame. Scars ran across his face and back, and his once powerful wings were tattered.

Lucifer looked upon the Arelim and pitied him. Righteous anger flooded his soul, anger that a God who would dare demand fealty and righteousness would subject his own creation to such cruelty of spite.

"Ashtaroth!" Lucifer yelled.

The Issi came into his master's bedchamber and bowed at the open door.

"My Lord?" He said.

"Tell the elders of my return to Athor and command them to bid me audience within the hour. Let them know I have returned with Abaddon and a plan for our control of Heaven."

"Aye my Lord," Ashtaroth said and quickly left.

****

Charon trudged into Hell's belly and looked to find his captive escaped. Enraged, he raised his skeletal head and roared his outrage. In fury, he lifted his hammer-like fists into the air and slammed them down into the eyed floor. The eyes popped like melons thrown against concrete and Hell screamed in agony.

Charon's eyeless skull slowly scoured the cavern to see any sign of his foe, and with maggot, infested flesh: the half man, half mount of a creature managed to utter a sound to this cousin of the Kiln. The walls of Hell's stomach bubbled in acidic retort, and magma fell back upon itself to reveal the stone and charred floor of Hell's belly, a wound inflicted by the power of the living God to form a Ladder to another realm.

Charon lowered his equestrian nose to the floor and with nostrils that did not exist snorted to sniff out his prey, now rogue. Then a circular scar in

Hell's flesh appeared: a wound that could only come from a Ladder.

Instinct drove Charon, chains shot from his body, and he latched himself in the stone floor and wall as if feeling the scar. Dredging for clues to his quarry's whereabouts, he searched with manacled antennae and noticed something foreign on the far wall. Picking up the soft object, he eyed a tattered and charred piece of cloth of a presence alien to his prison.

A piece of robe — a trespasser of royal blood—the Chief Prince.

Once more with head arched back, Charon raged into the air.

He found the scent of Abaddon. His angelic flesh was familiar to the warden, and there were still pieces' of Abaddon's flesh lodged in the barbs of Charon's manacled whips. Now with this new piece of evidence, the pursuit for his captive could commence.

Charon placed the tattered piece of purple cloth in his breast and retracted his torso chains into his chest. He raised his hammer like arms into the air and struck them together. The sound reverberated within Hell's belly. He struck once more and a spark ignited for a moment, and then quickly dissipated.

Again, he pummeled his stone arms together, and again a flash ignited and then snuffed out. With a cry of rage and invocations of unintelligible retribution, Charon slammed his own arms against one another as a flint would smite a rock, and a spark ensued.

The spark morphed, and lightning suddenly filled Hell's belly. The white light of a Ladder encircled Charon and washed him in iridescent heat. Hell convulsed and groaned her innards of brimstone, magma, and flame once more invaded by the creative power of the living God.

Crackles of lightning streaked across the chasm and arched back unto Charon. His iron and manacled body kissed and welcomed each charged embrace. Wider the electric field grew and arrayed the cavern in tentacled streams of plasma.

He raised his mighty arms of hammers and slammed them into Hell's floor, and bolts of lightning struck the cavern floor. Hell wailed, her cry soared to the ears of the denizens of Heaven itself, thunder rocketed across the sky, and all looked to see the mountain rumble and quake.

Charon pummeled the floor of the mountain once more. It cracked, and lightning walloped the spot and left its mark deeper in Hell's flesh.

Again, he struck the ground. The living mountain screamed and wailed its disapproval and cried out in pain.

Fractures appeared, and Hell heaved as magma splashed around the mighty warden of torment. Again, he crashed his arms into Hell's floor, and the might of his stroke broke through the charred and rocky ground and gave way.

The mighty angel fell as the floor beneath him buckled, and the Ladder collapsed and converted into a chute of fire and brimstone. A shaft, which funneled its way through space and time and pierced the barriers that divided the Third Heaven from all other realms and Charon fell.

Earth and Elohim smote one another as the impact of Charon's arrival bore the crust of the planet. He was welcomed with dirt, rock, and dust flung high into the air and the shattering sound of a thousand trees.

Hell's fire soon followed him, and where the fire of the physical universe sat quietly in consumption of air and carbon: Hell's fire was not so. The very ground liquefied, the air disappeared, and sulfur unpacked its bags and lined the brimstone filled crater with her stench and yellowish touch.

A pillar of fire stretched as a tower might pierce the atmosphere and found its home in Hell's paunch; its heat wilted and blackened the ground for miles. Earth retreated as life and color quickly raced to escape the perimeter of the flaming entrails that hung from Hell's belly.

Smoke and heat emanated from the crater, and newly created birds and beast were intelligent enough to remove themselves from the vicinity.

Charon lumbered forth from the freshly minted hollow; his manacles dangled as they touched the soft earthen soil. He lowered his skeletal nose to the ground, captured the scent that his barbed chains had left in Abaddon's flesh, and rose to look across the horizon.

A city stood many miles away. Less than a day's journey for the elephant paced angel. Nevertheless, time held no meaning to an immortal: and he would see Abaddon ferried home.

Charon had come to Earth for his prisoner and Hellfire had come with him.

****

"Bear witness to the impotence of El," said Lucifer. "A creator of a prison that I can enter and leave with its captives at will. Behold! I give you Abaddon and know that nothing is impossible to them that believe!"

Abaddon walked before the elders of Athor. The abrasion's and lesion's on his skin gave testimony to the harshness of Hell's bondage. Although scarred, he was unbowed and spoke. "The Chief Prince has apprised me of his plan. I was catalyst for his actions: his need to question the goodness of El. Question no more! See with thine own eyes the pity of our God!

"Grigoric history tells of Argoth and his supposedly prophetic declaration of the person of the Lord. According to him, when the Lord created him, and he looked upon his maker for the first time, he was so stunned, so overwhelmed that he was as a man in a trance and walked to the edge of the mountain of the Lord, looked out over the expanse of the Kingdom of Heaven and proclaimed…"

189

'The LORD, The LORD God, merciful and gracious, longsuffering, and abundant in goodness and truth, Keeping mercy for thousands, forgiving iniquity and transgression and sin, and that will by no means clear the guilty, visiting the iniquity of the fathers upon the children, and upon the children's children, unto the third and to the fourth generation.'

"What need have we of prophecies? What other lies have been told us? Are my lashes evidence of His mercy and graciousness? Are *my* shred wings testimony to His goodness and truth?"

"I was once Apollyon. I am now Abaddon, the Destroyer. I side with Lucifer and pledge myself to *he* who relieved me of the torment of Hell's belly. I will not serve a master that will not answer prayer, nor submit to a Lord who will not be found when sought. I stand here before you due to one who did not despise my cause. I was sought of one who braved the monster Charon and has returned!"

Abaddon turned to Lucifer and pointed at him.

"He will be my God and King!"

Abaddon turned again to face the assembly.

"Who among you will stand with us, or will you continue to cower under the shadow of the Almighty? Let go of this fear and break free of El's shackle and serve the Chief Prince!"

The great assembly hall was quiet. The gravity of the words spoken, and the actions taken would ring through Heaven and they all knew it. No one moved and no one spoke.

Suddenly, the assembly doors opened, and without invitation: Ashtaroth walked through the center of those gathered within the hall and marched to approach his Lord.

Lucifer eyed his servant and was silent.

"How dare he!" said one attendee.

Ashtaroth did not speak but continued and upon reaching his master's feet, knelt in common formality as was his custom, then rose.

"Remove this vassal," said one.

"He has no place here," said another.

The group became more unruly over the intrusion.

Lucifer raised his hand to silence them, and Ashtaroth looked into Lucifer's eyes and spoke.

"Cans't thou truly do as thou hast said?" Ashtaroth asked.

"I can," Lucifer replied.

Ashtaroth then bowed his face to the floor. He laid prostrate for a moment, then rose to his knees and spoke, "My Lord and my God!"

He turned to face them all that they might see and ripped his robes from his breast to reveal the sigil stone that bared his name. He reached into his chest to remove it, held it high for all to gaze, and carved in it a new name.

Slowly he dug his fingernail into the stone, scratched from its face the name given to him by El in the Kiln, and wrote a name of his own choosing. Each etch of a new letter caused him to change physically before their eyes.

Slowly, the slim and nimble Issi grew large. His flesh turned dark and spiky, and bony protrusions erupted from his flesh. Fire flared up around him as the sigil stone of fire melted his features and reformed him after a new image and a new likeness. His frail butterfly wings changed and grew transparent as like a dragonfly, and he stopped writing and held his stone up for all to see. His voice clearly changed as he spoke in a deeper bass.

"I am Astarte, Governor of the House of Lucifer, my Lord and my God."

And as the muscular insectoid creature stood before and held up his sigil stone: Tiamat, Mammon, Zeus, Cadfiel, Asmodeus, Dagon, Thammuz, Murmur, Mephisto, and countless others removed their sigil stones, held them high, bowed before Lucifer, and began to etch and alter their stones.

Lucifer beheld as each one transformed before him, and when the transformation of all was complete, and the elders had bowed before him. Lucifer looked upon the first of those that he would rule and smiled.

"I see a glorious day when the Creator will hang from a tree. Let us usher in that day now. Here — in this hall." He said.

Abaddon looked upon his newly appointed Lord and spoke.

"What is thy command, my King?"

Lucifer looked upon them all and replied, "Secure Athor. Gather those loyal to our cause and assemble in the great court."

"And what of those that will not serve?" Abaddon asked.

Lucifer was somewhat slow to reply.

"Then dissolution awaits them."

Abaddon smirked, and his eyes gleamed with anticipation.

"Thy will be done Lord King."

****

"Report," Michael said.

Gabriel had come from Mt. Hell and panted frantically.

"Charon has left the maw. Hell's mouth stands unguarded!"

"Are you sure?" asked Jerahmeel.

"Aye, I saw Charon move deep within the mount…his destination — I cannot say." Gabriel said.

Michael turned to look at Raphael. "Can you track him?"

"He has no Grigori; hence, he has no log," replied Raphael.

192

Michael thought for a moment and paced the entry steps to the temple.

"What is it Michael?' said Talus.

Michael stopped to reply.

"We must locate Lucifer. Jerahmeel go to his palace and seek query as to his whereabouts. Raphael and I will track the Grigori of Athor and its vicinity. The rest of you return to your assignments. Creation still needs governance, and nothing must be undone while El is on Sabbath."

Each angel took to the sky as Michael and Raphael reentered the temple palace.

"Have you shared with the others what you shared with me?" queried Michael.

"No," Raphael replied. "Only the Lord, you, and I know the extent of what Lucifer and Lilith have discussed."

"Then I think we should delve deeper," said Michael.

"Agreed." replied Raphael.

The two brothers made their way into the room of the Zoa and Michael moved with greater swiftness in his steps than before. Upon entry to the Hall of Annals, Raphael pulled Lucifer's tome, placed it on a podium, and the room turned white. The tome levitated in midair and then Raphael spoke to the room.

"Rescind to Third Heaven: Current location of Lucifer Draco."

The room flashed multiple colors and then went white.

Raphael looked perplexed and repeated his command. "Rescind to Third Heaven: Current location of Lucifer Draco."

Once more, the great room flashed in response. Colors, of the rainbow arched across the walls, floor, and ceiling, stopped, and then white stained the entire Hall.

"Uh — Raphael?" Michael said.

"Hmmph," said Raphael. "Regress to last encounter with El."

The room flashed to obey. Reds, blues, and greens washed upon the wall until an image displayed. Lucifer was shown as bowed before El and pleading for Apollyon's release. El's admonition to grieve silently replayed for the duo and then the room went white.

"Curious," said Raphael.

"What is it?" Michael asked.

Raphael lifted his finger to urge Michael to wait.

"Regress to last known presence in Third Heaven," said Raphael.

Again, the room flashed the colors of the spectrum and Michael's eyes darted to see what the chamber would show next.

The same image flashed of Lucifer kneeling before the Lord, pleading Abaddon's case.

"That's not right," said Michael.

"Aye," Raphael replied. "Lucifer was at the communion table with us before El dismissed him to do whatever he was assigned to do."

"Then where is the rest of his record?" Michael said.

Raphael rubbed his chin in thought. "Based on what we have seen here, there is no record from this point onward."

"That's impossible," said Michael.

"No," Raphael said. "Not impossible, just highly improbable."

"But who could change — wait — *no!*"

"Lilith has altered Lucifer's tome," said Raphael.

Raphael looked curiously at the image on the wall and spoke.

"Reveal: Grigoric tome: Ashtaroth," Raphael commanded.

Immediately a new book appeared on the podium.

"I have a concern that more might be amiss than I was lead to believe," said Raphael.

"Oh?" Michael said.

"Indeed. Ashtaroth is always near his master or has knowledge of his whereabouts. If I am correct we have a larger problem than just Lucifer and Lilith," said Raphael.

"Rescind to Third Heaven: the current location of Ashtaroth," spoke Raphael.

The room exploded in color and then flashed to white.

"As I feared," said Raphael.

"What?" Michael said.

"Regress to last known presence in Third Heaven," said Raphael

Again, the room burst forth in colors, and images raced across the room and stopped at Ashtaroth's encounter with Lucifer at the temple waypoint: after the Chief Prince had returned from the completion of Eden.

"We have a serious problem, Michael."

"What do you see?"

"My concern is what I *do not* see. Ashtaroth's record has changed. The record shows that he greeted Lucifer upon his return, but if this is his last known presence, then when does it show him leaving the Third Heaven?"

Michael stared at the image. "You're right. If he left Heaven, this surely was not the time it occurred."

"Indeed," said Raphael.

Michael stared at Raphael, "What else is wrong?"

"Michael these records are not just altered. A Grigori has rewritten history. Our problem extends greater than simply Lucifer at this point. These two records indicate that a plan is underway to rewrite history and or to conceal current information. This does not bode well."

"Lilith?" Michael asked.

"He and others I fear," said Raphael. "I suspect Lucifer and Ashtaroth will not be the only ones whose tomes have changed. Michael, someone has knowingly ceased documenting history. This incident is not just a coincidence with Lucifer but extends to his servant as well. I fear that this is an attempt to conceal information, from me."

"But why," said Michael. "To what end?"

"I do not know exactly," said Raphael, "but I intend to find out."

"How?"

"I will go to Athor and most likely find Lilith there. There can be no other way to investigate this other than by addressing the source."

Michael looked at Raphael curiously. "Go to Earth—you? You have never left the capital, my friend. Besides, there are few who have Elomic commands to travel, and I know that you do not possess one."

Raphael laughed. "I have seen the far reaches of creation and El has not limited travel to an Elomic command."

Raphael clapped his hand and the room flashed white.

"Reveal: Grigoric tome of Athor."

Immediately the room changed colors, and the three-dimensional landscape of Athor became visible. Raphael's tome and inkhorn appeared, and he took his stylus and wrote the words, 'Enter'. Raphael then walked into the wall and stepped onto a field that was just outside the city. Michael was stunned, for he never had seen this form of travel.

"Michael I shall return soon, but I suggest that you proceed to the Maw."

"Why?" Michael asked.

Raphael continued to walk while half of his body seemed to be in two

196

places at once as he spoke.

"Hell's tome glows with activity."

He pointed to a book on his shelf; it flared as if the contents would explode. Michael turned to his rear watching the tome grow larger.

Raphael engulfed fully in the wall appeared as if he were a part of a painting and spoke from within the image.

"Take the tome with you, for it will protect you from what lies within, and allow you to freely travel within Hell. Find Charon. I do not know what would move him from the maw, but if he has disappeared from his charge something is terribly wrong."

"Agreed," said Michael. "But what of you?"

"I will search for Lilith; determine the extent of the corruption to the Grigori and of their tomes. Be careful my friend," said Raphael.

"Be well," Michael replied.

Michael watched as Raphael floated further into the picture on the wall as the room erupted in color once more and then went white.

****

Lucifer sat with his newly appointed court. His home in Athor was large and palatial. Its quartz walls pulsated with the sun's light and refracted it in brilliant color.

"Now," said Mephisto, "explain to us your plan. How would you bring down El?"

Lucifer leaned forward in his chair and spoke.

"El's forces are scattered across the three heavens, but only those within the capital concern us for now, of which only a quarter of all Elohim reside. We on Athor and Earth alone comprise a third while the rest are strewn throughout the realms. We have numerical superiority on our side."

Dagon shifted in his seat and replied. "We do, aye, but only until word of our actions reaches the host in the second heaven. Once they realize what has transpired, they will surely overwhelm us."

Lucifer smiled. "That too I have carefully anticipated. You see Lord Dagon; to fight Heaven head-on is foolish. We would surely perish, but what if Heaven were made to battle against herself?" Lucifer grinned.

Tiamat raised his head. "Intriguing—say on."

"There has existed a growing schism between house Arelim and Issi since Saesheal's demise. We shall exploit this void of fellowship amongst the brethren and fill it with something else."

Thammuz looked at Lucifer and spoke, "Lucifer do not speak in riddles; speak plainly!"

Lucifer smirked. "We will fill it with murmur."

Murmur raised his head. "My Lord?"

Lucifer laughed at the irony. "We will set brother against brother, Issi against Arelim, and we will wait until they themselves eat away at their own strength, and at the pinnacle of their division, we will strike, sweeping aside any that would oppose us. In their confusion, they will reel before our attack. If we move quickly we can circumvent the loss of brother or significant damage to the city."

The lieutenants sat quietly and nodded. "There is wisdom in your plan Lucifer," said Zeus. "Yet there is still much work to be done."

"Indeed" replied Lucifer. "Ashtaroth and I will return with Murmur; our assignment will be to provoke the Princes Talus and Sariel to engage. We will incite the two great houses to attack one another. Once the battle has begun, Abaddon will assault Heaven at the place of my choosing. The rest of you will protect the waypoints. No Ladders can be made into the realm or Heaven's legions reinforced until we have accomplished our mission.

Cadfiel looked unconvinced and spoke, "And what is *your* mission Lord King?"

"I will enter the Kiln, secure it, and awaken the God Stone within. Once I possess the power of El, I will create a new race of Elohim who will be unleashed throughout all three heavens to do our bidding. By the time El awakens from his rest it will be too late."

Cadfiel laughed mockingly. "This is your plan? We have but one day to accomplish this and if we fail: when El awakes, He will but snuff us all out with a thought! Alas, even if you might do as thou hast said and become as El when he awakens he will of a surety seek our destruction."

The lieutenants looked at one another with concern. Lucifer eyed them and spoke.

"Nay Lord Cadfiel, he will do no such thing. El will be given a choice, for when all things have been set into motion, he will abdicate the throne. If he does not capitulate then I will destroy his beloved creation, starting with his prized possession: the humans. We will garrison the Earth, the garden, and Athor. If I do not arrive, you will see to its destruction. I bargain that El will not let his creation be destroyed. I realized this when he created Hell as opposed to oblivion for Abaddon. You see Lord Cadfiel, El loves. His love and readiness to spare will be his undoing. No. El will yield; He will have no choice when He sees all of creation threatened. And on that day my brothers, we will serve the triune God no more!"

Michael climbed down from Mt. Zion, flew across his great city, and landed at the steps of the Maw. The silicate breath of the caves entrance stung his eyes and scratched his throat. The heat belched from the great cavern, and fire leapt to lick Michael's face. Hell seemed agitated, and lava oozed across her black gums. He looked through the steam and saw that Charon was absent from his post.

I will be protected, thought Michael.

Michael swallowed hard and stepped into the fires of Hell. Fire and brimstone washed over his body as Hell's saliva of sulfur and magma cleansed her palate to consume the Elohim. The giant ferrous, black stalagmite teeth shut tight behind him.

The heat intensified and Michael began to understand the horror that Abaddon must have felt. He looked at his hands as the flames attempted to broil the flesh from his bones, but Hell would be denied this day as Michael stood his ground in the midst of Hell's maw.

"Oh, mount of anguish and torment hear me! I come neither guilty nor with guile. I seek thy ward Charon! Deny me not, for I come in the name of the Lord of Hosts!"

The ground buckled, and Michael lost his footing. Red-blistered eyes lifted from beneath the magma and stared at him. Orifices protruded from the walls, hissing and bearing razors for teeth. Pyroclastic forms bubbled from the surface of Hell's floor and made their way towards the Chief Prince. Each slid and hissed as they did. Michael clutched Hell's Tome and stood his ground eyeing the encircling creatures rising from the floor.

"Attack me at thy peril, creature, but thou hast been warned!"

Hell was a living mountain whose consciousness was aware on only the smallest of levels. All it knew was that within its maw was Elomic flesh. Hell hungered, and it would engorge itself on this little angel.

Tendrils shot out from the walls and flame, magma, and ash flared up in front of the high prince. A tendril of fire wrapped around Michael's legs and lifted him high into the air. Michael wailed in pain and clutched the book. Another tendril reached out to clasp his hands and then another. Michael thrashed as a fly captured in a spider's web as dozens of tendrils shot from the walls and enveloped him in a cocoon of magma. His clothing burned, but when the tendrils of heated flame touched the pages of the tome Michael carried, Hell screamed.

Hell's coils quickly retracted, and Michael fell hard to the ground. The eyes in the floor glared at him with pupils' red with rage and hissed at him.

"Yes, creature I carry thy tome. Now I query you again! Where is Charon?"

The mountain rumbled, and the antigens of lava melted into the floor. The hiss of steam subsided, and all the tentacles pointed deep into the darkness that was Hell's throat. The magma on the floor parted and revealed dry, black ground underneath. The lava pillowed up to the sides to form a pathway.

Michael followed the trail laid before him. Walking carefully, he ventured to neither the right nor left. The lava flows gave off a reddish-orange glow just bright enough to see. On both sides of him were rows of eyes and orifices that gnashed, spitting out ash and sulfur. Michael wheezed and coughed, and the smell and heavy fumes filled his lungs. His clothes blackened; and like a grey ghost, the Prince of Heaven walked the empty floor of Hell.

Deeper he traveled into the hallways, making note of his whereabouts and observing each corridor and cave. Cavern after cavern bubbled with fire and the walls oozed with sticky goo, ready to imprison and feed off any soul damned to abide inside. Michael then began to understand the wrath of the Lord.

His vengeance on any who do him or his own harm: would find themselves spending eternity in a living monstrosity consumed for all eternity. They would broil mingled in the fires of the Kiln that sustained life, and roasted in the fires of the Hell that took it. In that moment, Michael understood both the goodness and the severity of God.

Oblivion would not be an escape, and dissolution would be denied. For here within the hollow of the beast, one would be damned to live forever only to die as fodder for a creature that lived off the tortured agony and eternal spirit of its host, surrounded in the flickering light of flame for an eternity only to watch one's flesh slowly eaten alive. Michael marveled at the thing that was Hell and quickened his pace. He did not wish to remain there long.

Michael traveled over some floors soft and others of firmness, walking through branch, pipe, and conduit until finally in the distance. Michael could see light and relief flooded him.

Closer he came to a huge chamber and it was there that he saw it. The Bowel, a massive walled cavern of living fire, lined with eyes and latticed with teeth, and he could tell it was here, within the deepest pits of the mountain the true horrors of digestion played themselves out. For on the lining of Hell's stomach, images splayed themselves before Michael of all Abaddon's doings.

His first consciousness of waking from the Kiln, his accolades as Son of the Dawn, his judgment as he fell screaming into the pit of Hell, all that was his life played out before him. Moreover, Michael saw that Charon was not just a warden but also an instrument of vengeance, that deep within the belly of this beast of fire and brimstone, he replayed for his victim his life, a moving mural painted for Abaddon to relive. Hell feasted on regret and nourished herself off anguish and remorse. It was here that Hell grew obese from the weeping and gnashing of teeth.

Tattered remains of clothing and regal garb littered the floor, and Arelim flesh was stuck into the walls. Michael snapped from his staring as lightning arched across the ceiling and shot out from through the floor. He rushed to the sparks source to see moving in the center of the floor a whirlpool of lightning, fire, and brimstone that drained into a shaft of light.

A Ladder, he thought but unlike any, he had ever seen.

He looked into the great vortex, and it was as a funnel that ran from Hell's stomach through space itself. Hell lurched, and shook, and, the mountain groaned, and its guttural displeasure echoed throughout the cavern, and the mount expanded.

Charon was gone. Michael covered his eyes to see against the lightning, which arced within the cavern. He moved and flew above the edge of the "chute" and could see the Earth in the great distance at the bottom. The horror of the situation grabbed him. Hell had enlarged herself and had made foothold on Earth.

****

Raphael saw Elohim go about their business on the streets. Each took their assignments from their Archons, as his people dutifully took note of their surroundings and hovered ever so silently out of sight in the presence of their charge.

Nothing seems amiss, he thought.

Raphael passed into the street unseen to all, but his own people. Various Grigori bowed and or acknowledge their Lord. Some looked at him and others stared, but all continued in their duties. Looking around, he made out Ashtaroth in the distance and ran over to get a closer look.

What is this! He has no Grigori to accompany him!

Raphael turned to one of his fellow Grigori. "Tell me, have you seen the Grigori for Ashtaroth?"

The Grigori smiled and floated away after his charge.

Raphael gawked at the behavior in disbelief.

"My people," Raphael shouted speaking into the ether so that only his kind could hear. "Where is the steward for Ashtaroth?"

Each Grigori continued to float past their Lord, and Raphael looked on in amazement.

Ashtaroth then stopped, turned around, and looked squarely at Raphael.

Immediately dozens, then hundreds of other angels stopped and turned or stood to look at him as well.

Raphael's eyes darted across the street and he noted that all had ceased moving and slowly started walking towards him, and Raphael backed away. From the court behind Ashtaroth, the doors into Athor's castle opened. Lucifer, Zeus, and Mephisto stepped into view, and all of their assigned Grigori floated behind them and walked through the center of the street straight towards Raphael's path: and Lilith smiled at Raphael as they approached.

A group of angels landed, barred his path and encircled him.

"There is no need to yell or leave my prince. In fact…," said Lilith, "we insist that you stay."

Raphael began to run.

"Restrain him," Lilith said.

Grigori in the vicinity swarmed over their Prince, tackled him, and held him down to the ground. Raphael struggled to rise, but their grip was strong, and they were too many.

"Lilith, what is the meaning of this outrage! All of you release me immediately or incur the wrath of a High Prince!"

Some of the Grigori loosened their grip, and Lilith hurried to their side.

"Do no such thing," said Lilith.

Lilith raised Raphael to his feet and searched his person. He reached and confiscated his inkhorn, stylus, and tome, and upon doing so, Raphael immediately became visible to all.

"Ah much better," said Lucifer. "Raphael, it is so good to see you, my brother. However, I must admit I am disappointed that you felt it necessary to be secretive of your presence here. It was not necessary I assure you."

"Your hospitality Chief Prince means little to me when I am forcibly held."

"My apologies my friend — perhaps if you had been more forthright in your own activities, mine own actions would be less circumspect? Of course, I'm sure if I just *chose* to walk into the Hall of Annals, you would equally great me with such *hospitality*?"

"The Lord rebuke you, Lucifer Draco," said Raphael.

"Not today my little prince…," said Lucifer. "Not today."

Lucifer turned to walk back into the palace, and his entourage followed.

"Bring him," said Lucifer.

Raphael struggled as his captors held him tight. Lilith walked before him and spoke.

"Raphael, why do you resist? We will not harm you. Surely, you know that. After all, are you not the Prince Lord of all Grigori?" Lilith laughed mockingly.

Raphael smirked and retorted, "If I were *your* prince, then this conversation would be but imagined. You are a disgrace to our species."

They entered the palace and Lucifer directed several of his attendants to other tasks.

"Lilith, have Raphael brought to my chambers."

Lilith frowned. "Lord King it was my desire to query him before…"

"Enough Lilith: you may sport with him later. Bring him now."

"Yes my King," said Lilith.

"So," said Raphael. "You lower yourself from the position of Watcher to that of dog only to take orders from a rogue angel?"

Lilith moved closer to whisper in Raphael's ear.

"Pray that Lucifer will be merciful, for I most assuredly will not."

Lilith shoved Raphael down to the floor and closed the door behind him leaving Lucifer and Raphael alone within Lucifer's chamber hall.

"Are you hungry?" asked Lucifer. "We are not graced to have manna which grows on Gaia, but I would be remiss if I failed to show hospitality even at this juncture."

"Keep your bread, 'Lightbringer'. I am not here to dine with you, and what is Gaia?"

Lucifer put down a glass of water he was preparing to drink. "Ahh, yes, I have determined that Earth is too trite of a name. Gaia would be more appropriate for my home. Of course, that leads us to the real question my brother: why are you here?"

"You are filled with wisdom Lucifer, but for all your fullness, you have filled yourself beyond measure. Save your melodious pretense. I know of your words that you have echoed about El, and more importantly 'Lightbringer', the Lord himself knows."

"Ah, so you have come to reason with me? Or perhaps you come to incite the 'fear of the Lord', into me?"

Raphael spoke condescendingly. "The fear of the Lord does not dwell

206

in this place Chief Prince."

Lucifer laughed. "Indeed, it does, for my citizens clearly have demonstrated their ability to serve me, my friend."

"What do you want with me Lucifer?"

I, Raphael, desire nothing more than your allegiance. What is thy desire? Are you truly satisfied to sit in the Halls of Annals and live vicariously through others? Would you not prefer to explore the stellar phenomena that you see through your great hall? I, dear brother, can offer you that. Observe and document?"

Lucifer chuckled.

"Imagine a world where you might add your own ideas and opinions to that which you see. How more colorful and varied such a universe would be to explicate and not just simply to document? Have you no judgment on El's actions towards Abaddon? Was he not wrong to give the Earth to the humans? Or are you simply resolved to sit idle and watch our kind dissipate into oblivion only to serve as chattel? *We* are the superior beings. The strong ought not to bear the infirmities of the weak. Yet El would have us prattle to these creatures of mud and clay. Follow me Raphael, and we shall rule the heavens together."

Raphael watched Lucifer and was silent in his response.

"I will leave for Heaven shortly. I leave you to Lilith who is most anxious to assume your role upon my ascent to the throne."

"You are mad Lucifer. You will never usurp El," said Raphael.

Lucifer turned to leave and looked at his brother.

"What is madness? I merely speak those things that be not as though they were."

Lucifer closed the door behind him.

Lilith walked with Lucifer as his master prepared to depart.

"He is dangerous Lucifer. His presence could be disruptive. I would take his stone now."

"No. He is my brother and a Chief Prince. There will be time soon enough for dissolution, and when and if it comes it will be at my command."

"Yes Lord King. But may I suggest that a watch be placed to guard him?"

"Very well, you and Abaddon see to his keeping. However, once you are done with him, I expect you and Astarte to return to Jerusalem."

Lucifer turned and raised his finger to Lilith's face. "And Lilith…"

"Yes, Lord King."

"Raphael is not to be harmed."

"Yes, Lord King."

Lucifer and Lilith continued to walk and entered the room where several of Lucifer's lieutenants were laying out their plans.

"Report of thy stewardship," said Lucifer.

Zeus was first to speak as Abaddon and several other angels looked on in smiles.

"Our brother Cadfiel has developed a tool to assist us in battle."

"Really?" Lucifer said. "Show it to me."

Cadfiel came forward and placed before his master a plow shear, the blade had been straightened and beaten flat. It possessed a razors edge and the handle was stout and strong. Cadfiel laid it at the feet of his master and stepped away.

Lucifer picked up the blade, held it high, and examined it as he turned it from side to side.

"My brethren behold. An instrument of peace and toil now conformed into a weapon of liberation. This tool shall be a sword and the symbol of our righteous cause. Well done Cadfiel. You and Zeus see to it that our legions are outfitted accordingly. Spare no resource. You Cadfiel, I see have a unique gift. What name hast thou selected to dispense the stench of El's ownership from thy stone?

Cadfiel spoke immediately, "Ares, my Lord."

"Thou hast chosen well," Lucifer replied, "And war chieftain shalt thou be."

"My Lord King," said Zeus.

"Yes, what is it?" said Lucifer.

"How will we succeed in our invasion of Heaven? As the waypoints prevent our entering the realm en mass"

Lucifer smiled. "You will not Ladder to a waypoint, my friend. No. You shall bombard Heaven herself with our Ladders and within the great city walls and our legions shall appear and wreak havoc."

"Do you know what that will do the landscape and denizens of Heaven?" Zeus said.

Lucifer frowned, "Yes, but it must be done."

Abaddon laughed.

****

Michael landed on the spot where Charon had fallen. His entrance was less traumatic to the ground than Charon's own fall. Smoke hissed as the Ladder of fire and brimstone reached into the sky. The inferno of Hell's entrails dug deep into the Earth's crust.

Soon she will hit the core and when that happens, he thought, Hell would have home on two planes of existence. He wondered to himself how a Ladder could be made within the belly of Hell and only one word came to the forefront of his mind—Lucifer.

Michael moved a little away from the heated flue that towered into the sky and began to survey the area. If Charon had come here, where would he go? Michael turned to the east of where he stood and saw Athor gleam in the distance. He looked down at the ground and saw the long trail left from the heavy manacles that dragged behind the body of Charon. He followed them and the trail lead directly to Athor. Intuitively he lifted his body into the air and flew.

Faster his wings carried him, and in the distance ahead he saw him. Hell's warden marched on a path directly towards the quartz city. Charon's trail was easy to follow as boulders and trees were smashed in his wake. The mark of his presence being the long segmented trail of his chains, as the barbs attached to the ends, plowed themselves into the earth.

Charon was easy to find.

Michael thought to himself. God help him whom Charon finds. Michael had now caught up with this Elomic bulldozer. He hovered above him and examined the beast so unique among Elohim. Charon was unresponsive to Michael's presence, his skeletal face vacant of any expression. There was no smile, no flushed cheeks, nor raised eyebrow that might cause one to perceive emotion. There was nothing but the continual plodding of the giant, and where Charon was headed, Abaddon could not be far.

Michael continued on his journey and began to approach the city limits. He settled down far enough and landed behind a tree to conceal himself.

My clothes — surely I will be recognized.

Michael stripped off his royal robes and laid them under a rock. With the colors of the Builder of Heaven from off his body, he pulled his cloak over his face and walked the rest of the way to Athor. Moving through one of the side city gates, he watched the hustle and bustle of the angels as they ran to and from their assigned tasks.

Michael walked up the glass-lined street and saw Lucifer and Ashtaroth make their way to the front of the city gate. Several archons accompanied him including Murmur. Michael followed them as they made their way outside the city. He closed to within earshot and overheard Lucifer speak.

"Lilith you may remove Raphael from my hospitality and find a room suitable for him. Since he has refused to worship me, you may dispense with him as you see fit. Are the swords ready?"

"Aye Lord King. Zeus and the others are distributing them as we speak."

"Excellent," said Lucifer. "You have done well."

Michael watched as Lilith bowed and left to attend to Raphael.

Lucifer and his entourage leapt into the air and Ladders formed which lifted the trio out of sight.

Michael turned to follow Lilith. His thoughts raced as to why his brother would be confined against his will. *Was Lucifer seeking worship?* Michael continued to follow Lilith through the various streets and avenues of the great city until a center palace was come upon. He watched as Lilith opened the palatial doors and walked inside.

Michael studied the building and noticed it had few windows except at its peak. The whole structure had a transparency within it. Michael watched as Lilith ascended a spiral tower to the tallest room of the palace. The room was not transparent, and he wondered to himself if this was Lucifer's private chamber. From the entrance of the room, Abaddon stepped out smiling and laughing.

Abaddon has escaped, thought Michael. Michael looked up at the sun and realized that it was close to noonday. Charon would be within the city limits soon. Michael thought of a plan to secure Raphael's release. He would use

Charon's presence as a distraction to secure Raphael's freedom.

Quickly he moved to an alley where he could not be seen, and dashed into the sky. He then landed by the tree outside the city limits and found the stone where his royal robes lay. He dressed himself and made sure that his regalia would be noticed.

Michael then launched himself back into the air and concentrated: moments later a Ladder formed. Michael entered the cone, and sound and lightning flashed behind him. Traveling beyond the speed of light, he turned his direction back towards Earth and focused his entry to the courtyard. *There must be no mistake that the Builder of Heaven has arrived.*

The Ladder turned upon his command, and the planet loomed before him as Athor's central court quickly sprinted into view. The sonic boom of thunder clapped, and Michael materialized in the center of town for all to see.

"Hail. I Michael of the Kortai have come with words for Lucifer. Make way for the Prince of Heaven."

Immediately those that saw Michael looked as if they were undone. Some bowed, others looked frightened as if caught doing something amiss, but all stopped immediately to stare at the High Prince.

Good, he thought. *They were not expecting me.* He spoke again, "To Lucifer's quarters. You steward, attend me. Direct thy prince forthwith."

A Kortai warrior came quickly at the High Prince's command and replied.

"This way Lumazi."

Michael walked behind the angel, and they hastily came to Lucifer's palace.

"What is your name Kortai?" said Michael.

"Iofiel, my Prince."

Michael looked again at the transparent quartz, diamond, glass, and emerald palace made to house the glory of the Lord. Now it was Lucifer's home while away from Heaven. Abaddon was nowhere to be found.

He should be here shortly, Michael thought.

Iofiel knocked on the doors, and both Michael and he could see that several of Lucifer's vassals came quickly to answer the door.

Michael dismissed him. "Thank you Iofiel you may return to your tasks."

"Thank you High Prince," came the reply, and Iofiel paused, looked warily at Michael as if to speak, and then flew out of sight.

Immediately the door opened, and Michael walked through not waiting for an invitation and spoke.

"Hail. The Builder of Heaven command's audience with my brother Lucifer. Where is he?"

Startled and tripping over themselves, the house angels stumbled over their words.

"High Prince Michael," said one.

"Oh my," said another.

Several bowed as was custom when in the presence of a Lumazi; the others stood and spoke.

"He is not here my Lord. The Chief Prince has taken leave of the palace, and we do not know of his return or of his…"

Michael interrupted.

"Your knowledge is not necessary. I will wait. Escort me to the guest room as my journey has wearied me, and I long for rest before my return, and I would see the palace designed for El once more before I take my leave to Heaven."

213

Michael immediately stepped to enter the winding staircase, and several of the angels scurried to go before him to slow him.

"Ah my Lord, perhaps it would be best if thou retire to the main chamb..."

"Nonsense," said Michael. "Would you bar access to he who stands before the presence of God?"

"Uh, of course not my lord," said one.

Michael reached the top of the steps and began to turn the handle of the door.

"My Lord, please allow me to acquire linens and fresh manna for thy visit," said the attendant.

"You may depart," said Michael.

Quickly they ran back downstairs to parts unknown. Michael opened the door and stepped in.

Raphael sat across from him, his hands were shackled, and his mouth gagged. Lilith stood over him and held Raphael's inkhorn, stylus, and tome.

"What is the meaning of this outrage?" Michael demanded.

Lilith smiled and spoke, "Please come in High Prince and join us."

"Explain yourself Grigori! Release the High Prince or be judged."

"Oh I think not my prince," said Lilith.

Raphael's gag muffled his speech, but his warning to Michael was clear.

Michael heard steps behind him and then a thud. Pain raced across the back of his head, and he fell hard to the floor. As he looked up, he saw the face of Abaddon who had pummeled him from behind with a statue. Michael smiled as he hit the floor and went unconscious.

His plan had worked perfectly.

Chapter Seven

Nothing Covered…

End of day Six.

"Astarte we must complete the task for which we have arrived. Go to Talus; he will, of course, be surprised to see you. When you arrive, let him know immediately that you have word from me. Let him know that Abaddon has escaped the bowels of Hell."

Ashtaroth's eyebrows rose and he cocked his head and spoke. "My Lord, I do not understand. Your desire is to *inform* him that Abaddon has been released?"

"Yes, Astarte inform him. As his mind is so clouded in his blind allegiance to El, he will not be able to conceive of such a thing and will un-doubtedly accuse you of false assertions. His temperament is such that he will become agitated over such accusations, particularly from an Issi. He will temper his remarks at first, but press him Astarte. Press him and give him no quarter to mask his contempt for thy kind. Indeed, let him know the fullness of both Abaddon's, and your own disdain for his leadership. Make him aware of his failure as a leader. Make note that the, first of all, Elohim ever judged spring's from his house. Provoke him Astarte. Deride his race and his need for respect will incline him to lose reason, and when his reason is lost to him. He will be ripe for my plan."

"And what are your plans my Lord?" asked Ashtaroth.

"Civil war my dear Astarte, civil war. For it will be in that moment that Murmur will escort Sariel to the house of Talus. Your timing must be precise, for I fully expect the words that I shall put into Murmur's mouth to provoke Sariel and Talus into confrontation. When that occurs, we will move against

Heaven. In their confusion, we shall overtake them, and Heaven will be ours to control. Now go and delay not, for the time of our ascension is nigh."

Astarte bowed. "Yes my Lord." He departed from the palace to make haste towards Talus' abode.

"Murmur come with me," said Lucifer. "I desire that we use your gifts of encouragement and your ability to affirm to a different use."

****

Ashtaroth went to the mansion of Talus and knocked on the ivory doors.

An attendant answered, "Yes herald of Lucifer, to what does the house of Talus owe for this visit?"

Ashtaroth bowed respectfully. "I bring grave word for High Prince Talus. My master would bear him news as to the happenings on Earth."

"Indeed? Very well then," said the attendant. "Please come in."

Ashtaroth made his way into the palace and entered a room of white. Ivory and pearls adorned the walls, and the ceiling was translucent to the sky; the furniture plated in silver. Ashtaroth sat down and waited for the Prince.

He did not have to wait long as Talus promptly entered the living room and greeted Ashtaroth with a smile.

Ashtaroth stood immediately upon his entrance and bowed. "Lumazi."

"Please. Please." Talus motioned for Ashtaroth to sit. "To what honor do I owe the herald of Lucifer, and an Issi no less that he would come to my home?"

"I bring you grave news of Abaddon my Lord."

Talus frowned when he heard the name, his countenance visibly disturbed.

"And what of our brother?" Talus asked.

"Word has come from my master to inform you that Abaddon has escaped."

"Escaped?" Talus said. "Impossible! Escape is not possible from that realm. El has set at the Maw of the great mountain an Elohim who watches the way that none may enter, and that none may pass. You are mistaken."

"But my Lord, my message has come from the Chief Prince himself. I simply carry his word."

Talus rose from off the couch where he sat and towered in front of Ashtaroth.

"El's will be done. El has designed a creature who consumes the life of Elohim, a prison fit for one who cared not for the life of his own kind. No, my friend, there is no escape from the creature. Abaddon is lost, for there can be no evasion from that which El hast made."

Ashtaroth rose to his feet, his face red with anger.

"Mistaken?" Ashtaroth said, his voice echoed irritation for Talus' suggestion that he spoke in error. "Nay, Lord Prince I am not mistaken, but thou hast confirmed what I have long suspected. You are robust in strength and power, but bereft of knowledge. I come to thee with word from the Chief Prince himself, and you would toss my words aside as if they were dung. My master has well spoken of thy kind. You are indeed deserving of the destruction that awaits you. For even now while we speak; the seeds of thy downfall are at work, and know oh great prince that thy end lies not far behind."

Talus looked on Ashtaroth with shock and teemed with anger that he would be spoken to in such a manner, but Ashtaroth did not stop and continued in his berate.

"Even now as El is at rest in Sabbath, even now the Chief Prince moves to wipe from the heavens the stench of your foolish rule. Even now, Abaddon waits with a third of Heaven's legions to overthrow you. Yet I stand before you as a clarion call to action, and you still stand resolute to die in ignorance."

Talus glared at Ashtaroth and his eyes were wide in astonishment and disbelief. "Would you provoke me Ashtaroth? Have you come to make light of El's rule and of my own house?"

Ashtaroth looked upon Talus and smirked, "Nay Prince of Buffoons. I would not make light of so contemptible a house absent of dignity and intelligence. Oblivion indeed awaits thee, and may it embrace you and all your kind."

Talus lunged at Ashtaroth; his anger boiled as a cauldron within him. Ashtaroth stood defiant and with a pleased look on his face waited for the blow that was sure to come. Talus with the back of his hand slapped Ashtaroth across his jaw and knocked the angel hard to the ground.

Fueled by offense and insult, Talus' eyes flared, and his voice turned heavy in warning. "I know not what breach of protocol you inflicted with Apollyon, but you stand before a Prince of God, continue to speak words of treason and division and know of a surety that dissolution awaits you," said Talus.

Ashtaroth looked upon the great prince. His eyes narrowed, and his mouth bled, and his bruised cheek ached, swollen by the impact of Talus' blow. Ashtaroth spit blood on the floor, and looking defiant and unbowed, struggled to his feet. With resolution, he looked into the eyes of his prince and spoke.

"I am not hesitant to answer thee on this matter, O prince. For know that although I be smitten by thy hand, your title is onerous to me, for thou art neither worthy of honor and are empty of distinction."

Talus hovered over Ashtaroth his hands raised to deal a blow of dissolution to so scornful an angel. Fists clenched and with a wail of rage, the mighty angel lifted his great hands to bear down on Ashtaroth.

Talus in his anger did not hear the door open and failed to notice that the attendants' of his house, Sariel, and Murmur stood in the doorway and watched in shock as Talus pummeled Ashtaroth with his bare hands.

****

Slowly Michael opened his eyes. His head was still sore from Abaddon's blow. Groggy he awoke to see that he was not alone.

Raphael reached with his manacled hand to hold Michael's arm.

"Move slowly my friend. You were struck from behind."

"Ah," said Abaddon, "the prince has awakened. Thus begins the descent of the first of the High Princes. Your collaboration with El will soon come to an end."

Abaddon sat on top of a table, his mouth filled with manna leaf. He crunched as a cow that chewed the cud, and he leaned over on top of a long metal plow shear that had been beaten flat; its edge sharp as a razor.

Michael slowly rose to his feet, but his strong arms were constricted by the chains, and shackles that gripped him tightly.

"How long have I been unconscious?" Michael asked.

"One hour," replied Raphael.

Michael looked at his friend and whispered. "We must leave with all haste, for Charon will be here soon."

Michael then looked upon Abaddon and spoke. "You are a fool Destroyer, yet I know that nothing but destruction can be spoken from thy lips. Release us I command you, and perhaps I will bring petition before the Lord God that He might spare thee from His wrath, which is sure to come."

Abaddon placed his hand on his stomach and broke out laughing.

"You think I hold El in such esteem that I would entrust my fate to a

God who would destroy me? Nay High Prince. I will never again bow the knee to such a being that would do nothing while my kind wastes away, yet has the power to prevent it. Never again will I worship a creature that would imagine so abominable a thing as Hell. I spit on his mercy. I have tasted his wrath, and I shall not taste it again. Soon He will be brought low. For the Chief Prince himself will take up my cause, and he will be God!"

Michael looked on Abaddon and studied him intently. "Your doom is certain, and your conviction is sure. You simply do not know it yet, but rest assured your sin shall find you out."

Abaddon laughed and let out a loud burp from the volume of manna leaf he had digested.

"Do you know what I have learned Prince of the Kortai? I have fellowshipped with Lilith, and he has gone to great lengths to show me the uses of these instruments of Raphael: his stylus, inkhorn, and tome: such a wonderful *gift* from the Prince of all Grigori. However, Prince Michael, I had never thought I would be blessed to hold within my hands the Tome of Hell itself. My Lord King will enjoy this I am sure"

Michael panicked for a moment, and then discreetly felt the inner folds of his robes. The key ring with the keys to Death and Hell were still fastened safely against his skin. He breathed a sigh of relief and glowered at Abaddon.

Raphael spoke, "Abominable creature, I do not fear thee. The Lord rebuke you!"

Abaddon laughed, picked up the stylus in his hand, and twirled the writing instrument between his fingers playing with the captured.

"Are you aware Michael, that Raphael has the power to know all things present and that contained within this small tome, he carries the knowledge of all things? His tome is connected to all tomes. His is the sum of all knowledge that may be known. If I were to write in its pages, I may create using the power given to him by El. Did you also know Michael that Raphael was *Sephiroth*?"

Michael looked at Raphael. He had remembered the living statue and the inscription at the bottom emblazoned at the base. 'S-e-p-h-i-r-o-p-t-h' it said, but he did not have time to question Raphael. Charon would be here shortly and escape was paramount.

Raphael opened his mouth to speak. "You creature have not the wisdom to behold even a jot of the knowledge of God. May you find its value useless to you."

Abaddon replied, "Ah— that Grigori, is but a thin hope indeed, but fear not. After we have extracted from your tome all the information we seek. Know of a surety that thine stone shall belong to Lilith."

Abaddon moved from sitting off the desk, rose to his feet, and walked over to glare at Raphael.

"This tome is also a witness to the conspiracy of God. Contained herein lies the truth of the God king's plan to supplant us. For from the foundations of the world, were we created to serves as ministers to the clay-borne, and this Raphael, Prince of all Grigori — you knew."

Abaddon slapped Raphael across the cheek, and the blow made blood splatter across Michael's face.

Michael jostled to Raphael's defense, but his manacles tightened fast around his ankles and wrists.

"You will pay for this Abaddon. You debt shall be hung as a sign about thy neck!"

"Not today great prince," said Abaddon. "Not today. Yet take comfort that both Raphael and you shall live to see the fruition of our cause. His tome will be kept safely in the hands of Lilith so that we might monitor the happenings of all things."

Just as Michael moved closer to see to Raphael's wound, the door opened. Lilith walked in, and Abaddon gave him the Tome of Raphael.

Lilith thumbed through its pages, and his eyes were aglow with the excitement that a child might display upon the opening of a Christmas present. He leafed through its pages and turned to look back at his captors. "You do realize Raphael, that we will never serve the clay-borne. We will frustrate El's plans and bring to naught all those that would side with the God king and his plans to enslave us."

Raphael looked upon Lilith with a scowl. "You serve what is now a lap dog, one who would betray his own father. Would the creature say to the creator why hast thou made me thus? Yet you rebel against the glorious plan that El hast made thee partaker of. El knows of your plans. Would thou hope to battle with God?"

Lilith and Abaddon looked at each other and laughed.

Lilith spoke on the duo's behalf. "You have yet to grasp the extent to which we will not submit to his will on this matter. El will not battle us, but will abdicate the throne voluntarily. You see my prince; we know that El cannot be defeated by strength of arms. Although by force shall not the God-king be overthrown, but His own love and compassion shall be his undoing. For God so loves the world that he would lay down his own life. This *Sephiroth*, you know, and this weakness we shall exploit.

"We are meant to rule—not serve. El has lost His way and in doing brings ruin to us all. No, my prince, El will not be swayed through reason or force of our hand, but by His own free will, shall our bondage to his will come to an end."

At that moment, an explosion rocked the building, and screams could be heard coming from outside. Abaddon moved to the side of Raphael and Michael, to prevent any means of their escape, and to see to their security. Lilith raced towards a window to look outside.

"What is it?" cried Abaddon.

Lilith looked outside and saw the destruction to a section of the city's wall. Guards with newly minted swords valiantly attempted to do battle with a figure cloaked in dust, fire, and smoke. Manacled chains dropped from its sides, and its roar and the thunder of its hammer-like arms rang throughout the city courtyard. It raised its arms and fire and brimstone enveloped and engulfed all those that stood in its way. The guards were immediately consumed in fire, and small pyres of bodies lined the ground. As each Elohim fell, a huge vacuum of flame, magma, and smoke engulfed and swallowed up those who dared to interfere with the creature's progress and a wall of flame followed it and anything caught therein smelted in its wake.

With one chain like tentacle, the Elohim held a guard by the throat and tossed him effortlessly into the fires with others. The dark cowled creature lashed and beat Elohim senseless, and they were dragged alive screaming into blackness and flame.

"Lilith?" said Abaddon.

Lilith turned from the window and quickly looked at Abaddon in panic.

"We must leave for Heaven now!"

"What is it?" Abaddon roared back in frustration.

Michael chuckled and looked Abaddon dead in the eye. "Your sin has found you out."

Abaddon quickly left Raphael's side, raced to the window, peered down to look in the distance at the spectacle below. His eyes grew large, and his flesh turned pale. Panic gripped him.

Charon had come to claim him and Hell had followed.

****

Sariel looked upon Talus in disbelief and disgust and spoke angrily to his brother. "Would you bring dissolution to even more of my kind?"

And with a swiftness that belied his frame, Sariel flew to the aid of Ashtaroth, and Talus smote the Prince of Issi and knocked him to the floor. Sariel's flesh was torn, and his face was bearishly marred from the raw and bestial swipe of Talus' blow.

Talus paused as the realization that he had struck Sariel settled upon him, and he moved to see to his brother.

One of the attendants of the manor looked on the duo with eyes wide in disbelief and spoke. "In El's name — he struck the High Prince!"

"What manner of conduct is this?" another yelled.

Ashtaroth lay next to his prince, lifted his head unto his own lap, and berated Talus. "Once again your kind's buffoonery so legendary and pronounced has caused hurt. Who else must suffer at thy hand *both* foolishness and injury?"

Sariel shook his head as if to prevent himself from sleep from the blow dealt by Talus. He slowly pushed his torso up from off the floor. Ashtaroth loosened his hold, and Sariel rose to his feet and looked upon his brother to speak.

"Restraint is not in thy kind. Destruction swells in thy loins and ruin follows thee."

Sariel then hurled himself into the bosom of Talus and the two great princes slammed through the front door of the manor and rolled into the courtyard. Each attendant scattered to flee from the chaos as shrubbery and inden-

224

tations in the lush soil of Heaven ripped apart. Boulders were thrown high into the air from the commotion, and a cloud of dust smothered the grounds as the mighty angels wrestled in Heaven's lush dark earth. Arelim attendants ran to assist their prince, swarmed over Sariel, and struggled in vain to have him loose Talus.

Sariel's sigil stone suddenly glowed brightly within his chest. The innate power of El visibly pulsed from him, and three of his attackers were repelled back and hurled through windows, shrubbery, and the manor walls.

Ashtaroth rushed to block an Arelim attendant from accosting Sariel when his attacker was launched into the air by the force of Sariel's blow. Ashelon was his name, an attendant of Talus' house who now found himself uncontrollably thrown into the air. Like a cat, he twisted and contorted his body in vain to avoid the pearl spires that protruded from the court grounds. But speed was not his ally and the force of his plummet only hastened his impalement on one of the spires that raced to pierce his angelic flesh. With a thud, his body was run through, and his blue blood soiled the white pinnacle that flew the banner of house Arelim.

His body twitched and hung like a standard in the wind as the life force that animated from his stone slowly drained from him. Cobalt blood that flowed through Elomic veins pooled on the manicured grounds and stained the ivory pearl of the heavenly spire. He cried in anguish as the sound of gurgled blood choked his last breath. Ashelon pierced all ears with his death cry. "What have we to do with the house of Issi, and who shall take up mine cause?"

Ashelon released a final gasp for air, and the embers which fired his stone heart faded, and his heartstone became black as night.

On looking Arelim and Issi attendants stopped and looked on Ashelon's form; some revealed smug satisfaction while others boiled over in a potpourri of grief and rage, yet each was equally distraught and looked on in bewilderment and confusion as Ashelon's elements slowly dissolved and returned to fires of the Kiln. The great spire outside of Talus' home now stood stained and pooled with the blood from Ashelon. A monument to the blood spilled on his soil, a testament to a house known as the house of Apollyon — not Talus.

Talus and Sariel continued in heated battle, blind to the dissolution which stood about them and oblivious to the corruption and gathering storm of angels that stood in their midst.

Ashtaroth smiled at Murmur from across the grassy knoll. Murmur nodded in acknowledgment and smirked in approval as hundreds of Elohim flocked to gather to view, aid, and or stop the escalation of hostilities between the two princes and their kind.

Murmur looked on in quiet satisfaction. *Lucifer would be pleased,* he thought.

Civil war had begun.

Chapter Eight

And there was war in Heaven...

Charon's roar deafened the ears of his combatants and like fleas that irritate skin. He flicked away all who stood between him and his quarry. His face bent to capture his renegade charge. Charon was the personification of the vengeance of God, and only God could help anyone who crossed his path.

Abaddon had escaped and sought refuge within the quartz walls of Athor. The scent of Abaddon littered the whole city, but the odor was most concentrated in the crystalline structure that stood in Charon's path: the house of Lucifer. Citizens came from across Athor to protect the home of their King; alerted that Lucifer's stronghold might come under assault.

Athor's protectorate hovered and stood ready as one man. Each equipped with new swords to stop Charon. A line of Elohim one thousand strong resolved to face the Warden of Hell and keep him from setting foot on the palace grounds.

Each angel of the line watched the black wall of acrid smoke and rubble. Winds rife with sulfur irritated their ears and skin. Yet bravely they waited and wondered who this day among them would experience dissolution. Could they stand against the living manifestation of the vengeance of God?

Anxiety filled them all as they watched the oncoming cloud of noxious gas and smoke draw closer.

Screams and cries of anguish emanated from the dark soot that billowed before them. The agony filled wails from those first fallen to encounter the myrmidon of Hell. Wisps of orange and red flickered from the black smolder and flames leapt into the sky.

The ground shook with each step of Charon's advance.

Each one could sense that Charon was closer now. His every footstep felt in the vibrations in the ground. Angels grew tense and braced themselves. Several tightened their hold around the grip of their swords and anxiety leaped from angel to angel like an airborne virus, infecting all with fear.

Again, the ground shook.

Cacian an angel of the line looked at the tall dark wall of smolder that loomed before them. Ash littered the air and made it difficult to breathe. Each angel coughed and sought to wave the air clean and in vain straining to peer into the distance.

Slowly marching from the midst of the tender and smoke, Charon appeared as one might step from behind a curtain. The ferryman of doom approached, cowled in a black leather like robe of Elomic flesh and with a mare's skeleton for a frame. He dragged from rusted iron chains the screaming bodies of Elohim who had dared to defy him. As fish caught in hooks squirming for release, their wails of torment filled the air. Each was engulfed in flames and charred, yet somehow alive. The fires burned to the sky but did not extinguish. Each captive thrashed and screamed for release as they writhed in pain: eaten alive by the digestive flames of Hell.

Hell was alive. She had minions that fed her from afar. Each blistering maggot leeched the life force of the Elohim dragged in Charon's wake. Closer Charon marched trailing bodies behind him: an army of one poised against a legion of angels.

Cacian saw the bodies dragged by Charon and digested by Hell's flames. He reached up to feel the ash that fluttered in the wind and his eyes grew wide in terror, for the ash was the consumed flesh of his fallen comrades. In that moment, he beheld in revelation the entirety of who Charon was and screamed.

"Flee!" said one.

"Stand thy ground!" yelled another.

"Bring him down!" Taurus commanded.

Commander Taurus of the newly formed Athan army looked to his air chief Xercon. "You know what to do," He said.

Xercon nodded and rose into the air.

Xercon oversaw the command of the south wind and the storm. He raised his hands and spoke to the listening jet stream, who obediently hearkened to his command and quickened her pace. Large cauliflower clouds quickly converged over the assembled army and the sky darkened and grew greenish in color. A cumulous pillar of white clouds rose into the heavens; carried aloft by columns of rotating air until the very top of the cloud canopy sheared itself against the upper atmosphere and became as an anvil. Lightning streaked across the belly of the pillowed mountain and illuminated the now darkened sky. Thunder crashed off eardrums and shook the ground. Water droplets swelled in the folds of the infant storm, grew obese, and threw themselves from the heights to pummel and drench the ground below Charon's feet.

Charon continued his snail's pace forward as the soil beneath him saturated with water and the ground engorged itself on the pounding rain. The earth beneath him became soft and muddy. Charon's movement slowed, hindered by Xercon's command of the wind and rain.

Lightning brightened the sky and the denizens of Athor covered their eyes as the storm suddenly unleashed crackling white arms of voltage and pummeled the ground where Charon stood. Shockwaves echoed off the sky in a drumbeat of outrage, bass, and destruction.

In a dance of terawatted ferocity, strokes of lightning discharged from the sky and embraced Charon in their fury. The power of the mile long bolts heated the air around him to twice that of the sun and vaporized all things. The muddy ground beneath his feet instantly turned to glass and sealed the Warden of Hell fast. The vacuum created from the superheated air clapped its hands, and great booms of thunder raced as a sprinter out of his blocks and dashed across the city and into the regions round about. The sound shook the foundations of buildings and knocked individuals off their feet.

Xercon spoke the Elomic command to the south wind, and ever attentive to her master's cry. The great beast upon which the clouds rode hearkened to his call. The vast jet stream invisibly wrote into the ground with her finger, and a cyclone lifted itself from the dust of the earth and yawned as a man awakens from slumber. Again, bolt after bolt rained down upon Charon. Electric current flowed through his body and traveled through him to find release in the ground. A target Charon became: a conduit for all the wrath of the living sky. Pleased to see the myrmidon stagger, Xercon continued to assault him from the heavens.

Black finger like clouds reached down to grapple Charon and appendage after swirling appendage dropped as tentacles from the sky and touched the ground. They howled and wailed dissolution to all that would dare cross their path.

Xercon motioned with his hands and with a thought commanded the funnels to collide with anything that walked the trail of Charon.

And so they did.

Screaming wrath and destruction, they squalled as they hammered Charon. Winds ripped trees from the ground, and loose shards of quartz rose and darted towards the Warden of Hell. The twin sisters of wind waltzed around each other; launching shrapnel of wood, metal, and flesh as missiles. Their impact was ferocious and Charon stood as a nail hammered into the embracing arms of the earth. The cracking of great oaks and the roar of winds gone mad filled the air. Blackness from the immense clouds masked the eyes, as fine grains of sand ground flesh. Rain and gale torrentially beat structure after toppling structure to powder.

Charon's tentacles of rusted metal flayed in the tempest winds and with his great legs, he stood trapped, snared deep in the ground now turned to glass blasted by wind and quartz.

Xercon satisfied that his minions of air and water had pummeled the warden into submission, raised his sword and dove to fall upon Charon from the sky, and like lightning from heaven, he plummeted into the morass of rain, smoke, and the rage of cyclones gone amok, and fought to battle Charon in hand to hand combat.

Thus, the angels of the line watched in hopeful anticipation that a prince of the power of the air might slay the Warden of Hell; looking on as the very forces of the troposphere were unleashed on their behalf.

Deep at the base of the supercell of vortices, they fought as streaks of lightning bulleted across the city and smashed Athor and the land roundabout. Thunder burst the eardrums of angels who watched the shimmering outline of the two titans gripped in mortal combat.

Like a hurricane feeds off the waters of the mighty sea, the south wind churned and lifted buildings, trees, and boulders and threw them against Charon. Smoke billowed from the center of the struggle, and suddenly without warning fire exploded, and like a pebble tossed in a basin of tranquil water. The ripples of the shock wave rocketed through the land. Buildings flung outward in all directions, flung aside as trash. Smoke and debris filled the city and covered the angels of the line as each one looked to see who would survive the havoc of wind and storm gone mad.

Slowly the gusts subsided, and the roaring columns of cyclonic air slowed, dissipated, and lifted themselves into the sky. The rain stilled its torrential pour to a wimpish drizzle, and buildings, trees, and debris fell from the cleared sky and crashed to the ground.

Angels at the line strained to peer through the smoke and fire: to see a lone figure that stood at the center where cyclones and lightning once played.

Cacian peered through the hazy veneer of black smoke and trembled as he saw the shadow of he who marched towards them; his tendrils flailed with the familiar sound of rusted chains. Chains that now dredged against ground now turned to glass. Charon dragged the charred body of Xercon. And his captor's muffled screams filled the air. Cacian watched in fascinated horror as the maggots of Hell burrowed through Xercon's mouth and ears; watched as Xercon struggled to breathe as the worms filled his lungs. His body aglow now torched with the fire of Hell's flames.

Like the morning dew that settles across a valley, fear fell over the soldiers of the line.

Cacian looked to make out the boneless features of the myrmidon of Hell. Charon's fleshless skull expressed no emotion. Yet the pace of his quickened gait made clear that one sentiment governed his march ever closer toward his foes that remained.

Rage.

Lucifer made his way quickly from the central city towards the northern gate. His eyes darted nervously to each citizen, and he wondered if any suspected what he had planned, but each bowed as was custom when he passed. It was a normal thing for the Prince of Heaven to exit Jerusalem to depart for Earth. Lucifer traveled closer to Heaven's entry gates and ruminated to himself on the task that lay before him.

For the forces of Heaven not to overwhelm his strike force, he must hold the waypoints shut. There could be no Ladders into Heaven while his campaign was afoot. The Kingdom of God must be cut off from the rest of the multiverse. To accomplish this end, he must somehow usurp the guard at each of the four gates; then, with his own hands, he would cripple Heaven.

Finally, his feet brought him to the pearled walls of Heaven and the post of Deramiel, guard of the northern gate.

The great pearled gates towered before him, a massive structure of whitish black pearl, and ivory with a wall 24 feet wide and a thousand cubits high. Two solid gold doors latticed with drawings of two silver lions' heads, stood regally etched as living portrayals and roared the praises of God whenever the gates opened. Set between the gates with a flaming spear was Deramiel: ever vigilant to guard and watch over the bridge that connected Heaven with the rest of creation. Lucifer had always thought it curious that God would station guards at the entrance to Jerusalem. For Heaven had no adversaries and the Elohim were the pinnacle of creation.

Lucifer knew that El's thoughts transcended more than just the present but easily penetrated all possible futures. Lucifer conjectured in that moment that God had anticipated his plan and knew that the city itself would one day be besieged by its own. His mind raced in nervous anticipation as he approached Deramiel.

How to circumvent the Almighty? Would Deramiel turn to our aid?

He would not leave such decisions to possibility. No, he would assure the completion of his plan even if it meant his brother's demise. Thus, Lucifer plotted the destruction of Deramiel as he elucidated kindness from his mouth.

Deramiel recognized the Chief Prince as he approached. "Hail Lucifer Draco, Prince of Heaven," Deramiel said. "How fares the Archon of Earth?"

Deramiel also was of House Draco, one of Lucifer's own kin. Their affinity ran deep. *Surely,* Lucifer thought. *He will come to my cause.*

"All goes well my friend," Lucifer replied. "I have come with urgent word and am in need of thy strength to assist in that which is to come."

"The High Prince in need of me?" Deramiel said with a puzzled look on his face. "Why in El's name would you have need of me? Speak Lumazi and it shall be done."

Lucifer replied. "There has been counsel among the chief houses concerning the creation of the man. The Royal court is now split in its allegiance to El. Even now, I have come to learn that two of the great houses: Arelim and Issisi are in open conflict in the outskirts of Jerusalem. El Sabbaths and has left a divided council over the service to man. I but seek to maintain the word of our Lord whilst he rests, for all seek their own and not the things, which are El's. Therefore, I now come to thee 'watcher of the way,' for I have no man likeminded that I might attend to this affair and who will naturally care for our state."

Deramiel's eyes lowered as if sadness would overtake him; then he spoke. "If El is on Sabbath, and the court's leadership is divided, then Heaven itself is at risk. What would you ask of me, my Prince?"

"Indeed," replied Lucifer. "As the center guard over the northern gate, you hail the others if anything seems amiss to you. Yet of all the guardians of the gates of Heaven, thou art the only Draco and are chief guard; thus brother, thy House Lord and Prince calls on you now to stand by me and uphold the word of El. I have forces on Earth that will rally to our cause to assist with the quelling of the feud that now roars unabated in the way. Perhaps we might yet quell the division that has stirred Heaven to fight against herself. Those that are against us number more than those who are for us; thus I require your aid, but we must move quickly and quietly to bring them low, or else all that El hast spoken and our house has done to uphold his word will be lost."

Deramiel bowed to his Prince. "El's will be done. What would thou have me do?"

Lucifer looked at him and replied, "Go to and secure the eastern wall. Tell the gate captains that there is a disturbance at House Talus, and the court requires all officers of the realm to appear at Talus' grounds and to render aid and quell the disturbance."

Deramiel bowed. "But my Lord — please be not angry with thy servant. If I leave who will watch the eastern wall? For Heaven hast no appointed guard but I. To abandon the word of El, to '*Be still at this gate*', would leave Heaven without a watchman on the wall."

Thoughts quickly raced through Lucifer's mind, and he looked upon Deramiel with sadness and said, "I fear El hath left us no choice, for Heaven dost battle against herself. And lo, wherein thy sight doth danger lurk? There is nothing but thee and I that stand here at the gates. There exists no adversary in thy sight, yet furlongs away in the burbs past the Elysian Fields, two of the great houses bring dissolution to the realm. If it seemeth good in thy sight to question thy Prince's wisdom while El himself Sabbaths, then stay. And if it seemeth good to thee to stand idle while thy brothers raze each other in dissolution then stay, but know this. Although I might command thee as high prince, instead I would adjure thee by the love of God, that thou not stand idle whilst thy brothers fall. Fear not, for thy post, shall not be without guard. I will stand in thy stead and be a watchman on the wall until thou hast returned. I will not fail thee, and all shall be well."

Lucifer placed his hands on Deramiel's strong shoulders, looked him straight in the eye, smiled, and spoke. "You believe in God, believe also in me."

Deramiel reluctantly but subserviently turned to go and said, "As you command my prince."

Deramiel raced off to the northeastern section of the wall to accomplish his Lord's will.

Lucifer watched him go and stood as a sentinel to guard the gate of Heaven. Lucifer smirked when Deramiel was out of sight, pleased that his plan was coming to fruition. He turned towards the bridge of Heaven and recited the words that would allow him to open the city's waypoint into the realms.

A causeway to allow the forces of Abaddon, and Lilith to penetrate the city.

****

Lilith walked towards Raphael and lowered himself to whisper into his ear.

"I will take your tome my Prince and use its knowledge against you. Yes, I will leave you alive in knowledge that there is quickly coming a day that at my name, you shall bow, and with thine own tongue, thou shalt confess that I am thy Lord. Yes, to bring dissolution to thee would rob me of this pleasure. Thus, I will await you in Heaven. Follow me that mine wish might be fulfilled."

Lilith gloated at Raphael and rose to speak to Michael. "Archon I take my leave of thee. I go now to lay waste to thy home. Until we meet again — oh wait, Abaddon would you like a word with Michael before we depart?"

Abaddon quickly walked closer to Michael and towered over the arch-angel of Heaven. His claw-like hand unsheathed, and Abaddon slowly ran his talon across the cheek of Michael's face.

"Ah, my prince I leave thee a token of my love for thy God in thine own flesh."

Michael looked at him and stared deeply into his eyes. "Thy fealty to Lucifer will be thy undoing. Walk in thy calling '*Destroyer*', but know the end is not yet thine."

Abaddon angrily dug his claw deep into the epidermis of Michael's face and gouged a piece of flesh from his cheek. Michael grimaced in pain and let out a scream of anguish as angelic blood poured from his wound and raced to color the floor blue.

Abaddon smiled at his handiwork, looking on with glee as Michael held his palm over his wound, and glared at him in pain.

Abaddon turned to go and recited the ancient tongue to summon a ladder. He and Lilith stood in a bubble of power as the Elomic command to part the heavens peeled back to reveal the stars, and in the distance the eastern jasper gate to the great city of Heaven, and Michael could see that Lucifer stood at the gates.

An explosion shook the house and the walls quaked around them.

"Goodbye Prince of Heaven," said Lilith. "We go to confront the God King."

Suddenly the prismatic funnel of light and heat from a Ladder spread through the room, rocking the foundation of the house. Michael rose to his feet, raced towards Raphael with his bound hands, and jumped to cover his friend.

The walls collapsed to the floor, and the ceiling quickly followed.

With his great wings unfurled to protect both him and his brother. Michael huddled with Raphael. The constructed quartz buckled around them. The sound of timber and glass filled the air, and then the room went black.

****

"What have we to do with the house of Issi, and who shall take up my cause?"

Ashelon's death cry pierced the campus grounds of Talus. His lament for vindication traveled through the air and captured the ears of Heaven's citizenry. Like a siren that warned of an impending storm so too did his lament draw notice from the host of Heaven, and as one man, each angel paused to consider.

It was a moment never to be repeated in all the days of Heaven. A day when angels would reflect on whether to follow a cause apart from El's. Clarity of consciousness spread through the masses of Heaven, a rally to answer a question: whom this day would one serve? Like wildfire, the violence that raged in the courtyard of Talus moved as a pandemic across the topography of the Third Heaven as Arelim struck down Issi, and Harrada engaged Kortai.

Jerahmeel and Gabriel had worked tirelessly to clear and repair the damage caused by Apollyon's earlier rampage, and like all of Heaven, they heard the death cry of the anguished angel ring throughout the air.

"In El's name," said Jerahmeel, "go to, and look to the house of Talus!"

Gabriel nodded in acknowledgment and with a flash of light was gone. The Leopard of Heaven raced towards the quarters of his brother, and the ground moved as a blur beneath his winged feet. Hazy shadows of Heaven's citizenry zoomed past him, and in the distance of the multicolored grass that was Heaven's carpet stood the house of Talus.

Gabriel could smell the perspiration in the air, and the ground reverberated with the heavy pounding of angels trampling and wrestling on the ground. Gabriel came to the manicured lawns of house Talus, his eyes looked upon the countryside and with each batting of the eye, he beheld as angels wrestled one another in a death grip of bloody combat.

Each Elohim was lost in rage and offense; interlocked in a choreographed dance of fists upon beaten skulls. Wings whirled in acrobatic movements of evasion, and gusts of wind lifted up dirt high into the air as throats were slashed. Bones cracked as the concussive force of tackled bodies echoed across Heaven's tundra.

Yet Gabriel had not come to partake in madness. He came to see his brother Talus. Great drops of sweat fell as pearls from his muscular frame, and with determination of purpose; Gabriel darted amongst the enraged combatants. He dodged and weaved past blow after evaded blow from angels who were oblivious to his presence.

Suddenly a wave of energy traveled across the lawn, and the energy signature of the pulse was unmistakable. A Prince Lord was in exertion. Faster now the Leopard of Heaven ran, quickly he darted between torn wings, leapt over torsos, and ran closer to the center of the blast's origin. Traveling between the hordes of angels, he stopped to gawk at the sight that now stood before him.

Talus and Sariel grappled with one another, arms interlocked, each using knee and elbow to buffet each other as two rams might butt heads. Blood spurted from large gashes torn from the wounds in each angel's flesh. Lacerations drained as water from a faucet, and from Sariel's face hung flesh torn by his brother's assault.

Gabriel looked and saw that neither cared for the destruction that raged about them. His ears burned with the sounds of hate. Verbal assaults filled the once peaceful air of Heaven. Hatred rose as leaven into the sky and was palpable. Like a lanced boil of evil, it seeped into the corners of the realms now that El's presence had withdrawn. His influence so powerful a force that it kept in check avarice and hubris, for in His presence was fullness of joy.

But alas, the glory of God had departed. The Almighty was seemingly asleep to the goings on in His realm. Now new sounds filled Heaven. Heaven was now void of God's influence for the first time, and the silence of sanctification wrought nothing but violence in its wake.

"Let the Arelim bleed," cried one.

"Dissolution to the House of Sariel and his lackeys," was the retort.

In that that instant, Gabriel knew that madness had infected Heaven, madness as viral as the flesh-eating bacteria that lined the orbs on a million worlds, a bacterium of madness that exchanged reason for hate. Gabriel then knew what he must do. He and Jerahmeel must restore the soundness of mind to the horde, or oblivion awaited them all.

Gabriel watched as Sariel grabbed Talus by the chin with his left hand and used his right wing to knock the prince backward. The Prince of all Arelim staggered seemingly surprised that a species other than his own could yield such power. Quickly he rose to his feet, his cloven hooves firmly positioned on the ground for support. Sariel sensed an opening and leapt forward to press his attack. Wings arched back as he dove as a bird of prey with taloned hands outstretched. His hands purposed to smite his brother quickly and remove the stone from his flesh. However, the task would be denied him. Gabriel launched his nimble frame into Sariel's body and slammed deep into his chest.

Sariel soared backward against a wall and smashed through brick, pearl, and mortar. Crystal and all color of precious pearls fell from the crum-

240

bling wall.

Quickly Gabriel turned to face his brother Talus.

"Ahh welcome my dear brother Gabriel! It does my heart well to see that you have come to my aid. Of course, our brother must be shown the error of his ways. Come and we shall dispose of him together! What say you?"

Gabriel cocked his head to the side and looked upon his brother as he would upon a stranger.

"I think not brother, and I will take no part in this travesty. Ye both have caused great harm this day, and this madness must come to an end now."

Talus laughed defiantly. "*End*? Indeed today, we *shall* put an *end* to the problem that has plagued Heaven for far too long. Today we shall see the fall of the house, Issi!"

Gabriel realized whatever blood lust Talus had; was now in control of his ability to reason.

Gabriel turned to his left and noted the legion of angels that now approached him. All paused in a mass intermission of hostilities. A thousand eyes bored down in recognition to take note that a Malakim was in their midst. Each within his vicinity paused to determine if he was friend or foe, and Gabriel saw that his every move was watched, as both house Issi and Arelim studied to see for whose cause he would fight.

Gabriel saw that they too were lost in madness, an infection of revenge that manifested itself throughout the throng and was now as a stench wafted aloft in full bloom. Offense, anger, and retaliation raced through the crowd that Gabriel had dared handle Prince Sariel, dared that he would raise his hand in defiance to the prince who now lay unconscious. The swelling throng then gave voice to what he knew permeated their hearts. Cautiously they inched towards him; eyes ablaze that he had dared challenged their Prince.

241

"He has raised his hand against an Issi," said one.

"Then cut off his hand," yelled another in reply.

"Another lackey to the God King," said another.

Gabriel in all his seasons had never experienced the sensation of alienation that now overtook him. It was a new thing this awareness, an overwhelming sense that his difference created exposure, and that exposure posed danger. A danger that emanated from those he would call brethren. The thought of this cognizance, this — division chilled him to the bone.

In Heaven, there was neither male nor female, no recognition of an identity apart from El. But El's Sabbath had created a vacuum in the spirit, a swirling void that bled dry Heaven's holiness and cohesion, and instead ejected disunion, strife, and hate. An absence that created a consciousness of an existence apart from the living God, and in this new atmosphere, order degenerated into chaos. Gabriel noted that fear now settled over him, as night would overtake the escaping sun.

Gabriel was a Malakim, a messenger forever called to deliver the word of El. There were few of his kind in the Third Heaven, for many were off throughout the second heaven holding up all things by El's word. The need to be with his own kind gripped him. As a man slapped to prevent unconsciousness, so too was Gabriel now aware that here under the golden hued skies of Heaven he was not safe.

Gabriel looked at Sariel still unconscious. He moved quickly, and placed him over his shoulders tucked securely with two of his four wings within the cleft of his back.

The sound of outrage echoed roundabout him as he handled the prince.

"And where do you think you are going with him?" Talus said.

Gabriel stood mute, leaped over Talus, and with a flash of light, the

Leopard of Heaven fled. His available and unencumbered wings unfurled and hurtled Gabriel at breakneck speed back to Jerahmeel. There was strength in unity and the place of unity was where he needed to be if he and his brother would stop the insanity that plagued the great houses this day. So the Leopard of Heaven ran to escape those whom he called brethren, and whose minds were now gripped in madness.

As a cheetah moves through the plains, Gabriel raced back towards the direction of the city. Gabriel flew with ankle-winged feet over the grassy hills and to the woods of Mirabelle. Mirabelle, a forest of honey trees, filled Heaven's air with the scent of cinnamon from their bark and bled sugar from their porous leafs. Their sweet aroma hit Gabriel, but he could not pause to enjoy the pleasures of Heaven this day. Nay, leisure to taste and be dazzled by their multi-colored beauty would be denied him, as he wove a path, and dashed between the trees. Gabriel's heart pumped fast and the strength of his gait drowned out all things as he ran across the forest floor to return to the solace of Jerahmeel. The canopy from the tall manna leaves loosed golden rays of light. For a moment, relief filled him knowing that just beyond the acres of Heaven's foodstuff. Jerahmeel stood within the city gates ready to assist him.

Gabriel briefly allowed himself to hope until from his hind his peace dissolved as broken branches woke him from the illusion that safety was yet to come. Runners are warned never to look back; so as not to lose focus on the prize that is set before them. Gabriel did not so, but now turned rearward to hear the thunder of wings and the stomp of hooves behind him.

The ground shook as the tumult of hoofs pummeled the earth in pursuit of the Leopard of Heaven, and he saw their dust trails litter and begin to gray the golden sky. As a pack of jackals might hunt a fox, a hundred thousand angels ran hot in pursuit of Gabriel. A hundred thousand rabid Arelim and Issisi hooves crushed the soft petals of Mirabelle and manna leaf below their feet. Each one with eyes ablaze, set to overtake him at all costs.

****

They attacked, the guardians of Athor did. From the sky, they dove to smite the Myrmidon of Hell. In wave after endless wave, they accosted Charon. With newly minted swords, they assailed him in droves.

"Bring him down!" Taurus yelled.

Jaredeem of the house of Draco lifted his voice and like all Draco unleashed a roar of a sonic boom that he might bring Charon to his knees. The concussive wave of sound made its way through the air only to flow around Charon's frame as water glides around the belly of a goose on the surface of the water. The air was meaningless to a creature birthed within the Kiln. Charon unleashed barbed tentacles from his equine body and wrapped Jaredeem in coils of punishment for his folly.

Jaredeem fell to his knees in agony. His hands held his throat as he gurgled from the blood that now filled his lungs, and his body contorted in pain. Pain, an experience he was never designed to know. Pain that coursed through him like a thousand needles that stabbed into him at once. Pain as the flames of Hell liquefied his esophagus. Pain because he had a mouth, but could not scream. The vocal cords which before had been used to sing the praises of El used to assist Heaven's and Earth's various choirs in song were now dangled as soiled menstrual rags to be discarded in Charon's tentacled hand. Now tossed to his rearward where the remoras of Hell feasted on all things angelic.

Hell tasted angel flesh and multiplied her fiery maggots, the horrific fiery worms that did not die, bred by the tainted flesh of changed Elohim who would now eternally be cremated in Hell's fire.

Charon marched towards Lucifer's chief palace, unstoppable and undeterred by the thousand arrayed against him. Charon was an army of one, a mobile force of nature whose very breath immobilized those in front of him. His socketless eyes pierced and brought his enemies to their knees to sob uncontrollably. Angels whose eyes locked with his stood dazed as if looking into nothing, but seeing played before them the futility to fight. Many knelt in the hypnotic trance of despair and wailed as the flames simply overtook them where they cried.

Angel after angel was rooted in shock motionless as their very flesh was eaten away only to create and ignite even more pyres, they stood transfixed in horror at the image they saw of themselves in Charon's eyes. Engorging Hell's taste for the delicacy of Elomic flesh, the devourer of angels craved more. For Hell was lust. She was oblivious to all but one thing: she must feed, and the legions, which dared to interject themselves in Charon's path, provided her sustenance.

Charon ripped stones from flesh and provided Hell morsel after delicious morsel, and with each stones' destruction, the trail of angelic dust littered the ground like freshly packed snow.

"In El's name, he cannot be stopped!" yelled one.

Taurus who had observed the battle from afar realized the true nature of Charon. If they attacked in mass, more tentacles sprouted from his body to repel them. For every attack directed against him, he simply grew stronger. It was then that Taurus knew that against this abomination from the Kiln resistance was futile. With hammers for hands, Charon smashed his way against the throng, and bodies sailed in all directions. Forward still Charon marched and with barbed tentacles, he whiplashed angel after angel into submission. Others he picked up and flung headlong into buildings and trees. Some asphyxiated, for

Charon suffered none to bar him. Stones were smashed and throats cut. Nothing stopped the force that marched only hundreds of yards toward the palace walls. For Charon moved without pause and trod over bodies piled underneath him.

Screams filled the air. Smoke and flames jetted across the sky, and angelic blood flowed as rainwater might pour through the drains of a city. Hell's fires advanced as waves that crashed against the shore. Like storm surge, the flames moved and followed Charon on his path, and with every living thing the fires touched, life drained, and agony ensued.

For once entrapped in Hell's unforgiving embrace; the flesh festered releasing hundreds of new parasitic worms that raced across the Athorian battlefield. Taurus realized to fight against Charon was to battle Hell itself. Nay, for Hell and Charon, were but mere, singular and localized manifestations of the wrath of God. Taurus sighed in the light of this revelation; in the knowledge, that perhaps to follow Lucifer was indeed to have followed madness. Nevertheless, he was Elohim, and Elohim did not defer to failure and in that instant, Taurus gave the order that would seal his own doom.

"Bring him down whatever the cost! For freedom — for Lucifer!" Taurus shouted.

The battle cry carried across the field of Athor, and angels attacked with desperate ferociousness in the knowledge that to attack Charon was perhaps never again to breathe Earth's air. Using all means available to them to slow, nay stop the Warden of Hell, they threw themselves at him, a phalanx of wings, muscle, and swords to take down he who would trespass the ground of their Lord's house.

The land rose in upheaval and shook its objection, as Elohim who could control the ground brought their powers to bear, and the Earth itself rose as an enemy against the myrmidon. Charon latched his great tentacles as anchors in the earth's flesh, and they bored until he hit rock, and, as a surfer would ride the waves of the tide. Charon strode upon the back of the land. As the earth opened to bury him, Charon launched more anchors to pieces of ground that were undisturbed. Unstoppable, he inched closer toward the Athorian wall before him.

As ants fight off an attacker to their nest: so too did the Elohim launch wave after endless wave against him. And for each Elohim that engaged him, he slowed, his advance postponed until there were no Elohim left to fight.

The angels buzzed like a swarm to Charon and commanded all the elements to engage Him. From the scorched flash of lightning to the rumble of the earthen floor, each converged to the place upon which Charon stood. A great cloudburst of rain poured upon Charon, and the droplets fell from the sky. Each bead designed to extinguish hell's flame.

Steam wafted into the sky and the hiss of evaporation against the flickering tongue of the inferno's heat made the watery cloudburst of no effect. This was hell fire. It kindled off the flesh of Elohim–birthed from the cauldron of the Kiln itself. It could not be extinguished, and it would never go out.

Charon's eyeless sockets gazed upon the battalion sprawled before him. With gaps for ears, he heard the wails and cries of battle as they moved closer to engage him. They ran, flew, and galloped. Issi, Arelim, Harrada, and Kortai. Elohim of every race and station leaped to smite the warden to no avail. Charon simply marched ever forward.

For on this day, he who would bar the path of Charon only hastened his own doom.

"Are you alright?" Michael said.

"Aye," replied Raphael, "Yet my leg is pinned somehow; I cannot move it."

The dust slowly dissipated as Michael and Raphael moved gingerly among the rubble strewn over and around them. Charon's assault was closer now, his presence nearer to the origin of his prey.

"I too am bound by these shackles yet still. My hands are not free to lift the beam from off you."

Suddenly there was a pounding on the chamber door.

"Prince Michael, Prince Raphael! Can you hear me?" said a panicked, shrill voice.

"In here!" Michael replied. "Quickly in here!"

The door flung open and wood and metal flew across the room. Arms grabbed the sides of the door jam, and a figure stepped into the room and carefully walked over debris that lay strewn across the entryway.

"Prince Michael?" said the voice.

"Aye — but who art thou? And art thou friend or foe?"

The dust settled, and it became clear to Michael that the figure, which raced over towards Raphael, was a Kortai his brother in league to the city of Athor: Iofiel.

"My liege let me assist you." Iofiel raced to his Lord's side and picked up pieces of rubble strewn on the floor from the collapsed ceiling.

"Hurry!" said Michael. "Charon's path will bring him here soon; we cannot delay."

Iofiel reached Raphael and lifted a large beam from over his waist, freeing the Grigori.

"Ah, much thanks," said Raphael.

Iofiel nodded and turned to free Michael. Grabbing him with his great arms, Iofiel hoisted him up from off the floor tossing rubble to the side.

"Can you break the shackles?" asked Michael

"Yes, stand still and stretch out your arms," Iofiel replied.

Michael did so, and Iofiel with a swipe of his hand smashed the links that held the cuffs tight. Michael flexed, and the shackles snapped free, leaving broken links dangling from his wrists as an ornate set of bracelets.

Michael rubbed his wrists to massage them and spoke. "Thank you, my brother. Come, we must go quickly before the Warden befalls this place. We must warn the princes in Heaven of Lucifer's treachery before he has time to launch his assault." Michael nodded to Raphael and turned to go when Iofiel grabbed Michael by the arm to stop him.

"But, my Lord, there are those here on Earth and in Athor who require aid, for Lucifer hast moved all those that would oppose him to a camp deep beneath the Earth. We cannot abandon them!"

Michael eyed Iofiel curiously. "A camp?" Michael replied. "What do you mean he moved them? How many?"

"The exact count is not known, my Lord. However, several thousand have not bowed their knee to the Chief Prince. What I do know is that Lucifer has sought to imitate El and hast made an abode where all those that would defy him would dwell. He views his prison, his 'Tartarus' he calls it, as benevolent in comparison to Hell. He is mad I tell you, simply mad. He announced to all those within Athor that he would bring justice to our realm."

"He said to us all, 'peace', 'peace', yet destruction swiftly followed for all those that would not bow the knee and abdicate allegiance to El. He and a host surrounded us and with his voice, he caused the earth to shake beneath us, and when the ground opened her mouth to swallow us, he had Lilith, the rogue Grigori, create an abominable Ladder that transported everyone to a wretched place of darkness. A new realm within the Earth itself made he and thus imprisoned those who had once helped raise the very stones that decorate this fair kingdom.

Those who tried to reason with him he set as an example to us all. He publicly lifted Crocellus of the Kortai from a tree and had Abaddon chain him thereon. When the restraints were sure, Abaddon gouged with his bare hands the stone of God from his flesh and crushed it into powder. We watched as his stone became as sand in the wind.

Lucifer smiled at us and said that if we would not serve, then dissolution awaited us, or we could accept imprisonment as an act of his mercy. An imprisonment he called Tartarus, yet it is more than a prison; it is a camp of dissolution, a place that in darkness he brings to naught all those that might stand against him. Therefore, we must go far below the city's foundations, near the center of the Earth's heart. There he hast hidden Tartarus from the gaze of those in the Third Heaven."

Raphael spoke. "How is it that thou hast managed to escape Lucifer's gaze? Surely, he would smite thee if he knew of thy aid to us."

Iofiel replied, "I have learned in these dark times to feign fealty to the Lightbringer that I may in some fashion bring to naught his plans. I waited for an occasion to act and watched as he brought you here and stayed near in hopes to succor some opportunity that I might give thee aid. Behold, now my cowardice and failure to act sees the very vengeance of God at Athor's doorstep ready to destroy all that my prince had commanded me to build. For this I am ashamed."

Michael spoke. "Do not be deceived; cowardice on your part doth not bring Charon to Athor. Nay but the Destroyer he hunts, and will do so until Abaddon rests within the bowels of Hell once more. Cease to wonder if your actions bring dishonor, for who knew that for such a time as this hast thou come to this place to save us? For El's thoughts are marvelous, and his ways are past finding out."

Iofiel bowed and replied, "Then I adjure thee by the living God, do not deny your servant this request. But let us go quickly and bring relief to those trapped in the confinement of Lucifer's making, for I would seek how we might frustrate the cause of he who is now the King of Falsehood."

"No," said Michael.

Raphael looked at his brother with a puzzled look. "Michael, what do you mean 'no'? If Lucifer has entrapped our brethren ..."

"Lucifer would not do such a thing! He is Lumazi, he is Chief Prince, and he walks amidst the Stones of Fire"

Pleading Raphael spoke, "But Michael you saw where Abaddon's Ladder ended and who stood there waiting to receive him. What further proof do you need that Lucifer has betrayed us? Did not the Father tell us so?"

"Enough," replied Michael.

"Michael—I know this must be hard to hear, but whom else but Lucifer could free Abaddon? You know this to be true."

"That's enough!" Michael yelled.

Iofiel walked towards Michael, touched his lord softly on the shoulder, and tried to appeal to him. My Lord," said Iofiel "I saw Lucifer order the dissolu..."

"I said, that is enough!" Michael shouted.

Michael shoved aside Iofiel's hand from off his shoulder, turned and grabbed him by his throat, lifted him off his feet, and heaved him hard against a wall.

"I said enough! Do *not* continue to speak falsehood of my brother!"

Iofiel struggled to breathe, and Raphael yelled at Michael to release him, but Michael would not hear.

Raphael ran to them, pulled at Michael's arm, and screamed at him, "What are you doing?"

Nevertheless, Michael's hold was sure, and his hands wrapped tighter around Iofiel's throat.

Iofiel gasped for air as Michael squeezed his throat to silence him, but Iofiel fought to speak reason to Michael. "Have you too left El —to follow after the path of Lucifer?"

Michael's eyes immediately grew wide, the tension in his jaw loosened, and with a look of confusion, he released Iofiel, who fell to the floor wheezing and gasping for breath. Raphael pushed Michael aside and rushed to aid Iofiel. Michael staggered backward as a man dazed, shook his head in disbelief, and stared at them. He then spoke, "What have I done?" Then turned and quickly ran out of the room.

Raphael reached down to assist Iofiel to his feet. "Are you alright, my brother?" he asked.

"Nay," Iofiel replied, still coughing and massaging his neck. He turned to look into the dark hallway that Michael had run into. "My Prince and Lord of my house stands between two opinions. No, my prince, I am not alright."

Raphael nodded, looked into the darkness, and called out to Michael, but Michael would not respond.

Raphael lowered his head, and his face was grim as he stood to his feet and slowly helped Iofiel up. "Let us go. We need to find our trapped brethren."

"And what of the prince?" Iofiel said.

Raphael strained to see through the dimly lit hallway and saw a figure sitting on a wooden beam, his face in his palms and weeping uncontrollably. Raphael turned back to Iofiel and spoke softly. "There are some battles that must be won within before one can fight without."

The two turned to leave and left Michael to his sorrow.

****

Gabriel felt his pulse race as he ran through the Elysian Fields. The earth underneath his feet shook violently from the pounding hooves of his pursuers that closed swiftly to overtake him. His breath grew shallower, and his lungs burned from carrying Sariel. Gabriel was fast, but even the Leopard of Heaven could not escape his stalkers with such a weight to shoulder. He slowed, and he knew he could not outrace them. The wind felt good against his cheeks. The gentle breeze ruffled the fine tall stalks of manna leaf that carpeted open plains and acres of tilled land sprawled before him. The terrain proffered no advantage that he might conceal himself. There would be no hiding this day.

Closer the horde came, offended. Because he succored the Issi high prince, and in doing so, he made mad his brethren with even more rage, igniting the fury that now caused two of the great houses to hunt him. Their cries of dissolution to Gabriel drew nearer, and Gabriel knew that they would stop at nothing to capture him. They would pursue him to the gates of Jerusalem if he allowed them too. Gabriel could not bring such madness to the city of God.

I will make my stand here, he thought.

Gabriel's feet slowed, the tiny beating of his winged soles ceased, and his sprint through the golden hued fields of manna that he plowed underfoot came to a grinding halt. He eyed a gourd in the distance and gently laid the still unconscious Sariel to the ground. His back ached from carrying his brother. Ga-

253

briel stretched his wings, which prior had been taut, and his muscles celebrated the respite. With that momentary pause, Gabriel allowed himself to enjoy relief as he kneeled on the soft ground to stretch his legs. But only for a moment, as he turned his head to face the horde which now distanced only 50 yards away.

"There is no escape, High Prince," a pursuer said.

"We will have the high prince's head!" said an Arelim.

"Or we will have yours!" said another.

Gabriel stood to his feet and turned to face his pursuers. With grit of purpose, he unsheathed the iron swords which El himself had trained him to fashion, dipped the tip of one sword into the deep dark earth before him, drew a line for his attackers to see, and yelled to the legion who now stood paused to flay him. "I stand before the presence of the Almighty and mouth the voice of God! Hear now *this* message and never forget. The Lord hath not given me a spirit of fear; for if thou would seek a head to roll this day, you would do well to see to thine own!"

With those words, Gabriel launched himself at full speed towards the mob; wings unfurled and swords raised to attack a Legion.

The mob stood momentarily stupefied, taken aback that they now were on the receiving end of an attack by a High Prince of Heaven. Some moved backward unnerved in expectance of the high prince to surrender and surprised that this one angel would have the audacity to fight a multitude. However, for others who watched an epiphany occurred: the revelation that greater love had no man than this, that a man would lay down his life for his friend. For Prince Gabriel, many would wager, would die this day, yet they saw that he would sacrifice all to protect his brother who lay unconscious just yards before them.

Others were unmoved and raised their swords in kind to destroy the High Prince.

With a roar, Gabriel cried aloud, and the swords that he carried burst into flames as he threw himself towards the throng and set fire to the manna leaf to his rear creating a wall of flame. Flames that now barred the path of anyone that would seek to move behind him. The tall stalks of cinnamon smelling leaves burned instantly, their flames leapt high into the air, and dark smoke flooded the plains. Gabriel flexed his great wings, captured a gust of Heaven's wind, and shoved the same towards the wall of fire, launching a tidal wave of spark and tinder that raced towards the surprised mass.

Many on the front panicked at the wall of searing heat and fire that sprinted towards them and attempted to flee while those in the middle of the great morass were crushed between those who still pressed forward and those who sought to escape.

Gabriel sliced through the thinning throng, hacked limbs, and threw himself against Arelim, shattering breastbone and bursting ligaments, which held wings to flesh, slashing at anything that rose to take up arms against him.

Deftly, he weaved and dodged foes, shifting between his humanoid and cheetah-like form at will. He knew he must keep them off balance. The throng found themselves assaulted from every side as the speed of Gabriel's attack went unchecked against them. To his attackers, Gabriel appeared as if the God King himself had touched him, for he was omnipresent and everywhere at once, such was the ferocity of his attack.

Their screams rocketed to the sky from the heated wave, which launched against them and rolled across the golden fields. Panic and rage united in song with the cries of those whose limbs hung now severed. All joined in harmony in a horrific melody to create a new sound in Heaven. The horde wailed in lament for the lash that was Gabriel. A collective groundswell of underestimation journeyed across the mass. A miscalculation that was but momentary, as gaps in lines filled, and the thought of dissolution at the hands of Gabriel steeled the resolve of many; the corporate consciousness of the swarm knew that Gabriel could not fight if he could not move. Closer each angel moved towards one another. Closing their ranks tighter, they swung at the blur that was Gabriel, who still he evaded all touch.

Nevertheless, they were many, and he was but one. Gabriel now set in the center of bodies both maimed and dying knew that in his race to cut down all, he had left himself no room for retreat. They encircled him, menacingly creeping forward on his position, a blockade of Elohim all seethed with rage to silence the voice of God. When Gabriel saw that he would fall to the throng: when he perceived that he was trapped and that less than a hundred yards his brother lay unconscious, he reached to his side, lifted to his lips the Trumpet of Israel, and blew into the golden vessel. Its sound dashed through the air like racehorses into the golden blue skies of Heaven. The ears of all combatants burst, torn asunder by the blast of so powerful a sound that they fell to the ground, stunned and dazed, and in the moments that occurred between the bat of an eye, the clouds opened up, and the sky grew a putrid dark green.

The horde, which sought to slay Gabriel, gawked as they turned their gaze upward. For with the eclipse of the sun and through pierced clouds, they saw Ladders burst open across the lid of Heaven. Thunderous booms littered the peaceful skies while lightning strokes raced across the firmament to embrace each other: for upon winged gryphons rode legions of mighty Malakim. Thousands with unsheathed swords and spears descended upon them like locusts atop a field of defenseless corn.

****

Jerahmeel huffed as he entered the Hall of Annals, panting as he looked at the clear wall that separated him from the Zoa. He was always jovial and knew that levity could release tensions. Yet as he stood within the confines of the Hall of Annals, there was nothing that could generate lightheartedness this day.

Raphael had brought him to this place once before.

El hast decreed that you be given access to this place, but, alas, tread carefully, for within are the tomes of all creation. Within thou might know the invisible things from the creation of the world.

All right, Raphael. Jerahmeel thought to himself. *You said this was important. I hope you were right.*

Jerahmeel poured over the room and tried to remember all that Raphael had shown him. He stepped up a flight of stairs past the volume of books that floated and lined themselves on shelves and entered a room of pure white.

Ahh, this is it, he thought as he opened his mouth to speak to the listening room. "Location of Gabriel?"

The room flashed the colors of the spectrum, and Jerahmeel stood as if he was in a dream when suddenly under his feet the dark rich dirt of the Elysian Fields appeared. Jerahmeel beheld as Gabriel stood surrounded by a legion of Elohim ready to pounce upon him. Gabriel panted, and the blood of Elohim stained the golden hilts of his flaming swords and splatter was awash over him. His eyes glowed with a crackling light, and power dripped from his body as sweat beaded and glistened from his muscular form.

In El's name! Jerahmeel whispered aloud. "Gabriel! Gabriel!" he yelled.

Yet it was to no avail. Jerahmeel watched as the sky opened to reveal that the Malakim Gryphons fell from the skies and that House Malakim rode upon them to do battle on their Prince's behalf.

"But where is Michael?" Jerahmeel wondered aloud. The room unable to recognize if Jerahmeel posed a question or directed a command responded. The image of Gabriel disappeared from view, and the great room displayed Michael weeping uncontrollably alone.

"Argh, ya stupid room! I didn't say change the scene! Show me both Gabriel and Michael!"

The walls of the room obeyed and displayed on one wall Gabriel and the Malakim now locked in heated battle with house Arelim and Issi. The other portion of the wall displayed Michael weeping alone in a dark room.

"In El's name! Half of Heaven is in battle in the Elysian fields!"

Jerahmeel watched helplessly at the twofold scenes before him and wondered how he might provide help.

****

"We are almost there my prince," said Iofiel.

"Good," said Raphael. "We must quickly return to Jerusalem and make haste to find Lucifer."

The duo moved deeper into the cold and damp filled emptiness. With each step, Raphael followed Iofiel into the shadows, their hands outstretched reaching to feel their way against the cold rocky wall. Raphael noticed that his vision grew dim; his ability to see lessened with each step.

Raphael followed Iofiel and he led him deep into the bowels of Athor to a circular stairwell that lead into the depths of the earth past the foundations of the gleaming city; darkness became their third companion. The blackness reached out to ensnare and entangle a blackness that became tangible to the touch and enveloped them like a well-worn robe. The darkness hung oppressively upon them, suffocating and heavy. It was then that Iofiel suddenly stopped.

"What is wrong?" said Raphael.

"We are here, my Lord," replied Iofiel. "Look."

Raphael strained to see through the deep fog of blackness, but despite his vision, even he could not peer through the veneer that lay before them, and the light that emanated from his own body no longer was able to penetrate the darkness.

"Look at what? I see nothing but blackness roundabout. To what should my eyes gaze upon?" he said.

"Try again, my Lord, but look not with your natural eye but with that which we see in the spirit."

"Wait...I see it," said Raphael. "Lucifer was wise to conceal his actions on this wise."

Slowly, Raphael made out that darkness writhed within the darkness. Then Raphael saw the onyx door and the seal of Lucifer Draco. It was a strange thing, oval in shape, but the oily blackness which was before him was so dark, so devouring of light that it made the surrounding darkness seem as light. Slowly the depth of Lucifer's sin saturated Raphael's understanding. For to conceal oneself was to attempt to deceive God. Raphael began in that moment to grasp the gravity of Lucifer's cunning, a cunning that would seek to pluck out the very eye of the Almighty. For where in the multiverse would one run from God? Nevertheless, here within the bowels of the Earth, Lucifer sought to create a place of shadow to hide his atrocities from Heaven.

Raphael put his hand to the door, and it was icy cold to the touch. His breath turned to vapor in the damp and musty air. He intuitively knew that within

259

the confines of this door was another realm, a realm where the presence of God did not bring warmth. Iofiel stepped to the side, and Raphael turned the handle and pulled the heavy and onyx door. The seal of the First of Angels had been broken. Raphael jerked even harder, yet the door resisted and became heavier. Iofiel came to assist, and the duo pulled as one. The door creaked in reluctance, then gave way and opened to them. The seal of the chamber ripped and a hissing sound filled the air; and the cavern smelled with the stench that Raphael had only smelled prior when the blood of Corlus had spilled on Heaven's soil — dissolution.

****

"Why is this door thus that it refuses to open?" said Michael.

Raphael and Iofiel turned to see Michael standing behind them, studying the dank dark door and the structure over them.

"Are you ok?" asked Raphael.

Michael looked at his brother, nodded and then turned to Iofiel. "I repent of my actions earlier. I ask your forgiveness."

Iofiel placed his hands on his leader's shoulder. "My concern is for my Lord's welfare. I would see you whole."

Michael smiled. "Thank you my friend."

Michael turned to look at the huge door and felt its surface. It was cool to the touch and had a rough feel as if he was touching the exterior of something made of coarse rock; there were also ridges to it.

Michael leaned closer to inspect the door. Slowly he approached and placed his cheek against the wall. He lifted his head, and his eyes darted to make out an outline and the rise and fall of something — breathing.

"This is no door," said Michael, and he quickly backed away.

But it was too late, for Iofiel had already dug his hands deep into a ridge and used his weight to pull against the door and lurched the gate open, ripping the hinges from the sidewalls. Screams and wails then filled the corridor. Suddenly, light shined from two slotted sources above them. The 'wall' moved, buckled, and turned inside out to reveal an Elohim now towering above them. The dark figure had four arms, his back was like the shell of a tortoise, and Iofiel had ripped from the creature a scale that he himself had thought to be a door. There was no door. There was but an angel, disguised and concealed, who barred the path of anyone who might dare go further.

Michael looked into the body that was the creature and gasped, for within its bowels were the bodies of Elohim trapped and pushing against its flesh to escape. Each soul was emaciated beyond recognition, and their wails and groans filled the cavern as they pushed against the translucent skin of the creature. They were as bones heaped upon one another, refuse to be discarded, living angels crushed under the weight of one other, suffocating within the innards of the angel's flesh.

"I know thy scent, Michael of the Kortai. I am Minos, and though thou be the Builder of Heaven, you are not welcome here. For respect of thine office, I offer you passage to go whilst you may still leave, but know of a surety dissolution awaits you if you abide here. Tartarus is for the enemies of the Chief Prince, and my orders concerning intruders are clear."

Michael was quick to speak, "Who art thou to do harm to your own kind? Release those within I beseech thee. This ought not to be."

"Nay," replied Minos. "For the God King has himself created a realm that exists to consume Elohim, and we are told that the very fires of the Kiln have ceased to ignite our kind. We will not become lackeys of the Clayborne, nor will we bow the knee to El who would sentence us to slavery."

261

Michael winced as the groans of those within Minos cried out for relief.

Michael replied, "I am not slow to answer thee Minos, for I am on the Lord's side and forever shall I stand with El." Michael turned to look at Iofiel and smiled. Iofiel nodded knowingly.

Minos retracted his arm into a pocket of his flesh, and from within the deep folds of his arms, appeared a long scythe, which glistened and dripped with mucus. "Then come," he said, and know that Tartarus awaits you."

Minos heaved his scythe over his head and slammed the blade into the dank ground, and the steps underneath the trio shattered.

Iofiel quickly placed his back against the wall, missing the blow by inches; the breeze of Minos' forceful strike cooled his face. Raphael and Michael both jumped clear of harm's way while a shower of rock and debris exploded around them and sent small pebbles like shrapnel into their bodies. Michael sprinted and hurled himself into the air to grab the hand of Minos, struggling to use his weight to pull the creature's arm behind its back. Yet, Minos was too strong and flung Michael over his shoulder as one might swat a gnat. Michael careened into the dark stone wall, and with a great thud; hit the damp rock and fell violently to the ground.

"I have moved the stars into place on El's behalf. You are nothing to me, Prince. In vain, do you fight against me."

Minos lumbered closer to Michael who lay helpless on the ground. Michael's shoulder and back ached and throbbed, screaming out for relief.

The giant black Arelim moved in closer for the kill.

If dissolution is the Lords will,– then I will face it standing. Michael thought and struggled to rise to his feet.

Minos stood with his scythe gripped tightly and raised the weapon to cut Michael down; he placed his foot on Michael's chest pinning him to the ground.

"Goodbye Prince of Heaven," said Minos.

Michael closed his eyes, content in the knowledge that dissolution awaited him, but in the moments that the blow was destined to connect, the crash of falling rock thundered and the chasm's ceiling cracked. Light flooded the chamber, and Minos leaped to avoid being crushed as angel upon angel fell upon a singular hooded figure whose whips for arms flayed them to, and fro.

Michael rolled out of the way and marveled that the battle above to stop Charon had reached Tartarus itself.

Oblivious to all the angels that sought to bring him to a stop, Charon eyed the massive body that was Minos. His gaze fixed on the black onyx figure of he who would pretend to stand as a guard to a nether realm, a pretender to a throne that was his alone. Charon moved and dragged with tentacled arms a multitude of angels behind him, and Hell was awash in ecstasy. In a heated lust of engorgement, dangling angel flesh near and far, and like an intoxicated slut, she had her way upon the flesh of Elohim that dared to strike the Warden of Hell.

Without slowness of gait and without sound or pronouncement, Charon marched towards Minos to confront the imposter as warden of the nether realm. For in all the multiverse, there could be only one.

Minos had heard of Charon; yet, the report had not done Charon justice. Minos was Lucifer's answer to Charon, and Tartarus a mere projection of the realm of Hell, a prison made after the fashion and likeness of Lucifer's schemes. Watching Charon, Minos knew that Lucifer had established him and Tartarus as counterfeit.

"I have no quarrel with you ferryman. Do not force my hand, for my allegiance to the Chief Prince is clear, and this realm is shut by my hand and opened by none other. You may not pass, for I am the Maw here."

263

Charon did not speak. He only moved, plodding closer to confront this imposter. The worms, which did not light on Charon's body, slithered away from his flesh and crawled to the ground as if commanded by some unspoken voice. Creating a veil of fire that allowed none to pass or else risk consummation; they formed a line between him and the squadron of angels who now lay behind him in ruin.

Michael skirted backwards as Minos focused his attention on Charon, this new threat absolute. Minos walked to meet the Warden of Hell.

"Raphael! Michael! Come quickly!" called Iofiel. Motioning with his hand, Iofiel stood within the cleft of a rock, and Raphael and Michael joined him.

"Michael, are you alright?" asked Raphael.

"Aye," said Michael grabbing his arm that still was sore from his impact against the cavern wall. The trio hid and watched as the lumbering giants of Minos and Charon approached one another.

****

Jerahmeel looked as the forces of Heaven locked themselves in mortal combat. Malakim warriors filled the skies. Each rider strafed the ground, grabbing Arelim and Issi warriors. Flying high into the air, and then released them. The gryphons grasped their prey in their talons and flung them to the hills. Angelic bodies lined the once peaceful fields of manna, and the bluish silver blood of Elohim saturated the ground.

"He said to find the inkhorn and stylus," mumbled Jerahmeel.

He turned from the scene, which stretched for miles, and rushed to the desk and shelving in the library. Jerahmeel pulled down from the shelves above him, tome after tome. "He said it was hidden."

He searched through drawers and flipped over shelves. Tables fell to the wayside as book after book became as litter on the floor. As he hurried to search, he could hear the screams and curdled cries of his brethren on the battlefield. Jerahmeel sweated in anxiousness knowing that he held the promise to put a stop to the madness.

After pulling out a final drawer latticed with gold, he found it: the golden inkhorn and stylus of Raphael, the badges of each Grigori's honor and power.

Jerahmeel looked at the small pot and stylus. They seemed unremarkable. No different from what he had used countless times writing on manna leaf. However, he did not have time to dote; his task was to succor his brethren. He looked at the glowing inkhorn and remembered what Raphael had told him. *Speak the word, return, and break the container, and all realms will open that I might be brought home.*

Therefore, Jerahmeel took the stylus and broke it, and smashed the inkhorn into the ground. The floors, walls, and the ceilings above him suddenly disappeared. The room became as nothing, as color washed around him, and the sound of a rushing wind swept through the chamber. It was then that he heard the voice of his friend Raphael.

"It is time to go, Michael."

****

Lucifer met Abaddon and Lilith as each angel stepped through the Ladder. "Are you ready to begin?" said Lucifer.

Abaddon laughed. "They called me '*Destroyer*'," said Abaddon. "Let us then commence with their destruction!"

Lucifer moved to place his hand on his comrade's shoulder. "Nay, we are not here to obliterate the city and those therein. Do not forget our mission.

We are here to offer peace to those who seek solace under my banner and war only against those who align themselves to the perverted purposes of El. Are we clear?"

Lucifer eyed Abaddon as the giant of an angel snorted, shook his head in the affirmative to his new king, and reluctantly showed compliance. "For now, it shall be as you wish Lucifer."

"Nay," said Lucifer. "It shall be as I wish yesterday; today, and forever, for there can be only one God. Either thou art with me or you are against me. Come, for we have much to do."

The army of Lucifer Draco marched across the bridge and poured into Heaven's gate from the Ladder of Lucifer's making. They came as ants might overrun a carcass. Legion upon legion marched on translucent streets of gold, and the ground shook as their numbers rivaled the stars above, an army of Draco, Arelim, and Issi warriors, all with swords and blades fashioned after the imagination to destroy: pikes, polearms, shields, armor covered wings of leather, feather, and transparent wings as dragonflies. They marched this horde, marched and flew in columns of precision bent to stop El. An uprising of citizens united in their noble cause to usurp the dictator El at all cost. They were the spring, the dawn of a new day, confident that the Firstborn of all Angels would lead them to freedom.

When Deramiel came back from his errand to return to his post, his eyes looked upon the throng that massed before him: a cloud of Elohim who had not returned home to sing the praises of El. It was his inner knowing, his intuition. The look in Lucifer's eyes that made him know clearly that he had been betrayed. The gravity of his brother's deception fell upon him as a stone about his neck, and Deramiel fell to his knees. Lucifer saw the angel in his path and raised his hand to signal all to stop, and the armed warriors whose cadence made the ground shake came to a thunderous pause.

Lucifer walked before the throng and went to pick his weeping brother from his knees. He placed his arm around him to help him up. As a man might assist one with a disability, so too did Lucifer raise Deramiel to his feet and kissed him on both of his cheeks.

Deramiel looked upon him and said, "Come thou to betray the kingdom with a kiss?"

Lucifer paused, shaken at the words leveled against him.

"Nay, Deramiel. What thou seest before thee are those who have chosen to live free, to deny El usage of us as slaves to the Clayborne. Would you have our people debased into extinction? Do you not see? El hast made man to replace us. Why else enlarge the city? Or create a mote in the realm of all space that will not grow manna? Do you not see?" Lucifer held on tightly as the two embraced each other, their heads resting on each other's necks.

Deramiel sighed then replied. "What I see all too clearly is the heart of he whose consumption is for more than his station. I see a mighty son who would betray his own father. I see the creature risen up against his creator who hast done nothing since the day of your youth but elevate you on high. Yet despite all this, a multiverse with which you may enjoy, you would instead gaze on the one thing you cannot have, the throne of the Living God. This — my *friend*, is what I see."

Deramiel gently released Lucifer, and Lucifer sullenly nodded and said to Deramiel, "Then see no more."

With a swift turn of his diamond-laced wing, Lucifer sliced the neck of Deramiel. Deramiel's head severed from his body and fell to the ground. For a moment, the consciousness of Deramiel was there, and his eyes were spasmodic. Then they stopped and focused on the person of Lucifer. The gaze of Deramiel's pupils fixated on the beautiful eyes, of Lucifer. Lucifer peered past the blue eyes of Deramiel, but the look of betrayal that marked Deramiel's face etched itself into the High Prince's mind.

Lucifer turned to look away, stunned at the sense of shame and guilt that overwhelmed him. For a moment, he thought that perhaps he had leaped into the most terrible mistake he and Heaven had ever known; despondency and anger flooded his soul, but he hardened his heart, buried and suppressed any feelings of shame and guilt.

"El, I lay Deramiel's dissolution at your own feet," he whispered. "You have brought me to this." As Lucifer murmured his curse, Deramiel's stone flickered and went out, and his body slumped to his knees and fell at Lucifer's feet.

Lucifer turned to face the army that was behind him, straightened himself, and spoke for all to hear. "All will serve the cause of freedom or all will likewise perish." He waved his hand for the mass to follow and turned towards the city. The head of Deramiel became as sport to kick as the hordes' cadence became a quickstep, and their march to the city gates once more made the streets shake.

****

The two titans of the underworld clashed. Minos with his muscular arms and tortoise-like shell smote Charon with his fist, and the crack of bone filled the cavern. Never had Michael seen Charon stumble so. The Warden fell backward, his tendrils flailing and fire engulfed him as he crashed to the cavern floor. The impact sent great plumes of smoke and debris flying across the room, and the throng, which looked beyond the veil of fire, bleated from afar and cheered as the warden smashed into the dank earth.

Minos spoke. "I have been appointed the judge of the dead in this realm, ferryman. Hell hath no claim on Tartarus here. Fight me at thy own peril and risk my judgment as well."

Charon staggered to his feet as his tentacled body pushed him up from the floor. The warden again moved to engage his foe. Minos looked stout, his face resolute, and the scythe with which he carried; he swung around his body to smite Charon. The blade cut through bone and marrow, slicing off an appendage. The warden screamed, and the long flaming tendril fell to the cavern floor.

Like a child whose arm had been scraped on the harsh rock so too did Charon now nurse his wound. Minos pressed forward, and again his scythe carved through the air and came down hard on the shoulder of Charon, and once more, the personification of the vengeance of God fell to his knees and black fluid oozed from the wound.

The liquid saturated the blade, and the dark blood, different from that of other Elohim, solidified and wrapped itself around the edge. Charon looked up at Minos, and the face of a mare, the dead skeleton grinned! Minos looked as the blood moved, and like a snake, the blood coiled itself around the blade of the scythe and moved towards the arm of Minos himself.

"What trickery is this?" said Minos?

Michael watched from afar. He was there when Charon was created. Only he who was there from his creation truly understood that Charon existed to exact the vengeance of God. It was then that Michael realized that God was not asleep. He had no need for rest; fatigue was beyond the living God's necessity. He could not overextend himself. Charon was his mouthpiece against all those that would come against the will and word of God. The unstoppable, slow marching eventuality to all who resisted his will.

Minos was merciless in his fury. His scythe moved in a waltz and carved through flesh and bone of the warden. So it was that when Charon screamed, Michael knew that these were no ordinary screams, but cries of pleasure—the orgasmic and masochistic moans of a creature who fed off torment only to reflect it back upon the bearer.

Minos raised his mighty arms high above his head to bring dissolution to Charon, his scythe found its mark, and the blade came down straight on the equine skull of the Warden. As a pick might thud against ice, so did the sound of the cracking of Charon's skull fill the room. Charon roared in anguish and then grew still.

Onlookers cheered in glee at the destruction of the Warden. Praise for Minos filled the massive cavern, and applause echoed through the dank, smoky, dark cave.

"We must leave this place quickly," said Michael to his brethren. "Minos does not understand the nature of what Charon is. The more he resists, the more powerful the creature becomes. Charon cannot be destroyed except by submission to the Lord's will." Gingerly, the trio attempted to climb up the stairwell from which they came.

Minos looked over his defeated foe, and a smile escaped from his lips. The arrogant grin of pride marked his face, and he spoke. "The God King has no voice in vengeance, for Lucifer is the one true God."

A noise suddenly came from the rubble, and the ground beneath Charon stirred. Bones sliced apart earlier now moved, joint connected to joint, and the sinews grew before the eyes of all. Flesh carved away suddenly rejuvenated and reattached itself. The skull of Charon ignited, and fire shot from his eyes. The massive creature rose to his feet, and the worms of Hell, which never die, poured as blood from his body.

Charon turned and slowly marched again towards Minos, the chains for arms trailed behind him, and massive waves of flame leaped to engulf his path as he walked.

Minos beheld a new thing, a creature that knew not dissolution. Nevertheless, Minos was Minos, the guardian of Tartarus. He was the handle to the door to the lost souls within the black door, which was his very flesh. The way was shut, and he would allow no passage save his Lord King himself.

Minos turned to face Charon once more, lifted his scythe, and brought it square onto the shoulder blade of Charon.

The cries of the creature smote the eardrums of all in the cave. Michael and the host of angels covered their ears.

Charon staggered. Blood leapt from his body as a wellspring, and tentacles of bone and barb and the worms of Hell moved towards Minos.

Minos drew back so not to be touched by the leeches of fire. Yet it availed him not, for the blood of Charon was as a living thing. It moved in a serpentine fashion and flowed to the foot of Minos and then to the ankle.

Minos sliced at the blood, but with each stroke against the liquefied attacker, it dispersed as a mist and then reformed to pursue him the more. When it reached him, it solidified and grabbed his heel, as ropes would lasso a stallion. Minos struggled, struggled to overcome the solidified blood that slowly began to consume him, as the worms found him quickly, and they fed, for Minos was an Arelim, a mover of stars, and the worms engorged themselves on the angel who thought to undue Charon.

The reality of his foe confronted Minos, and he sought to flee, but the long trail of blood followed him as the worms of Hell moved and attached themselves as leeches upon the angel, burrowing into him to consume him alive.

As a murderer stalks his prey, Charon followed Minos. The mighty Minos pleaded for his life and screamed in tortured anguish as the worms and blood feasted on him.

All looked and beheld the true nature of Charon: he was consumption, a plague, and one angel coined a new term to give words to what he saw.

"He is not dissolution…he is *Death*."

The throng turned from their cheering and now clamored for escape.

Yet it was too late. They had fallen into the lower parts of the Earth, trapped in the prison of Lucifer's corrupted mind and caught between the vengeance of God, and the maggots of Hell. Each larva moved to feed, to sustain mother Hell, and provide life and strength to the warden.

Minos looked at Charon and spoke. "What is this that thou hast no stone, nor gem which animates thee? What art thou?"

Michael watched from afar, and he knew Charon was not fueled by God's love, like the host of all Heaven. Nay, Michael was there when God gave rise to Charon; a creature fueled by God's hate, his very life tied to the Kiln. Where there was the Kiln, there would be Charon.

The arms of Charon reached from his body and latched their barbed claws into Minos' shell, and Minos was held fast, pinned as he attempted to claw his way to safety. It was a pitiful sight, a mover of stars struggling to escape the power of the living God.

"*Death*," Michael had heard an angel describe Charon. It was a good name.

Dissolution indeed sounded too trite for whom Charon was. He was Death.

Charon then lifted Minos high into the air and ripped his shell from his body. Minos screamed, and the worms enveloped him. His body burned but was not consumed. His beating stone, the engine of life, which El gave to all, pulsated still, infested with worms of fire and sulfur. They crawled through nostril and mouth, and Minos gurgled, choking as they passed through orifice after orifice and attached themselves to his lungs and heart and breathed for and through him, worms that through their burrowing created new orifices.

As the pieces of Minos' now broken shell lay on the cavern floor. Charon looked down on the mass of burning flesh and flayed the skin that surrounded Minos' heart of stone. With a brutality that defied all that Heaven had seen, Charon slammed his tentacled arm deep into the chest of Minos and pulled from his chest his living stone. The worms still latched on it dangled from it and fell to the cavern floor as linguini.

Minos was key to Tartarus, and Charon now held his Heartstone in his hand. He gazed upon the black onyx rock that looked so much like his own. The monster took the stone and ingested it, taking its essence into himself.

The cavern shook, and Minos' shell began to glow. Heat emanated from it, and hands reached from inside his body to pry open the shell. Angels poured from it coughing; dozens at first, and then hundreds stumbled and hurried over one another to find release from the prison of the netherworld that Lucifer had created in secret, a realm where Minos himself was both door and key.

Michael yelled to the throng that poured from Minos' now lifeless body. "Come to me all who bow the knee to El; come to me!" Those who had not sworn allegiance to Lucifer went to the side of the familiar voice of Michael, and he spoke to the freed masses of angelic warriors before him. "See now the treachery of Lucifer usurper to the throne. See now as his allies clamor for escape. Go to and smite them. Look to those who cared not for your imprisonment, nor show them any quarter."

Lucifer's minions moved with haste to escape the march of Charon as he returned to the surface. They turned to face the released captives and knew that to fight Charon and their brethren was futile. Some sought to escape while others turned to face this new enemy and attacked.

The cave exploded with violence as angel attacked angel, each grappled in hand to hand combat, and stones were torn from chests, smashed to the ground, and dissolved to ash.

Jerahmeel within the Halls of Annals saw that Raphael and Michael were deep in melee combat. Michael was too far to succor, but Raphael was within reach; he would know how to stop the onslaught that approached Heaven. Jerahmeel reached within the image of the wall, grabbed the arm of Raphael, and pulled him from the dimension of Earth into the Hall of Annals.

Raphael screamed with pain, for his body was simultaneously present in two realms at once. With a great heave, Jerahmeel pulled Raphael, and they fell backwards to the floor. Raphael looked at Jerahmeel with a smile and whispered as he faded into unconsciousness, "What took you so long?"

****

Lucifer belted out from his restored balcony and looked upon the great city of Jerusalem. The inhabitants scurried about, for they did not know that dissolution dwelled within their walls, but the citizenry was curious about the warriors with stave and spear, sword and shield. Never had they seen such instruments, and Lucifer knew that in moments, their decisions if they were wrong would shed their naiveté and Heaven would be at war.

I must convince them of the rightness of my cause, for I will not stand to see, my brethren to fall to the lie that El hast propagated.

As the pipes in his belly gave the clarion call to the city as he had in so many times past, Lucifer trumpeted once more for all of Heaven to assemble before him to meet their God.

They came, as was routine. They came because the First of Angels called to them. They came because they knew they would meet God. They were each surprised in what they saw and heard. Thousands looked up in wonderment and in silence to the balcony of Lucifer's abode. Shimmin a Harrada was the first to speak.

"Your majesty, forgive this outburst, but why hast thou assembled the host of Heaven, for El rests, and the God King abides in his temple. Why then are we here?"

Lucifer looked upon the crowd and spoke. "Hear me, host of Heaven. From the start of our kind, thou hast seen my face, and I have called thee to praise the name of El. From the beginning, I have seen you birthed from the Stones of Fire. From the beginning, I have presented you to El that He might announce his word to you.

"But no more. For even eternity must end, and an end has come indeed. I have not borne witness to another Elohim since the creation of man. Nay, the Kiln burns no more to ignite the stones that animate our kind. Instead, we hear in the distance the hunger pains of the abomination of Hell. A new furnace the Lord hast made to consume our kind! Is this to be our fate? We are now commanded, we who stand at the apex of creation, the firstborn of all things, we who uphold all things by the word of his power, are now asked to set aside for another! We are destined to teach, nay to serve, this flesh borne thing of mud and clay. Indeed, with every beginning, there must be an end, an end to the lie that we were made to move stars, to breathe life into creation. Nay, the true revelation of our purpose is now made clear with the creation of the Clayborne and the construction of Hell. We are to be slaves, and this, despite my love for El, I will not stand for. I cannot stand for! I will fight Him; fight this trickery of He who would subjugate us for all eternity. Join me, and we shall usurp El, and free ourselves of his leash. Go to the mountain of God with

275

me, and we shall rule the heavens, and I will guide you as I always have, and my face shall be to you as beloved, and ye shall know peace.

"But know this, El's power and this realm of Hell are not to be feared. I would not stand for false judgment on our brethren, and thus, I, the First of Angels, have braved the maw and have returned. See the impotence of El to construct a prison that can be escaped."

Abaddon moved from behind Lucifer and stood by his side, and many in the crowd gasped and stood stunned, but the gravity of Lucifer's words rung true to many, and the rumblings of discontent and dissension grew among different ones in the crowd.

"I cannot understand why God would make a Hell for us!"

"What is the man that he is mindful of him?"

"El hast gone too far!"

Finally, one word among all others rang out toward the balcony and hit the earshot of both Lucifer and Abaddon.

"Traitor!"

Lucifer scoured the crowd to identify who would blaspheme against him. Soon the word spread from one voice to another, and one could no longer make out who was on the Lord's side and who sided with the cause of Lucifer.

Abaddon looked at Lucifer waiting for permission to do what Lucifer was hesitant to do.

"You see, God King, there can be no turning back now. Would El tolerate such blatant disregard for his rule? If you are to be King, then you must do what must be done."

Lucifer grimaced at Abaddon's words and tightly closed his eyes. *Why do they not understand? Do they not see that blind allegiance to EL means enslavement to man? Why must it come to this?*

"Traitor!" was the cry of the multitude. "Traitor!"

"Abaddon is a murderer, and El is the living God," said an angel, "I will not abandon my God!"

Lucifer's eyes widened as he gazed the cityscape, and he lifted up his hands to quiet the crowd.

Yet the throng failed to silence, and the more Lucifer gestured for calm, the more they clamored for his own removal.

"You are *not* a friend to God!" said one.

They then mocked him as a herald for daring to pretend that he stood for the cause of El.

Others came to his defense, and they argued with each other, but it was clear, many would not be turned. Lucifer's heart quickened, his stone glowed, and he could not resist the urge to scratch at his chest. His face contorted in anguish and grief, and a tear ruefully fell from his eye at his decision and the scene that now played before him. His lips moved cursing El unconsciously as he spoke. Lost in bitterness, his mind frustrated over goals denied. The hosts of Heaven were not united in their love of him over El. Lucifer seethed as his ears received a call for his own imprisonment for betraying El. Distraught, he backed away from the balcony so as not to be seen and covered his face with his hands.

Abaddon looked down from the balcony upon the restless crowd and then turned warily to his master. "Lucifer!" said Abaddon. "What is thine command? You desire to lead us. Then lead!"

Awakened from his ruminations, Lucifer wiped the tears from his eyes. His brow became hard, and he turned and spoke firmly to Abaddon.

"Destroy them."

Abaddon leaped over the balcony and landed among the crowd; his feet made the ground shake and cracked the golden glass street below. Silence overtook the throng, for his presence was imposing, and whispers were all that was heard. One angel looked in defiance at the great Arelim and walked directly to face him.

"You, 'Destroyer,' are a blight in Heaven and why El consigned you to Hell. Your very presence is an offense to me."

Abaddon was want to correct him, but simply grasped the angel by the stone in his chest, crushed it within the palm of his hands, and threw the lifeless body to the ground.

Like wildfire, the throng scattered while others leaped to attack him; violence erupted round about. And from the great Chittim balcony that was his perch, Lucifer, Son of the Morning Star, watched as Heaven degenerated into civil war, watched as brother fought against brother, watched as his plan for Heaven's control took shape, and watched as angels battled each other to dissolution. Lucifer clenched his teeth, tears filled his eyes, and he muttered, "El, you will burn in the very Hell thou hast made for our kind, for know of a surety that I come for you."

****

Michael moved and ducked kicks and punches thrown wildly at him. He grabbed the wings of one angelic combatant and flung him into another. The underworld was rife with battle and the smell of dissolution was in the air, but it was Charon who was the source of all things chaotic as the lumbering giant of God's vengeance made his way to the surface; nothing stopped him. He merely consumed whatever stood in his way.

Charon seemed preoccupied, oblivious to all others around him, and attacked only if attacked. Angels in their collective wisdom moved from his path and steered clear of him, focusing instead on one another. Charon was a force to himself and not to be interfered with.

Thus, the former prisoners of Tartarus and Michael fought against those loyal to the cause of Lucifer. The cavern shook, for it could not contain the violence, and upon the surface of the earth, the ground swelled upwards and erupted in volcanic ash and thunder as the ground exploded, and Elohim after Elohim burst from the ground locked in combat. The ash of clouds mixed with Elomic blood as bodies filled the air and the surface of the ground around Athor disintegrated into a morass of angels slashing, hacking, and swinging against their foes.

As Michael surveyed the scene, he saw that the Earth had also erupted in madness, the natural response to Elohim no longer watching over seedling and animal. Vegetation itself had arisen against friend and foe alike, and the sky darkened with winds run amok as the elements themselves were unleashed to battle on each one's behalf.

Michael beheld that the Earth was in agony, her body ripped to shreds as Elohim at cross-purposes with one another used her to do their will. Smoke filled Athor from the distance, and Michael discerned that the battle was planet wide. Michael could only imagine what the heavens looked like. He looked skyward and knew that somehow he must bring the madness to an end. He knew that Raphael had escaped, dragged into the great walls of the Halls of Annals by a force unknown. He knew that only in Heaven could he cause the battle here to cease; therefore, he looked to Iofiel who stood fighting off enemies of the state. Michael ran towards him, ducked, and weaved among angels until he reached his side.

"I must return to Heaven. Only there can this be stopped before the Earth itself is torn to sunder. I leave but place thou in command of the host here. Fear not, for the Lord, is on our side."

Michael turned himself skyward and uttered the Elomic command to open the realms and create a Ladder to Heaven. He lifted himself to depart, broke the atmosphere, and found himself hurtled past cloud and into the darkness of space. The Ladder twisted, turned, and arched to the Third Heaven, and in the distance, Michael saw it, the waypoint of Heaven, but the way was shut, held in check by an Elohim with a flaming sword. Within seconds, before he crashed into oblivion, Michael violently turned his body to avert his own dissolution, arched the Ladder back towards Earth, and crashed like a meteor into her waiting arms. As an artillery shell finds its target, Michael flung himself into a group of Lucifer's forces. The blast of the Ladder's energy blew apart ground and flesh. All Elohim in the vicinity of the impact found their stones shattered or cracked, and they fell to the ground in agony or were vaporized. For a moment, all had stopped fighting to see the site, as the charred ground and smoke revealed the white-hot glow of the Builder of Heaven. As smoke wafted through the air from the crater that now adorned the ground, Michael rose from bended knee and spoke high into the air so that all could hear.

"Heaven is at war, and the way to her is shut."

****

Lucifer quickly left his bedroom and headed downstairs; his entourage of Ashtaroth and Lilith accompanied him. The walls shook, and dust fell from the ceiling, for the battle for Jerusalem had begun.

"My Lord, your plan for Heaven is coming to pass," said Ashtaroth. "The fighting in Elysium and on Earth hast divided Heaven's forces. With El himself withdrawn from battle, He hast made it possible to strike at the Godhead, and in his weakness, we shall be made strong."

Lucifer frowned and spoke, "No, my plans are not as I desire. For brother is set against brother. This is not my perfect will, and I will see it end. Lilith, secure the library that we might have knowledge of our enemies' movements. Ashtaroth, continue to walk with me." Lilith left his master and motioned two guards to accompany him. Lucifer watched until they were out of earshot.

"I have a task for you, one unique to your abilities and one I can impart to none other." Ashtaroth stood silent, bowed his head, and waited for instruction.

"Go with Abaddon. He will need to be brought into remembrance of why we are here. Stay with him Astarte, remind him that we are *not* here to obliterate all that exists. I fear that without my influence, he would bring ruin to us all, and our plan would come to naught. Do whatever thou must to keep him in the way."

"And if he rebels against thy will, Lord King?" asked Ashtaroth.

Lucifer paused, his brow wrinkled, and his eyelids closed. He turned, looked sternly at Ashtaroth and spoke without fluctuation. "Then let dissolution be his end and assume the head of the army in his stead. Are you clear in your purpose, Astarte?"

"I am clear, my Lord." Ashtaroth bowed and set himself to leave his master.

Lucifer watched as Ashtaroth walked away, looked towards the mountain of Hell, spread his wings, and lifted into the sky. Lucifer flew towards the Maw and thought to himself, *It is time to bring this sad season of El's reign to a close.*

Abaddon and his cadre smashed their way through throngs of angelic resistance. With his great sword, Abaddon cut down soul after anguished soul. Limbs flailed as all who stood within his path were hewn asunder. Abaddon gloated as each angel fell before him. His lips curled in a smile as his sword drew Elomic blood

The denizens of Heaven were not prepared. They had never known violence. Now violence was unleashed against their own, by their own. Surprise and confusion were the tactics of choice Lucifer sought to use in his battle against the populace. Yet, surprise and confusion quickly dissipated as allegiances formed across Heaven's landscape. With battle lines drawn and bodies assailed against body, Elomic blood spilled onto the golden streets like water from a tap.

Each angel's special ability was unleashed in the termination of eternal life. Their Elomic gifts used not to build but to beat back horde after oncoming horde of angels who defied El's will. The streets of Heaven filled with those using their hands, feet, and wings to defeat those who held sword and spear.

Across the cityscape they parried and thrusted, ducked and weaved, and flew at each other, stopping swords with clasped hands, kicking, and punching until Heavens ranks began to decimate; until the countless could be counted. Heaven's air filled with the clouds of dissolution and the ground with the blue blood of Elohim lined the streets.

The armies of Abaddon marched from the palatial abode of Lucifer through the residential quarters of Heaven and set fire to home and estate.

"Burn them with fire!" commanded Abaddon. "Let it all burn."

The officers of Abaddon obeyed, and Ares was swift to carry out his master's commands. Each dwelling that they passed was set to flame, and smoke rose high into the air. Abaddon moved with speed, his effortless ability to destroy now increasingly evident as he cut down all who stood in his way.

The army of Lucifer continued its march through the burbs of Heaven and made their way to the Golden Path, the center lane that would take them to the throne of the Mountain of God itself. Abaddon looked ahead and saw nothing but the towering spires and the multitude of angel fold before them. He looked upon the masses of oncoming angels that raced towards him and knew that more were with El then were with them. There were simply too many to kill, too many who had jeered and mocked the Son of the Dawn, but enough to enact his vengeance; to mete out his punishment to all who witnessed his humiliation at the hands of El. Like perfume, Abaddon smelled the fear that invaded the consciousness of beings who knew not trembling. He wallowed and smiled in gleeful intoxication and marched towards his audience with El where Lucifer and he would bring justice to the God King.

Abaddon smiled and waved to his ground soldiers to advance the burning of Heaven. The smell of house and fallen bodies filled the air. The crack of timber and rock and the screams of angels echoed in Abaddon's ears.

Ashtaroth had made his way to catch up with the front and looked to see all that was wrought. He saw the destruction of Heaven's habitations and the bodies that lined the ground in the wake of Abaddon's march. He pushed through cadre after cadre of angels aligned to their cause, and it was then that he saw Abaddon reach for the horn to signal what Lucifer had forbidden.

"Abaddon no!"

Abaddon turned to see Ashtaroth, and their eyes locked. Abaddon smiled and put his lips to sound the Horn of Lucifer to summon the legions who waited on Earth.

Lucifer's horn pierced the ears, and immediately the sky filled with what looked like falling stars. The boom of a Ladder opened up above them and then another, and then as far as the eyes could see. Ladders dotted the sky and explosions reverberated throughout the city. Thousands of angelic troops poured into Heaven from Ladders directed into buildings, and those not behind the safety of Abaddon's troops were obliterated as the first and Third Heavens attempted to occupy the same space.

Angels upon gryphons and other winged steeds and Elohim that flew descended from the portals that opened in the midst of the sky; they came through as bees whose nest had been disturbed. Those that once thought to fight Abaddon scattered; as everywhere about them reality was warped, and new legions faithful to Lucifer attacked without mercy, striking down whoever did not wear their Lord's mark.

Abaddon looked to Ashtaroth and spoke. "Isn't it glorious? Let it burn, Astarte! Let it all burn!"

Ashtaroth looked upon Abaddon as spittle dribbled from the Destroyer's mouth and knew that Lucifer was right to send him.

Abaddon must be stopped at all costs.

****

Raphael ran towards the back of the Hall of Annals as the mountain shook.

Dust and rock fell from the ceiling as the rumble of battle could be heard from outside.

"We must work quickly," said Raphael. "To secure this place, for it surely will be a target of Lucifer to hold its secrets."

"But why?" asked Jerahmeel. "Why this place?"

284

"Because in this place, the hidden things even from the foundations of the world can be made known, and El hast decreed to whom might know these things. Lucifer in his grab for power would of a surety have this place. This must not be. Come quickly; I must show you something."

Jerahmeel quickly followed Raphael deeper into the catacombs of the Hall of Annals and pulled from a sealed glass cabinet a tome of record. Each leaned to brace himself as books fell to the floor, and the booming thunder became louder.

"What is this?

"The Tome of Iniquity," said Raphael. "El has purposed it sealed and to be opened only for such a time as this."

"Wait," said Jerahmeel, "El knew that all this would happen?"

"El knows all. We are merely a witness to what he chooses to reveal, and there is much that lies within the mount: those things that are past, those things, which are, and even those things that are yet to be. This tome El trusted to be shown now. What you will see hast been seen only by El, Lucifer, myself, and now you.

Raphael reached into his cloak and pulled a key and with it unlocked the golden seal that encased the Tome of Iniquity.

Raphael moved to exit from the room. "Observe quickly; we must depart soon. The rumblings of the mountain can only mean that Lucifer's forces are close. When you are done, we shall plan how to defend against this threat."

Raphael closed the door behind him.

Jerahmeel looked at the book. It sparked and glowed. Smolder and heat lifted from its thick bound cover. It smelled of fire and brimstone and stunk. Jerahmeel approached as he covered his nose and began to cough; his throat scratched and phlegm settled in his throat. Waves of nausea overwhelmed him with each step that he took. He reached forth his hand to touch the book, and it festered and sizzled with boils as his fingers lighted on the cover.

The book flung open as if with a life of its own. Images of its contents drew Jerahmeel into the scene and he was afraid, for around him was fire, smoke, and flames that engulfed him. His stomach churned and vomit bellowed from his mouth; the stench of decay and heat was unbearable. But he knew this place. He had seen it before from afar. It was the inside of the Kiln, but this view was like none other: for the vantage was from none other than El himself. For God hath kept a record, and Jerahmeel realized that what he was about to witness was something that not even the Almighty would let slip without testimony. Jerahmeel was undone to know that for these brief moments he beheld what God himself had seen in the Kiln.

Jerahmeel was overwhelmed with the sights and sounds that flung at him, for about him were color and sound that even he with his ears had never heard: it was both beautiful and terrifying all at once. The Lord and Lucifer stood within the Kiln, and God motioned for him to pick a stone.

The stones were vibrant, and each alive with the colors of the rainbow. Each one sang harmonic melodies asking God to allow them, "to be." All living stones of flame, stones that represented all the elements that El had made, set here as it were in a storehouse: the Kiln. It was here that Jerahmeel knew that God had simply stored a fraction of who He was in this place.

El watched as Lucifer picked up the stone that He had commanded.

"The time hast come to promote thee, even to be as one of us. For we have chosen thee to become one with us as God. But another must hold now the title of the Morning Star. Now," said El. "gently place the stone in the wall's flesh."

With his palms outstretched, Lucifer received the large stone that El had given him and noted how similar it was in size and shape to his own. He gazed upon it, and a frown showed upon his face. He lifted up his hands and flung the stone. The gemstone smote the wall, and like flint, it sparked, chipped, and cracked in three places and unleashed sparks to ignite flame within the flames. The stone ceased in its melodic song and let out an ear-splitting wail, and Jerahmeel covered his ears from the pain.

And the thing which Lucifer did displeased the Lord.

The Lord knelt down and took the wailing rock, and immediately its cries diminished but did not stop. Then the Lord himself tucked the stone gently into the folds of the wall's flesh while Lucifer looked on.

And the Lord spoke to the rock, "Thou art beautiful and strong, as the diamond, you must be resolute to uphold the brightness of my coming, for if thou canst surpass the inner wail of thy spirit, know that thou shalt herald me as the Son of the Dawn, even as this one who now stands beside me. Rise, Apollyon, and take thy place amongst the stars. Fail me not, and thou shalt be exalted among thy people, but be thou warned, that if sorrow persists, then on your shoulders shall indeed a new dawn come, the breaking of a new day. And he to whom you would seek solace shall be your true King, and your infamy shalt be known even unto the end of days."

Jerahmeel watched as God constructed from the wall the form of a great Arelim, and God then caused a deep sleep to overtake Lucifer. The Lord took the splintered shard of Apollyon's stones from the floor and grafted a shard into Lucifer's stone. When he awoke, Lucifer could feel the hurt of Apollyon beating within him and scratched hard at his chest.

The Lord spoke, "Because thou hast chosen not to honor me, know that you shalt forever feel the pain of purpose marred. For if thou will not be faithful in that which is another man's, who will make you ruler of that which is thine own? For lost now thou art to promotion, for we had chosen thee to become even as God, but because thou hast chosen to embrace iniquity, then iniquity shall be thy schoolmaster, for when thou dost move to remove the mar in he, then know that thine own sin shall then be healed, and restoration shall come to you both. For alas, thou art now linked, for the strong ought to bear the infirmities of the weak."

Then the Lord turned his back on Lucifer, and Lucifer clutched at his chest. The fires of the Kiln grew dim, and nothing remained but the two angels. Apollyon towered over Lucifer and looked straight-ahead as a machine ready to receive instructions. Lucifer gasped for air and knelt on the floor while one hand grasped at his now hurting chest, and he yelled for the Lord God to hear.

"Am I my brother's keeper!?"

The Lord stopped to turn and said, "No, my son, he is yours that thine iniquity might be purged."

With those words, the vision that Jerahmeel beheld came to a halt, and the images whirled around as if drained and funneled into the pages of the book that Jerahmeel held in his hands. The tome closed with thunder, and lightning flashed; Jerahmeel dropped it to the floor and fell backward on his hind in astonishment.

"El hast known since the beginning!" said Jerahmeel.

"Aye," said Raphael. "And more importantly, he knew what Lucifer and Apollyon were capable of."

"Does Abaddon know that Lucifer flawed his purpose?"

"No. There is no record in Grigoric history of this revealed outside of El, Lucifer, and us. This book has been sealed."

"Then we must see to Abaddon; perhaps he might yet be reasoned with?"

"Nay," said Raphael. "He is as you have said, *Abaddon*. The fracture has run its course and cannot be repaired. He is lost."

"But…" said Jerahmeel. "Apollyon…I mean Abaddon was to replace Lucifer, and Lucifer knew about the replacement and marred him. I cannot believe this, Lucifer…Lucifer was to be one with the Godhead!"

"In the mind of our brother, there could be only one. El sought to teach him that in a universe of plenty, he had no lack. Nothing would have been denied him, for he was the beloved of the Lord. El had willed Lucifer to be imbued with the powers of the Godhead, and they being three would be four. But lo, in his blindness to see only what he was, he lost sight to that which could be. He was afraid of loss, and in his fear, he was the first to lash out in anger, the first to do Elohim harm from the womb of the Kiln. He was a murderer from the beginning, and the Lord pardoned him."

Jerahmeel looked on in stunned disbelief, trying to comprehend all that he had seen and heard.

"And did Lucifer know that you knew?"

"No, he only suspected. This is why I suppose he had such a desire to see into the Hall of Annals, that he might divine its secrets and to wrest from me the extent to which others knew of his iniquity."

"Why show me this, Raphael? To what end does this help our cause and stop the fighting of our kin?"

Raphael turned. "I cannot do what must be done here. The Hall is not designed to display its secrets in mass. We must go to the Library in the city, and from there I can take the tome and show it, for I intend to broadcast the truth of he who would be God to the people. Let them decide if this is whom they shall serve. El has rejected him. Now the people must know why."

"And then?" said Jerahmeel.

"Then…" said Raphael, "They shall know the truth, and the truth shall make us free."

****

Michael looked in the distance as Charon had stopped at the fiery plume and extended his hands into the tendril of Hell. Hell hearkened to her master, reached for him, and lifted the warden into the air to return him into her bosom. Michael watched as Charon vanished into a whirlwind of fire and knew that on the other side of the unimaginable heat Charon walked the belly of Hell, an antibody as at home in the digestive tract of brimstone and fury as any microbe within the intestine of a cow.

Can I survive this journey? Michael thought to himself.

He knew that he could not form a waypoint, for all entrances to Heaven were shut. To form a blind waypoint could destroy the very ground of Heaven itself. Michael's mind raced as he watched the fire slowly begin to dissipate.

"You wouldn't dare?" said Iofiel who stood beside him coming to realize what ran through Michael's mind.

"There is no other way," replied Michael. "Do you have a better idea?"

Iofiel looked at the flame ascending into the sky beyond the first heaven past the clouds, looked at Michael, and offered his hand.

"When you open the gate of Argoth, we will come."

Michael paused, looked at Iofiel, took his hand, and embraced him and spoke in his ear. "Hold this ground for El, and we shall celebrate our victory over a banquet of manna."

Each beheld the landscape before them as plumes of smoke and fire rose into the air, and Athor burned as the war to retake it from those aligned with Lucifer waged on. As Michael prepared to depart, they heard without warning

290

the sound of the Horn of Lucifer crack the heavens, and as if on cue, legions that were preconditioned to worship upon the sound, fell to their knees. It was the clarion call to worship, and Michael and Iofiel watched as angel after angel kneeled to lift their voice to sing the praises to El. Yet on this day, neither angel could bring himself to do so, for they knew that today this sound was something else and that their kind had been tricked.

Then they saw it…the flash of a Ladder. Then another, and then hundreds, nay thousands, and the vacuums created ripped the ground and made the air crackle with lightning and thunder. Iofiel fell to his hind blown back by the multitude of Ladders that reached to the sky, and then he looked upon the ground. It was marred as far as the eye could see as each Ladder dug into the earth and cauterized the ground into glass. Iofiel noted that everywhere their enemy had vanished; gone home to wage war, each angel a weapon of mass destruction let loose upon the unsuspecting people of Heaven. He knew that Heaven could not survive such an assault.

Iofiel fell to his knees, rent his clothes and wept that Heaven was being destroyed.

Michael frowned and looked resolutely at the ascending funnel cloud of fire and flew quickly to intercept the tendril of Hell, to allow hellfire to touch him once more. As he approached, he could feel the heat, and his body began to glow. He prayed, asking El for courage, and closed his eyes as he flew into the cylindrical pyre. Hell knew that angel flesh was in her grasp and coiled her lanky vines of fire around Michael and pulled him towards her.

Michael felt himself lift through the heavens, pulled by the force of God's punishment to all who would seek to defy his will. The fire bit at him and burned him. His body convulsed in pain as his lungs filled with the gas of brimstone, his eyes grew blurry, and his body contorted as he flung through space and time. A shard of nourishment lobbed through the boundaries of the cosmos to feed the stomach of Hell. Michael heaved, and his flesh gave way to the heat as he moved from one realm to the next.

Agony rippled over him, and he cried out in pain. His mind became clouded, his vision darkened, and Michael lost consciousness, but only for a moment, for Hell would not let angel stuff of this sort die. No, she must suckle on him, to fan her flames. Michael's life force was different from the rest; he was a Chief Prince, one of the Lumazi, and Hell would savor her meal.

The long tendril slowly receded itself, and with thunder and the snap as if of a thousand trees, Michael fell hard on soft, wet, warm ground. He could hear the gurgle of the giant, and the life ebbed from him as she fed upon him. Michael knew that perhaps he had done nothing for the cause of Heaven save hasten his own demise. As he flickered back and forth between states of consciousness, he saw the hooded figure that was Charon. His equine skull could not be mistaken as the warden towered over him.

Michael could feel the chains of the Watchman of Hell wrap around him; the breath of the beast floated as toxic poison on the air. Michael moved his face as far away as he could as Charon sniffed at this intruder. The flames had somehow died down, and Michael could feel that he was held aloft by Charon's might alone, for no tendril touched him. Sweat beaded on his brow and flowed from his face. Michael coughed as the haze, smoke, and brimstone made what little breathable air acrid to swallow. Michael coughed and wheezed as Charon continued to view this angel.

Charon knew Michael's scent. He gently placed the Chief Prince on the ground and stood silently over him. His black cloak draped over him, but Michael could dimly see through its folds that eyes upon eyes looked at him. Tongues salivated within razor sharp teeth, and ooze coated the ceiling and walls, yet Michael remained unharmed.

Then Charon let out a roar, and the sound made Michael cover his ears; it was a bestial sound. A sound that mimicked the great creatures Michael had seen on the Earth. A guttural sound that made him cower. Charon's tendrils flailed about him, and he raised his hammers for hands and flung them into Hell's belly. Hell convulsed and yelled her displeasure with a sound that could not be described. Michael could only perceive that it was one of pain.

Michael discerned that Hell and Charon were at odds over his presence, for he sensed that at any moment the salivating tongues, which were just outside of his reach, might devour him, tongues with eyes that looked at Michael, hungry to consume him.

Hell's eyes looked at Charon and backed away deeper into the heated darkness outside of view: afraid to cross the warden.

Charon uncovered Michael, looked upon him and reached to touch his forehead with a skeletal finger. Afraid, Michael backed away. Charon lifted his hand and turned his palms upward as if to give Michael something. Michael moved closer, and Charon reached with one finger and touched Michael's forehead, like a drill. Then suddenly a voice as of a serpent spoke to him.

"Whyyyy haveeee you followed meeeee, Michael of the Kortai?"

Michael looked at Charon, but the warden's mouth did not move, but Michael responded. "Charon?" You...you speak?"

"Ayeeeeee." said Charon. "To thossssse whom wordsssssss need be spokennnn...wordddds, I will muster. You, angel of God, ssssshould not beeeee hereeeee ."

Plumes of fire jumped off Charon as butterflies might dance around a flower.

"I am in great need of thine help," said Michael. "I come this way only because there wast no other choice. The waypoints are shut. Lucifer in his deceit can be the only cause for such a barrier. He must be stopped."

Charon nodded. "The princccccce of pridddde is *not* my chargeeeee. Hissss actionsssss have yet to bring him within my gazzzzze. He would be wisssse to not have my eye sssset upon him."

"And what of Abaddon? He hast escaped a second time from thy grasp."

With his chains, Charon lifted Michael high into the air. Michael felt Charon squeeze him, and the archangel winced in pain. Suddenly, the tongued eyes of Hell made their appearance. Charon flung Michael to the ground and spoke.

"Wouldddd you dare mockkkk the Vengeance of God within the bowlsssss of a creature that at my whim would consummmmme you alivvvvve?"

Michael lifted his hands in abeyance, "Nay, great Charon, to mock the vengeance of God is to do so at one's own risk. I have seen they might and know of a surety that all those who stand before thee must eventually fall. Yet Abaddon is not within his cage; he runs amok. I can only imagine on the streets of Heaven itself."

Charon laughed, and Michael opened his mouth in shock. Never had it occurred to him that the creature could know humor.

"He fleessss what isssss the inevitable. Some sinsssss are opene beforehand, going before to judgment and otherssss follow after. He has been horded ssssimply closer to my domain that he might be corralled. He will be with usssss sssssshortly."

Michael looked upon the giant puzzled. *"Us?"*

Charon roared, the heated darkness of the cavern grew ever brighter, and Michael saw what none else had ever seen. There was no dissolution. Embedded within the walls of Hell, were thousands of Elohim. Each eaten alive and their stones drained of life. They cried and wailed; their agony let loose for Michael to hear. The screams of torment brought him to his knees.

Michael, consumed so much in his own pain, had been oblivious to that which lived within the very walls and floors. Everywhere the eye could see, Elohim of all races were mangled and digested alive by the fiery worms of Hell. The living dead, each a morsel to nourish the villi of Hell's very bowels. Their cries filled the cavern, and Michael covered his ears and eyes that he might shield himself from the site.

"Please make it stop. It is enough," said Michael.

Charon roared again, the cavern grew dim, the bodies of all the living receded into the walls flesh, but Michael could still make out the faint cries of those damned to have followed Lucifer.

Charon lifted up his nose and turned; his hand closed into a fist and smote the wall. Hell groaned her displeasure.

"He issss here," said Charon.

"*He*," said Michael. "Who is here?"

Charon touched the wall, and immediately it became transparent, and Michael could see. Lucifer was within Hell itself and fought through the creature. Michael's mind raced with awareness.

"Of course: it was *never* about the city."

Charon's hand moved from the wall and the image disappeared. The giant began to move towards the direction of Lucifer.

"Wait!" said Michael. "Do not destroy him; I have an idea that might remove this breach from your domain."

Charon stopped and turned. "Ssspeak."

"Lucifer cares neither for Heaven nor Hell. He cares for one thing and one thing alone. Power, he comes for the Kiln Stone. If he can enter the Kiln, he can be like God and cause those things that are not as though they were. He can from the Kiln speak and build a new creation. Don't you see? Each of the stones contains the very power of El himself. He cannot destroy El, but he can use the power of God himself to fight the Almighty. He will use El's own power against Him. Only there and there alone can he gather the might to battle El. He must be stopped."

Charon replied, looking at the angel from over his shoulder. "And what do you proposssssse, Builder of Heavennnnn?"

"Allow him to pass; do not attempt to stop him. For of a surety, he has not planned that I would be here. But go and arrest thine charge Abaddon. Bring him to naught but leave Lucifer to me. I understand now why El allowed me to enter the Kiln and see thy creation. I can stop him. Allow me to pass. I beseech thee."

Charon stood silent for a moment, gazed upon Michael, and then spoke. "And if you fail?"

"Then we are all undone, for even the vengeance of God cannot hope to stand against God himself. For a house divided against itself is brought to desolation, and behold what Lucifer himself has wrought with his division."

The great cavern shook, and then Hell let out a scream of anguish and pain. The Warden fell to his knees, for he and Michael were knocked off balance. Charon touched the wall once more, and a vision of the mountain materialized on the creatures flesh.

Michael saw that a portion of the great mountain of Hell had been obliterated. A Ladder formed near and sliced through the mountains flesh. A piece of the mountain face sheared off from the familiar signature of a Ladder.

Michael knew that Heaven was under siege with blind jumps from rogue angels who cared not for the protocols to keep Heaven and her denizens safe.

"Behold," said Michael. "Even Hell herself cannot stand against the power of a Ladder. What, pray tell, would Lucifer accomplish with the Stones of Fire the very source of thine creation?

Charon stood and walked towards Michael, and looking up at the giant, Michael backed slowly away. Charon reached into his robes and pulled out two glowing keys that were on a chain of fire and handed them to Michael to take.

"You will not ssssurvive Hell absssssent my pressssence," said Charon. "Only Lucifer and few of his kind have the power to traverse this realm and not perish, and even they cannot do so unssscathed. Buttttt your fleshhhhh is not like the Chief Princeeee, sooo I giveee to you the keyssss of Deathhh and Hellll. With them, you may pass through Hell unharmed, and the power to bind and loose those within are yours."

Michael reached up to grab the key ring, which blazoned with fire and heat and dripped as sweat beads from a tired soul.

"Gooooo to and sssstop thy brother. Do not fail me."

Charon turned to walk away, and as he did, a wall formed to separate Charon from Michael. Darkness enveloped Michael as he stood alone with the glowing keys of Death and Hell in his hands.

****

Lilith and his men made their way through the damaged city and entered the Great Library. "Secure the premises," said Lilith.

Lilith's minions made their way to the two doors that lead into the building and stood watch to protect their master within.

The attendants of the hall looked at the invaders, stopped what they were doing, and stood silently. Lilith approached the desk and spoke to the Chief Keeper.

"You are Hariph, Keeper of this Library…"

Hariph lifted his hand and interrupted him. "I know thy works. Lilith of Lucifer. I know that thou hast left thy station as his Grigori, but know that we who work this great Hall will not leave our post to serve. We are the librarians of Grigoric history storing the chronicles of all things. Even now, we continue on our charge. We shall not be moved."

Lilith smiled at him, "Then continue, but you will provide me with the information I need without delay, and if thy service displeases me, then know that thine own story will end this day. Am I understood, Chief Keeper?"

"All stories end, Lilith. There is no story but El's, for only He is the Alpha and the Omega, the beginning and the end. We are but paragraphs in his tale. But come, I know what you seek. I am bound to assist all who inquire within. Your war does not concern me save it prevent me from my charge."

Hariph spoke angel-speak and a book lifted from a shelf and floated to the stone and golden counter before Lilith. Lilith quickly turned its pages to the latest entry, frowned, and spoke aloud.

"How can this be? Michael was left on Earth, yet even now makes his way to the Kiln!"

"Perhaps," said Hariph, "your plans are not as sure as thou hast hoped?" Hariph grinned.

"Wipe the smirk off your face, Lord Keeper. Bring me the tomes of all the Chief Princes immediately!"

"And what of thy Master Lucifer?" asked Hariph.

Lilith realized that he had disturbed the order of the Lord. By not documenting, he no longer could know how his master fared. He was blind to his chief's actions. He smiled—it was a liberating feeling. To be free of this shackle, and no longer required to chronicle the exploits of another. *I will have to thank my Lord properly when I am lord of all Grigori. This is how Raphael feels...to know all, yet never required to himself chronicle.*

Hariph's work was complete, and the books of all six princes were before him save one.

"Where is Raphael's!" yelled Lilith.

"Ah, yes," said Hariph. "You see Prince Jerahmeel came to us not long ago and held a scroll to release the tome to him. His lordship has taken it; to where we do not know."

"How can such a thing be? No one is allowed to remove a tome from this Hall!"

Hariph nodded in agreement. Lilith reached over and grabbed Hariph by his shirt, "You will tell me on whose order did you release this tome. You claim to stand neutral, yet you deny me my ledger!" Lilith released him, and Hariph slammed hard against a wall.

"Croganus, attend me and rid me of the Lord Keeper."

Croganus moved from the doorposts, unsheathed a flaming sword, and approached Hariph. Hariph waved his hands and spoke. "Would you kill me before knowing who ordered the release of Raphael's Tome?"

Lilith motioned for Croganus to stop.

"Speak, brother. Reveal what is chronicled."

Hariph rose to his feet, brushed himself off, opened a drawer behind him, removed the scroll and he handed it to Croganus who in turn gave it to Lilith.

Lilith saw the prismatic and red clay mark that had the Seal of El and unrolled the scroll to read. The document was like golden paper, its ink was as a mixture of onyx and surrounded in silver and written in angelic script.

To the Lord Keeper,

As thou hast been charged since, thy creation with the keeping of all tomes within the Hall, and to wit war has come upon us, you are requested and required in the name of Lord of Hosts to release the Tome of Raphael to the bearer of this scroll.

For two days hence, thou shalt be besieged upon, and Lilith will come to claim it. Lo, it cannot fall into the enemies' hands.

Be swift in thy duties and remain faithful to the end, and thy reward shall be given after thy dissolution.

Lilith's eyes grew wide for the writing was penned with the finger of God and signed by El himself.

He dropped the scroll, and it burst into flames. Hariph laughed aloud.

"You art a fool to think that the creature might outwit the creator. For even the foolishness of El is wiser than your wisdom. El hast known of thine treachery before thou hadst even set foot in this very room."

Lilith slammed his fists on the stone table, shoved the books to the floor, scowled, and grabbed Hariph. "Who am I to deny prophecy?" Then he looked at Croganus. "Kill them all."

As Lilith bent down to pick up the books, the screams of those felled by Croganus' sword mingled with those who fell in battle outside the library's walls. Lilith thought to himself.

Are we undone?

****

Jerahmeel rocked to the side as the cavern shook as the mountain rumbled from the thunder outside its walls.

"Raphael, we must act quickly. Can the mount withstand a Ladder directed against it?"

"Nay, it cannot. However, El lies within its center. I am of a surety that although nothing may bring Him harm, the same cannot be said for the rest of Heaven. It is clear that Lucifer intends to pummel the realm into submission." Raphael raced to the great wall and spoke. "Reveal Third Heaven."

The wall complied, Jerahmeel and Raphael watched in horror and astonishment, for Lucifer had placed guards at the four gates into the realm, and each had an open Ladder that prevented other Ladders from forming. They beheld that angel after angel fell upon Heaven as falling stars, and like meteoric lightning, they blasted the landscape around them. Heaven filled with craters from the destruction, and wave after endless wave destroyed buildings and friends. The skies bled with the blood of angels caught in each blast's wake.

Their aim was true, and the duo looked as the firmament rained with angels who fell from the skies, each a missile of destruction as they landed in their Ladders. Like beams of death, they fell upon all things and blasted the mountain of God and the temple. The rock face roared its objection. As one angel landed to unsheathe sword and destroy those who did not possess the mark of Lucifer, another angel materialized to bombard the mountain. It was ugly and imprecise. Even the Seraphim were under siege as Lucifer's soldiers were sent to breach the temple doors. The four mighty creatures battled with light and sound, cutting down all who would seek to enter without invitation, yet they were but four against a Legion which sought entry into the mountain. Raphael

301

and Jerahmeel took in the scene in disbelief, and for a moment, despondency overtook the affable Jerahmeel who looked at the images before him and hope melted away.

"It is only a matter of time before they overwhelm even the Seraph," said Jerahmeel. "What can we hope to do?"

Raphael smiled. "Have faith, my friend. We are not without arms, yet I must concede our brothers genius," said Raphael. "Lucifer has cut Heaven off from the multiverse. He prevents the totality of Heaven's might to engage him. Those that resist, he blasts into dissolution thinning our ranks here and forcing us to battle one another. Yet to what end? How does he expect to conquer El? Nor can he hope to keep the entire host away forever. By now throughout the realms, all have realized that they are stranded from home. For when they return, they would strike him down. What does he hope to gain?"

"Can you track him?" asked Jerahmeel

"Nay. Lilith no longer chronicles his charge. Lucifer is invisible without a Grigori to….wait…that's it…."

"What is it?

"There are Grigori throughout the realms. We can find where he is by looking where he is not."

Once more, the great cavern heaved and bucked, the ceiling cracked, and the image started to fade for a moment.

"Shay-t-zune-zi-t-al whey" spoke Raphael.

An image of Heaven showed on the wall and its topography showed throughout, and there were swathes of red, except in one place.

"Oh my God!" said Raphael. "He wouldn't dare!"

"What is it?"

Raphael showed his brother the red that outlined the whole map and pointed to the sole dark void where no red existed.

"These are the Grigori. Even in battle, there are those who have not wavered in their duties to record all that transpires around them. Through them, I may see all that transpires here. Lucifer does not exist within the sight of my brethren because he is here in the void."

Jerahmeel looked at the map and saw that there was blackness in but one area in all of Heaven — Hell.

"He moves to the Kiln," said Jerahmeel.

"Aye, and once there, even I do not know what might transpire. But lo, we have yet hope, for I see we have a standard raised even now against him. Reveal Athamas."

Once more, the wall obeyed and the image of Michael and Asthmas came to the fore. The room itself grew bright, and Jerahmeel could feel the intense heat that emanated through the portal into the room. They watched as Michael moved with all swiftness through the organs of Hell as fire enveloped him, and hundreds of angels cried and begged him for release. Raphael watched the internal digestion of Hell, and it was gruesome to behold. The smell was putrid; Raphael could only imagine how his brother fared.

"Michael somehow knows Lucifer's plan. He moves even now towards the Kiln. There is yet hope that he might stop him."

Michael turned and saw that there was a light against the wall, and he strained to see that Raphael was watching him and Jerahmeel stood to his side.

"Canst thou hear me?" yelled Michael.

"Yes, brother!" said Jerahmeel. "Lucifer aims to capture and awaken the Stones of Fire! You must stop him!"

"I know!" yelled Michael, "I have…"

Suddenly a tendril of fire leapt through the wall, and heat and flame engulfed Jerahmeel and Raphael. Each screamed in pain as the flesh of Hell and bodies' still alive, but digested; seeped through the wall to consume them.

Michael moved quickly, placed the flaming keys of Death and Hell into the mountains organic wall, and spoke. "Retreat into thine own sphere I command thee! Do them no harm!"

Upon command, the cancerous tumors of living bile, brimstone, and flailing arms of Elohim retracted back into the wall as the tendrils with razor like tongues hissed and eyed Michael with hatred.

Raphael rose to his feet and held his arm, now burned, and shook his head, groggy from the sensation of being eaten alive. Jerahmeel also came to himself.

Raphael spoke. "Go quickly, Michael. Godspeed. We will bring to naught Lucifer's plans." Michael nodded and turned to continue his journey through the razor sharp teeth of bile-infested intestines of flame and magma.

Raphael spoke angel-speak and the image of the wall grew dark.

"We must stop this madness before it can grow further," said Raphael.

"But how?"

Raphael eyed the glowing glass wall that separated the Zoa from them and was struck with inspiration.

Jerahmeel looked at his brother knowingly. "That is not funny, Raphael. I did not intend for you to fight madness with madness!"

"I intend to give our people who hold to El a chance at survival. The Zoa are as the Ophanim; they cannot be harmed by our kind. It is time we showed Lucifer's legions that they have reason to fear what lies within the mountain. I need to get to the Library. Can you open the waypoint of Argoth? We must secure a passage to bring the legions."

"Aye," said Jerahmeel. "Lucifer has but one guard at each, portal. We only need one portal to bring in reinforcements."

Raphael moved to the wall and spoke. "When I go through, you must speak the words to image the cliffs of Argoth. If you do not do so in time, well, the Zoa will have you to feast upon, and I would very much like to see you again."

Jerahmeel chuckled. "Kick Lilith's butt for me."

Raphael smiled and turned to place himself in front of the wall. Jerahmeel moved to the side so as not to be in the line of sight of the Zoa and ducked behind a bookcase.

"This ought to be fun!" said Jerahmeel.

"Only if we live to tell about it," said Raphael.

Raphael then spoke the words that brought down the barrier that separated the Zoa from them, took a tome from off a desk, and threw it into the cavern. Jerahmeel watched from a distance as the ceiling slowly moved, and the creatures awakened at the sound and movement of the thrown book.

Raphael spoke the words to the wall, and it revealed the street and entryway to the Great Library He tucked the Tome of Iniquity within his robes, grabbed another book, blew upon it, and then threw it into the Zoa filled room. Fire raged about, and the sound and movement from the fighting in the streets caught their attention. They saw Raphael throw another book, and a Zoa burst into flames and roared. They charged towards Raphael. Quickly he turned to run and immediately passed through the wall. Running into the street and dodging combatants, he sprinted to the Great Library.

Like a pack of elephants, several of the Zoa ran after him and leaped through the wall to overtake him only to find thousands of angels spread before them.

The throng looked about them curious at these new things. With its barbed tentacles, a Zoa grabbed a soldier of Lucifer, pierced his chest, lifted his body into the air, flung him around, and pounced to tear his limbs with its teeth. The populace raced every man for their lives as the giant creatures filled the streets. Each stung their prey and then devoured them.

Raphael looked to his rearward and saw that the creature that he had burned with his book still followed hard after him.

Maybe this was not the best idea.

Raphael saw that an angel blocked the doorway to the Library. And when the angel saw that Raphael raced towards him, he shut the door, and Raphael slammed hard against it. Seeing the creature upon him, Raphael leaped to his side, and the elephantine Zoa barreled through the door, smashed its way inside, trampled on the guard and crushed him underfoot.

Raphael entered in after it and saw Lilith with a look of petrified horror and anger on his face.

Raphael spoke. "You didn't think you would get rid of me that easily, did you?"

The Zoa looked at them both with saliva and angelic blood dripping from its mouth ready to consume them.

Chapter Nine

No other God before me.

Jerahmeel peeked over the table sprawled with books and cautiously moved to the wall. Raphael's handiwork rampaged through the street as the Zoa that escaped: crushed Lucifer's soldiers underfoot and tossed foes into buildings. He remembered that his role was to close the Ladder at the Cliffs of Argoth and spoke as commanded by Raphael the words necessary to bring the waypoint into view.

Movement from out of the corner of his eye confirmed that Jerahmeel was not alone. He turned to look to his right and creeping towards him was a Zoa. Its mouth opened wide to reveal the razor-sharp teeth. Spittle dripped from its mouth as it hissed at Jerahmeel, poised to pounce.

"Now, I know I look tasty, but soon there will be a nice strong angel over there?" Jerahmeel pointed at the guard whom the wall had brought into view. "Now that fella, yonder — he's got good bone structure and lifts stars; yep, there is way more meat on him than...."

The Zoa roared and leapt at Jerahmeel who ducked out the way and rolled over books and fallen brackets. The momentum of the creature sent it careening into shelves. Massive stone bookcases broke, crashed, and toppled down on the creature, burying it under piles of books.

Jerahmeel smiled as he surveyed his deftness and quickly remembered that the Hall of Annals contained the tomes for all things. Quickly, he ran towards a bookcase looking frantically for the creature's tome.

Even the Zoa have a tome. If I can but find it, perhaps—yes—just maybe.

He pulled book after book off the shelves, searching frantically, and sighed a sigh of relief when he saw the volume.

Suddenly his feet left him, and he fell with a thud as a tentacle wrapped itself around his leg and lifted him dangling into the air. Like a wrecking ball beheld by the end of a crane, Jerahmeel was swung headlong into the stone stable, and it broke in two with his fall. Books flew everywhere, and the hiss of the Zoa vibrated in his ears. Jerahmeel groggily opened his eyes to see three of the beasts fighting to be the first to devour him. He lifted himself to the ceiling with his great wings, and the creatures slammed into each other in their attempt to capture him.

Jerahmeel moved lower to the ground: the projection now in full view of the Cliffs of Argoth. He then flew within mouths reach of the creatures to draw them to follow him. Hissing, they did, roaring and lumbering to devour him. Jerahmeel reached into the wall and disappeared to the other side.

Lucifer's assigned guard over the waypoint concentrated on keeping the Ladder he had created from closing when he saw Jerahmeel suddenly fly straight towards him with a giant book in hand and appearing from nowhere tentacled creatures running after him. The guard panicked and tried to move, but it was too late. Jerahmeel had grabbed a hold of him, and a Zoa had grabbed them both. They rolled over one another and toppled off the cliff of Argoth, and the guard screamed as they all plunged into the swirling Abyss below.

****

"Behold, Astarte; Heaven falls before us!"

Ashtaroth, who with sword in hand cleaved at foes whom just days ago, he called brethren, frowned at the destruction and bloodshed before him. He huffed as he fought alongside Abaddon as the citizenry of Heaven came as a flood to stop them.

308

"Nay, Abaddon. Lucifer would *not* approve of this scale of dissolution. He would find another way!"

Ashtaroth swung his sword at an angel and brought it hard into its chest, smashing its stone; it turned to powder before him.

Abaddon laughed and reveled in his freedom to destroy and then took pause as creatures he had never seen came galloping on tentacles with mouths filled with razors. Like a herd, they felled everything that stood before them. Tossing angel after angel behind them and ripping to shreds those that carried the mark of Lucifer.

"Lo. See the handiwork of our brethren for they bring beasts to deter us!"

"They fight with beasts because we have become as beasts. Look about you! Our city burns, Abaddon, and the golden streets run blue with our blood!"

Abaddon turned to Ashtaroth and spoke. "From the day I was called DESTROYER, this ceased to be my city. Let it burn, Astarte. Let them all burn, for they watched El consign me to burn and be eaten alive for eternity. They are all but kindling for my wrath."

He eyed the new creatures that moved towards them and pulled open his breastplate to reveal his cracked God stone. He removed a shard, spoke angel speak, and tossed it into the sky.

"See now the true meaning of the 'broken stone'… and tremble."

Ashtaroth and the other generals watched as the shard pulsed in the air and grew dark. Giant globules of black separated from it: one, three, then nine, and suddenly it burst and millions of locust-like creatures filled the sky and cast a shadow over the great city.

The shape of the locusts was like unto horses prepared unto battle, and on their heads were crowns like gold; their faces were as the faces of men. Each creature had hair as the hair of the human female El had created. Their teeth were as the teeth of lions. Each held a breastplate of iron, and the sound of their wings was as the sound of chariots of many horses running to battle. Their tails were like unto scorpions, and they had the power to paralyze and torture all that they attacked.

Abaddon commanded them to strike at all who bore not the mark of his Lord and to attack the oncoming Zoa.

They descended upon the Zoa with ferociousness and stung them and anyone bearing not Lucifer's mark. The people writhed in agony and cried out in pain, for El to save them.

Smug with satisfaction Abaddon mocked the tormented, "Yes where is that God who would save you from me? El has abandoned you, yet you refuse to bow! Refuse to surrender!"

The locusts were as a cloud that moved throughout the city.

Ashtaroth looked at the suffering of those before him and noted even the Zoa stopped and convulsed in agony on the streets. The creatures grew limp and motionless against the onslaught, but Abaddon watched in glee, watched as angel after angel pleaded with him to make the pain stop. Each tormented soul prayed and cried out to El for relief. The locusts landed on each man and stung them over, and over, and the whole of the city was filled with screams and wails.

Ashtaroth beheld his brethren and was moved with compassion. He turned towards Abaddon and said, "Retract thy army! We cannot rule if there is none to obey!" He pulled at the arm of Abaddon to make him look at him. "For the love of God Abaddon, stand down!"

Abaddon turned towards him wroth, and struck Ashtaroth across the face, and he fell to the ground.

"You would adjure *me* by the love of God! *Me*? Do not *ever* touch me!

I tolerate you because Lucifer tolerates you."

Ashtaroth rose from the ground, spit blood, and glared at Abaddon. "We are all but servants to our Lord King. We bear his mark, and his will is to subjugate the populace not to destroy it."

Abaddon laughed. "Then our master's plan is flawed. And you are a fool Astarte; there can be no subjugation without destruction."

"Stand down!" Ashtaroth warned once more. "Or be removed from thine office."

Abaddon laughed. "And who do you think will follow *you*, Astarte? Will *you* remove me? Only the God King commands me, and you vassal are not he."

Ashtaroth's brow grew tense, "Then you leave me no choice." and he turned to the army of warrior angels behind him.

Ashtaroth raised the crescent seal of Lucifer for all to see.

"By order of his majesty Lucifer, Son of the Morning Star, whose seal I now bear. Abaddon is hereby relieved; he is no longer in command. Arrest him. If he resists—kill him."

Many paused, as Abaddon stood at the head of the army. With this new displayed power to summon a swarm of angelic locusts many were afraid to move against him.

He laughed.

"You see Astarte— you possess authority but lack the might to enforce it."

He then placed his hands on his hips and chuckled. "Now all of you obey me, or you too shall likewise perish!"

Ashtaroth looked at the indecision and hesitation of those he command-ed and then looked at Abaddon who haughtily laughed at him. Without warning,

Ashtaroth threw himself headlong into Abaddon, and kicked him in the jaw knocking the giant Arelim to his knees, and pummeled him until Abaddon's face hit the ground.

"I speak for Lord Lucifer! No one defies his will! I said arrest him!"

Emboldened, Ares rushed with several others to bind Abaddon with chains of iron, but Abaddon struggled to his feet and flung his apprehenders to the side. More immediately came to subdue the great angel.

"Enough!"

Abaddon then spoke the words to open a Ladder, and those who held him attempted to cover his mouth and silence him, but to no avail. The multitude that followed looked in horror as a giant funnel cloud opened above Abaddon. All fled to escape, but it was too late, for as the vortex of the Ladder touched down and disintegrated his captors. It blew those in the immediate vicinity back, and all crashed hard into buildings and walls. The vacuum of the Ladder retracted, and many fell screaming as they were lifted and sucked into the burning whirlwind.

The smoke cleared, and Ashtaroth emerged climbing from under debris and rubble. He looked over the army and lo, friend and foe alike had been vaporized in the wake of the Ladder's blast. The great city smoldered, and a third of it had been destroyed. Stone, wood, and angelic debris fell from the sky as spire after city spire was in flames, and explosions rocked buildings.

Ashtaroth looked at Abaddon in disgust and spoke so that all nearby might hear. "You are hereby deemed traitor to the cause of Lucifer. Let Heaven herself spit you out, and know of a surety that you have no country, no home. You are in league with no one. You are the Destroyer, and you will not be allowed to live." He spoke to the warriors near him and said, "Kill him."

Upon command, warriors of Lucifer attacked Abaddon, and he fought them with sword and with brute strength, picking up angels and using their bodies as a shield to protect him against the horde that now attacked him.

When Abaddon saw that all of Heaven arrayed itself against him, he summoned his legion of locusts, and the wasp-like creatures that had just attacked those without the sigil of Lucifer now attacked indiscriminately all that moved.

Ashtaroth's face grew grim as he entered the fray, and took up his sword to destroy him.

****

Gabriel looked down at his hands. The powdered dust of stones he had shattered from the chests of his fallen brethren covered them, hands that had spilled Elomic blood. He surveyed the scene about him, and tears poured from his eyes, at the carnage that strife had ravaged on the Elysian Fields. The gryphons of Malakim filled the skies; the manna fields burned and its lush soil turned upside down.

The groans and screams of the battlefield echoed across the golden hued skies and a fog of dust and flame settled above the Elysian Fields for as far as the eye could see. Gabriel saw angel after angel locked in armed and unarmed combat, each combatant locked in fury to the dissolution of the other. The cracking of bones, the ripping of wings, the shredding of throats, and the smashing of stones all joined in a cacophony of sound. Row after row of Elohim clashed using the powers given them by El to bring to naught one another. Gabriel wondered how they all had arrived at the point of self-genocide.

"I take it, Gabriel, that my brethren and the Arelim did not take well to your touching me?" said Sariel who slowly regained consciousness.

"Forgive me, brother, for I would not let you harm our brother nor

313

would I see harm come to you," Gabriel replied.

"Then you have bested me in obeying the Lord. Your act has brought me shame, but it was a noble act, and it is I who am sorry for the hurt I have caused."

Sariel viewed his brethren locked in combat, Arelim fighting Issi and Malakim.

"We must find Talus," said Sariel. "Only the three of us can end this folly."

Sariel rose to his feet, and he scoured the landscape. "Do you see him, Gabriel?"

"Aye, to the hills on the eastern edge of the forest."

Sariel followed the path of Gabriel's fingers and saw in the distance Talus encircled by powerful Arelim guards, watching the battle that encompassed the fields of manna.

"We must go to him," said Sariel.

Gabriel looked at him as if he was mad, "But he will of a surety attack us."

"Perhaps, but we must seek reconciliation or risk a wider war with the other great houses. The burning of the fields must have caught the attention of those within the city by now."

Gabriel motioned to the gryphons guards that encircled them and they lifted themselves into the air, an entourage to provide escort for their leaders as they flew over the battlefield, towards Talus and his guard.

The guards of Talus came to attention, and with wings unfurled, they covered their master and prepared themselves to battle the incoming wave.

"Stand down," said Talus. "They mean us no harm."

The guards of Talus relaxed and kept a watchful eye on the giant gryphon riders that descended with their trident spears and landing just feet away. Sariel and Gabriel walked from the midst of them to approach and Talus moved his guardsman aside to greet them.

The three stared at each other in silence until Gabriel spoke for them all. "This conflict must end, or Heaven herself with be brought to naught let alone the multiverse of El's creation."

Sariel eyed Talus warily. "I agree the blood spilled between our houses must end here before it reaches beyond the fields of Elysium."

Talus looked at his brothers and said, "I could have descended upon you with my forces well before you greeted me here, Gabriel."

"You could have tried, brother," Gabriel replied.

Talus smiled. "But instead, I chose to remain and wait to see what thou wouldst do. When I saw no intent to do me harm, yet you still protected our brother, I was brought low and ashamed by thine example. Therefore, I sought to recall my people from battle, to have them stand down, but to no avail, for the battle hast taken a mind of its own. Vengeance and blood are all that consumes my people now. They seek to remove the stain of Apollyon and the disgrace he has brought on our name."

Gabriel replied, "How can such a thing be done?"

Talus looked upon the battlefield of Elysium, now drenched in Elomic blood. He surveyed the might of Heaven unleashed, the very ground beneath them scorched. "They seek to eliminate his memory from the minds of those who remember."

Sariel interrupted, "They cannot destroy the entire lot of Elohim!"

"Nay," replied Talus, "They cannot, but as a mover of stars, we can diminish the numbers of Heaven. Therefore, we must quell the horde before they do the unthinkable."

315

Gabriel said, "They would not be so foolish!"

"I know not what my people driven mad by anger and hubris would do, Gabriel. I only know that a Ladder formed outside of a waypoint would bring dissolution to multitudes, to friend and foe alike."

"Then speak to them through me," said Gabriel, "before pride and anger give way to further destruction. Perhaps if they see us together, if we were to speak as one man, then madness might give way to reason, and the horde might be stilled."

"Look about you Gabriel," said Sariel. "How can we communicate to so many?"

Gabriel looked and saw the swells of angels over the fields were as the sand upon the seashore. They covered as far as the eye could see, and the food-stuff of angels, the source of Heaven's provision, was destroyed. Gabriel's face frowned, a tear flowed down his cheek, and thoughts of despair began to flood him. Quickly, he shook himself from despondency and said, "Take my hand, the two of you, and rise with me into the air"

Clasping hands, Gabriel, Talus, and Sariel took to the skies with their guard's surrounding them. They moved towards the throng, and when they had settled over the midst of the battlefield, Gabriel took his horn and blew to recall the Malakim riders that had come to their master's aid.

The blow from the Trumpet of Israel was recognized, and immediately the Gryphon riders took to the skies to depart. All in combat took notice that the skies filled with the creatures and their riders, and those who had been fearful of the Malakim spear; relief flooded them.

The Malakim came towards Gabriel, and the sky filled with their steeds. Gabriel reached to his brothers' chests, placed his hands on their stones, and motioned for them to touch his stone. When they did, they became as one being, and Gabriel spoke so all could hear. When his lips moved so too did the lips of his brethren, and they spoke as one man.

"Mighty host of God, thou who hast moved stars and carried the voice of El throughout the corners of the heavens…legions, hear me! Cease and desist and lay down thine arms, for look about you and behold what your anger has done to Heaven; see what your rage hast wrought!

"For pride hast laid waste to reason, and strife has eaten at our souls: and to what end? That we might destroy each other for no cause? This is not why El hast made us; this is not what El would tolerate. These are not the acts of a child towards his father. We are Elohim, and we were created for more than this."

The host paused to weigh the words spoken, and warily eyed one another. Weapons slowly lowered, and fists gradually unclenched. Hands, once raised in battle, now offered handshakes of peace. Gabriel and his brethren smiled, for they had quenched the rage that hovered over the throng; a sigh of relief came over them all.

The sky then turned red in the distance, and bright lights engulfed the city of God. The booming sound of thunder cracked ears, and shockwaves rocketed across the plains. Sonic tidal waves of force slammed headlong into the mass of angels assembled in the field and all were blown back by the blast.

The concussive gust smashed into Gabriel and his brothers, and they fell hard to the ground. The rush of debris and manna leaf sliced cheeks, and the heated wind ruffled hair. Gabriel, sore from his fall turned towards the direction of Jerusalem. Fires and black acrid smoke lifted high into the air and the despondency filled him, as he knew the unthinkable had happened. A Ladder, no hundreds of Ladders, flashed throughout the sky, and Jerusalem burned.

He rose to his feet and spoke to them all. "I will not stand here and fight

317

amongst my brethren while treachery seeks to destroy our home. We will face this threat, and bring it to naught. Come, therefore, and we shall smite those who would do such a thing."

Gabriel lifted himself, and Talus and Sariel followed him into the air. The three great houses trailed their leaders into the sky, and those that could fly flew, and those that raced along the ground galloped, a mighty army of thousands upon thousands bent to exact vengeance on those who would defile their home.

****

Michael moved gingerly through the foul smelling intestines of flame. Arms and wails of devoured souls clawed at him, as Hell's teeth bit, repeatedly, into angelic flesh.

Hell was different somehow, larger, more ferocious in her attempts to smother Michael, but he held the keys to Death and Hell, keys that would if he commanded, force her to regurgitate any and all he desired. He was a deputy of Charon now, a guardian to the souls that lay therein, and she would obey him.

Finally, thought Michael.

The umbilical to the Kiln came into view and Michael could hear the roar of the Stones of Fire: the source of Hell's power. As Michael entered the Kiln, he heard the clamoring of sounds, the echoes of stones vying for his attention, ready to mold as he willed. The stones sang to him within the furnace of fire, each in a melody unique to its properties. Prior when El had created Charon, Michael had not noticed the songs that radiated from them: he had been too overwhelmed by wonder and fear.

As the glowing, heated gems of orchestral chorus filled the cavern with melody, Michael noticed harmony in the fire. Hymns like none in all creation, he closed his eyes to listen and savor their tune.

He listened; realizing that within the melody there was one stone that did not sing as the others. A larger stone that sung a song in harmony yet unique from the others He had never noticed it before, being too overwhelmed by the presence of God and being in the Kiln to witness the birth of Charon. Nevertheless, it was clear to him now, a much larger stone in the center of the room: a Primestone. It called to him, nay beckoned to him with the singing of its melody. A melody from which he realized all other melodies sprung. The Primestone glistened in the fire, moist despite the heat and flame, and where the other Stones of Fire called out, *"to be,"* this one was not so. It simply sang, *"I am."* Then Michael understood the secret of the Kiln. Here, within this fiery cavern, God did not just fashion his ministers of flame. Angels alone were not this crucibles function. Nay, here hidden alone to all but the most worthy of Elohim, to he who was Chief Prince, El granted one power to join the Godhead—to be as El.

Michael knelt down and placed his trembling hand over the stone to touch it. He listened to its song, and its refrain called for him to cup it in an orgasmic embrace and partake of its "fruit."

When he saw that it was pleasant to the eyes and a stone to be desired to ascend to power, he reached closer to touch it: a touch that he might be as El and possess the power of the Almighty.

The Primestone crackled with energy, and tendrils of plasma rose from the gemstone and reached up to embrace his fingers.

Perhaps El would have me be God — to use his own power to defeat Lucifer?

Michael knew now why Lucifer would not cede his position. He understood why Lucifer was so obsessed when he heard that Michael had gone into the Kiln. It was clear for, unbeknownst to all of Heaven, yeah even Raphael, God held within the Kiln a secret that only He and the Chief Prince knew, that within this chamber, one might become God. Michael was humbled that El would reveal to him such an intimate truth.

The giant gemstone called to him, and Michael dreamt of what he could do with such power. Those fallen in battle he could resurrect; perhaps he might make a universe after his own likeness, and after his own image. He could force those who sided with Lucifer to reason. More and more his thoughts raced with how God could change all things, and then he understood that the stone was more than just a receptacle to contain and dispense God's power. It was a test, and the words of Iofiel flooded back to his remembrance.

'Have you too left El to follow the path of Lucifer?'

His failure to control himself with Iofiel haunted him. He pulled his trembling hand back and scooted away from the gemstone. He shook himself to gain composure and marveled that the Lord would leave such power within his grasp.

"No, there is no God but El," he said to himself.

Perception dawned on him that Lucifer saw the stones as common, as things to use for control. He remembered what El had taught him when Lucifer departed from the communion table.

"And it shall come to pass when thou must confront thy brother, do not confront him alone, for you will speak to the stones, and they will be. Charge them, Michael of the Kortai, and they will aid thee. But beware, for within lies a token of my faith in thee. Fail me not, and thou shalt be Chief Prince."

"But Lord why must this be at all?"

"Fear not, for there must need to be a falling away first, that the man of sin might be revealed, the son of perdition, who opposeth and exalteth himself

above all that is called God, so that he as God sitteth in the temple of God,

showing himself that he is God. For even now the mystery of iniquity doest

already work, and for now, it must be, and I must be taken from out of the way,

but, alas, the Wicked shall be revealed whom I will consume with the spirit of my

mouth and shall destroy with the brightness of my coming."

Michael rose to stand and anger swelled within him.

Lucifer cannot be allowed to have the Kilnstones.

Michael reached down to grab a stone. It was as hard as polished diamond and its brilliance gleamed. It sang soprano throughout the cavern when held, and with the other hand, Michael picked up another stone. It was black iron and a deep bass resonated from its song, a low hum that made one's chest vibrate. Each had a different song, and as he touched them together, their songs changed from unison to harmony and merged to form a new element mixed with the properties of diamond and iron.

He placed it within the Kiln's fleshy walls and spoke angel speak. The Kiln hearkened to the word of El and took from Michael's mind the image that he desired to fashion within the cavern's womb: an angel of power with which to match the First of Angels.

The walls rumbled, and the wall took the stone. A bulge formed from within and grew immense. A membrane of mucus like substance appeared and dropped to the floor, a great sac with a dark figure within burst, and the newly formed angel fell to the fiery floor. Michael stood up to give it charge.

"Rise Ouranos, Titan of God, for you shalt be a standard to aid me. For the Prince of Angels comes to secure power, and we shall stand between him and the Lord."

His head was that of a man, his arms as great oaks, and he shown as the sun in the sky, a brightness that could reflect all light and sound and wrap the

321

light around his person. He looked down at Michael, and his whole body was like a mirror; Michael could see himself in the angel's skin. The great behemoth stood in front of Michael with four great arms and eight flowing wings of light, and his legs were as that of a bear.

"Lo Titan, our enemy will be here soon. Go to and conceal thyself within the wall. Come when called for, and let thy aid be swift."

The creature plodded to the back wall and like a chameleon, melted into the background, waiting silently for Michael to give command. Michael positioned himself in the center of the Kiln, kneeled, bowed his head, and prayed

Lord El, I face my brother to prevent this usurpation. Give me strength. Forgive thy servant and hold not this charge to my account. If there be other means whereby this might end, let it be, but if not... Michael paused, grimaced, and swallowed hard. *Then let my sword be swift, and thy will be done in all things.*

He stood, lifted his hands, and pointed to the stones about him, and they rose from the floor, hovering, and as Michael spoke the Elomic word for destruction, the stones lifted into the top of the fiery chamber and embedded themselves into the ceiling, germinating to become as willed by Michael, their songs changed to reflect his will. They seethed in the ceiling above and hissed as if simmering.

Michael knelt then removed from his folded wings a gemmed scabbard and unsheathed a double bladed sword of fire made by the Lord himself. He struck the blade into the burning floor and imaged the Ophanim. Suddenly, hands rose from the ground to grasp the sharp blade. Blue coils of electric current wound themselves over the steel, and the fire of the sword turned from red to blue. Seven stones rose into the air and attached themselves like iron filings drawn to a magnet; and when all seven had attached themselves: the steel cracked. The sound of a thunderclap burst through the cavern and Michael was knocked back. He eyed the sword as it rose from the ground spitting arcs of lightning. Two eyes and teeth materialized within the blade. He reached out to touch the hilt, and the blade split into seven swords, each alive with eyes that moved within the blades. The blades sang to him in the fire and floated in the air above him.

Michael marveled at the swords, when he lifted the blade they encircled him, and when he swiped, they mimicked him. He thought of himself sheathing the blade, immediately they flew to him, reconnected to the sword, and it vibrated in his hands. He could feel the current race around him as he held it. Michael stood waiting. He gripped the hilt of the sword and closed his eyes.

El thou knowest what is at stake. I will not allow Lucifer to command the God stones.

Michael's face grimaced as he heard the sound of familiar music from the opening of the umbilical to the Kiln. A glowing figure stepped into the fiery furnace with him. He opened his eyes and looked into the fire.

Lucifer had come.

****

Abaddon lifted himself into the air with his great wings and flung from his back those who dared to strike at him. A swarm of angelic locusts surrounded him, and those that attacked him were stung and fell to their knees writhing in pain.

Ashtaroth lunged at Abaddon, and he too was stung and fell back. Abaddon yelled to him and pursued him as he fell to the ground. "Now I will bring your miserable life to an end, Astarte. From the onset, this is how it should have been. There will be no Michael or Lucifer to save you from my hand this time!"

Ashtaroth fell hard into the ground and swerved to his side as Abaddon crashed into the earth, barely missing him. Ashtaroth rose quickly to his feet, and with wings spread before him, he used them as a shield to protect his face from the locust swarm that encircled his foe.

He drew his sword, struck at Abaddon, and clipped his leathery wing. The Arelim yelled in pain, stepped back, and then laughed maniacally.

"I am going to enjoy this."

Abaddon motioned with his hand and the swarm which before had attacked Lucifer's foes now arched and raced to fall upon Ashtaroth. They fell upon him and stung and bit into his flesh. He attempted to wave them away, but it was to no gain as his vision darkened, and he fell to the earth writhing in agony and screaming. The locusts covered his body so that naught but a thrashing shape twisted on the ground.

"Now Astarte, you shall know pain. Let anguish be thy companion, for it is not yet my desire to kill you, but to savor and to feast upon your suffering with my own eyes, for *you* to taste what it is to be savored by Hell."

Round about them both, warriors attempted to strike at Abaddon but a wall of locusts kept them at bay, and those that were not in liege with Lucifer still fought to fend off his legions. The clash of steel could be heard in the distance. As Abaddon knelt down to gloat over the convulsive body of Ashtaroth, he pulled his sword from its sheath to behead him.

Ashtaroth saw through the veil of carnivorous like insects that Abaddon lifted his sword to cut off his head. In terrified agony, he reached out to him to spare him, only to see the Arelim jolted and thrown back by a blur from behind him.

Abaddon hurtled backwards against a wall, and a hazy like figure pummeled his face, and then kicked him in the abdomen. Abaddon curled up in a ball and vomited. Coughing, he shook himself and stretched out his wings attempting to take flight, but a hammer like blow fell on his back and knocked the wind from his lungs. He smashed into the ground, wheezing as the blows came as if from nowhere and assaulted him from every direction. He held his hands over his face for a defense. Light flashed before his eyes, and he beheld a bright, glowing figure enveloped with the presence of God standing before him.

Gabriel, staff in hand, stood over him and spoke, "I have a message for you." The archangel then took his staff and swung it as a bat into Abaddon's face, and great drops of blood and spittle flung from his cheek.

Abaddon fell hard to the earth. Groggily struggling to regain himself, he stood and sputtered blood as he spoke. "You do me great honor High Prince, but it will take more than that to defeat me."

Gabriel nodded in agreement then motioned his hand skyward.

"Behold."

Abaddon looked up, and lo the heavens swarmed with Malakim and Gryphon Riders, and at their front, Talus and Sariel plummeted from the sky with an army of angels all headed straight towards him.

****

The Zoa looked at them both, and its mouth opened to reveal rows of razor sharp teeth. Spittle fell from its mouth, and it tentacled arms and legs tensed as it eyed them. Like one of the sea predators of Earth, it slowly encircled them. Eyeing its prey, it hissed at them menacingly.

Lilith backed away slowly and pulled from his cloak the tome he possessed, quickly found the section on the Zoa, and wrote in angelic script the word *deletion*.

325

The creature then raced towards them, and Raphael ran, dived over a table while the Zoa leapt after him, jumping over the table and smashing into chairs and streams of books.

Lilith completed his writing, and the creature turned to consume him, for he was closer, but as the Zoa approached, it began to fade. It roared.

Howling, it reached to grab Lilith, and Lilith instinctively changed to his gaseous form. The creature stung him, Lilith cried out in pain, and the Zoa disappeared from view, but not before Lilith clutched his arm, now sore from the welt that burned him.

"Stings, huh? I always wondered what would happen if one of those things actually touched me. I've learned something new today." Raphael laughed.

Lilith scowled at him and spoke, still clutching his arm. "Laugh as you like, for you will not laugh long. I am pleased that I have the chance to finally deal with you as I see fit," said Lilith.

"And in what way would an errant Grigori deal with the Prince of Chronicles?" replied Raphael.

"Let us just say I seek to rewrite the tale of thy existence."

Lilith lifted his pen, and it transformed into a dagger. "I now wield the Pen and Inkhorn of God. I am now he who writes creation. Your inkhorn and stylus belong to me now."

An explosion rocked the building and both swayed to their sides and lost balance. Raphael smiled. "Aye, you do have my belongings, they were handed to me by El himself, and I would see them returned. Raphael held his dagger; his inkhorn floated by his head.

Lilith took the tome still in his hand, inscribed in Elohim the words for delete, and looked at Raphael giddily.

"Goodbye, my *Prince,*" Lilith said sarcastically.

But nothing happened, and Raphael moved closer towards him holding the hilt of his dagger in hand and chuckled. "Perhaps...," said Raphael, "my name is not spelled correctly. Did you check your spelling or is the grammar not clear? Or pray tell the Elomic language has escaped you?" Raphael laughed mockingly at him.

Irritated Lilith looked down at what he had written and quickly wrote the verse again to delete Raphael, but nothing happened, and his face soured with disapproval and anger.

"You see, Lilith; to be Sephiroth, to command the power of El to create and delete from creation, one must have three elements: the Pen of God, which you do possess, and the Inkhorn of God, but they are of no use unless you possess this."

Raphael lifted from the inside of his breast a gilded edged tome for Lilith to see; it gave off a golden hue and pulsed, as Raphael held within his hand his own beating heart shaped in the form of a great book. Raphael smiled and placed the tome back snuggly within his chest.

Lilith frowned and raised the dagger he held.

"Then —" said Lilith, "allow me to relieve you of your Heartstone."

Lilith assumed his gaseous form, vanished from view, reappeared behind Raphael, and thrust his dagger to stab him in the back, but Raphael turned and parried. Attempting to strike in return only to hit ether as Lilith quickly turned to mist.

Lilith and Raphael attacked one another. Daggers sparked as steel clashed with steel. Raphael deflected each attempted strike and ducked and weaved to avoid being cut down. Raphael moved quickly and leaped over the stone table, and upon it were books spread out, but Lilith was there to meet him.

The Grigori caught Raphael by the face and slit his cheek, and blood poured from the wound. Raphael cried out, pressed hard against his nerve, and wiped blood from his face.

"Yield to me as Chief Chronicler, and I will allow you to assume the mantle of poor Hariph here," said Lilith.

Raphael saw the steward of the hall lying face down dead and said, "Look to your own fate Lilith. You desire to be Sephiroth, and like your master, you lust for position above your station. If power is what you seek, then by all means take it." Raphael then pulled from the tome of his own heart and let Lilith see it beating; its sheets moved as new text formed on its pages. He threw the book into the fireplace within the room, and as it began to burn, Raphael staggered and collapsed.

"No!" cried Lilith and he vanished to appear suddenly bending over the now burning book to remove it from the flames. As he reached to grab the tome, Raphael pounced upon him and thrust his dagger into Lilith's hand. Lilith screamed in pain as the dagger pierced his flesh to find its tip in the book now ablaze.

Lilith tried to mist, but he could not for the blade of Raphael held his hand in the book.

When Lilith reached to grapple with Raphael, Raphael forced Lilith's hand to write in the flaming book the angelic script for his name in his own blood. Lilith repeatedly pummeled Raphael to break free but could not, for Raphael held fast and scratched into the burning pages, *delete.* When the last character was entered, Lilith screamed and slowly began to fade from view.

Raphael looked upon his brother, released him, and spoke. "Let the memory of the just be blessed, but the name of the wicked rot and your memory cut off from the realm forever."

Lilith struggled to switch between mist and solid form but could not. His body grew grey, and he writhed in pain while from the sole of his foot to the crown of his head. He turned to ash, the remains fell to the floor, and the wind swept the embers away.

When Lilith was no more, the Inkhorn and stylus of God fell to the floor. Raphael picked them up, lifted the tome of El and, doused the cinders that fell from its cover, and placed it back securely into the folds of his chest. His strength slowly returned to him, and he sat to rest against a wall. Through the windows of the building, he saw Malakim gryphons descend from the skies to smite those with Lucifer's mark, and his spirit lifted.

Gabriel had come.

****

Lucifer stepped into the Kiln, and he could hear the siren songs that the stones sang to him.

Soon the very power of creation will be mine to command, and I will make a new Heaven and a new Earth.

Lucifer looked to the center of the Kiln, and standing before the Prime Stone with a sword bathed in blue flame was Michael.

Lucifer smiled. "Brother, so you *have* supplanted me as the Chief Prince, yet it is of no consequence. Bow down and worship me; pledge to me thy fealty, and even now offense shall be forgiven, and all shall be thine."

Michael answered and said unto him, "We have not spoken since the Lord's supper, and after all this, your first words are of your station, but naught for the destruction you have caused. I would know why."

Lucifer looked upon his brother in anger. "You query *me*? *Me*? Am I a dog that I must give answer now? Hast thou risen to prominence that I should

329

be questioned?" Lucifer guffawed. "Very well then, know that I oppose the enslavement of our people, and I will be a slave no longer. I would have what El would deny me. Yet it is not seemly that I should take your life, Heaven cannot afford the loss of so great a servant to her cause."

Lucifer moved closer to Michael, his hands folded behind his back watching him.

"Even now, you threaten to take my stone?" Michael replied. "I have in vain held back the truth of your treason. I have told myself there must be just cause for your deeds. That what Raphael and Iofiel said about you were amiss, but out of thine own mouth, you stand condemned. I have loved you, yet you would seek to destroy me to achieve thine own ends, and there is a part of me Lucifer — that would let you."

"So brother," said Lucifer. "Then my words fall on deaf ears, for thou hast eyes yet cannot see, and ears yet will not hear. I had sworn that I would never leave thee nor forsake thee, yet now my own brother lifts up his hand against me. Am I hated thus?"

Michael lowered his gaze, frowned, grabbed the hilt of his sword, pointed its blue blade at Lucifer, and looked him squarely in the eye. "I do not hate you brother." Tears fell from Michael's eyes. "I hate what I have become because of you."

Lucifer stopped his walk and closed his eyes, a tear ran from his eye, and he spoke. "What is done is done. It is too late for returning; too much has transpired. To see freedom, there must be a new God. This has grown beyond you and me." Lucifer scowled, his voice changed to a heavy base, and the sound pounded with the force of a drum.

"Move aside. My accession to the Godhead has been delayed for too long, for despite El, I will be God."

Michael stood his ground, his sword locked and pointed at Lucifer.

"I will not allow you to take the God Stones. I will see dissolution before you assume the throne."

Lucifer stood mute for a second, his face stoic and grim. He looked at his brother, studied him, and then slowly nodded. "So be it."

Lucifer opened the pores of his flesh and immediately detonated in light: the colors of the rainbow were as a thing alive and wrapped themselves around Michael blinding him. Lucifer inhaled and belted out a roar that sent Michael reeling and he was thrown back and crashed into the great cavern wall with a thud.

Lucifer walked confidently towards the Prime Stone and spoke.

"Thou art a fool to withstand me. You cannot hope to best me in combat. Bow down and worship me, and even now I will spare thee."

Michael lifted himself from the floor and held his abdomen now sore. In a voice low and deliberate, he gave the command. "Ouranos, destroy!"

Like a dog unleashed, the giant golem broke from its embedded slumber and raced to charge into Lucifer.

Lucifer looked at the gargantuan Elohim that ran towards him, and again confidently opened the pores of his flesh. Light lifted from him as the surf upon the ocean and crashed in all directions.

The waves of multicolored force bathed itself over Ouranos, but the golem continued his charge unabated. He lumbered as only a giant could and raised his hands to smite Lucifer.

Lucifer backed away and opened his mouth to speak. He shouted to the creature to stop, and the echo of his mighty voice reverberated in the Kiln, causing the mountain to shake from within so that even those outside felt the bass of Lucifer's voice vibrate their chests.

But Michael knew his brother, and El had prepared him. Ouranos was unmoved and slipped through the sound boom as through water; he came for the Chief Prince with hands lifted to strike. Lucifer grew pale as he looked at the behemoth.

Lucifer drew his sword, but it was too late. He felt the crush of Ouranos' fist slam his head into the ground, the weight of the creature was such that the Kiln floor yielded and cracked as Lucifer's body crumpled underneath the creature's hands.

Lucifer, however, was the First of Angels, and he lifted his wings to cover his face. His scales retracted into his body to reveal the diamond armor surrounding him. His legs and arms grew muscular, and with the revealing of his talons, he completed the transformation into the warrior angel necessary to survive the environment of the thing El had called space. He lifted the great titan from off of him, swung his sword at the creature, slicing into its chest.

Stunned from the blow, Ouranos fell to the ground. Lucifer retracted once again the armor from his body and opened his mouth to blast the creature with the power of his voice.

Michael now recovered; flew to assault his brother, and with a sword in hand; struck Lucifer across his neck, and sliced his esophagus. Blood spewed into the air as a mist. Michael landed on the floor and turned to attack his brother once more. Lucifer's eyes grew wide as he gurgled on his own blood and for a moment staggered, and fell to bended knee. Ouranos stood to launch himself at the Chief Prince again. Michael also turned and leaped into the air to bring dissolution to his brother.

Lucifer grinned and stretched his hand to touch the Prime Stone. With vocal cords embedded in his forearms and ears, he spoke over it. *"Ehyeh asher ehyeh,"* Which means in Elohim, 'I will be what I will be.'

Immediately both Michael and Ouranos were repelled, flung hard by an invisible hand against the cavern wall.

When Lucifer spoke, the god stones quieted, stopped their singing and rose from the cavern floor. *"Ehyeh asher ehyeh,"* he spoke again.

With each chant, every stone changed its song and sounded like the voice of Lucifer, so that when he spoke, all stones spoke, and the disparate songs of many became the unified song of one. Each gemstone then moved towards him and attached itself to his skin.

Lucifer opened his arms wide to receive them as each stone slowly melded into him. He began to gleam as the brightest star and changed before Michael's eyes. The power of God resident within the stones poured into Lucifer and the gash across Lucifer's throat healed itself.

The elements of all creation danced around him, and he changed in appearance with the addition of each stone: his head became as fine gold, his breast and arms of silver, his belly and thighs of bronze, his legs of iron, his feet part iron and clay, and all stones sang the song of Lucifer.

Lucifer basked in the power that flowed through him, shimmered and became opaque. For in that moment he was in the Kiln but was not, and on Earth, but was not. Present in Heaven, but was not.

The power of El to be everywhere coursed through him and the host of Heaven saw Lucifer's image in all places. Many wondered at the sight, for only El ever displayed such power, and Lucifer relished in the sensation of omnipresence. El's power crackled and sizzled and the ground shook as the universe witnessed the ascension of Lucifer to the Godhead.

The Kiln erupted in even more flame, and Michael and the juggernaut drew back from the heat and lightning that sparked across the chamber.

Lucifer then grew in stature, and his body convulsed and changed.

Legs like that of the reptilian earthen creatures sprang from him. His twelve wings merged to become two wings of leather. His body elongated, and his shoulders cracked and budded heads like unto serpents. Lucifer fell to the ground and writhed, as he became a beast with seven heads and upon each head were ten horns. His translucent skin turned dark crimson, and he arose from the Kiln floor as a great dragon and spoke. "Behold the First of Angels my brother! Behold thy new God!"

Lucifer's voice modulated all things within the Kiln, and the sound was as thousands speaking at once.

The fire that raged in the room swirled in vortices. Lucifer inhaled the flames: swallowed them into himself, reared his head back, and spewed at Michael living fire. Michael, sweltering under the heated blaze, raised his sword and wings to cover and anchor himself into the floor, and watched as Ouranos slowly turned to slag.

Michael turned his eyes to the boiling stones he had planted in the ceiling above him. Stones that sung not the song of Lucifer nor joined themselves to the Usurper. Stones that sang the song *he* had given them, stones needed to complete Lucifer's transformation. Michael watched as his brother exulted in triumph, and waited for his opportunity to attack.

****

Jerahmeel hung for dear life to a cropping of rock as the swirling abyss of the bottomless pit awaited him below. The henchman and he struggled to climb up to the edge of the cliffs and out of reach of the Zoa that somehow also had escaped destruction. Its teeth snapped at them and tentacled appendages sought to capture them.

Lucifer's guardian of the waypoint kicked at Jerahmeel, and Jerahmeel slipped. The Zoa's tentacled arms reached to grab him by his ankle and drag him into its jaws. Jerahmeel kicked at the creature below while the guard kicked at Jerahmeel from above. Nevertheless, Jerahmeel held fast and pummeled the creature. Struggling for release, he tugged at the heel of the struggling angel, pulled from his robes a dagger, and plunged it into the guard's calf.

The angel screamed, slipped, and then fell plunging past Jerahmeel into the waiting mouth of the Zoa. The Zoa's teeth clamped deep into the angels abdomen and would not let go, and Lucifer's henchmen screamed in agony.

Jerahmeel grabbed a tentacle, and with it jumped and swung from it to another portion of the cliff; his momentum caused the creature to slip, then fall, as Lucifer's guard screamed as he and the Zoa fell, grappling one another into the swirling Maelstrom of the bottomless pit, and disappeared into the blackness.

Jerahmeel pulled himself upward, his muscles ached, and his tendons strained to sustain his weight. Determination and survival fueled him, and with hand over fist, he climbed to pull himself up to the firm ground of the Cliffs of Argoth. Turning over on his back, he caught his breath, and while upside down, he noticed the waypoint was still sealed.

He lifted himself to his feet and ran to turn the lever that deflected all Ladders away from the area. As the seal fell back, it crackled with energy and the buzzing sound of a Ladder could be heard. Suddenly, a vortex of light and fire opened and then another, and instantly angel after teeming angel fell from the sky and the cliffs became full of the angelic host. Jerahmeel allowed himself to let out a sigh of relief as Iofiel and others across the realms Laddered into the waypoint. Chronos, the keeper of Time in the second heaven, approached his prince, extended his hand to raise Jerahmeel from the ground, and asked, "Why hast Heaven been barred from us?"

Iofiel rushed to Jerahmeel and spoke, "Forgive me, my Lord, but I

335

inquire of Prince Michael? Is he safe?"

Jerahmeel looked at him. "Aye, he travels to the Kiln."

Iofiel let out a sigh of relief.

Breathless, Jerahmeel pointed towards the heavenly city. "Alas, we are at war, for the Chief Prince has sought to overthrow El and has conspired to prevent all opposition. Go to and open the way to Heaven, and smite them that would oppose El."

The legion stood speechless and in shock at the smoke and flames in the distance.

Chronos was unique as an Arelim, for as Lucifer's body was filled with tabrets and pipes, Chronos' was replete with hourglasses and instruments to measure all units of time.

"To arms," he yelled. "Let us secure the gates so Heaven will never be sealed again!"

The chronometer within the forehead of Chronos quickened, and energy flashed about him and enveloped those on the rostrum of the cliffs. In seconds, they were all gone and immediately reappeared at the next waypoint. One angel guarded the gate and kept it shut. When he saw the multitude teleport from nowhere: all hovered and stood with arms raised, he trembled in fear.

Chronos spoke authoritatively as he stood behind Jerahmeel. "Stand aside or know dissolution."

Jerahmeel just smiled and said, "I think he means it."

The angel bowed and moved away from the lever, and Jerahmeel re-leased the locks and the shield that deflected all Ladders. The shield was drawn back, and the Northern gate suddenly filled with Ladders as angels poured in with questions; angered that they could not come home. Some became incensed that Lucifer would strand them in the realms without means to return. Soon the legion became legions: and Chronos transported the horde to each of the remaining waypoints until all were secured.

When the last of Lucifer's lackeys was shackled in chains, Jerahmeel turned to the mass of Elohim, which were as the stars, for they were too numerous to count, and asked Chronos, "Can you hasten the multitude to speed us to the city?"

"Nay, for we are now too many. Even I have limits to my power. We are almost the whole of all Elohim."

Jerahmeel patted his young brother on the back, nodding, then moved to set himself so that he could be seen of the entire host and shouted to the multitudes before him, "Lucifer in his arrogance has sought to displace El, and make himself King over us! Our brother has become awash in his pride! I say that we show him that we are not traitors to the father!" Jerahmeel raised his bloodstained dagger into the air for all to see and roared, "I say we show him the error of his ways!"

The mob thundered their approval and chanted, "El! El! El!"

Jerahmeel shouted, "Let all who bear the mark of Lucifer Draco be brought low! Now, go to and let us see this end!"

As one man, each used the various modes that were available to him - to run, fly, gallop, or teleport into the city of Jerusalem, fists and weapons raised: a legion of legions with but one purpose: to bring to naught every shred of rebellion that kept them from their home.

Sariel watched from afar, as Talus grappled with Abaddon for control of his sword. He studied him, for Abaddon had adjusted his attacks to combat Gabriel's speed and tried to anticipate where Gabriel's next attack would come from. Abaddon surrounded himself with his shield of locusts; they encased his form as an exoskeleton and gave him strength. Sariel watched as the sword of Abaddon sliced through angel after angel. Watched as Abaddon's foes fell maimed, and crippled before him screaming in pain. Abaddon controlled the swarm as a thing alive. Using the insects like a living whip, he extended the swarm by his will and wrapped Talus and Gabriel in a tendril of stingers until each became immobilized in pain.

Sariel noted their folly: for they did not attack him as one man; instead, each sought to take him down solely. None took the time to note that Abaddon adjusted in time to their strength and speed

He considered that Abaddon was a mover of stars, thus one of the strongest of Elohim. Abaddon was not a mere angel; he was the Destroyer, for he was Charon-like in his ability to withstand blow after blow dealt to him. He could be slowed, even redirected, but he could not be stopped, not man-to-man. Sariel admired his strength. There was something hidden, regal about Abaddon. Sariel had never noted it before, but seeing Abaddon in combat, Sariel knew that El had originally more in store for this angel, but whatever purpose was his genesis, it now was lost, for now, he had to be stopped.

So Sariel studied him, and watched as gryphon riders fell upon him only to be cut down and slaughtered. Abaddon himself took up a rider's trident, and with a sword in one hand and trident in the other, he dismounted a rider and mounted his gryphon and launched himself into the sky. He jousted with riders, who sought to fell him, and he speared them through to a man; all that tried to face him in battle were cut to the ground in blood.

Sariel noted that whenever Abaddon extended himself, his broken stones glowed brighter. The swarm moved around him, and he grew stronger as they attached themselves to the very gryphon he rode. He animated the creature with an unholy power, making it even stronger as Abaddon's own power coursed through the gryphon's veins. Sariel watched the havoc around him. Those with the mark of Lucifer fought with those who had none, and all fought to stop Abaddon.

The stench of blood permeated the air. It ran as rain into the drains of the golden streets and splattered like graffiti on the walls of now burning and broken towers and buildings. The air was full of the sound of moans, screams, the clanking sound of steel, the thuds of bodies slammed to the ground, and the swift breeze of foes that bobbed, weaved, and sliced through the warm air. The sounds of anger and bitterness filled the air as brother fought brother. The hatred towards El and Lucifer's hubris were as the smell of charred rubble, a palpable odor that choked the lungs.

In the epicenter of all the chaos was the rogue angel Abaddon, defiant, standing against attack after attack. Sariel stepped back to dodge a foe thrown across his path, slipped on blood and fell backward. Suddenly, an angel hovered over him and Sariel beheld the mark of Lucifer burned into his attacker's stone. The angel had a sword to smite Sariel but recognized him for who he was and paused.

They looked into each other's eyes. Sariel stood to his feet, and the glory of God still shown on him. Sariel saw his hesitation. For deep within the breast of his brother was shame. The angel lowered his eyes to the ground and bowed his head. He hobbled as he backed away from his prince, and dropped

339

his sword to the ground.

There will be many hearts singed with regret this day. Sariel thought.

The angel turned to fly away; the reality of what he was about to do, weighing heavy upon him. However, the moment that he arose to leave the field of battle; a spear pierced his back. His great wings curled as if broken, blood spewed from his wound, and his entrails hung from the spears tip. Standing behind him was a member of Sariel's own house. Gripping tightly the spear he had moments ago lunged into his brother's back. He pulled it from the angel's backbone and the wounded angel fell as a bird to the ground. Without mercy or compassion, he raised his spear a second time and shoved it into the stomach of Lucifer's henchman. The light dimmed from the fallen angel, and movement stopped.

Sariel became enraged and leaped to the aid of the angel who even now dead gurgled blood from his mouth. The Prince with deftness of hand disarmed his younger sibling, and with tears and anger in his heart swung the tip of the spear across his brother's face and sliced open his jaw. His house brother fell back, his eyes wide opened and confused, for he had been struck by one who did not have Lucifer's mark.

"If I have done thee wrong, then bear witness to my misdeed, but if not, why smitest thou me?"

Sariel replied, "Is it not enough that a foe would lay down his arms to flee? He who would live by the sword shall die by the sword!"

Sariel then raised the spear over his knee, snapped it in two, and threw the pieces to the ground. He looked away into the sky; he knew that to destroy the Destroyer, there would need to be a sacrifice. He could not stop him—this he knew. However, he could bring Heaven to pause, to ponder his doings, that to defeat this foe required the laying down of one's life. Sariel then took to the skies and flew to Abaddon to do battle.

Fear and peace fought with one another in his mind, only to be scolded by the resolution to be silent,

Thy will be done, my Lord.

Like a streak of lightning, he flew into the army of locusts, and they immediately stung him. His body became inflamed, and he generated fire from his own body. The creatures seared themselves as they touched him and fell as dross. He smashed into Abaddon, knocking him from his gryphon, and they wrestled as they streaked through the smoke filled air.

Each grappled and contorted to gain an advantage, pulling, twisting, and struggling to gain submission.

Abaddon pummeled the jaw of Sariel, and they fell as comets from the sky. Sariel held fast to Abaddon and did not let him go. He reached with his fiery hand into Abaddon's chest and ripped the second broken stone, tearing the angel's ligaments. Abaddon cried out in agony.

Immediately, the locust swarms lifted from their prey, releasing whomever they held and came en masse to aid their master. A black cloud of biting teeth and stingers descended to envelop and swallow Sariel and their master in an embrace of venom-laced stings.

Sariel crushed the beating stone in his hands. The swarm reached their master in smoke and fire, set upon Sariel, and injected him with their venom. But Sariel had done what he had set out to do. He released Abaddon and allowed the swarm to have him. The two angels plummeted towards the ground. Abaddon's chest seeped spark and smoke, and he dripped fire as blood, for his innards was open for all to see. He was molten on the inside, and dark ash poured from his mouth.

Abaddon gripped at his chest as he fell and opened his mouth to swallow the swarm. They swirled within him, and as a thing alive, arms and hands reached for Sariel as they fell to the earth. Abaddon wrapped his hands around Sariel's neck, and like a boa constrictor tightened his lock on the prince as they smashed headlong into the ground. The explosion knocked back those that stood near. Buildings collapsed, and rocks and debris flew across the city. Smoke sprinted and blanketed all in dust and ash.

In the smolder a figure stood, seen through the cloud to drag another. The form lifted the motionless angel and tossed him from the bellows. The visage of Sariel could be seen, and he was broken, his spine extended from his back, and from his lifeless body; locusts poured from his mouth, nose and ears, for he was stung from the inside, and his body was as a pustule waiting to burst. Abaddon shouted as a deranged man, spread his great wings, placed his foot over the face of the dead Sariel, and screamed to all in defiance.

When Talus and Gabriel saw their brother dead: they went mad with rage and launched an attack upon Abaddon in unison. In a choreography of death, swords swung, parried, thrusted, and dodged.

Each pressed their attack

Talus matched Abaddon's strength, for he was Abaddon's prince. He backhanded the rogue angel and sent him reeling into the ground. Gabriel was swift to take advantage of his brother's attack, and before Abaddon could respond, Gabriel's staff had smashed itself into his face. Abaddon screamed and sought to flee, but Gabriel was everywhere and kept him off balance. When Abaddon predicted where Gabriel would be next, Talus caught up to them and again punched Abaddon with such force his chest cavity caved, and his bones splintered. Abaddon doubled over in pain, stumbled back wheezing, and opened his mouth and chest plate to unleash the swarm to attack them.

Talus lifted up his hand to protect himself and be overwhelmed when

Gabriel suddenly appeared before him and spun his staff and wings so that the swarm could not touch them. Still they moved towards him, undeterred, stopping for nothing but the cessation of Abaddon's heart. Lo, they fought him even as one man, each using the other's attributes to keep Abaddon off balance, to beat him into submission, to defeat the Destroyer.

While they pressed him, the battle waged citywide. Ashtaroth having charge of his troops held back to survey his army from on high. He saw that with the addition of Talus and the horde from the Elysian Fields, the battle still favored his cause. He smiled knowing that his master had succeeded in drawing all attention to the city while he himself was set to the true prize.

"Note brother, how the princes smite Abaddon," said Asmodeus.

Ashtaroth chuckled. "They know not that they merely act in accordance with the master's will." Ashtaroth smiled as he watched the princes subdue Abaddon and hold him fast with chains of iron, yet they struggled to contain him, for the battle still raged about them.

Ashtaroth smirked, sighed, looked up, and breathed in Heaven's air, now filled with smoke and the ash of the broken and crushed stones of his master's adversaries. As he watched a flock of gulls that hovered over the battlefield, his eyes strained to see flashes of what seemed like balls of lightning coming towards them.

The luminescent birds of Heaven flew over the city, squawked at the bodies of the fallen, and wailed for the dissolution that was beneath them. Manna fields burned to the east, black smoke filled the sky to the south, and below them, the dead lined the streets as fallen autumn leaves waiting to be raked.

As a school of fish flees a predator, they too dispersed as the air crackled with thunder and lightning as Chronos and a host of angels that possessed the power of teleportation fell to the ground shouting a cry of battle. Thousands descended like electrified hailstones onto the city streets and instantly took up arms to fight those who possessed the mark of Lucifer.

With the landing of Chronos and the host, the clouds themselves gave up the ghost. Each opened their mouths to whisper the word, "Woe," between them until it covered the whole of Heaven. When their sadness had pillowed to overflowing, rain fell from the sky, for the clouds were alive and cried tears. The angels had taken no notice of their presence and pierced them with Ladders so that their wounds were such they now bled out as it were great drops of foul smelling vinegar. A filmy liquid that splashed from the sky of Heaven and the birds cawed and sought escape, for they found themselves now covered in slime. Many dropped from the sky while others flew to hide themselves for the whole of Heaven's armies had gathered themselves to war, and none considered that reality had begun to tear at itself.

Brother slew brother, and with each angel felled, Heaven's glory diminished. The celestial realm became unhinged and with the loss of each Archon, planets were decimated, and great tears in space opened to swallow galaxies whole, for there was none to watch over El's word, and none looked to keep it. Creation groaned, for her stewards had turned their face from her. Each looked to his own, and none cared for the things that were El's. They left their first station to clash with one another.

Darkness reclaimed realms that once gleamed in light, and even the Earth convulsed as continents shifted and leviathans and dinosaurs assailed by earthquakes were buried beneath rock, sand, and water.

The great armies clashed steel against steel. As the rage of angels burned towards one another, Asmodeus frowned as he looked about him, for he saw that the way to the Kingdom of Heaven was open and the legions of El had found passage. He looked disapprovingly at Ashtaroth and said, "Did we cause with Lucifer to bring asunder the very fabric of all things? Behold the host has come. We are undone."

"Nay— not yet," replied Ashtaroth. "There is still the master." Ashtaroth then pointed towards a giant protrusion that swelled from the mountain of God.

Without warning, a great shock wave burst through the air, and trees, rock, and fire streaked across the sky. The ground itself heaved, buckled, and caused all to hesitate and stop to see this new thing. A blast of thunder and rock erupted to the north, and each beheld with mouths agape: all now frozen in awe at the mountain of God and the source of their birthplace.

The Kiln had exploded.

****

Jerahmeel ran into the Spire of Tomes and yelled for Raphael. "Raphael, are you here? Where are you?"

"Over here!" cried Raphael, "in the steward's room."

Jerahmeel ran past desks and tables with maps, parchments, and volumes tripped, and fell to the floor, landing with a great thud. He pushed himself up and looked behind him to see that by his feet laid the dead body of Hariph sprawled behind his help desk.

He died even at his post. Jerahmeel raised himself to his feet, continued to walk, and entered into the steward's room.

The room was as a dome with a pinnacle that shot high into the sky. Round about the dome were projections of all the happenings in all realms.

Raphael stood motionless and watched the panoramic display of galaxies, stars, and life across galaxies begin to deteriorate, for Elohim, who were charged to watch over the course of all things, were now vacant from their posts,

345

and with El's and their absence, the realms slowly fell into ruin.

Raphael stared at the projections and said, "All things are upheld by the word of His power. But El stands mute, still in Sabbath, and the stewards appointed have left their first estate."

He pointed and they both watched as a planet seeded with life ripped apart, for the star which orbited it went nova, and its Archon was absent.

"We must hurry Jerahmeel, or there will be no multiverse when El awakes from his rest."

"Will El return? And what will be his mind when he sees what the people have done?"

Determined to bring sanity to the madness, Raphael took the Tome of Iniquity and quickly set it upon a golden pedestal in the center of the room. Then faced his brother and spoke.

"He will be wroth."

****

"In El's name!" said Chronos. When he spoke the clocks within him stopped, and suddenly around him, all things slowed. He moved to knock a brother from the path of a large boulder that had ejected from the Kiln, and when the angel was safely out the way, the clocks within Chronos moved again; the giant boulder then resumed its original speed and smashed behind them barely missing them. When Chronos looked down, he had saved his comrade from destruction. Noting that he bore the mark of Lucifer, Chronos rose from atop him and asked.

"Whom do you serve?"

The angel replied, "I am with El, but my deeds have brought me shame."

Chronos hugged him and covered him with his own body as fire fell upon them all. The skies lit as fireworks as the ejected Stones of Fire cooled and dropped upon them, obliterating all that they touched.

"We are undone, for the God stones fall on us," cried Chronos. "I know not what this day will bring. Nevertheless, thou shall not be brought low by my hand. Take heart. For God is with us."

The heavenly host, which had assembled in the city, ran for fear as pyroclastic bombs of rock and smoke jetted from the mountain's side, and hurtled across the cityscape, smashing into buildings, and set shop and angel ablaze.

The Kilnstones landed as falling stars, living things, which hitherto fore had sung, 'to be." Now removed from the heated womb of the Kiln, they echoed their terror and wailed in anger across the land. Each swallowed into great light anything that they touched, and angels and every living thing ran from them, for their yearning "to be" disintegrated all that was.

From the side of the mountain, a dust cloud billowed into the sky, and two bright lights streaked like lightning across the sky. In the midst of the tumult, Michael and Lucifer plummeted towards the temple.

Lucifer, scarred from battle, was unlike anything the host had ever seen, for though his sigil was clear. He was a huge dragon with 10 heads, and he flew with wings to hold up his monstrosity of a body. He had two tails with barbs that protruded from their tips, smoke and fire simmered from his mouth, and another larger stone that sung pulsated within him. Fire belched from his carnivorous mouth, and he flew through the sky raining flame upon all that he saw. He twisted falling out of control as he hurtled towards the ground.

Atop his back was Michael in white robes encircled by seven blue swords and each was as the Ophanim but smaller, and they sliced through Lucifer as the brothers plunged to the earth. Michael rode Lucifer as a beast and struck his sword deep into one of Lucifer's skulls, and the great dragon roared in pain.

They fell from the sky headlong into the court of the Burning Ones, crashing into the steps of the gates and blasting into the doors of the throne room and into the Holy of Holies.

All of Heaven watched as Michael with seven levitating swords fought Lucifer. When Michael pointed at the neck of his brother, a sword flew through the air and embedded itself into his throat, causing Lucifer to let out a gurgling scream. The concussion of his voice knocked the Seraphim to the ground, and their flames extinguished because the blast was of such force. The temple doors creaked from the impact of Lucifer's cry: all onlookers knelt and covered their ears.

Michael then leaped towards his brother, grabbed a sword, swung from it, and pulled with his weight until it tore Lucifer's flesh open as a zipper would a coat. Lucifer roared with pain, and with one of his great heads fired, a mouth of flame at his own neck to cauterize the wound. With another head, Lucifer opened his mouth, and a blast of sound screeched towards Michael and knocked him back.

Michael raised his flaming sword that El had made him and flung it into the mouth of Lucifer. The great dragon let out a scream, the pillars of the holy place smashed, and the temple began to shake as if to collapse. Lucifer choked on the sword and attempted to withdraw it from his mouth. Michael seized his opportunity, with his thoughts, sword after sword lodged itself as a stepladder, and Michael climbed them. With each step taken, a sword retracted, and Michael climbed higher upon Lucifer and continued to stab at him.

Michael reached the neck of one of Lucifer's heads and raised his hands. The swords flew through the air and into his palms, and with them,

Michael sliced through one of Lucifer's necks and the great appendage fell to the ground bleeding fire. Lucifer roared in pain and turned over to crush Michael under the weight of his hulking body.

Jerahmeel viewed the images on the Library's Dome. He watched helplessly as the God Stones fell and destroyed all things. He anxiously watched Lucifer and Michael battle within the temple gates and knew he and Raphael had little time.

"Hurry Raphael, the throne room, hast been breached. I do not know how much longer Michael can withstand Lucifer!"

Raphael slowly began to speak angel-speak over the great volume. The Tome of Iniquity glowed a bright orange hue, and as its pages opened, each page ripped from the book and plastered itself to the domed ceiling of the Great Library.

The dome burst forth into color and erupted with images that began to pulse upward when suddenly a blazing white light screamed and hurtled into the dome-spire, and glass fell upon them in great shards. Jerahmeel leaped as panes of crystal crashed to the floor below. He lifted his head and turned to look for Raphael, and despair filled him.

"No!" He screamed.

Raphael was sitting up; his inkhorn and stylus floated near his head, and he coughed up blood. His hands covered his abdomen as blood oozed from his stomach. Jerahmeel beheld that he had been run through with a great pane of glass, and in the middle of the room, a Kilnstone glowed and slowly was digesting him, taking back the very life that El had once given, and absorbing all things into itself. Jerahmeel screamed running to succor him.

Raphael still conscious motioned him to stay away.

"No!...there... there ...is not much time. The dome...destroyed, and

349

I am to return soon to El. Take the book, my …inkhorn, and stylus." Raphael removed his tome from within his chest and the items floated to Jerahmeel. "Go to… quickly now…awaken Argoth. The people…my people–they will hear… they will listen to him."

Jerahmeel picked up his brother's instruments and tucked them into his robes.

Raphael smiled at him.

"Fear not; all is not lost. Go…," said Raphael. "Quic…" He beamed at his brother, and his eyes widened; smiled and then spoke no more.

Jerahmeel fell to his knees and watched as the Kilnstone consumed Raphael and all that it touched. Raphael's stone hummed and sang with the same pitch of the stone, which now absorbed him. The melody was soprano and melancholic in tune. Jerahmeel wept, and Raphael's tome ceased writing pages.

Jerahmeel gathered himself, for he could still hear the explosions and the sounds of battle outside. He scooted away from his brother as the Kilnstone reached out for him. Jerahmeel ran back into the front room. When he had come to Argoth, he took the inkhorn, stylus, and the tome of Raphael and placed them in Argoth's outstretched palms.

When he did, Argoth moved and took them into himself, stepped down from his pedestal, and without speaking walked past Jerahmeel who stared at him.

Jerahmeel put his hands on his hips, "Hmmph, Not even a thank you?"

When Argoth walked to the steward's chamber, the Kilnstone glowed at his presence. Raphael's body still lay on the ground. Argoth paused and nodded at his fallen brother as if to pay respect, and when he did, he looked upwards and flew into the sky. Set high above the great library, he was awash in color, and light ejected from his person so that all of Heaven stopped to see. Argoth's presence radiated with the glory of the Lord, and his voice boomed as he spoke so that all could hear.

"For nothing is secret that shall not be made manifest; neither anything hid that shall not be made known."

The domed wall suddenly erupted in multicolor, a rainbow shot up from the tower's spire, and lo, all that battled saw it and paused to ponder the meaning of this strange new adversary.

The light shot high into the heavenly sky and spread out as an umbrella. Each Grigori became visible and with tombs opened, suddenly illuminated, and all volumes released their pages and everywhere projected the image. Nowhere in the multiverse was there not a Grigori that did not display it, and image after image paraded itself across the canopy of Heaven's sky. The sound was such that all could hear. The volumes of all Grigori hovered in the air, and their pages showed the image.

Each angel beheld that El and Lucifer were within the Kiln. Apollyon's stone was freshly cut, whole, and made by the hand of the creator. All Elohim watched in fascinated horror as Lucifer took Apollyon's stone and bashed it against the Kiln wall breaking it into several pieces. Across the emporium, and throughout the city, all let out a collective gasp that the Chief Prince had marred the purpose of God's creation. One by one–the words "iniquity", and "blasphemy" was mouthed, in hushed whispers.

Lucifer beheld the image above the skies, his secret now revealed for all the realms to see. His face contorted with a frown of shock, and chagrin, that his secret was exposed. Lucifer's muscular ribcage spasmed and he clutched at his chest in pain. The agony was overbearing and he could no longer hold his draconic form, and changed back into his angelic appearance. Abaddon's eyes were wide in disbelief and his mouth agape, and all hostilities had stopped to see the great images in the sky.

When the last page of the tome plastered to the wall, the great prismatic beam retracted into the spire, a thunderclap reverberated across the realm. The sky returned to its normal hue, and all eyes turned and fixated on Lucifer and Abaddon.

Abaddon whose head still looked to the sky lowered his now grim gaze and turned to look at Lucifer. "It was you! My stone was broken because of you! My birthright— of that too you have robbed me. El knew the thoughts he had towards me, for they were always of peace and not of evil, to replace thee as Lightbringer. All, this time, you have been but false to me — all this time you knew!"

Abaddon's countenance changed. He roared with anguish, and his anger was such that he bucked as a wild stallion. Talus and Gabriel struggled to hold him but could not, and he broke free. Abaddon grabbed a sword from its sheath and rushed towards Lucifer. His stone that remained glowed, his form grew black, and from his innards spilled bile. The swarm of stinging locust poured from openings in his flesh, and he charged to cut Lucifer down.

Suddenly, from his rearward, chains of rusted black iron wrapped themselves around him. He turned to see who would stop the Destroyer, and with horror, he saw the Warden had reach of him. In terror, Abaddon attempted to back away but it was too late, for Charon held him fast by his legs and arms. Abaddon fell forward, and he was dragged screaming as he clawed at the ground straining for escape.

"Nooo!" He screamed. "Nooo! I cannot go back!"

Then he howled, for the worms of Hell consumed alive the stinging locusts and bored themselves into Abaddon's flesh. All onlookers moved away from Charon's path, and none interfered as he pulled at the writhing angel who

352

struggled to breathe. Charon dragged him kicking and screaming, and none dared to stop him. The fires of Hell licked and jetted out from his cowled equine body; his molten footprints scarred the ground.

"Help me!" screamed Abaddon, but no man came to his aid. In desperation, he sought to unleash the swarm on Charon, but they melted when they touched his form. The worms of Hell feasted on them as appetizers, for the manacles wrapped around Abaddon were as straws to Hell. As she siphoned Abaddon's power, his features deteriorated, and he wasted away before the eyes of all. Charon then turned to drag him to the Maw and return him to its bowels. Abaddon kicked and screamed, both pleading and enraged.

"Lucifer! Lucifer! I will have you! Do you hear me! Your day will come King of Lies! I will have you! Lucifer! Arrrgghhhhhh!"

Lucifer smiled. "Thus ends my pretender to the throne."

Lucifer then turned to gaze upon Michael who stood between him and the throne of God and spoke.

"You cannot defeat me brother, for I and the Kiln Stone are one. The very power of El resides within my bosom. Stand aside, for I go to claim what is mine."

Michael sword in hand barred his entry into El's presence. His seven floating swords gyroscopically whirled around him in light and blue flame.

"No, brother."

Lucifer stepped closer, "I am now He who can be all things. And who now shall save you from my hand?"

Michael replied. "Never was my task to bring you low but only to forestall thee. For thy treason and thy crimes can only be judged by another."

Michael smiled and pointed to Lucifer's rear. The First of Angels spun around to see that the constellations of Heaven had turned. The stars had

353

changed their alignment, and in the distance off to the horizon. The Shekinah glory raced as a great incoming wave across the land. It illuminated all in its wake, covering everything in a trail of brightness. Color returned to the land, and it meant but one thing.

The evening and morning were the 8th day.

Chapter Ten

The Sins that Follow After

The Shekinah glory roared across the land as waves that crashed along the sea, a white blinding force of holiness that heralded the return of the Lord of Hosts.

It was clear to all who gazed that in a moment, the Lord of all things would awake. Panic suddenly gripped those who had fought against El.

Lucifer turned to face Michael and transformed into pure light; desperately crazed to smite El while he still slept. He waved his hand and a flash of light blinded Michael. Lucifer then used the sound of his fingers and flung Michael against a marble wall. His head hit hard against a pillar.

The light of the new day and the Shekinah had now reached the outer burbs and quickly made its way towards the city.

Lucifer rushed to El's throne and took from his sheath a golden sword of light to smite the Almighty, and as he raised his hand to bring it down, the Shekinah then enveloped the temple, sprinted into the holy of holies, and surrounded El. The mountain shook, and the colors of the rainbow jetted in all directions so that even Lucifer covered his eyes, for the brilliance of El's glory, was too much to behold.

The light of El reflected off everything, and the whole of the city was awash in white so that all that dared to look in the direction of the mountain cried out with pain, for the glare was too bright to view.

El's eyes then opened, and when his gaze sat itself upon Lucifer, he knew what his oldest child had done, and he stood.

Lucifer ran with sword raised swinging wildly and struck the Lord in his heel. Blood flowed from the wound, but not as the blood of Elohim; for the blood of angels was blue. El's blood was as crimson: and it pooled at his heel. The Almighty winced and felt pain. The Ophanim that had been asleep immediately came to life, surrounded El, and created a wall so that Lucifer could no more approach.

El was wroth, and from his mouth, a great sword emerged. Then he spoke. "Because thou hast not heeded my words and hast said in thine heart, I will ascend into Heaven, and will exalt my throne above the stars of God.

"Because thou hast said, I will sit upon the mount of the congregation in the sides of the north.

"Because thou hast said, I will ascend above the heights of the clouds, and that I will be like the most High. Thou shalt be brought down to Hell, even to the sides of the pit.

"They that see thee shall narrowly look upon thee and consider thee saying, is this the man that made the Earth to tremble and that did shake kingdoms; that made the world as a wilderness, and destroyed the cities thereof, that opened not the house of prisoners?

"For behold, thou art as the spit in my mouth and an offense to me; a Satan to be no more in my sight."

As the Lord spoke, Lucifer cried out in agony. The Prime Stone he had stolen from the Kiln burst from his chest, ripped through his skin and rocketed into the waiting palm of El. Lucifer's features grew dark and pale, and he lost the power to reflect the glory of the Lord. El walked towards him, and as he did — Lucifer was forcibly repelled from his presence, and the Ophanim whizzed outside the temple like dogs unleashed. The whole of Heaven bowed and covered their heads, and the colors of El were such as he was as a thousand suns. The Almighty held Lucifer suspended in the air, choking and contorting in an invisible grip, and the whole of Heaven saw the Lightbringer, as he was— a creature forever subject to the creator.

The presence of God was palpable, lightning and seven thunders echoed, and the Seraphim were ablaze again. They stood and resumed to shout HOLY! HOLY! HOLY! Their voices boomed across the court, and El's majesty was such that wherever He walked those that had fallen to dissolution immediately rose to life, choking and gasping for air as if rescued from drowning.

El looked at his children and the great destruction to the city of Jerusalem. He frowned and then said, "Charon, be thou still."

Upon command, Charon stopped his march to the Maw of Hell and tightened his clutch around Abaddon who struggled to obtain release.

The Lord then pronounced judgment on Abaddon. "Thou shalt yet serve in the last days, and your wrath may then be quenched, and justice even then shall be thine, for that which was taken cannot be returned. Because thou hast fallen from thy glory, ye shall fall until the end of days as thy rage knew no bottom, nor shalt thy fall from my sight."

The Lord then pointed to the Abyss.

Charon then took Abaddon, who kicked and screamed, and walked him over to the cliffs and the raging winds of the Maelstrom that swirled below. Charon then lifted Abaddon above his head and tossed him flailing into the bottomless pit. Abaddon clawed against the winds of the chasm of endless space, and his cries for mercy echoed in the air as he fell. Black, acrid smoke rose up from the Maelstrom as he descended, and the locusts followed their master.

The Lord then created a golden seal with a key, placed it over the Abyss, and shut it, so that none might fall therein, and nothing could escape. Moreover, when the seal covered the Abyss, the muffled screams of Abaddon ceased. For as the closing of a flue, so too did the smoke billow no more into Heaven's air.

The Lord returned his gaze to Lucifer, still suspended in the air for every eye to see. Lightning crackled around him, and the Lord spoke. A Ladder then instantly formed in front of Him, a vortex of such size and power that Heaven had never seen anything like it before. It ejected lightning and fire before the Almighty. Lucifer became as lighting himself, cried aloud, and was flung across the skies of Heaven and cast out.

Lucifer screamed curses at the Lord, and writhed as he was expelled to parts unknown; his wails carried across the sky.

The Ladder, however, did not close, and the multicolored vortex, whirled and suddenly became black as night. Then, without warning, all that bore the mark of Lucifer were entangled with black tendrils that reached for them from the ground. The tentacles burned, and the whole of Elohim who sided with Lucifer were seized.

Some struggled to escape, and others sought to hide, but the black held them and found them no matter where they hid; curses, howls, and cries for mercy echoed across the city.

Chronos' face grew grim as he looked at his brother whom he had just aided. Iblis was his name. He locked his eyes on Chronos, and his countenance was one of resignation to his fate, for he neither struggled nor resisted as large black tendrils clutched him and dragged him into the ground.

"I am sorry, my brother," said Chronos.

"As am I," said Iblis. "I will not forget your kindness."

Chronos shed a tear as the tentacles enveloped his brother and dragged him into the depths of the floors of Heaven, and when Iblis was pulled through Heaven's crust to the roof of the second heaven he was ejected with legions of others as they streaked across the lower spaces and plummeted throughout the realms below.

Many in the city wailed and cried aloud, for judgment had come. The giant Ladder split with a great explosion and spread across Heaven like a spider's web cocooning each traitor in blackness. For all that had espoused Lucifer's cause were cast out and fell to the heaven's below; the storm of El's fury was such that He banished all those who bore Lucifer's mark or failed to take up His cause, so that when He was done there were none left in Heaven but those who were on the Lord's side.

The heavens shuddered for the legions of Elohim that streaked through the realms. Some were flung and became locked in the depths of great seas; others were thrown to burn in the center of stars, fated to encircle the universe until the end of days. While those who were too powerful to roam free, El let them pass through the atmospheres of frost planets, where they took the form of ice and judged to hurtle through the heavens encased until the last days. Still others were propelled to celestial corners where their Kilnstones changed and became so heavy that they were entrapped: crushed by the dense weight of their own sin: so that not even light could escape their reach. They consumed all things, a celestial warning forever for other Elohim.

Those that were fortunate fell to the planet El had created for the humans. Imprisoned in mountains, trees, and the lower parts of the Earth reserved until El's wrath had subsided. The Lord set aside those who had entrapped his people on Earth to Tartarus, the realm of Lucifer's own creation and sealed them within the Earth.

El then turned to those who had been prime evils in aiding Lucifer and said, "Thus saith the Lord, for three transgressions and for four, I will not turn away the punishment thereof because thou have threshed Jerusalem with threshing instruments of iron and have been chief to set brother against brother."

Then Murmur, Ashtaroth, Zeus, and Ares were cast as one man tied to each other in flaming chains and were hurtled across the arc of space, exiled to Earth, and sealed in the great river Euphrates. When their bodies crashed into the river, a third part of the fish in the river died. The Lord then set a watch over the mouth of the river so that if they ever sought escape, they would perish by an Ophanim he posted over the river. He sealed them deep within the mouth of the river until the end of all things.

Thus, the Lord chastened the sons of God that they fell as a great torrential rain unleashed from the sky. The Earth became without form, and darkness covered the face of the deep: as the loss of so many Elohim had turned the works of God back upon itself. The continents were ripped from the upheaval, for there were many that had turned away to watch El's word. The Lord then placed a living mist around Eden to protect it and shrouded the man he had created from harm.

The great Ladders that had been sprawled across the face of Heaven then faded into nothing, and when the crackling of lightning had disappeared, seven thunders uttered. "It is done!" The Ophanim then rushed to El and surrounded the Lord in a great light. The Lord's features were visible by all, and He was as a great lion with wings.

When El had stopped in the pronunciation of judgment, the sky returned to its golden hue, and El changed, as a man ancient in years that walked with a limp, for the injury to his heel was clear. All wondered as they saw the blood and pondered. *Can God be hurt? Can the Eternal One be destroyed?*

Michael, like all of his kind, bowed his head before the Lord, and when the Lord walked past him to return to his throne, Michael turned to God and said, "Will not the judge of all the realms do right? For thou, my Lord could have prevented such a thing. To what end does the loss of the realm's children serve?"

The Lord stopped, sighed, turned to face his son, and walked towards him. Michael was afraid for the power of the Lord and the Ophanim was still a thing that made the air crackle. Michael knelt and bowed his head and the Lord knelt to touch Michael's forehead.

"See O beloved of angels, the things that are yet to come."

A shimmering globe appeared in El's hands, and Michael gazed into the giant crystal. It displayed images similar to the walls within the Hall of Grigoric records, but these images were different, and Michael perceived that what he watched were images that were of the future. For the Earth below him was populated with the humans and they multiplied as the stars in the sky. Michael peered deeper into the orb and watched as thousands of humans escaped a land that had kept them in slavery for 400 years, brought out by the mighty hand of the Lord. He watched as the seas swallowed their pursuers.

Moreover, men named Abraham, Isaac, Jacob, and David lived and died to serve El's cause, and Michael watched as they fought to scrape out holiness in lands that had begun to worship the very ones El had just ejected. And Michael beheld as many a nation rose and fell by the command of the Lord. Finally, the great orb revealed a man whipped and beaten, and a crown of thorns was placed on his head. Michael looked away from the cruelty and destruction that the Adam and his kind could inflict on one another. Yet the brutality that this man took upon himself was somehow different. Michael looked on in horror at what he beheld, and he stared into the eyes of a man who hung on a cross.

It was the eyes of the man that told him who he was.

Michael fell back on his hind and waved his hand over his face to deflect the image he refused to see.

"….no….no…" and Michael shook his head in denial, placed his face in his palms, and wept. For Michael saw through the flesh of the man and

361

looked into his eyes to behold that the man was El—hung by Adam's kin on a cross.

The orb then grew dark and disappeared. The Lord stood mute looking down at his son.

Crying, Michael looked up at the Lord who smiled at him, and stroked his head as a father might his young child. El turned to walk away into the throne room. Blood trailed the transparent golden glass, and El walked slowly with a limp into the palace, until the great doors closed.

Michael staggered to his feet, still reeling from the images El let flood his mind. He stared at the throne room doors that shut behind El and looked at the trail of crimson blood left behind. Tears continued to fall from his eyes, his thoughts still racing and his heart filled with emotion.

But Lord...why must you die? But there was no reply to his thoughts.

As Michael stepped away from the Holy of Holies, he walked outside the temple to face his brethren and to do the will of his master. He was the Builder of Heaven, and his duty was to build the city. He looked upon the ground, and saw that broken into pieces was the key ring that Charon had given him. Yet, the keys to Death and Hell were not there. He looked to recover them until he saw that his brethren approached. Grief redirected him away from the search of lost keys to his kin. Jerahmeel came carrying the ruined body of Raphael, and Gabriel walked through the crowds holding the fallen Sariel.

Michael's mind turned to grief at the loss of his brothers, and as he beheld the Kingdom of Heaven, which now lay in ruins, resolution gripped his face. He wiped his tears and marched out from the palace towards the destruction to assist his people.

Epilogue

Lucifer awoke groggily from his slumber, his eyes crusted over with ash and blood. His muscles throbbed and agonizingly objected with each attempt at movement. Pain bit at his jaw, and he instinctively reached to touch his face. Anger swelled within him as he felt the long scar left by his combat with Michael. He knew his visage was disfigured, and he calculated reprisal.

Michael would not go unpunished.

Slowly the mighty dragon rose to his feet and surveyed his surroundings. Smoke and burning embers served as his linen, an impact crater his mattress.

How long have I been unconscious?

Gingerly, he clawed his way up the steep sides of the charred earth, as gravel slipped beneath him. The fallen prince struggled to lift his tender frame, but determination enabled him to reach the crater's edge. He dragged his body forward and fell face down into the cool soil of the black earth. Steam hissed from the crater, and smoke, dust, and haze shrouded his view. His eyes slowly adjusted to his surroundings and began to filter out the debris, and his clarity of mind sharpened.

Lucifer looked at the scene before him and saw the mighty Euphrates only a short ways removed. The sun's zenith informed him that mid-day was upon him. He followed the sun's trail leading west to Athor, his mighty city.

He strained to see but was only able to spot several landmarks that lead to Athor. He followed them with his eyes as they piloted him closer to his own current location and curiously not further away.

Questioning, he turned to his east and saw the lush green of Eden beyond; his delicate handiwork crafted with love, unspoiled and spared from destruction. Still he looked for his earthly home and found nothing.

Slowly his intuition spoke to him and informed him that something was amiss. He moved farther away from the crater. Walking, almost stumbling, he finally mustered enough strength to use his great wings to lift him airborne. Higher he rose that he might gain a better perspective, but each increase in elevation brought with it an equally painful and horrific realization.

Denial of the truth assaulted him. The hard guttural ache he felt as he surveyed the ground below would not stop. The truth assailed him and could not be denied. Athor was razed; its majesty obliterated.

Athor once stood as a beacon that magnified the very beauty and power of Lucifer, its triangular opulence designed to exalt him. Everything was now gone, wiped out by the very fall of Lucifer himself.

His once great city blotted out by the destructive power of Lucifer's own descent. Even in exile, El would have no monument that glorified his adversary. He had used Lucifer's own person as the explosive device to wipe the Earth clean of Lucifer's legacy.

Lucifer had wrought destruction in Heaven, and El saw that Lucifer reaped at his own hand the ruin of his kingdom.

Lucifer's anger swelled within him and despair pulled the once mighty prince to the ground. On bended knees, bitterness rose within him as he grasped the soil of his city now laid waste.

He stood defiantly to his feet and raised his tightly clenched fist high into the air, cursing the creator of the universe and spouted obscenities not pronounceable in the tongues of men.

He surveyed his once magnificent home, as bitterness and anger became his comforters. Seething with hate for his father, Lucifer's tears fell into the dark earth.

He slowly gained his composer, wiped the tears from his eyes, and rose to his feet to behold the river Euphrates and the region roundabout. His gaze followed the waterway's course toward the expanse of the great Garden of Eden off in the distance.

Lucifer's eyes fixated menacingly on the tropical paradise's pristine beauty — beauty wrongly denied him; his thoughts became ravenous with greed.

Looking down beneath him, he saw two keys protruding from the earth; each etched with the sigil of Charon and glowing with fire. Lucifer reached down to pick them up and beheld them. The souls of Hell displayed themselves within one key screaming while the other dripped black with oil and sulfur. Lucifer smiled, and thoughts upon thoughts filled him. He reached within the folds of his robes and withdrew the Tome of Hell that Abaddon had confiscated from Michael.

Vengeance soon came along as a hitchhiker requesting transport, and in Lucifer's desire for companionship, he embraced the emotion and consorted with her like a familiar lover.

With his thoughts filled with bitterness and retribution: his heart discovered comfort, and a smirk found the mouth of the King of Lies.

I will secure your downfall through the Adam.

Lucifer smiled and salivated with lust for the garden in the distance and blithely transformed into a winged serpent. His great wings caught the breeze, and he drifted upon the wind.

Like the fine filament of a dandelion seed carried aloft by the breeze; his mind desired to disperse his seed-bearing parachutes of sin and iniquity. He was eager to bore himself into the innocent life of the human female, to supplant and choke the light from all things.

The warm spring wind proffered him to welcome the Adam and the Eve; the humans El had placed within the garden, these contemptible pretenders to royalty: a species of earth and clay, oblivious to all that truly lay around them.

He would welcome them indeed, for little did they know that something wicked their way comes.

The End

Glossary

El or Jehovah
The name that angels have given to God and by which he has revealed himself to them. Triune in nature, El is often seen in a singular bodily form. On rare occasions, his triune nature is revealed as three separate distinct personalities (Father, Son, and Holy Ghost); collectively they are called the Godhead.

Elohim
The collective name of all celestial kind.

Godhead
The Trinity composed of the Father, the Son, and the Holy Ghost.

Chief Prince
An honorific title given to one of seven angelic princes who stand before the presence of God and receives instructions for their race. The Chief Prince is entrusted by El to walk within the Stones of Fire and to protect the secret of the chamber, the Primestone. A repository of Gods power where one may become as God. Lucifer is the Chief Prince of all Angels.

Lumazi
The group of seven archangels who stand before the throne of God.

Archon
The highest-ranking angel over an assignment.

Ladder
A mode of transport utilized by angels to travel between the realms.

Tartarus
A prison designed by Lucifer to dispose of those who opposed him.

Hell
A living mountain that serves as a prison. Designed originally with angels in mind, it lives off the eternal spirit of Elomic flesh. It possesses the ability to reproduce similar to an amoeba and can grow. Hell has grown to hold captive Humans.

Dissolution

Death to a celestial being is called dissolution.

The Kiln

A furnace from which El creates all celestial life and the storehouse of the Stones of Fire; the living elements of creation. At the heart of the Kiln is the Primestone and the ultimate test for angelic kind.

Elomic Command

A vowel, consonant, or phrase allowing the power of God to be invoked by a delegated authority.

The Abyss

A gulf of nether sometimes referred to by humans as Limbo or by demonkind as "the wilderness". It is a realm that separates the Third and Second Heavens. Failure to bridge the realms without a Ladder or direct intervention from El can cause one to be entrapped within the winds of the nether. The winds are referred to as the Maelstrom. Kortai builders frequently build near the edge of the Maelstrom expanding the landscape of Heaven. The Abyss is also referred to as the "bottomless pit." Mortals cannot pass through the abyss without shedding their corporeal shell. Only Death or direct translation by God allows passage past the Abyss into the spiritual world.

Waypoint

A designated area where travel between two points was allowed by God. Failure to utilize a waypoint could displace the Third Heaven with the second or vice versa causing untold destruction.

Manna

The food that angels consume. Grown in the fields of Elysium, it is must be shipped to the four corners of creation to supply angels with sustenance. When harvested it instantly grows back. During the exodus of the children of Israel, the nation was temporarily fed this food. Exodus 16:15

Creatures

Cherubim
A type of angel having great power; but not necessarily governmental oversight.

Seraphim
A heavily creature designed to serve as voice to the holiness of God; also called a "burning one" a creature of great power. There are 4 in existence, and they stand before the temple of God.

Virtue
A living sentient aroma that lives before the throne of God and perfumes the throne.

Ophanim
A heavenly creature designed to serve as guard to the presence of God.

Zoa
A heavenly creature designed to serve as guard to the secret things of God.

Stones of Fire
A living sentient element of God, which can be molded in the Kiln to create celestial life. They are also called Kilnstones or Godstones.

Shekinah Glory
The residue of God's breath, equivalent to the exhaling of a human's carbon dioxide; a living cloak of breathing light that envelops and irradiates the person of God; Primarily a localized phenomenon. Those that come near the Lord are irradiated by the Shekinah leaving an afterglow on their own person for a temporary period. The Shekinah can manifest wherever the holiness and righteousness of God exist.

Angelic Rankings

Chief Prince
El's designated angelic leader over all Elohim.

The First of Angels/The Sum of all Things
An honorific title given to Lucifer.

High Prince
Seven angels in existence who speak for all their kind. (Collectively they are called the Lumazi and sometimes referred individually with that honorific title.)

Archon
A sole high-ranking governing angel who directs a specific assignment or regions of a territory(s). Sometimes referred by humans as archangels.

Principality
A sole mid-ranking governing angel who administers more than one territory.

Powers
The lowest ranking governing angel overseeing one territory.

Prime
A non-governing angel representative of a particular virtue. (i.e. love, justice, etc.) After the fall, some angels were designated as prime evils.

Minister
A non-governing angel who serves the cause of El.

Demon
A fallen non-governing angel who serves the cause of Lucifer.

Specter
Fallen Grigori sometimes referred to by humans as Ghosts.

Shaun-tea'll
A group of angelic warrior dispatched to bring truth to the Grigoric records of fallen Grigori atany cost.

Thank You

Ready to read the continuation of the series? Check out Book Two!

The Third Heaven: The Birth of God

More books are coming in this series! You can sign up for my mailing list to be notified of new releases, giveaways and pre-release specials by! checking on updates at my website!

http://donovanmneal.com

Thank you for allowing me to share my writing with you. If you loved the book and have a moment to spare, I would really appreciate a short review on the page where you bought the book. Your help in spreading the word is gratefully appreciated and reviews make a huge difference to helping new readers find the series.

Please keep in touch with me on the following sites.

Guess what— I answer my emails! Email me at tornveil@donovanmneal.com

Facebook   Donovan Martin Neal

Twitter.com @ Donovanmneal

Thank you again dear reader and I hope we meet again between the pages of another book!

Donovan

About the Author

Donovan Neal M.S.N.P. is a graduate of the University of Michigan, Ann Arbor, and has a Masters of Science in Nonprofit Management from Walden University.

He has functioned in the ordained ministry for over 20 years and has previously served in such capacities as dean and instructor in his church's School of Ministry. Donovan has taught on a host of subjects ranging from Apologetics to Leading Different Personalities.

Donovan is a prolific songwriter and singer having written over 50 different songs of praise worship for the local church and has performed in various schools and churches in the Ministry of Christian rap.

Donovan's heart for ministry has carried over into his secular pursuits and he has worked with countless abused and neglected children, adults with developmental disabilities, and women who have been victimized by domestic and sexual abuse. He currently works to help end hunger in his community.

Donovan has three saved children Candace, Christopher and Alexander: each is involved in ministry. They currently reside in Michigan.

Read More from Donovan Neal

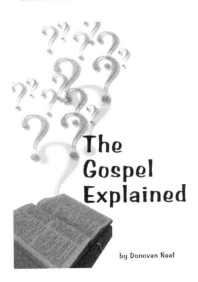

The
Gospel
Explained

by Donovan Neal

In our day of religious pluralism; and where almost everyone proclaims to profess, and to preach the gospel: it is necessary to make a differentiation between that which is "the gospel" and that which is not.

It is for this reason that I have attempted to place on paper what the scriptures state as being "the gospel". It is in hopes that by doing so. The unbeliever will consider the gospel and be moved to make a commitment to accept Jesus Christ as their Lord and Savior.

As for the Christian, it is hoped that this book will provide a tool to be used in evangelistic and discipleship endeavors, and provide a deeper understanding of what it means to be "saved".

Available on Amazon and Lulu.com

Remember that if you have enjoyed this novel please leave a review on Amazon to let others know. It's one of the greatest ways you can help an author!

Made in the USA
Columbia, SC
08 April 2023

14578353R00228